Chapel Springs Revival

by Ane Mulligan

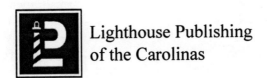

Lighthouse Publishing
of the Carolinas

PRAISE FOR *CHAPEL SPRINGS REVIVAL*

"With the charm of the Mitford Series, the humor of I Love Lucy, and the heart of Andy Griffith's Mayberry, Ane Mulligan's *Chapel Springs Revival* is sure to be a hit with fans of Debbie Macomber and Jan Karon. Reading *Chapel Springs Revival* is like coming home to the place you wish you were from, to the friends you know and love."

Gina Holmes
Award-winning author of *Crossing Oceans & Wings of Glass*

"*Chapel Springs Revival* creates a touching story involving real women who face crisis, love, doubt, and desperation with love and humor. Together, they survive when courage calls."

DiAnn Mills
Christy Award-winner and author of *Firewall*

"At last the world has a chance to relish the wit and wisdom of Ane Mulligan with her debut release of *Chapel Springs Revival*. You'll laugh at the antics of the southern folk in this sleepy town that might look a lot like yours, and when the dust settles, you'll wish you could go back and visit, maybe have a pastry at Dee's 'n' Doughs or slip off your shoes and walk along the boardwalk. A fun and heartfelt story from a masterful storyteller."

Carla Stewart
Award-winning author of *Stardust* and *The Hatmaker's Heart*

"*Chapel Springs Revival* is delicious, and it has so many of the elements I love in a fun read: A heroine I relate to? Check. A big, lovable dog and some baked goods? Check, check. Quirky humor, a thread of faith and a nice injection of Southern charm? Check, check and check. Mulligan's focus on studying her craft and perfecting her style is evident in her debut novel. We'll want to watch for much more from this writer."

Sandra D. Bricker
Author of Live-Out-Loud fiction and the *Jessie Stanton* series

"Reading *Chapel Springs Revival* is like going to visit an old friend in her hometown--you recognize the people and want to get to know them better and you are fed a lot of delicious meals. This is a small-town story with big-hearted characters."

Southern novelist Judy Christie
Author of *Magnolia Market*

"In her heartfelt debut novel, Ane Mulligan completely charmed me! Claire Bennett is a hoot as she sets out with her friends to revitalize Chapel Springs. The fun, quirky cast of characters leap off the page and into your heart, and their lively misadventures are anything but ordinary. Filled with snappy dialogue, wit, poignancy, humor and romance (and even some terrific recipes), *Chapel Springs Revival* will settle in your mind and heart. Bring on the next novel, Ms. Mulligan, so I can revisit my new friends!"

JoAnn Durgin
Author of *The Lewis Legacy Series* and *Catching Serenity*

"Ane Mulligan's debut novel, *Chapel Springs Revival*, is a humorous look at old friends dealing with serious issues—in their own quirky ways. Patsy, the more mature of the two, spends most of the book trying to keep her best friend Claire from getting into messes. Mulligan combines all of this in a delightful and compelling novel that will make you both laugh and cry."

Robin Patchen
Author of *Faith House* and *One Christmas Eve*

"Novelist Ane Mulligan's quirky humor and love for life (and dogs) shines through in *Chapel Spring Revival,* where the characters are engaging—and the food enticing. A story complete with recipes and a reminder of following God's plan for our lives."

"A story full of small-town charm and big-hearted friends. *Chapel Springs Revival* is Southern Fried Fiction, a taste of a community that will be transformed through the devotion of a group of friends and God's guidance."

"A story filled with faith, friends and food—all appealing."

"Small-town Southern fiction filled with faith, friends and food—and what more could a reader want?"

Goodreads

CHAPEL SPRINGS REVIVAL BY ANE MULLIGAN
Published by Lighthouse Publishing of the Carolinas
2333 Barton Oaks Dr., Raleigh, NC, 27614

ISBN: 978-1941103418
Copyright © 2014 by Ane Mulligan
Cover design by Ken Raney: www.kenraney.com
Interior design by Karthick Srinivasan

Available in print from your local bookstore, online, or from the publisher
at: www.lighthousepublishingofthecarolinas.com

For more information on this book and the author visit: www.anemulligan.com

Brought to you by the creative team at LighthousePublishingoftheCarolinas.com:
Eva Marie Everson, Rowena Kuo, Barb King, Michelle Creech, Brian Cross, and Eddie Jones.

Library of Congress Cataloging-in-Publication Data
Mulligan, Ane
Chapel Springs Revival / Ane Mulligan 1st ed.

Printed in the United States of America

The particular charm of marriage is the duologue: the permanent conversation between two people who talk over everything and everyone.

- Cyril Connolly

Dedication

To my own dear husband, who still shakes his head and asks, "What did you say?" Thank you for pulling Chapel Springs out of my head and putting it on canvas for me. I love you.

Acknowledgements

People always ask where my characters come from. There is a tiny bit of myself, but, for Claire Bennett, I chose the most fun and quirky bits of three wonderful ladies it's my pleasure to be friends with: Carol Crosby, who is my workout buddy and is one of my most delightful friends. She gets into mishaps that leave me shaking my head. She truly *is* Claire. Then there is Patsy Hannah, whose "can-do" and "forward-ho" attitude fit Claire to a "T." Finally, there's Becky Thompson, who is a wonderful character in her own right. She keeps me guessing what she'll say and always makes me giggle.

I've always believed it takes a village to raise a novel. To my Silverarrows (a offshoot of Penwrights) Gina Holmes, Jessica Dotta, Michelle Griep, and Elizabeth Ludwig I owe you so much. You've stretched me and never let me get away with anything but my best. Without you, this novel would never have seen print.

To the other Penwrights: all y'all have been my encouragers and my best friends (Alphabetical by first name): Bonnie Calhoun, Chandra Smith, Cynthia Hickey, Eunice Matchett, Frances Divine, Kimberli Buffaloe (McKay), Linda Yezak, Patty Smith Hall, Pamela James, Pamela Meyers, S. Dionne Moore, Sharon Lavy, Terri Thompson, Yvonne Anderson, and our token male, Mike Ehret, who's the only guy who hung in there. We had a few others, but they couldn't take all the estrogen.

I have the world's best beta readers. A huge thank you to Ginger Aster, who catches every plot hole and missing word; Nora St. Laurent, who never fails to tell me if a scene doesn't cut it; and Barbara Davidson, for my tag line and punctuation.

Special thanks the members of American Christian Fiction Writers (ACFW) my professional writers association, for the training and networking they provided. These special, multi-published authors take the time to train and encourage new writers.

Special thanks to Sandra D. Bricker and the late Diann Hunt, who both made me laugh and showed me how to use my whacked sense of humor in my stories. To James Scott Bell, who taught me about story structure. I hope you like my Q-factor in this book, JB. To Deborah Raney, you made me fall in love with women's fiction and taught me so much, thank you! See? I said it takes a village.

To my very special agent, Sandra Bishop: you believed in me and found just the right place for me. Thank you for all your hard work! To my wonderful editor, who happens to be one of my early teachers, Eva Marie Everson. I've loved your books and love your editing even more. Thanks for finding my plot holes and making my story better!

Research is the foundation of a good story, and I must mention two special people who helped me with my geological questions, when I found myself typed into a box: Paula Turner, President of Geomodel, Inc., and author Linda Kozar's husband, Mike Kozar, that wonderful Geo-geek, who patiently answered lots of questions.

My family played a large part in putting up with dinner discussions of plots and characters, even when they couldn't follow what I was saying. Thank you for not having me committed. I couldn't have done this without your support.

Finally, I give thanks to God for the wonderful gift of storytelling. My teachers used to call it lying, but He kept it alive within me, until the time was right. And now, I'm a *professional* liar: a novelist.

Thanks for reading!

To see a map of Chapel Springs,
go to www.anemulligan.com/p/books.html

Chapter 1

Claire Bennett couldn't remember when the tradition began—meeting her friends at the bakery, *Dee's 'n' Doughs* before the workday started. It must have been after their nests had emptied since none of them had any tag-alongs velcroed to their ankles. Whatever the cause, stopping for a chat and a hot cup of coffee got her creative juices flowing. Okay, maybe that was the caffeine and sugar, but Claire couldn't imagine life without her girlfriends.

She wished she could share her deepest heart with her husband. She and Joel used to talk, sort of, but something had changed, somewhere between diapers and soccer. It was around the time she started going to church without him. She shuffled through a pile of leaves on the sidewalk, the dry crunch reminding her of their conversations. He wasn't much of a talker and never had been, but he'd become noticeably quieter lately.

A spring breeze played with the edge of her shirttails as she stepped up onto the boardwalk along Sandy Shores Drive. She paused and lifted her hand, shading her eyes against the rising sun and welcomed the tremolos and wails of the loons floating up with the mist lifting off Chapel Lake. She searched the reeds along the shoreline for their distinctive black and white neckbands. Like Yankees, they'd soon migrate back to the north. She'd miss their plaintive cries. Time and time again, she'd tried to capture the emotion in her pottery, but so far she hadn't found a way to translate sound into form.

Not seeing the loons, she scanned the width of Moonrise Cove for Joel's boat. Near its center, a lone fisherman—not her hubby—had anchored his dinghy in the fog. Joel was probably angling off Henderson

Island. But that lone boat in the foggy cove would make a melancholy painting. Maybe she'd suggest it to Patsy. With the image in mind, she hurried on to the bakery.

Soft light poured through the picture window of *Dee's 'n' Doughs*. As she pulled open the glass door, the brass bells attached to a quirky wrought iron hook shaped like a loon, announced her arrival. She paused on the threshold for a moment, closed her eyes, and let the heavenly aroma of yeast, vanilla, and almonds entice her. That indulgence alone would probably add another inch to her waistline. When she opened her eyes, her studio/gallery partner, Patsy Kowalski, was chuckling at her.

Claire dropped her black tote on a chair. Today, all the tablecloths were printed with woodland creatures. The ones yesterday had been fishermen. "Morning. We the first?"

"Aren't we always?" A tiny crease appeared between her eyebrows as Patsy sipped her morning French roast. "Hurry up and get your coffee. I've got something to tell you."

With intuition borne of being best friends since kindergarten, Claire sensed disquiet in Patsy's tone. The news probably had to do with one of the kids. Even though they were grown, worrying about them never failed to make that crease materialize.

Between Patsy's three and Claire's five, they had plenty to worry about.

She scurried over to the row of insulated airpots, selected the breakfast blend, and added a shot of cream. When she reached for a packet of sugar, a pan of warm, gooey cinnamon buns Dee had left out for them, leered at her. She squeezed her eyes to slits and tried to focus on the coffee, weighing size ten jeans against the taste of golden brown pastry laden with butter, cinnamon and rich, gooey icing.

No good. Those buns tempted her beyond reason. If only she had more self-discipline—like her friends. She bit her thumbnail. If she skipped the sugar in her coffee ... she snatched the clamoring pastry onto a plate, sucked the frosting off her fingers, and grabbed a packet of sugar substitute.

Clutching a napkin between now-sticky fingers, she slipped into the chair next to Patsy, ready for a good natter. "So what's up? You're worried about something. Is it the kids?" She pinched off a piece of the bun and popped it into her mouth, then moaned. Dee and her doughs should be on the Food Network. Either that or arrested for assault on

Claire's backside, which was exactly where this bun would end up.

Patsy's hazel eyes warmed, crinkling the skin around the edges. "No, kids are fine." Her expression changed, the light extinguished. "It's—"

The door opened, its bell jingle-jangling. Lacey Dawson strolled in, followed by her sister, the new widow who moved into town just a few months ago and was about to open a health spa. Claire zeroed in on the newcomer's flawless skin and svelte figure. Hmm, that spa might be worth exploring if she could shed those extra pounds hugging her hips and get her skin looking as young and fresh as the widow's. Then, maybe Joel might regain interest.

She smiled at their newest resident. What was her name? People referred to her as the widow on the hill, because she bought the old Wexler house atop the hill behind Warm Springs Park. Wracking her brain brought up nothing but dead space. She quirked her brows at Patsy, who obliged by patting the chair on her other side.

"Lydia, sit here so we can get to know you."

Lydia. Lydia Smith, the widow on the hill. She even looked like a Lydia. Chestnut-brown hair in a jaw-length bob framed an open and friendly face. Claire fingered the ends of her hair and repeated Lydia's name silently three times. Then once more out loud for good luck. "Lydia, are you settled in yet?"

Her shiny hair swayed against her cheeks as she nodded. "Pretty much. A few boxes got shoved into the mudroom. I'm fixin' to get to them later this week."

Claire scooted her chair over, giving them more room. "Where're you from, Lydia? Your accent sounds like south Georgia." The woman added extra syllables to every vowel and dropped so many word endings she could be fined for littering. North Georgia accents were a teeny bit more civilized.

"Close. Alabama. Mobile, actually. But tell me about you. I understand you're a potter?"

Claire blinked in astonishment. Lydia had moved the conversation away from herself pretty fast. "That's me. Patsy and I share the gallery, *The Painted Loon,* two doors down. She's an accomplished artist. Works in oils and acrylic."

"That's wonderful. I could use some pieces to dress up the spa." She paused and smiled. "I'm glad Lacey invited me. This is the first time I've had a chance to sit down and get to know y'all. She's been tellin' me that all y'all were raised right here in Chapel Springs. I think y'all are lucky, to live where you got your raisin.'" Lydia stopped and looked around the still-empty bakery. "I thought there were more ladies in this group, though."

"There are," Claire said, "but we're the early birds. Dee's in the back, baking, and the others'll be along directly, *if* they're coming today." They never were sure how many would show up on any given day. "The waitress starts at nine. Those of us who come in this early have to help ourselves."

"I wondered about that. Doesn't she worry about someone leavin' without payin'?"

Claire shot an amused glance at Patsy. Obviously, Lydia wasn't used to life in a small town. "Not Dee and not this early in Chapel Springs. Only residents and ducks are up before the sun here. She has a box under the counter for us to drop in money or an I.O.U."

Lacey appeared with two coffee mugs, a bagel with cream cheese on the side and a cinnamon bun. Lydia chose the bagel and ignored the cream cheese as her sister sat beside her.

Claire rolled her eyes. "You have more willpower than me." And a smaller waistline.

"Oh, I wavered, sugah, but with openin' a health spa, I have to be careful. I'm my own walkin' advertisement."

And quite the ad she was, too. By her designer warm-ups, it was clear Lydia's thighs were firmer than Claire's. Would Joel think she looked better than her in jeans?

Then Lydia's mouth turned down in remorse as she eyed the leftover pastry on Claire's plate.

"That I can understand." Claire grabbed a shaker, poured salt over the remainder of her bun, then pushed the plate out of both their reach. She brushed the excess from the racooned tablecloth.

Lydia stared at the plate, tilting her head. "Now, why did you do that?"

"To keep us both safe, girlfriend."

Lydia tilted her head. "I'm missing something."

Claire grinned. "When I need to lose weight, instead of a fixed diet, I cut my intake in half." She eyed the leftover bun. "All right, I ate more than half, but if I put salt on sweet things or sugar on salty things, it ruins them." She raised her hands, palms up, and grinned. "Voila! Diet success."

Patsy, who hadn't gained weight since high school, shook her head.

Claire scowled at her. "If it weren't uncharitable I'd ask God to zap ten pounds on you."

Her BFF fingered some crumbs from Claire's abandoned plate into her smirking mouth.

Brat.

Patsy braced her elbows on the table. "Lydia, what do you think of Chapel Springs?"

"I love it. It's exactly what I needed." She opened a container, shook out a breath mint and popped it in her mouth. "After Sam died, I rattled around in that big house. When Lacey got my daughter a job at the bank, she moved here. I decided I should too. I haven't regretted it for a minute."

Claire shook her head at the offer of a mint. Why ruin the lingering taste of cinnamon? "How's the spa coming along? Are you ready to open yet?"

"Almost, I'm waiting for monogrammed towels, and I want some custom lotions, but ..."

The hesitation in her voice tweaked Claire's emotions. She wanted to help and met her new friend's gaze. "But what?" If she helped, maybe Lydia would give her a discount.

Her new friend bit one corner of her lip and glanced at her sister, who shrugged. "Well, I don't want to turn your morning coffee time into a business discussion."

"That's okay," Claire said. "Don't stop now. You've got me curious. Did the mayor hold your business license ransom for more taxes?" He'd tried that on her, but only once.

Lydia twisted her napkin and bit her lip again, glancing between Claire and Patsy. "No, I've got that. It's the marketing I'm worried about. I planned to advertise on the Internet, using photos of the town to show off its peaceful beauty and play up the healthful benefits of the warm springs." She hesitated. "Look, I don't want to be seen as an upstart newcomer, but the town is a tad ... well ... drab."

"Drab?"

Hiding her smile at the way Lydia pronounced it "dray-ub," Claire took a mental journey down Sandy Shores Drive, which didn't take long. From the "Welcome to" sign to the one declaring "You're now leaving," it was one-and-a-half miles. Some people thought the tiny mountain hamlet was too small, but not her. The fact she could walk everywhere added to its charm, not to mention its clean air. But Lydia was right.

Their picturesque village lacked sparkle.

Claire wrinkled her nose. "It *is* dray-ub." Patsy kicked her under the table. Had she said that out loud? "I'm sorry. I wasn't making fun. I—"

Lydia waved her apology away and grinned. "And dreary. Why, the paint's peeling on a few of the buildings. Another one has a broken sign. Mostly, they just need some color. And flowers." She leaned forward, her eyes bright. "Definitely flowers, maybe window boxes. I think Chapel Springs needs a revival."

There was a good idea. "We used to have hanging flower pots. When Felix Riley campaigned for mayor, he walked around town, waving at everyone." Claire did a mock queen's wave. "Well, one day he wasn't paying attention and walked smack-dab into a lamppost. One of the flowerpots was loose where its holder had cracked. It wobbled and fell, landing on his foot. As soon as he got into office, he had them all removed."

Patsy sighed. "I miss those. They did a lot to brighten the town. You're right, Lydia, we need some sprucing up. And now that you mention it, we've had fewer customers in the gallery. I doubt Claire noticed. When she's busy creating new inventory, she doesn't see or hear."

"Oh, for the love o' Van Gogh. I notice things. I remember taking note of Happy's Hobby sign looking downright pitiful. I know our income's gone down, too. I had to get creative paying last month's bills." She scrunched her eyes and pictured the village again. "The more I think on it, there are a lot of places we could set large urns of flowers. And maybe even some colorful awnings." Visualizing them sent her creative juices into hyper drive.

Lydia chewed her bottom lip. "Please don't think I'm being overly critical. I love Chapel Springs. It's such a warm, inviting town and I want the spa—all of us—to be successful."

"You've made a big investment," Patsy said. "It's understandable."

"I love your idea about advertising." Claire leaned forward. "We can't afford to lose the tourist trade." She rose. "I need more caffeine. Anyone else?" She was ready to dive in. If this revival idea worked and business picked up, she could shed the stress of paying for multiple kids in college.

Three mugs thrust toward her. Laughing, she slipped her fingers through the handles then crossed the room to fill them. "Hey, Patsy," she called over her shoulder, "grab a pad to take notes. Dee's got to have one around here somewhere. Try behind the counter. We need to do something besides just talk."

Patsy went through the swinging door into the kitchen and returned a moment later with a notepad and pen. Claire handed the refilled coffee cups back to their owners and took her seat. Pulling the pad closer, she picked up the pen, lowered her readers from the top of her head to her nose, and listed the names of the shops on Sandy Shores Drive then stopped, the pen wiggling in her fingers. Lacey leaned toward her and eyed the pad, making Claire rethink what she wrote.

This wasn't enough. Sitting only made her antsy. "Let's move this outside—take a good look at the village to see what has to be done." She wanted to see the object of her intended work. "I'm so glad you moved to Chapel Springs, Lydia. You've lit a fire under us, one that needed lighting." Not to mention the one she lit under Claire to lose the extra pounds. "You can bring business ideas like this to our coffee klatch any day." She pushed her chair back and stood. "Come on, ladies, let's go."

"Wait a minute." Patsy's hand shot out, grabbing Claire's arm and pulling her back down. "Wouldn't it be better for each of us to take one or two places instead of all of us descending on the same one, so nobody feels—"

"Besieged. Brilliant, Pat-a-cake." Claire yanked the pen from behind her ear, and started divvying up the list. "We'll start at the south end with *Front Row Seat*." She glanced at Lydia. "That's the video store."

Lydia frowned. "Videos? Do those even exist anymore?"

"They do here." Claire grimaced. "Warren Jenkins, he owns *Front Row Seat*, hates progress. He has one small section of DVDs and clings to his old videos." She made another note. Best give him and Felix to someone other than herself. He'd be sure to pitch a hissy fit if she approached him.

"We need to get some other people on board as well," Patsy said. "We're most likely to meet some resistance."

"You're right, again." Claire nibbled the end of her pen. "We can count on Felix and Warren to lead it, too."

"I don't believe I've met them," Lydia said.

"Our illustrious mayor owns the ice cream shop, *Flavors*, and figures as long as it's clean inside, that's the end of his responsibility, and like a sheep, Warren follows whatever Felix does. Those two are a right royal hiney pain." She peered over the tops of her readers at Patsy, who folded her arms across her chest. Uh-oh. Claire knew that look. It meant she'd stuck her foot in her mouth, again.

Patsy wagged her finger. "Don't color Lydia's impressions. That's not fair."

"Oh, come on, Patsy. Felix and Warren would still have us all back in the fifties if the good Lord would listen to them. I'm sure they tried to bend his ear on more than one occasion regarding that. Hey, that gives me an idea." Claire jotted another note and shot her best "I'll fix their wagon" look across the table at Patsy. "We'll give those two to JoAnn." The pastor's wife was one of her biggest encouragers, and Claire adored her.

"That's the pretty redhead, right?" Lydia asked. "Why her?"

Claire nodded. "She's powerfully persuasive. If anyone can influence that old atheist, it'd be JoAnn. You'll learn all about her, after you've lived here a while."

Patsy rolled her eyes. "It's time for you to open the gallery." She slid her handbag strap over her shoulder. "I've got to go to Pineridge to see my framer. I'll be back later. See y'all."

After dropping her money in the box, Claire stuck her head through the kitchen door and shouted good-bye to Dee, then held the front door open for Lydia and Patsy. When she started to pull it shut, a hand grasped it.

Spinning around, Claire splayed her fingers against her chest. "Oh, my word! I'm sorry, Lacey. You were so quiet, I forgot you were here." She gave the young woman's shoulders a squeeze, waved good-bye, and turned toward the antique store, *Halls of Time*, next to the bakery. A brighter color around the windows, she decided, would frame its displays, making them pop.

She hummed a lively tune and continued along the boardwalk to her gallery-slash-studio. She'd heard the term "curb appeal" on HGTV, and that's exactly what Chapel Springs needed—some fresh curb appeal.

Arriving at the gallery, her keys jangled as she pushed one into the lock but stopped mid-turn realizing that she and Patsy never finished their conversation at the bakery. Claire twisted the key, opening the door and dug her cell phone from the depths of her tote. With one hand, she punched Patsy's speed dial number, but it rolled to voice mail. Her BFF had already driven out of range.

Chapter 2

The next morning, Claire stood in front of her walk-in closet door. "Something's wrong, Shiloh. I can't put my finger on it, though."

The big mastiff cocked his head then yawned.

"You're a big help. There could be a burglar in there." Claire pointed to the closed door. Shiloh rolled over for a belly rub. "Some watchdog you are."

She turned the knob and stepped inside. Something was not right, but it wasn't her clothes. They still hung on the hangers where she put them, at least the cooperative ones did. The defiant ones slid off onto the floor. But that was normal. Still, something bugged her. Yesterday, Patsy hadn't gotten back to the gallery to tell her whatever her problem was. Could that be it? She turned and surveyed the bedroom. Nothing was out of order, except Shiloh had lumbered up on her bed while she was in the closet.

"Get down, you goof." She pulled the mastiff's collar, but he didn't budge, and two hundred and twenty pounds of dog had to cooperate to move. "Come on, off the bed." She went around behind him to push. That's when she noticed their wedding photo while shoving against the dog's rump. She stopped.

That's what was wrong. It wasn't Patsy, it was Joel.

He didn't kiss her when he left this morning. In all the years they'd been married, he always kissed her good-bye. He'd snuffle her neck, tickling her awake with his warm, sweet breath, saying he needed some good-luck sugar before he went fishing. Okay, in the last few years, it had become more of a peck in passing, but still—had it come to this finally?

She dropped onto the bed beside Shiloh, absently scratching his ears. Her eyes narrowed. "Great Aunt Lola wouldn't have put up with it, y'know." Shiloh cocked his big head, stared at her, then licked her chin. She wiped it with the corner of her terrycloth robe. "You didn't know her, but family lore has it that the first morning her husband didn't kiss *her* goodbye she left him. Went off to Hollywood and became a big star in silent films."

Lola Mitchell never took second place to anyone or anything. She lived the high life, all right. Presidents and princes wined and dined her while all Claire got was a TV tray in front of a ball game. She missed her flamboyant great aunt and the stories she told.

Her sigh drew Shiloh's big paw onto her arm. "Doggone it—sorry, boy—but how could he leave without even an 'I'm outta here'? All I am anymore is a sheet-changer. A towel folder. A pancake flipper—and a bad one at that. I'm tired of being taken for granted." What happened to the romance?

She scratched beneath her dog's collar.

"Bev and Drew went on a romantic Mediterranean cruise last summer. We fished on the lake. Patsy and Nathan went to Europe—we went to Atlanta for the boat show. I want more than fishing and a boat show. I want to dance under the stars and cuddle in the moonlight." She wanted the romance back in her life.

Shiloh whined and laid his large head in her lap.

"Thanks, boy, but I was thinking more of cuddling with Joel. Somewhere in the whirl of twenty-seven years of marriage and five kids, I have become a LazyBoy recliner." A steady, comfortable piece of furniture. How utterly humdrum. Aunt Lola would shudder at what Claire had let her life become—reduced to talking to the dog.

She stared at their wedding photo on the dresser. Joel, handsome in his tux, gazed down at her with passion smoldering in his eyes. When had they lost that?

The heater kicked on, and a piece of paper taped to the dresser mirror fluttered.

He left her a note. Not a kiss, but a love note would work. She jumped up and quickly scanned it and her hopes died.

"He used to whisper sweet nothings, now all I get is a reminder to pick up fish bait."

Shiloh mumble-growled.

"Oh, you always take his side."

Claire padded back to the bathroom to get ready for the day. Three damp towels lay strewn across the tile floor. What would it take to get him to toss them into the hamper? A basketball net hung above it? When Joel had fishing on his mind, nothing got noticed, certainly not wet towels, never mind her.

She stuffed the towels in the wicker basket.

Dawn fishing was a collateral benefit of owning Chapel Lake Marina. Joel called it research. That always made her smile, but a couple of fat trout would make a mouth-watering dinner, and husband-cooked trout was her favorite meal. Okay, husband-cooked anything was her favorite. Her culinary expertise maxed out at Jell-O.

After getting her makeup on and her hair dried, she dropped the robe and reaching for her underwear, caught a glimpse at herself in the mirror. Ugh. Forty-seven didn't look the same as twenty-seven. Turning, she peered over her shoulder and sighed. She understood that gravity was important to the whateverology of the world, but—she glanced up at the ceiling—Lord, did it have to work on her body, too?

Determined not to stay in a funk, she threw on her favorite loose fitting jeans. Not too bad for her five-foot-seven frame, but without the extra fifteen pounds, she could fit back into her size tens. Maybe that would earn her a dawn snuffling. Joel always liked her in tight jeans.

She put the dog outside and closed the front door. Wispy ground fog drifted off the lake and curled through the streets of Chapel Springs as she rounded the corner of Sandy Shores Drive.

They said it was foggy the day Aunt Lola left town.

Being later than usual, Claire headed straight to *The Painted Loon*. The gals would have already left the bakery. After unlocking the door, she stood in the opening, pretending to be a customer. What would Lydia see here inside its doors? The warmth of the polished dark wood floors and Shantung Beige walls provided the perfect backdrop for the art. The overhead lighting, designed by an expert, enhanced the displays. What was not to like? The gallery welcomed her like an old friend. It was perfect. Well, the inside was anyway.

She tossed her jacket onto the coat tree, then went back outside and crossed the street. The sun had climbed high enough to take the chill off the morning. In these mountains, spring weather was unpredictable, but the day held the promise of mild temperatures.

Closing her eyes, she turned around and then opened them. Where were the bright colors? The tan building had brown trim. How utterly boring for an art gallery—especially for one with a name like *The Painted Loon.*

Okay, so the outside wasn't so perfect. She shoved her hands into the back pockets of her jeans and rocked on her feet. This section of storefronts wasn't too bad. Some had a fairly recent paint job, even if the colors were sort of "dray-ub," as Lydia said. Some colorful blooms would help tremendously.

Still, the street resembled her favorite old sweater, the one she wore in the studio. Shapeless with bits of dried clay clinging to the front and holes in the elbows, it might be comfy, but it sure didn't make a good impression. She always sloughed it off before going into the gallery to greet customers.

Did Joel view their marriage like a drab old sweater?

She shook the thought off and put her mind back to the trouble at hand. Not that marriage trouble wasn't important, but right now she had a town to revive. And as much as she hated to admit it, Lydia pegged it right. Even the streetlights had rusty spots. There was shabby chic and just plain shabby. No way would Chapel Springs slip into the latter. Not if she could help it. The town depended on the weekenders and summer boat people, not to mention the fishermen, although they didn't do much shopping except for bait.

No, if things didn't turn for the better, all the businesses would be closing their doors. So, how come the town council hadn't done anything about this? What did they do at their meetings? Play bridge? Whatever, it wasn't much town business. Claire narrowed her eyes. Those good old boys needed an attitude adjustment, and she'd be happy to deliver it. Maybe she'd earn some respect in the end. And Joel just might view her in a new light, too. That thought made her grin.

A moment later, the smile of anticipated victory slid off her face. Her husband's business would be included in their revival plans. What if he joined forces with Felix and Warren? She chewed a hangnail on her thumb. He wouldn't ... would he? He played chess with Warren but didn't share the man's politics. No, she was sure Joel would be an ally.

Claire ran back to the studio, grabbed her camera, and stormed down the street to *Front Row Seat Videos* where she snapped a couple of photos. Good grief, the *Halls of Time Antiques* matched its antiquated contents—before restoration. One picture was all she needed at *Happy's Hobby Shop*, which reminded her she needed to go by *The Happy Hooker* and pick up bait for Joel. She'd do that during lunch.

As she passed each building, she took shot after shot of the bland colors. *The Tome Tomb's* catawampus screen door resembled a book with a broken back. The boutique, *Sunspots*, had cute clothes in its window—if you could see through the glass. Like a sunscreen gone bad, the foggy glass made the shop appear dirty. All it needed was a little elbow grease.

With the exception of the restaurants on the square, the town reminded her of a garden going to seed, and she had a camera full of evidence to prove it. It didn't take a Harvard grad to figure out why the tourist trade had dwindled. When she and the ladies got finished with the revival, however, Chapel Springs would rival the lake when the water sparkled like diamonds in the late afternoon sun.

Thirty minutes later, Claire completed downloading the digital photos to the computer in one corner of their studio behind the gallery. Just as she pulled the first photo up to view, the front door opened, triggering the buzzer in the back. The brisk clack of Patsy's hard leather heels signaled her arrival.

"It's me." Her voice rang out from the gallery.

Claire turned in her seat. "Come see what I've got."

One corner of a large gray frame preceded Patsy through the door. Claire jumped up and helped her maneuver it into the studio, banging Patsy's elbow against the doorframe in the process.

"Oops, sorry." They leaned it against the wall. "Nice frame. Which painting is it for?"

"Loon Island." Patsy rubbed the offended elbow.

"Oh, I love that one." Claire stuck out her lower lip in a teasing pout. "I almost hope it doesn't sell so I can keep looking at it."

Patsy gestured to the large bank of windows covering one entire wall. "You've got the real thing right outside."

"Yeah, but I keep thinking if I study it long enough, I'll figure out how to capture the loon's song in porcelain." Claire pointed to the computer. "While you were gone, I took photos of all the shops on Sandy Shores." She sat in front of the monitor.

"I thought you were going to wait." Patsy pulled up a chair beside her at the computer and peered at the screen. "Whoa, is that *Halls of Time*?"

"You're darn tootin' it is. A couple of others look as bad. Wait till you see the bookstore." Claire opened the other photos and printed them off. "I'll ask Bev to make a PowerPoint presentation for when we go to the town council. Convincing them to make it an official town project will be the hardest part." She scrutinized the first print.

Patsy pulled the second one from the printer and studied it. "Since I drove to bring in this frame, on my way over, I went by Lakeview Cottages. They would look adorable with bright pots by their gates. I think we should talk to Glen about them, though, and not just take pictures."

"You're probably right. He's a reasonable man, not a bit like Warren or Felix. Maybe he'd paint the little porches to match the flowers."

"Why do you think Felix and Warren will be against the idea?"

"Because it wasn't theirs."

"Come on, Claire. I think you're still carrying a grudge about Felix's son. They're not that bad."

"I am not. And they are that bad. They're stubborn and contrary, and you know it. Why, Felix could argue with a fence post and Warren would declare him the winner."

Patsy clapped her hand over her mouth, giggling. "I have to admit you're right. About that, anyway."

"Come on." Claire gathered up the printed pictures, slipped them in a file folder and stood. "Let's go call on each of these folks."

"Hold on, Claire." Patsy stepped in front of her. "You're charging off again like an ambitious two-star general anxious for his third. Think first."

Claire folded her arms and jutted her jaw. "About what?"

"If you go on the attack, they'll go on the defensive."

"And ...?"

Patsy's shoulders dropped as she let out a huff. "They didn't hear our conversation at Dee's, so naturally they'll ask whose idea it was. I know you. You'll blurt out that it was Lydia's."

Claire shrugged. "So?"

"What would be their obvious reaction?"

Claire chewed on her friend's words for a moment. "Oh, I see what you mean. Lydia's a newcomer, and if they find out it was her, the old coots will make her life miserable."

Patsy nodded. "Exactly. That's why we need to practice a little psychology. Talk to a few of the reasonable ones like Glen Tabor and ..." a wily grin crept across her face, "Eileen Carlson. I happen to know for a fact that Felix is sweet on her."

Claire's jaw dropped. "No. Really? Oh, this is too good. The only thing better would be if he were sweet on Lydia."

"That's why you should stop and think before you blunder and end up with your foot in your mouth. Again." Patsy's wry smile softened the criticism.

Claire elbowed her. "I'll concede that I might, on occasion—sometimes—speak too quickly."

"Sometimes?" Patsy rolled her eyes.

"Moving right along, what do you think we should do?"

"Talk to the other merchants, one at a time and get them enthusiastic about the project. Show them how it will help business. Then we'll have more votes than those two do when the next council meeting rolls around."

"When's that?"

Patsy lifted the page on the calendar. Her eyes twinkled as her smile spread from today into tomorrow. "Girlfriend, you aren't going to believe this. It's April first."

"April Fool's Day?" Claire hooted with laughter. "That's too rich. A pair of old fools flummoxed on their special day."

"You're terrible." Patsy waved her away, but Claire caught the twitch at the corner of her mouth.

"Uh-huh. And you love me."

Patsy whirled and hugged her. "I do, and it's my life's mission, keeping you out of trouble."

"So, do you want to split up the list?"

"Uh, no. I told you, it's my job to keep your feet on the ground and out of your mouth."

"Very funny. But I have to admit we do make a formidable team."

Outside, the sun's warmth triggered a hot flash, so Claire reopened the door and flung her jacket inside. Patsy gave her the raised eyebrow thing, and she gave back the evil eye. She'd hang up the jacket later. Right now, she had a goal to achieve. Turning her face toward the antique store, she set her feet to moving.

Chapter 3

"Hold on." Patsy stopped. She needed to pull Claire back from *Halls of Time* and Eileen. She responded best to soft persuasion, and Claire had on her man-the-torpedoes personae. "Let's start with Tom Fowler. His drugstore is probably the best kept building in town. He'll support us from the get-go."

Claire stared up the street for a moment, and then nodded. "Good thinking." She swung around and charged toward Tom's.

Claire never stopped to think first. It frustrated the fire out of Patsy. She shook her head and hurried after her. "Slow down. You're a bulldozer when you're on a mission."

Claire pulled a face, scrunching her nose. "Your flattery leaves me flat. Besides, you avoid talking to people, so you need me."

"If I can keep you aimed in the right direction and under control, maybe you'll carve out a path to success for us." And the good Lord knew the town needed it. Maybe that was why he sent Lydia.

Now if he'd only send Patsy some help. Her heart slid to her toes. "Claire? Can we sit and talk first? I ... I need to tell you something."

Claire did an about face, nearly colliding with her, grabbed her arm and pulled her across the street to their favorite bench by the lake's edge. Now that they were there, Patsy wasn't sure she really wanted to share her worry. To voice it would give it reality.

Sitting silent for a moment, she watched a small gaggle of loons, making their way toward the shore. They'd soon be ready for the migration north. Once they left, the lake would feel empty and silent. Like her house.

She twisted the small diamond in her earlobe and whispered, "I think Nathan's having an affair."

Beside her, Claire gasped. "Nathan? I don't believe it."

A spark of hope flickered. "Why not?"

"Well ... he's just too ... Nathan. Solid. Dependable." Claire turned sideways on the bench, pulling one leg beneath her. "What makes you think he's having an affair?"

The loons swam close to the shore, eyeing them. One youngster waddled up the mouth of Chapel Creek, poking under a rock until it grasped a fat salamander in its beak. "He's still working long hours. Our plan was once the last kid graduated he could slow down, but ..."

"Are their college loans all paid off? I wish ours were."

"We didn't borrow that much. That's why we've worked so hard through the last few years and did without. We'd planned to travel." A lump constricted her throat, making her voice sound like it came through a funnel. "He ... doesn't talk anymore. And ... he hasn't touched me in months."

Claire gaped at her. "Months? Is this what you wanted to tell me yesterday? Whoa. Do you have any ideas of who it could be? I mean, Nathan doesn't know any unattached women, does he? I can think of a couple of married ones I wouldn't trust alone with any man. This is serious. Are you sure? I mean, could you possibly be mistaken?"

As Claire babbled, Patsy pulled a crumpled tissue from her pocket and dabbed her eyes. "I read a magazine article, 'Twenty-one Signs of a Cheating Husband.' He's done ... sixteen of them." Her breath stuttered as she tried to control her tears. "He's even working out and dieting. Then, last week, the phone rang and when I said, 'hello', the person on the other end hung up."

"That could have simply been a wrong number."

Patsy shook her head. "I thought so too, except it happened again this week, twice."

Claire's face hardened, her eyes narrowed and she gritted her teeth. Patsy's heart warmed. Everyone needed a loyal friend like her.

"That rat! How could he do this to you? Who could it be? Why I ought to—" Her jaw dropped again. Claire turned and faced the lake, her eyes growing wide and round. Patsy's heart beat faster.

"What?"

"Uh ... I don't know how to say this, honey ... but ... Nathan only works with men."

Patsy blinked, trying to clear her thoughts or her sight or whatever this cloud of confusion was. *Men*? She clapped her hand over her open mouth and, stomach churning, stared at Claire. "You don't think? He couldn't." Patsy shook her head. "I can't ... could he? Oh, my."

"Yeah—oh, my."

"Still, it *could* be a woman." If she hoped hard enough ... a woman Patsy would at least know how to fight against.

"Where would he have met her? You said he's always at work."

"Oh, right. He is." She twisted her tissue, shredding into bits. "Oh, dear Lord, why?"

Claire grimaced. "Forget why. What are we going to do about it? What would Aunt Lola have done?"

Stuffing the remains of the tissue into her pocket, not much came to Patsy's mind. She could hardly get a handle on the thought that her husband ... no, she couldn't even say it. Not even to herself. Had she done something to send him in that direction? Maybe if she—"What? I'm sorry, I didn't hear what you said."

Claire sniffed. "I'm not surprised. Your brain shuts off when you're overloaded." She stretched her legs out and crossed her arms. "I said Joel isn't exactly Mr. Romance any more. Frankly, I'm tired of being taken for granted. This morning he left without so much as a 'See ya.' We used to do things together, but now we hardly do more than eat dinner at the same time. I feel like a piece of furniture in my own home. I wonder if it's a phase men go through. Like menopause."

Patsy pulled her feet up on the bench and wrapped her arms around her legs, resting her chin on her knees. Was the change in Nathan due to male menopause like Claire suggested? A surge of self-righteousness buried the despair gnawing at her heart. How dare Nathan do this to her?

"I don't know, it could be, but ...." Patsy sighed. "Nathan just ..." Tears choked her again, drowning her anger. Sorrow—or was it self-pity—wrenched her gut. She preferred anger to this.

Marked lines appeared above the bridge of Claire's nose as her eyes filled with concern. Then, bless her heart, she snorted. Patsy smiled through the tears. No matter what happened, Claire could always make her smile.

"Pat-a-cake, you're not going to take this lying down. Together, we'll change Nathan's mind. At the same time, I'll add some zip to my own marriage."

Setting her feet back on the ground, Patsy put her hand on Claire's arm. "What are you thinking? I see that look in your eye."

"What I think is, like Chapel Springs, *we* need a revival. A physical revival. A make-over. From top to bottom." She jumped up and pulled Patsy with her. "We'll go to Lydia's spa and get the works, and then call Snips and make an appointment with your daughter. Coupled with some sexy negligees, we'll kick the humdrum to kingdom come."

Patsy narrowed her eyes. "And just why are we going to see my daughter?"

"For a makeover, silly. We're getting a new look, and Deva will help us. She's been after you to do something with your mop for ages."

"I like my hair the way it is, and besides, Deva would say something to her daddy about finally getting me in her chair."

"Hmm, maybe you're right." Claire snapped her fingers. "We'll do it ourselves. We'll go to the drugstore tomorrow. I need to do some research first, then after we tell Tom about the town revival, we'll look over his hair products." She fingered Patsy's short brown hair. "We'll do highlights on yours."

"I'm not so sure about this. What experience do you have with highlighting?" Besides, she liked her bed-head look. It's what her hair did naturally and for the first time in her life, she was stylish.

Claire waved off her objections. "I've watched Irma do mine for years. It can't be that hard. We'll pick up some new makeup too."

"You think doing this will help revive our marriages?"

"It can't hurt. The way I see it, men need something different to keep the marriage relationship adventurous. We just need to be sure we're the ones giving it to them."

Chapter 4

In her studio, Claire changed out of her good jeans and slipped on a pair of faded overalls. She had a list of commissioned pieces to make—the first being an alligator vase. After a moment of musing, she decided if she tilted his head upward, the flowers could go in the gator's open mouth.

She needed time at her potter's wheel to let its rhythm soothe her. The light from the wall of windows and three large skylights always illuminated more than just the room. For the past twenty-six years, the two places she thought and talked to God the best were here and out at Aunt Lola's grave site. Today, she had to sort her thoughts—separate them from her emotions, and there was no time to visit the cemetery.

Joel had been his Dr. Jekyll-Happy self last night. He grilled the bass he caught to a crispy and tender perfection that all but fell apart on her tongue. When dinner was over, however, Mr. Hyde made an appearance. With hardly a nod in her direction, he headed straight for the den to watch a ball game then went to bed after a reminder to turn off the lights. Like she'd forget.

He hadn't even kissed her goodnight. The dog gave her more affection. Always thrilled to see her, Shiloh lapped sloppy wet kisses on her face. She'd take even one of those from Joel at this point. Shoot, she'd settle for some real conversation.

Aunt Lola wouldn't have stood for being ignored like this.

After attaching a bat to the pottery wheel, Claire grabbed a lump of clay from the barrel, carefully closing the plastic over the remainder. Their marriage was about as dry as the hunk she left unfinished on the wheel last week. Tiny fissures had widened until they split the piece in two.

The fresh clay landed with a thud on the worktable. Punching her frustration into it, she created several fist-sized craters. Joel refused to talk about problems—thought psychology was hogwash. But if they couldn't talk about it, how would he know they had a problem? Her fists worked absently now, kneading the clay until it was pliable. If only Joel were that pliable.

Patsy's announcement that Nathan hadn't touched her in months had shocked Claire. Slapping the clay onto the center of the bat, she settled in with the wheel between her knees. He still gazed at Patsy with such love, Claire never suspected anything was wrong. Had he simply become a good actor?

She started the wheel spinning slowly at first, patting the clay and forcing it to the very center. She was positive—well, reasonably sure—that Patsy was wrong about Nathan. Claire moistened the clay, then put her weight into pressing the lump first down, then upwards, shaping it as it spun. The gator's shoulders emerged in rough form.

Nathan without Patsy was like Frosted Flakes without Tony the Tiger. Maybe she could help her best friend by doing some detective work. Of course, she couldn't follow Nathan into his office. As the vase began to take its initial shape, she created the open mouth. But she could follow him to lunch. See where he ate, with whom, and if she got lucky, get an idea of the problem.

She used her thumb and other hand to pull the mouth to its desired width. Too bad Patsy couldn't pull her marriage into shape as easily. However, once they knew what troubled Nathan, she was confident they'd find a fix.

Joel was another matter altogether. He'd gotten lazy with their marriage and was downright inconsiderate. When was the last time he opened the car door for her? She thrust her fingers inside the mouth to give it its width. He let his impatience rule him and his temper go unchecked. The mouth of the gator flopped.

Claire groaned. She stopped the wheel and slipped a length of fishing line beneath the ruined piece to release it. Now she had to start all over again. Checking her list, the next order was a set of decorative tile trivets for the Bed and Breakfast, *Sweet Dreams*. In her present frame of mind, she'd be better off working on those. She opened the barrel and removed a fresh lump of clay.

That's what she needed, something fresh to get Joel interested again. What would Aunt Lola have done? An image of a Victoria's Secret ad came to mind, making her smile as she slapped the softened clay on the wheel. Between her makeover and learning Vickie's secret, her husband wouldn't know what hit him.

The next morning, Claire hurried to *Dee's 'n' Doughs* with her dieting resolve in place. When she opened the bakery door, she wouldn't have any problem. The cotton wads, dabbed with Vick's VapoRub and stuffed inside her nose, should outwit any conniving aromas. Those extra pounds were on their way off her hips and thighs.

No one else had arrived yet. After pouring a cup of coffee and successfully ignoring today's platter of fresh strawberry Danish that Dee left on the counter for them, she sat down and pulled out the calendar book she'd bought in January but never used. Between reviving the town and her marriage, the calendar would fill up fast.

Chewing on the end of her pencil, she calculated the days left before the town council meeting. They had less than two weeks to get the other merchants on board with the program. She jotted some notes about flowerpots and awnings to dress the storefronts then pulled out the coupon for Lydia's spa she'd printed off the Internet. She'd give herself six weeks to lose the weight. Flipping the pages forward in the calendar, she marked May first with a red heart.

Patsy walked into the bakery a moment later. "Hey, girl."

"Hey, yourself." Claire grinned. "I've got a lot to tell you."

"Let me get my coffee." She dropped her sweater over the back of a chair. When she came back with a steaming mug and sat down, she wrinkled her nose. "You sound a bit stuffy. Have you got a cold?"

"Uh-uh."

"How come I smell menthol?"

"Oh." Claire pointed to the cotton in her nose. "I'm overcoming Dee's calorie-laden temptations. I'll lose fifteen pounds if it kills me."

Patsy crossed her eyes. "It may kill *us* first."

Claire shoved her calendar to Patsy. "Look what I found on—"

Bells jangled and Bev McMillan blew in like a nor'easter. She surveyed the table and chose a seat facing them. After a quick nod, she sailed over to get her coffee.

Claire eyed the green Prada clutch Bev ever-so-casually dropped onto the table top. "Eight big ones, ya think?"

Patsy slapped her arm. "Hush, she'll hear you. You are so tactless."

Bev returned carrying a plate loaded with three Danish. Her oh-so-proper Boston accent had always tickled Claire, and she waited for her to speak.

"My treat." Bev sniffed. "What in the world is that odor?" Her upper lip curled in distaste, and she lifted the plate to her nose.

She didn't disappoint, although the lip thing made her sound more Cockney than Bostonian this morning.

"It's Claire," Patsy said, snickering. "She's resisting temptation. It's creative, I'll give her that." She picked up one of the Danish and slid the plate back to Bev, who now eyed its contents suspiciously.

"I could use some help resisting Dee's goodies," Bev said. "What have you done?"

Claire pointed to the cotton in her nose. "I can't smell anything but VapoRub, and it's not exactly appetizing."

Bev twitched her nose. "Doesn't that feel uncomfortable?"

"Nope. Well, maybe some, but a girl's gotta do ... whatever."

"You don't have *too* much to lose." Bev gestured toward herself. "And you and Patsy are both tall. Not like me, anyway. I'm desperate to lose three pounds." She sighed and pushed the pastry away. "I'm so short every ounce shows."

For the love o' Van Gogh, where would those pounds come from? Bev looked as perfect as a woman could. Totally put together, like a fashion model. Except petite. Maybe *she* could give her and Patsy some tips. They hadn't known her all that long, three years at most, but maybe it was time to take her into their confidence. Keep the enemy close and all that—without giving away too many details, of course. Claire glanced at Patsy, who returned a half smile and a suggestion of a shrug.

"Bev, I don't know about yours, but our marriages need some refreshing, something to put the zing back." Claire took a mouthful of lukewarm coffee.

Bev's eyes opened wide and round, and she slowly shook her head. "You're not going to do something kinky like swap husbands, are you?" She put her hands out in front of her as if to stop them. "I'm not into that."

Claire spewed coffee and snorted. The cotton wads shot out of her nose and landed on the table. Patsy coughed and quickly set a plate on top of the soggy lumps. Bev jumped back, her eyes bugged even wider.

"Whatever gave you that idea?" Claire asked as she mopped the table with a couple of paper napkins. She tried not to laugh at the mental image of Joel and Nathan, befuddled as she and Patsy swapped keys.

"In Boston, a few of our friends decided to try it." Bev fanned her flushed face. "Thankfully, Andrew wasn't interested."

Claire couldn't help herself and her giggles set off Patsy. She must have gotten the same thought Claire did. Joel and Nathan would think they'd lost their minds if they suggested something like that. Then her mirth faded. They would, wouldn't they?

She wiped the coffee drips off her chin, wadding the napkin next to her cup. "Our idea of adding spice to our marriages runs more along the line of making ourselves over. Would you like to join us? It'll be fun. Have you met Lydia yet? She owns the spa."

"I made sure I did as soon as I heard that bit of news. This town needed one."

Patsy set the soggy napkins on top of the plate in front of her. "Speaking of the town, we want to start a campaign to revive tourism. First we have to get the stores repaired and painted."

Bev leaned forward, and Patsy winked at Claire. It was rare for Patsy to be so talkative, and Claire wasn't about to stop her. She smiled and sipped what was left of her coffee.

Patsy's attention returned to Bev. "I understand you've chaired a lot of committees. Would you consider leading ours?"

Bev's beacon-bright smile rivaled the searchlights at a Hollywood premiere. "I'd be honored. This town is in dire need of both refurbishing and some culture beyond the art gallery. I have a vision of concerts in the park," her hand swept in front of her, palm out, "a ballet, perhaps. I've wanted to introduce my son, Andy, to something more refined than fishing ever since I gave into Andrew's desire to raise our son here."

Claire tried, but seven-year-old Andy and ballet wouldn't compute. Last summer Andy and his dad, whom they'd gotten to know better at church, had gone fishing with her and Joel. Andy caught a huge largemouth bass, and his delight tickled her. Culture, indeed. That little boy loved it here.

Uneasiness gnawed at her stomach, and she studied Bev over the rim of her cup. What did they know about her anyway? She didn't come to church often. Seems she was one of those CEO Christians, attending church on Christmas and Easter only.

"Why don't you come to church with Drew and Andy?" *Ow.* Patsy had kicked her under the table. "I mean, are you coming on Easter?"

Bev pulled her arms off the table and put them in her lap. A stiff smile thinned her lips. "The church here is a bit ..." she seemed to consider her words, "informal for my tastes. Back in Boston they don't telephone if you miss a Sunday."

Claire imagined not. She pictured a large stone cathedral, cold and imposing, especially if Bev only went twice a year. Most likely no one even knew her. "Oh."

"Did Drew grow up here? I don't think I remember him," Patsy said while giving Claire's ankle another whack with her foot. Claire scooted her chair over a couple of inches to escape.

"They moved away when he was ten. For some reason, he seems to think this is a better environment than Boston. I'd do anything for Andy, but we could have had the same environs in Mazatlan, where I want a second home. There at least we'd be among expats whose social status was more like ours." She blinked and sighed. "Present company excluded, of course. Well, if I have to wait for Mazatlan, at least I can bring some culture here."

Of course. "Yes, well," Claire cleared her throat, "here's what we feel the town needs." She and Patsy laid out their plans. When they finished, Bev took possession of the list.

"Those are all good ideas, and I'll add a few of my own. Have you gone to the other shops yet?"

Glancing at Claire, Patsy shook her head.

"One change to the plans, I'd like to go with you. They might take the proposal better from me, since I'm not an owner, but one of their best customers." Bev blotted the corner of her mouth.

Claire could just imagine. The woman probably waved around money like a Southern lady waves a hankie, but she had a point. "Good thought, and since you've lived here for a few years, you pull more weight than Lydia."

Bev stiffened and frowned. Patsy rolled her eyes.

"What?" Claire glanced between them. "Bev's a good customer. They'll listen to her."

"I'd like to think so," Bev said, fingering her bracelet. "What about Dee and Lydia? Are they in on this?"

Claire nodded and pulled a folder out of her tote, which Bev eyed with a smile. At least the SAK passed her inspection, unlike the town. That still rankled. Claire hoped they hadn't misplaced their friendship.

"These are the pictures I took yesterday." She spread them out on the table and pointed to one. "This is the antique shop. And here is the bookstore. See that top door hinge? All the screws are missing but one."

"A liability to be sure." Bev picked up the photo, held it close, and squinted.

"Would you like to borrow my glasses?" Patsy asked.

"No, thank you. I have my own." She quickly shuffled through the other photos, squinting at them then handed them back. "I'd prefer to see the real thing."

See? The woman couldn't see anything. "Why won't—" Patsy's foot smacked Claire's ankle again. "What?" She shot Patsy as innocent a stare as she could muster. "I was saying why don't we go then?"

On the way out the door, Claire whispered to Patsy, "You keep rolling your eyes like that and one day they're going to get stuck."

Chapter 5

Claire picked up a box of hair color from the drugstore shelf while Bev explained their plan to Tom Fowler, who stood arms folded, pipe in one hand, listening. So far so good. They needed the pharmacist to help persuade the other council members. Claire continued pretending to consider the golden brown as an option for Patsy's hair, turning the box over and reading the instructions, all the while keeping one ear on the conversation between Bev and Tom.

She had to admit, Bev was persuasive. Maybe Claire should have Bev tell Joel. He hadn't paid much attention last night, when she told him about their plan. She didn't appreciate his teasing, either. How was she supposed to have known that sink hole would appear right where she'd told Warren to park his '52 Chevy?

"A fine idea." Tom clenched his pipe between his teeth. "I painted the drugstore two years ago, but the missus has it in her mind to redo the trim work."

Good, he bought the idea. But then why not, with Bev buying an expensive bottle of perfume during the exchange. Claire returned the box to the shelf. She'd come back later when she could concentrate, otherwise she might pick out the wrong formula. Bad hair was one of the three deadly sins, and she already struggled with the other two—she hated to cook, and with her foot in her mouth half the time, her manners were suspect.

Claire joined Bev and Tom. "Can Patsy and I help you choose the trim color? We'd like to brighten the shops a bit, bring them into the twenty-first century."

"Well now, I don't know, Claire. The missus has her heart set on pine tree green."

"Patsy did some drawings. See how cheery the stores look in this." Claire unfolded the sketch. "I love the stripped awnings she drew. Don't you think Raelene would like some of those?"

Using his wife's favorite colors, Claire drove for home. "They come in a dark and light cranberry stripe. Then with some pots of hot pink azaleas, and perhaps the windows trimmed in that pine green she likes ..." She held her breath. Tom's decisions carried a lot of influence. It would be impossible to move ahead without him.

"I like it. Bring by the samples, and I'll see to it."

Patsy elbowed Claire.

"Oh, right. There's one more thing. We want your help with the other council members. That's why we came to you first. The town needs this, Tom. Tourists are going to Lake Hartwell and Lake Lanier instead of coming here."

He pulled the pipe from his mouth and nodded. "Believe me, I've noticed a steady decrease in business this past year. I can see where we might have some trouble with the boys, though, since their stores aren't as tourist dependent as most." He peered inside the pipe bowl, tapped it against his heel, then stuck it in his lab coat pocket. "I'll lay a little groundwork before the next meeting. Now, was there anything else, ladies?"

"No, that's it." Bev held out a dainty hand which disappeared in Tom's large one. "Thank you for your cooperation, Mr. Fowler. Ladies?" She turned and sashayed out the door.

Claire stared at her back and shook her head. "I'll come in later for that hair color," she said to Tom and linked arms with Patsy.

Outside, the three made their way toward the boutique, passing the ice cream parlor, *Flavors*. It was painted stark white and showed every speck of dirt. Claire wrinkled her nose.

"This place is the worst of all. Felix refuses to spend money to make it more appealing. Why, the man is tighter than bark on a tree. It'd serve him right if we all changed to store-bought ice cream."

"That's pretty drastic, but it might be effective," Bev said.

"If we can get the other members on board, we'll have enough votes to overcome his and Warren's objections." Claire grinned. "I can't wait to see their faces when they're outvoted."

They proceeded on to the boutique, *Sunspots*. Nancy Vaughn, another council member and longtime friend, could be counted on to support the restoration plans.

Nancy's high-pitched, elongated hello greeted them as they strolled in. She could have been Julia Child's sister with that voice. "Well, bless my soul. Claire Bennett! I haven't seen you in my shop in ages."

"I'm on a mission, Nancy, but not a clothes-buying one. Sorry."

"Oh." Her face fell. "So why *did* you come?"

Poor woman. In her giddiness, she'd probably seen dollar signs before her eyes. Bev stepped around Claire, and Nancy's spirits visibly revived as her height gained a good inch.

"My favorite customer. I just got in a new shipment, and there's a dress that made me think of you as soon as I laid eyes on it."

Patting her hand, Bev led her over to a display of summer shorts. "Of course, I'm your best customer. I've never left *Sunspots* without purchasing something."

Her smile dazzled, her teeth were so white. She must use those strip things, Claire figured as she ran her tongue over her teeth. Maybe she should get some.

"And while you show me your latest shipment, I'd like to talk to you about an idea we ladies have."

Like a moth to a porch light, Nancy fluttered around Bev.

Patsy pulled Claire toward the door. "They don't need us. Let's wait out here and not remind Nancy of our wardrobe neglect."

They sat on the bench beneath *Sunspot's* window to wait. Across the street, the lake simmered in the afternoon sun. By the time Bev came out, arms loaded with bags and Nancy's declared promise to support their campaign, it was nearly dinnertime. They'd have to approach the other merchants tomorrow. Hopefully, with the same good results.

Walking home, Claire couldn't help but wonder how much the town's revival would cost Bev and ultimately, Drew. As she rounded the corner, Claire spotted her twin daughters' blue Toyota parked in the driveway. She sprinted to the door.

"Megan? Melissa?" Why had they come home again so soon?

"We're in the kitchen, Momma."

Claire hung her tote on the stairs newel post. From the looks of the set table and the appetizing aroma permeating the house, the girls had been home for some time. She wondered what they'd fixed. It didn't really matter, of course. Twin-cooked anything was her favorite. They definitely inherited Joel's culinary talents.

She peeked through the kitchen doorway and came up short. The twins stood shoulder to shoulder at the soapstone counter, chattering and working on dinner. When had they become women? In her mind's eye, they were still little girls in pigtails, pretending to be chefs beside their daddy, perched on stools to reach the counter. Now they stood on their own, making supper for her. The girls turned around as she approached.

"To what do I owe this surprise? Neither of you flunked out have you? Clemson's still standing?"

Megan laughed and hugged her. "Momma, you're silly. We just wanted to come home and—" Melissa, who'd sidled next to them, tapped Megan's ankle with her foot, catching Claire's in the process.

What was that about?

"Uh, to see Charlie and Wes," Megan finished. "We missed them."

"And you and Daddy," Melissa added.

Uh-huh. Claire leaned back and peered at Megan. They were home three weeks ago. Since when did the twins make a five-hour drive just for their brothers' teasing? No, she knew her girls. They had a secret, and she didn't like being left on the outside of secrets. Still, she was thrilled to have them home and pulled Melissa into the circle and hugged her.

"Whatever the reason, I'm glad you're here." She looked into the pot. "That's a lot of spaghetti. Did you invite Charlie to supper, too?" She hadn't seen her eldest son in almost a month, even though he lived less than a mile away.

Megan nodded, her honey-blonde ponytail bouncing. "Yes ma'am. He'll be here at six-thirty."

That gave Claire an hour. "I'll go shower and be right back down. I want to hear all about your classes and friends." She headed up the stairs then paused, listening for them to spill the beans.

"Hey, Momma, do you have any French bread?"

Rats. They knew what she was up to. "In the freezer," she called before running up the stairs. What on earth could the girls be hiding? She hoped they wouldn't keep her in suspense for long. She couldn't concentrate on anything else until she knew. After a fast shower, she slipped into a clean pair of khakis and a white cotton shirt and hurried back to the kitchen.

"What can I do?" she asked, tying on an apron. Why she loved this kitchen so much when she didn't cook, she had no idea, but love it she did. The first time she'd been inside the hundred- and-twenty-year-old house—back when it belonged to old Anna Schrecter—she knew she wanted to live in it. It came on the market after Miss Anna moved into assisted living in Pineridge, and Joel bought it for her.

Together they refurbished it but left the original architectural detail. The kitchen retained its stone floor and high tin ceiling. They put in new soapstone counters and sink, replicating the old ones that had cracked. Soft, buttery-yellow walls and paprika cabinets made her feel hugged when she entered. Sometimes, it even made her want to cook. Okay, maybe that was an exaggeration.

"You can sit and keep us company." Melissa handed Claire a cup of tea and tucked a towel in her apron. "No offense, Momma, but we have this meal all planned out."

"Yeah, yeah, I know what y'all think of my cooking. At least I can make good coffee."

"You may not be a great cook, Momma," Megan said as she washed a dirty pan, "but nobody's a better potter in the entire South. Did I tell you we saw one of your decorative serving platters in a small museum gallery in Charleston?"

The surprise fell on Claire like a warm hug. "I wonder if that was the piece I sold in January from my website. It shipped to a Charleston address. How fun."

Megan picked up the towel and wiped her hands. "The owner said she visited here last summer. She was only waiting for an opening in their inventory or something like that. Anyway, the building is tiny and only features Southern artists, but I thought it was cool."

Claire scooped coffee grounds into a filter. Joel would want a cup as soon as he got home, and she always had it ready for him. She set the timer to start brewing ten minutes before he walked in.

The next hour flew by in laughter. Oh, but it was good to have the girls home. The house was too quiet without all her chicks. Technically, their youngest child, Wes, still lived at home, but he spent all his time at the community college, with friends, or closed up in his room and on the computer, so she hardly ever saw him. The whole family would've been together tonight if Adrianna could have come, but her job in Nashville kept her too busy to get home much. Claire never could figure out how a computer scientist ended up with a job in the music industry.

"Can anyone join this party or is it just girls?"

Claire jumped. She hadn't heard the door close. Why did Joel have to sneak up like that?

"Daddy!" Megan dropped her spoon and flew into Joel's arms with

Melissa right behind. He might be an old grump sometimes, but no one could say he wasn't a good father. He gave the girls a squeeze, then opened the lids on each pot and inhaled its aroma.

"Ahh, the perfect amount of oregano. Is my coffee ready? When's Cha—"

"Sit, Daddy," Melissa interrupted and pushed him toward the built-in banquette table. "I'll bring it to you."

"Oh, right, uh ... sure, thanks." He winked at Melissa.

Whatever the twins had planned, Joel was in on it and not her. What was that about? It wasn't her birthday, so why couldn't she know? She lifted her lips to him, but his kiss landed on her cheek. He dropped his lunch pail, jacket and two magazines on the counter. She'd be the one who picked them up later.

He sat on the bench opposite her. "What did they tell you on delivery when you ordered the new winch?"

"What winch?"

"The one I asked you to order in the note I left you this morning."

Claire stalled with a sip of tea, running the note back through her mind. Could she have tossed it away before reading all of it, or was he trying to pick a fight to throw her off his and the twins' secret?

"It was yesterday morning, and your note only said to pick up bait, which I did. It's in the fridge—" Uh-oh. She grinned to soften her next words and avoid an argument. "The fridge at the gallery, but I'll go back and get it right after dinner."

"Sometimes I wonder about you." He shook his head. "I really need that winch. Will you order a new one?"

"I'll go online after I get the bait." She frowned inwardly; he wasn't totally inept at navigating the Internet. Why couldn't he do his own ordering? She always had to ask him questions about something or other. He claimed that "frustration" kept him from doing it himself. Well, what about *her* frustration? "Sorry I forgot it, but I got caught up in plans for sprucing up Chapel Springs."

He grunted as he opened the paper.

Claire tapped her fingers on the table for a moment but got no response. Finally, she'd had enough. "How's it going, you ask? It's going well. I'm glad you're interested."

Joel flipped one corner of the paper down, then folded it, and laid it on the table. "Go ahead. Tell me. I won't be able to read my paper until you do."

If he didn't have his elbow on that newspaper, she'd grab it and whap him upside the head. Instead, she decided the best way to punish him was to tell him. "I told you last night we were going to talk to Tom Fowler and Nancy Vaughn today. Well, we did and they're on board. I think Felix and Warren are in for a surprise at the next council meeting."

The twins whispered to each other. When Joel faked a cough, they stopped. Okay, this was beginning to get on her last nerve. She'd ruled out her birthday and it wasn't their anniversary. Being on the outside of a secret didn't suit her well at all.

"I can't believe Felix and Warren won't support it." Joel scratched the back of his head. "Warren's bed and breakfast can't be doing well."

She finally had his attention. Amazing. "It isn't. Gloria stopped by the gallery yesterday and mentioned it. How she puts up with his stodginess, I don't know. Anyway, she's going to do what she can to influence him." Claire snickered. "I have a feeling Felix is going to be royally outnumbered."

The front door squeaked open. "Anybody home?"

Melissa dropped the strainer in the sink. "Charlie's here!"

Laughing at Joel and the twins jammed in the doorway to the dining room, each trying to reach Charlie first, Claire slipped through the hall and got to the foyer before them. Shiloh beat them all and stood on his hind legs with his front paws on Charlie's shoulders, giving his face a thorough licking. Sandi stood beside him. At twenty-six years old, the two glowed with youthful vigor.

"Sandi, my goodness. When I heard Charlie's voice I didn't realize you'd be with him. I'm delighted to see you." But why did Joel and the twins try to keep their visit a secret?

"Down, Shiloh!" Charlie pushed the mastiff's paws off him.

The dog promptly dropped only to slather his affections on Sandi. Good-natured, she laughed and scratched Shiloh's ears. He finally sat with a thump.

Charlie put his arm around Sandi and pulled her close. Looking at the twins, he asked, "You didn't say anything, did you?"

The girls shook their heads.

Claire thumped her hands on her hips. "Okay, what is going on?" She wanted to know and know now.

Charlie's face grew pink. She hadn't seen him blush since he had to pin a corsage on Sandi at their high school senior prom. And her face matched his. Suddenly, a seed of enlightenment germinated, and Claire grabbed Sandi's hand and pulled it toward her.

There, on the third finger of her left hand, sat ... Great Aunt Lola's diamond ring. Claire stared at it. Her son had finally proposed. But how did he get the ring? Claire raised her eyes to his and caught the nervous tic at the corner of his mouth. Joel was in on this. She turned her head and gave him the evil eye. That was her ring to give. Sure, she'd planned for it to go to her firstborn's bride, but Joel had no right to take it out of the safe deposit box without asking her. Even for Charlie. She'd deal with her husband later. Without releasing Sandi's hand, Claire yanked the towel from her apron and threw it at Charlie.

"That's for keeping it a secret from me." She pulled her future daughter-in-law into her arms. "Welcome to the family, sweetheart."

Sandi's eyes scrunched like an elf's with her pleased grin, but it was Charlie who made Claire chuckle. He puffed out his chest, proud as a papa loon while he shook his dad's hand. With everyone hugging and backslapping, she stood remembering. He first puffed his chest like that when—

"Charlie looks as proud right now as he did once when he was eighteen months old and I'd delayed getting him up from his nap. He got bored and investigated his diaper. In a proud display of artistic talent, he painted the wall beside his crib with the contents."

Charlie groaned. "Ma!"

"One day, son, you'll have kids. I want Sandi forewarned in case they take after you." Laughing, she hugged him. Her firstborn. "Now, when's the big date?"

Charlie glanced at Sandi first before he answered, and a sharp dagger stabbed Claire directly in her heart. She remembered when she and Joel did that. When they became one mind. Only somewhere along the line their minds drifted apart.

"We're looking at dates in July."

Oh, dear. That didn't give them much time. "Where are you having the wedding?"

"We'd like to have it in the town park, using the gazebo."

"Lovely. Be sure to have your mother call me, dear." Doing a quick calculation, Claire walked into the kitchen. A moment later, everyone followed her and encamped themselves around the banquette Joel had built to accommodate a dozen people.

Excited conversation floated around Claire as she picked up the spoon lying next to the pot and gave the sauce a stir. She liked the kids' idea of a wedding in the gazebo. *If* they got council approval, it only gave her around fourteen weeks to complete the town project before then. The town *had* to sparkle for the wedding. She winced at the time crunch. With the crazy characters who made up Chapel Springs, who knew what would happen? And if anything went wrong, Felix would blame it on her.

The gazebo!

Her spoon clanked against the side of the pot, splattering spaghetti sauce onto the stove. She grabbed a paper towel and wiped up the mess. Just because last July's fireworks display had been her idea didn't mean the resulting *fire* was her fault. Felix never would admit his cousin wasn't a professional pyrotechnic. Now she'd have to add fixing and repainting the gazebo to the project.

Wes arrived just as they sat to eat. A bit of brotherly shoulder bumping preceded the blessing. Joel had always encouraged shoulder bumping but barely tolerated the food blessing, and then only because his children initiated it. Had it been her, he would've ignored her and started eating. Stubborn old goat. His hands were on the table but not folded. He was ready to grab the bowl of spaghetti. He caught her peeking at him and shook his finger. He was such a hypocrite.

At Charlie's "amen," bowls passed and plates filled amidst chatter and clatter. Claire loved the ping-pong conversation and dove right into the thick of it, telling the kids about their plan to revitalize the town.

"Are you going to advertise on the Internet like Mrs. Smith suggested?" Charlie asked.

"We are. I already emailed Adrianna. Your sister agreed to help us design a website and get it up."

He nodded. "The Internet is a great way to market the town and a lot cheaper than magazines. Cable advertising's another way that's not too expensive. I want to open my own agency here one day." He took Sandi's hand. "Then we'll be Bennett and Bennett, specializing in cable and Internet ads."

"That's wonderful. Maybe you can help us make sure this campaign works," Claire said.

Joel grimaced, the muscles in his neck tightening. "I'm not sure there's enough business in Chapel Springs to support an ad agency, son."

She wished he wouldn't be so pessimistic. He'd put a damper on

Charlie's plans.

Unperturbed, Charlie grinned. "Now, Dad, you haven't taken Momma's campaign into consideration. When she sets that mind of hers to something, nothing stands in her way to success. Why, she could put her boots in the oven and before you know it, everybody'd be calling 'em biscuits."

Joel snorted. "That analogy is a bit off base with your mother. If she put biscuits in the oven, before you knew it everybody'd be calling 'em boots."

Claire bristled but held her tongue. She couldn't refute her lack of knowledge or skill in the kitchen, but did Joel have to make fun of her over it? She was only six when her momma died. Daddy never remarried and when she took cooking in middle school, she approached it *her* way. That may have worked for Frank Sinatra but not for her. She failed home-ec. More than once.

Sandi said something Claire missed in her musing that made everyone laugh. Charlie threw his arm around Sandi and pulled her close, kissing her cheek. He wore his love so openly. Was this simply newly engaged affection or did it go deeper? What did Charlie know about love that his daddy didn't?

She yearned for Joel to love her like that. Oh, she knew he loved her but not as freely as her son. Maybe it was going to church that made the difference in Charlie. Joel wouldn't go, but the library had lots of self-help books. They must have some that taught men how to love their women. Come Monday morning, she'd make a stop there.

Plan in place, Claire gathered the empty plates. "Anyone for dessert?" She stopped and turned to the twins. "Uh, what is dessert?"

Before they could answer, Wes pushed his chair back and stood. "I've got some work on the computer. I'll eat dessert later."

After one of Dee's decadent cakes, the kids, except for Wes, went to a movie. Claire loaded the last glass in the dishwasher, then filled the sink to soak the pans.

"Okay," Joel said. "What's got your panties in a wad? You're looking as low as a toad in a dry well."

Claire squirted soap into the pan. "I didn't appreciate you giving Charlie *my* Great Aunt Lola's ring. It was mine to give, not yours."

"I thought that was it." Joel picked up a steel wool pad and nudged Claire to the side, stepping in to wash the pan. As if he thought that was going to make up for his betrayal.

She leaned her hip against the counter and folded her arms. "Well, I can just imagine your ire if the tables were turned."

"Charlie asked me to get the ring out and begged me not to tell you. He wanted it to be a surprise, honey."

"Oh, it was a surprise, all right." She picked up a dishtowel and dried the pan he handed her. "You'd think they'd know by now I don't like surprises. And I could have acted surprised if you'd have told me about it." She swatted him with the towel. "At least you'd have spared me an entire evening of mad."

Chapter 6

Patsy gave the fluffy duvet a final tug then aligned her and Nathan's pillows. The bed appeared department-store-perfect—nothing out of place. Beneath the top cover, the sheets hadn't been changed, but from the outside, all looked ideal. Hiding imperfections seemed to be the story of her life.

Nathan's wallet rested on the dresser. Folded tight. The shower still ran, and his singing echoed in the bathroom. She traced the wallet's stitching with one finger and glanced toward the closed door. Her heart picked up its beat. If she opened it, would she find a note or some memento? Did she want to? She pulled her hand back and turned away. She still needed to settle on tonight's menu.

A few minutes later, the bathroom door opened and Nathan walked out, dressed in a brown-and-tan striped golf shirt and Dockers, ready for work. His eyes fell on her, opened wide, and he jumped.

"What are you doing up so early?" At the dresser, he picked up his wallet, slipped it in his back pocket and buckled his watch. "You don't usually open the gallery so early on Saturdays."

"I'm not going in today. Don't you remember? We have company coming for dinner tonight."

Nathan stared at her. "We do? Who, Joel and Claire?"

Patsy sat on the side of the bed. "Of course, along with some of our other friends. The party's for Joel's brother, Vince, who's joining Daddy's practice."

He tapped his temple. "Oh, right. What time do I need to be home?"

He didn't remember at all. She resisted the urge to sigh. "Everyone's arriving at six. Can you please be here by four?"

"This is a busy time of year, Patsy. You know that."

She did and he had seven hours to work. That was enough. She clenched her lips shut against the words she wanted to say.

His sigh—the one he didn't resist releasing—carried an exasperated edge. Then he paused and smiled. "I'll do my best." He kissed her cheek. "What did you plan for dinner?"

Changing the subject was his standard method of avoidance, but for the cause of peace, she went along. "I took yours and Daddy's diets into consideration. We'll have wasabi salmon with orange-ginger sauce, fried Brussels sprouts with walnuts, wild rice with cranberries, and field greens for the salad. I'll leave the blue cheese off your salad."

He nodded and picked up his briefcase.

"I can't vouch for the dessert, though, since Claire's responsible for that."

"No problem, then. It won't be edible."

Patsy couldn't help laughing and threw a pillow at him. "You're horrible. She'll pick up something from *Dee's 'n' Doughs*. And that'll serve you right."

A shadow passed over Nathan's face then disappeared so quickly she wasn't sure if she imagined it since he grinned.

"We'll see who has the most willpower tonight, me or your dad."

After he left, the silence in the house echoed around her. Downstairs, she flicked on the television, tuned it to cable radio, and selected a classical music channel, steering away from movie themes and love songs. Those made her sad, and she needed to pray, not cry. And to do it right, she needed a soft rag and the bottle of beeswax with orange oil.

Her mama first taught her to combine prayer and housework, telling her talking to God took the work out of chores. Polishing the wood in her childhood home became a task she loved, and together, she and her mother had polished and prayed through this house until she married Nathan.

After Patsy gave birth to their third child and they outgrew their small house, her dad asked them to move in here instead of buying another home. This one had grown too large for just him and Mama. Nathan had left his old accounting firm to open his own business, so money was tight, and they jumped at the opportunity. Her parents moved into the apartment above Mama's art studio behind the main house.

Now, the house loomed large around Patsy. In the living room, she polished the built-in bookcases and prayed for Nathan, asking God to bring him to his senses. The way he was acting, people would think his cheese slid off his cracker—if they found out. Hopefully, no one would.

Moving to the fireplace mantle, she prayed for herself as she rubbed the oil deep into its crevices. Why couldn't things stay the way they were? Was it something she'd done? She knelt at the fireplace surround, dabbed more oil on her cloth and rubbed it into the clefts. She buffed the wood until it gleamed as she asked God to calm her heart and fix her marriage. By the time she finished praying, her chores were done, the house smelled of orange oil and beeswax, and she felt ready to face the evening.

With her great room a merry blend of music, voices and laughter, Patsy whisked the orange-ginger sauce and readied it to pour over the salmon fillets. The house had been quiet for so long, this was a welcomed change and filled her with hope.

The doorbell rang again, and Patsy welcomed the McMillans, fashionably late as usual. She closed the door as Bev presented her back to Drew, who helped her remove her coat. Set free from the wrap, she adjusted the sides of a short, tight fitting black dress then sailed into the living room. Patsy's long broomstick skirt, with its blues and grays, had looked so lovely when she put it on. Now, it seemed dull. Mousey.

"Something smells wonderful, Patsy," Drew said. "I'm looking forward to it."

Sweet man, he was a good friend. "Thank you. I'd better get back to it."

She hung their coats as Drew crossed the room to where Nathan chatted with Joel and his brother, Vince. What would it be like, having Vince work with her father? While she liked him, it felt really strange for Daddy to have a partner. He'd always worked alone, except for a nurse. It was hard for her to admit he needed the help. It meant he was getting old. Both her parents were.

Her dad joined the group of men while her mother stood chatting with Pastor Seth and JoAnn Hanson. Her mother must have told them a funny story because Seth threw back his head with hearty laughter. When Mama laughed, it always reminded Patsy of a bell, ringing melodiously.

She returned to the kitchen, where the aroma of oranges and ginger lent a festive mood.

"Our Vince has changed, hasn't he?" Claire picked up two plates to take to the table.

Vince's youthful face belied his age—thirty-eight, but changed? Patsy shook her head. "I don't know. He still looks wet behind the ears." She laid lemon wedges beside the salmon on the plates Claire held. "I just hope Daddy's patients remember he's not a kid anymore. Why did Vince leave Atlanta?"

Claire's smile faded and her voice became a whisper. "Ariel left him for the hospital administrator. Broke his heart."

Patsy gasped. "You never said anything." Poor Vince. At his wedding, the love gleamed in his eyes when he looked at his bride.

"We just found out the night he got here. He told us the bare minimum, and then said he didn't want to talk about it again. That's what I meant about him being different. He doesn't have the same joy d'verb he used to."

"*Joie de vivre.*"

"Whatever, he doesn't have it anymore."

Was every marriage doomed? Her parents were happy and had survived fifty years together, but what of the others? Patsy followed Claire and carried two more plates to the table.

Bev had joined the men, her animated face commanding their attention, even as her hands flitted like butterflies, punctuating her conversation. Mesmerized, the men hung on her every word, except Drew, who stood to one side, looking uncomfortable, causing Patsy to wonder about the state of their marriage. Would they end up a statistic, too?

Claire nudged her and, scrunching a goofy face, crossed her eyes. "Hey, Chicken Little, I'm hungry."

Patsy chuckled. "Okay, call everyone to dinner. I'll get the last two plates." Maybe her thoughts were too pessimistic.

In the kitchen, her mother stood at the counter with her back to the doorway.

"What do you need, Mama?"

She startled, and a knife and fork clattered to the floor. "Patricia Louise Benson! You scared the living daylights out of me. Shame on you."

Benson? A chill entered Patsy's heart. Her mother hadn't called her by her maiden name since the day she married Nathan. "I'm sorry. Can I help you find something?" She scurried forward to pick up the utensils off the floor.

Her mother waved her away. "No, I certainly know my way around my own kitchen. Go see to your friends."

"Are you feeling all right, Mama?"

Her mother turned and put her hands on her hips. "Well, of course I am, child. Whatever makes you think I'm not?"

Being called child for one, and this wasn't her kitchen anymore. It was Patsy's. Not wanting to alarm her mother, Patsy raised the corners of her mouth.

"Just wanted to let you know dinner's on the table."

A talk with her dad was in order. If she could stall him for a moment before he left, she could tell him about this so he'd keep a watch on Mama's behavior. After all, she was seventy now. The word Alzheimer's slipped into Patsy's thoughts. With her worries over Nathan, she didn't need that. Shooting a prayer heavenward, she pasted on a bright smile, and joined her guests.

Out the dining room's large bay window, light rain pattered against the panes, highlighting the cheerful atmosphere around her table. Good friends enjoying one another and good food warmed her heart. If only it would stay this way and never change, she'd be happy.

Through an open window—raised a few inches to let in the fresh air —the loons wailed in a perpetual conversation, reminding her. She and Nathan used to chat at the end of each day, sharing achievements and disappointments. Now the only one she talked to was Claire.

Down on his end of the table, he joined in animated conversation with Drew and Joel. She frowned and turned to Claire. "What happened to our normal guy-girl seating?"

"I don't know." Claire cut her fish. "This is great salmon. I remember trying to make this once, but mine didn't taste like yours."

"And I remember you didn't have any wasabi. Instead of going to Pineridge to buy some, you sprinkled green food coloring into baking soda and used that."

Claire, bless her heart, blushed. "Oh, yeah."

"That's your problem in the kitchen, my friend. You can't substitute things unless you know what you're doing."

She snorted. "Who made up that rule?"

"It's a matter of chemistry, not a rule."

"I failed chemistry."

"I rest my case." Patsy patted Claire's hand. "You have so many other talents, and since Joel loves to cook, you don't need to. Why take that from him?" Patsy speared a Brussels sprout. "Do you realize how many women would kill to have a husband who cooks?"

Claire's eyes grew soft as they traveled beyond Patsy. "I suppose you're right, but still ... maybe I should do something to make up for it."

She had her doubts about that. Knowing Claire ...

"Bev tells me," Drew used his fork to gesture to his wife, "that you've enlisted her in some campaign to beautify our sleepy town."

Vince paused, his water glass halfway to his mouth, and laughed. His gorgeous smile belonged in a toothpaste ad. A doctor shouldn't be that handsome. Patsy compared him to Joel. Brothers they might be, but Vince got the best of the family genes. She'd often wondered if Claire ever compared the two.

Vince blotted his mouth and turned to his brother. "I'd be willing to wager my sister-in-law is involved in this."

"Ya' think?" Joel chuckled. "No bandwagon has ever made it past my wife."

Water splashed over the edge of Claire's glass when she set it down. "You can't deny that Chapel Springs could use some sprucing up."

"Never argued the point." Joel raised his hands in surrender. "I'm on your side. Remember?"

Smart man. Patsy sucked her bottom lip in to keep from laughing.

"You should thank Claire instead of maligning her," Bev said.

Joel opened his mouth then clamped it shut and shrank into his chair in helpless resignation. Poor Joel had never come up against anyone like Bev. None of them had. While Claire tended to run over people unknowingly, Bev used logic and coercion, a lethal combination. Patsy still hadn't warmed to her completely. Something about the woman set wrong with her.

Bev gave a sharp nod in Joel's direction. "Our committee will bring about changes that will increase tourism and in turn, your financial worth."

"How do you propose to accomplish this?" Nathan asked.

With a coquettish tilt of her head, Bev beamed at him. Patsy, being a good Southern girl, had learned the art of flirting by the time she was out of nappies. There was social flirting, the kind every Southern belle did to get her way, but this was *not* social flirtin'. This was a come on if she ever saw one. When Nathan didn't respond, Patsy wasn't sure whether to be relieved or cry. And what must Drew think of his wife's blatant behavior?

"We've approached many of the merchants, especially those on the town council, and won them to our side." Bev beamed.

"Ha!" Joel's guffaw echoed off the high ceiling. "I'll bet you don't have Felix and Warren tucked in your pocket."

"Maybe not." Claire set down her knife. "But we'll outvote them by the time we're done getting our support in place."

"If Bev's doing the asking, you'll be sure to get those votes," Drew said with a note of pride in his voice.

His wife smiled at him then turned to Vince. "Tell me, Doctor, how are you adjusting to this small town?"

"What's to adjust? I was raised here."

Bev waved away the explanation and leaned forward. "But you've spent years in Atlanta." The deep V of her neckline revealed way too much cleavage. Patsy was embarrassed for Drew, who put his arm around Bev's shoulders and pulled her back.

Vince glanced at Claire and swallowed, his Adam's apple conspicuous in the motion. "I'll miss some of the readily available culture, but it was time to come back."

"And now it's time for dessert." Claire jumped up and grabbed her plate. "I picked up one of Dee's delectable death-by-chocolate creations."

Bev reached across the table and squeezed Vince's hand. "Don't worry, Doctor. I have plans to bring culture right here to Chapel Springs." She sat back. "Right after we ladies take on the town council."

Chapter 7

"Do y'all have time for lunch before you head back to school?" Claire glanced over her shoulder as she pulled out of the church parking lot and onto Cottage Lane. With Patsy's party last night, she hadn't had much time with the twins. "Pizza, maybe?"

Trees lined the left side of the road and on the right, Glen Tabor's adorable beach cottages. They didn't need much work, just some flowers to anchor their white picket fences. Each cottage wore colorful awnings and matching shutters, reminding Claire of kindergarten children in brand new clothes, lining up for their first day of school.

"Sure, we've got time." Always the people-pleaser, Melissa looked in the back seat at Megan. "That okay with you?"

"Sure." Megan put her hand on Claire's shoulder, her eyes twinkling in the rearview mirror. "Hey, Momma, Sandi led our college group this morning. She had us each make a list of the things we want in a husband. Then she said we shouldn't even date a guy if he doesn't match up to the list. Wild, huh?"

Melissa looked out the window. "Why risk fallin' in love with a boy if he's not husband material?"

Claire's momma-antennae vibrated with the memory of Melissa's broken heart when she stopped dating Felix's son, Billy. He'd refused to go to church with her, claiming religion was the opiate of the masses. Little snot couldn't even come up with an original excuse.

Megan rolled her eyes. "Who cares about falling in love right now, anyway? I just want to have fun."

Claire reached over and gave Melissa's hand a squeeze while

frowning at Megan in the mirror. She should know not to remind her twin of her heartbreak, but Megan wasn't as tenderhearted as Melissa.

"What else did Sandi say?"

Melissa turned, laying her arm across the seat back. "She told us to start praying for our future husbands."

Claire frowned. If they didn't—"How can you pray for a man you don't know yet? What did she mean by that?" She hung a right into the *Pasta Bowl's* parking lot and found a space near the entrance. "Well, looky here. For once we beat the Presbyterians to Sunday lunch. Will wonders never cease?"

Megan jumped out as soon as they stopped and ran ahead to get their name on the list. After locking the car, Claire linked her arm with Melissa, and they strolled toward the entrance. Jake must have painted the railings by the steps already, getting a jump on the revival. The buttery-yellow nicely offset the deep red of the azaleas in the restaurant's flowerbeds.

"Sandi told us God has a perfect mate picked out for each of us. By praying, we're telling God we want the husband he's chosen for us."

Claire nearly tripped over her heart as it zinged to her toes. Was that what was wrong with her and Joel? She had never prayed for a husband. Well, she *did*, but not like that. When single, she'd asked the stars to send her one. The day she met Joel, she fell in love and never looked back.

What did all this mean? Her heart must have returned to her chest because it pounded, and with each pulse, lodged a lump firmly in her throat. Inside the *Pasta Bowl*, she let the girls order for her. Her thoughts were so jumbled she'd probably try to order egg rolls.

Somehow she swallowed her pizza and sweet iced tea while listening to the girls chatter on about Sandi and her discourse on future husbands. When the waiter asked if they wanted dessert, Claire almost ordered Rolaids.

She hurried the girls home to pack. The minute they pulled out of the driveway, she ran inside to call Patsy. She needed to talk. Now.

"Hello?"

"Meet me at the bench."

Claire waited near the shoreline. Out on the lake, the loons swam in lazy circles, and a fish jumped in hopes of catching a fat bug. This was the place she and Patsy had met to cry on each others' shoulder and talk about heart issues since they were old enough to have issues greater than Raggedy Ann going bald. She sensed rather than heard Patsy's arrival.

The implications of what Claire had learned left her bewildered. With her friend beside her, lending strength in her silence, she leaned down and picked up two pebbles, rolling them in her fingers.

"This morning, Sandi—I told you she and Charlie got engaged—started a new topic at church for the college age girls. Dating and marriage. She told them to pray *now* for their future husbands." She turned and stared at Patsy. "Have you ever heard of such a thing?"

"Actually, yes. My daddy told me he and Mama started praying for my husband the day I was born."

Claire tossed the stones down. "And you never thought to tell me?"

"You wouldn't have listened back then. You were as much an agnostic then as Joel is now."

Why was Patsy always right? "But now I'm more than a little confused and worried. Sandi told them God had a husband picked out for them. One who shares their faith. All they have to do is ask and he'll bring the right one to them."

"That's what I was taught, too."

"You prayed and God sent you Nathan. Is this the happily-ever-after you prayed for?"

"We aren't promised happy-ever-after, Claire. What we are promised is help through the problems."

"Cheese-Louise, I'm as mixed up as a can of Planters."

"About what?" Patsy picked a bit of green paint from her cuticle.

"I never did that—pray for a husband, I mean—even after I became a Christian." Claire bit her ragged thumbnail. "Do you suppose ..."

She jumped up and paced in front of the bench. Running her hands through her hair, she pushed its layers away from her face. After a moment she stopped. With her fingers interlocked, gripping the back of her neck, she spun and faced Patsy.

"What if Joel isn't the right one?" There, she said it. Her hands fell to her sides. "We fell in love and got married. I thought that was what you did." She plopped back down on the bench. "What am I going to do? What if God never intended for me to be with Joel? He isn't a Christian, and ... but—" She ran out of breath and options.

"I don't know." Patsy's voice came out in a whisper.

Claire picked at the dry skin around her chewed nail. Aunt Lola had

had more than one husband. In fact, she'd had several. Did she ask God about them? Somehow, Claire didn't think so.

If she wasn't destined to marry Joel, then who had God picked for her?

"Oh, for the love o' Van Gogh, do you remember Benny Allgood in fourth grade?" She made a face, curling her lip. "His mother always made him my partner in square dancing. I couldn't stand to hold his sweaty hands, and even though Daddy was one of the chaperones, he wouldn't stand up to Benny's mama. I'll never forget my humiliation when the petticoat under my dance costume fell down and Benny stuffed it in his pocket."

Patsy snorted. "I felt so sorry for you when the woman calling the dance asked over the loudspeaker, 'Did you lose your petticoat little girl?'"

Her giggles grew into riotous laughter. Claire couldn't help herself and chuckled. It was funny now, but it hadn't been back then.

"That's probably why I hate square dancing."

Patsy finally mopped her eyes. "What made you think of Benny Allgood?"

Claire sobered. "What if God wanted me married to *him*?"

"Well, you'd never have to worry about losing your petticoats." Her lips flubbered as suppressed laughter burst out her mouth.

"You're terrible. I'm trying to be serious here." Struggling not to laugh herself, Claire slapped Patsy's hand. "This is a serious situation." Her friend's laughter didn't stop. "I'm serious, Patsy."

Wiping her eyes again, Patsy took a deep breath. "I'm sorry," a chuckle interrupted her, "but I can't get that image out of my mind." She leaned down and picked a dandelion then blew its seed-dust into the air. The gentle breeze lifted the miniature parachutes higher, scattering them hither and yon.

"So what are you going to do?"

Claire reached out to catch one of the floating seeds, but the motion wafted it away just out of reach. "I don't know. I keep thinking about Aunt Lola."

"I remember her trying to teach us the art of flirtin' with boys. We were all of about eight years old and not very interested, but she was so glamorous, even at seventy-five, that we couldn't help but listen."

"I can still hear her saying, 'Girls, you dip your chin down like this, then peek through your eyelashes like this.' We'd try it and she'd laugh and tell us we'd get it one day." Claire missed the old gal. "What I remember most is her telling me that a man should treat me like a queen. Never let a man put you second place to anyone or anything. Well, what if you're married to the wrong person, and what if he's putting you in second, third or even fourth place?"

Patsy reached over and gave Claire's hand a squeeze. "I know you're mixed up right now, but don't do something you'll regret. All those husbands of your Aunt Lola's weren't really such a good thing, you know."

"I guess I just need to leave my options open and wait."

Patsy's forehead wrinkled. "Be careful, girl."

Claire stood and brushed dandelion dust off her pants. "Don't worry, I will. If I'm not supposed to be married to Joel, I'm not even sure what I'd want in another man. Someone would have to knock me off my feet."

The sun dropped below the treetops, casting long shadows over the beach. Claire raised a hand in good-bye but didn't move as Patsy headed home.

What if, back when she was twenty, she'd found the man God intended for her? Someone who treated her like Aunt Lola said? Like a queen? Someone who appreciated her? Who talked with her. Shared dreams with her. Held her hand instead of walking off and leaving her behind.

Someone who didn't blame her for everything.

"Wes, I need to use the computer when you're done," Claire hollered up the back stairs.

"In a few minutes, okay?"

She plunged her hands back into the sink to wash the frying pan. "Just let me know." That kid was on that computer all the time any more.

The phone rang. She flipped the dishwater off her hands, grabbed a towel and plucked the receiver off the wall.

"Hello?"

"Claire, we haven't met yet, but I'm Zoe Walker, Sandra's mother, and she said to call you, and since we have such a short time before the wedding, I thought I'd jump right on it and call you tonight." The words came at breakneck speed. "I'm pleased about the children, aren't you?"

Whoa, Claire's breath came up short just listening to the woman. "Uh, yes. Excited, actually. We've grown to love Sandi." The question was would they grow to love her whirlwind of a mother? Claire had never heard anyone talk so fast without taking a breath.

"Yes, well, I must say, I cannot understand Sandra's decision to have the wedding in Chapel Springs instead of here. But, we'll move on. Right now, I need your list of guests for the invitations. Sandra insists on a small wedding. Oh, and the other big thing you have to do is the rehearsal dinner. That will be the night of the rehearsal, naturally. For some silly reason, Sandra thinks she prefers *simple* things."

Said like that, simple sounded more like last week's leftovers. "Uh, I'm not—"

"Oh, I'm sure you can manage a *simple* dinner, certainly. She's forever telling us how she loves the *simple* atmosphere of your home."

If she said "simple" like that again ... Aunt Lola had warned her about women like Zoe. Jealous mothers-in-law. What in the world was she jealous *of*? "Well, if—"

"Since Sandra has a maid of honor and five bridesmaids, plan on six ushers, too. Well, five really plus the best man, whom I'm assuming will be Charles's brother Wesley."

That was her idea of a small wedding? Claire gave up trying to say anything and instead tried to make sense of what the woman said. Jotting down "list, rehearsal dinner, and ushers" on the blackboard next to the phone, she missed something. What was it? "When do you need the list?"

"I'd like it by the end of the week, since we need to get the invitations in the mail, and did Sandra tell you we'll fly in the week of the wedding? And, of course, I'll come for any showers."

Fly in? "No, she didn't say anything about it. You don't live in Pineridge? I'm not sure we'll have enough room." Had Sandi told her parents about Shiloh? Not everyone liked big dogs, not to mention that Claire wasn't sure she wanted this woman staying with them. Her ears hurt with the mere speculation of a whole weekend around her.

"We lived there for only a short time, thankfully, while my husband helped a bank out of some little trouble. Did Sandra tell you he's a well-known investment banker here in Des Moines? We returned home to Iowa as soon as he sorted out the situation. We're by the country club where I was raised. Our families and all our old friends are here. Well, all but Sandra, of course. We'll be bringing those friends and family members with us. I remember how quaint Chapel Springs is, but if there is anywhere remotely suitable nearby, it would be helpful if you would make arrangements for us."

Thank the good Lord. Claire's head spun as she added "reserve B&B or cottages" to her list, which was quite doable. The dinner. That's what she forgot. "About that dinner, where did you say you wanted it?"

"Well, if I had my way, it would be at the nearest country club. But my daughter wants the *simple* atmosphere of your home. Can you handle that? But now I need to run so I'll be expecting your list soon. Bye."

Claire expelled a long breath. While she was glad her future daughter-in-law liked her, raving to her mother had not been such a good idea. Chuckling, she pictured Zoe in haute couture, throwing down a Gucci bag as a gauntlet for Sandi's affections. Silly woman.

A quick mental calculation of the guests, Claire figured the rehearsal dinner would be for at least twenty-four, more if the out-of-towners were included. She stood in the doorway of the dining room. Even with an extra table, extending the dining room into the living room, they'd never fit everyone in. She glanced out the large window to the backyard. The patio. Of course. They could serve outside. The weather should be nice enough.

That wouldn't be the problem. The food would. If only she knew how to cook. If Joel hadn't always hogged the kitchen, she might have learned. Right now, her problem was that he refused to cook for more than ten people. It wasn't fun, according to him. It was work, and he worked hard enough. This would take some finessing.

She walked into the den. "Honey?"

Engrossed in a basketball game, he hadn't heard her. Interrupting any ballgame was not the way to make her husband cooperate. While she waited for the commercial, she picked up a bowl Joel had left in the den last night, dumped the old maids of popcorn into the trash, and took it back to the kitchen. When she returned the game still blared, so she grabbed a Southern Living magazine off the coffee table and curled up on the couch.

She thumbed through the pages, flipping aimlessly. What would Joel say about hosting the rehearsal dinner here? He would think it had been her idea. Then if anything went wrong ...

Joel leaned forward. "He got fouled!" He looked at her. "Did you see that?" He turned back to the game, not waiting for her answer.

Patsy entertained large crowds, fed everyone and made it look effortless. So why couldn't he? Claire pushed aside the thought and focused on the magazine, flipping a few more pages until an advertisement jumped out at her. Henderson's Organic Market cooking course. If only she could take one and learn enough to pull off the rehearsal dinner. Pie-in-the-sky dreams. That's what her dad would say about that idea. She turned the page and read an article on azaleas.

The TV clicked off. "They lost. I'm going to bed. You coming?" Joel stood in the doorway.

"Huh? Oh, yeah. I'll be right there." She flipped the pages back and took one last glance back at the cooking school ad. If only …

That was one of Aunt Lola's favorite sayings. "Were ifs and buts candy and nuts, we'd all have a merry Christmas."

She followed Joel upstairs and down the hall toward the bedroom, flipping off light switches as she passed. With his team losing, she'd have to talk to him tomorrow about cooking the rehearsal dinner. She paused with her hand on the hall light switch. What if God had intended for her to have a husband who didn't cook? Would she have learned? Maybe Joel had been holding her back all these years. She stopped outside the bedroom. What if …

What if God had wanted her to be some famous cook like Sarah Lee, but she never discovered it?

Chapter 8

"Someone must have warned the council to prepare for lots of folks for tonight's meeting," Joel whispered in Claire's ear.

She counted the seats from the foyer of the bank's upstairs community room. Hopefully, they'd all be filled with her supporters. Chapel Springs needed this revival, and she intended to see it through until the town sparkled again. If the mayor and his cronies couldn't see that, they shouldn't be in office.

The hum of voices drew her into the room. "Felix is about to have his feathers and his second chin ruffled." She took a deep breath and pulled Joel through the double doors. "Come on. Let's find our cohorts."

She quickly spied Happy Drayton in a corner, head and shoulders above the crowd, talking with Earl Appling. Apparently those two hadn't even bothered to change out of their fishing vests, but came straight from the lake. They probably still stunk of fish, but as long as they voted with her, she'd overlook it. Joel raised his chin in acknowledgment to Happy's wave and headed toward the duo.

"Save me a seat," he tossed over his shoulder as he walked away.

It would be nice to have a husband who stayed by her side. Her nerves were strung tight as a fiddler's bow, and she'd have liked his support.

Patsy and Nathan hadn't arrived yet, but Nancy from *Sunspots* was chatting with the McMillans, probably tempting Bev with tidbits about new merchandise. Claire eyed Bev's fancy Italian pumps. Those had to have cost five big ones, at least. Drew must make an awfully good salary.

In front of the windows overlooking a meadow behind the bank, Ellie Grant, the librarian, and Tillie from *The Tome Tomb* used bookstore, had a lively discussion going, no doubt about books. That pair lived and breathed books. Whenever Claire picked up a new one from the library, Ellie gave her a review on it, whether Claire wanted it or not. She watched them for a moment. Both hand-talkers, she waited for one of them to backhand an unsuspecting passerby.

She quickly grew bored. Catching a whiff if fresh brewed coffee, she followed her nose to the refreshment table. Felix always provided dessert at evening meetings. The town could pay for cookies but not flowers? They weren't even Dee's cookies, so he couldn't argue support for a town merchant. Claire bent over the plate and inhaled. Nothing. Not a hint of chocolate or anything. She turned her nose up at the unmistakable store-bought cookies and poured a cup of coffee.

JoAnn came out of the kitchen with another coffee pot. "Claire, how are you?"

"Better question, did you get to talk to Felix?"

She shook her head. "I tried, but either he had a sudden meeting, or I had an emergency. It was very frustrating and strange."

Claire patted JoAnn's hand. "Don't worry about it. I know you tried. He'll find out tonight, though."

Warren Jenkins sauntered in, followed by his longsuffering wife, Gloria. How she put up with him, Claire didn't know. He made a beeline for Felix, leaving Gloria standing on her own, looking lost. Claire couldn't help feeling sorry for her. Gloria was so sweet and hospitable, how she came to marry Warren was a mystery. Maybe like Claire, she didn't pray about a husband. Of the town's two inns, Gloria's B&B, *Sweet Dreams*, was Claire's favorite. Victorian in style, it fit her image of the perfect Bed and Breakfast.

The other B&B, *Chapel Lake Inn*, built during the 1920s, was a typical old lakeside hotel. It was rumored—emphasis on rumor—that FDR had stopped there during one of his trips to Warm Springs. According to the owner, he wanted to try the waters of Chapel Springs. No one had ever validated the fact, but that didn't bother Faye. She had a commemorative plaque made and called one of her rooms the Roosevelt Suite. Claire sniffed. As if that made her boots biscuits.

"Who are you looking down your nose at now?" Patsy's eyes twinkled and her long silver earrings swayed just above her shoulders. A barely detectable scent of peach blossoms floated around her.

"You just get here?" Claire asked, ignoring the question.

"Nathan was late. Is everyone else here?"

"Just about. I was looking to see if our restaurant contingent is here. Jake arrived a couple of minutes ago."

Lydia stood with her brother-in-law and sister Lacey, who said something and pointed toward Claire. Jake looked up and bounded across the room as only a thirty-year-old man could, a piano-keyboard-grin adorning his face.

He pumped Claire's hand. "I'm excited about your plan. It's about time the town realized we depend on the tourist trade. My revenues have been down nearly forty percent. I had to lay-off two of my wait staff." He glanced at his watch. "We'd better find seats. The meeting will begin in a couple of minutes, if I know our mayor."

Not wanting to be under Felix's nose, Claire made her way to the sixth row followed by Patsy. A moment later, Joel and Nathan joined them.

Joel leaned toward Claire, his voice lowered. "Earl and Happy are on board."

She smiled her thanks. Twisting her neck a bit, she glanced at Nathan sitting on the far side of Patsy, his arm on the back of her chair. How could he sit there with his arm around Pat-a-cake, acting the loving husband?

Claire sat back as Felix lumbered to his seat at the table in front of the room. The other council members trailed behind him, their chairs scraping the floor as they moved into place. One by one, they sat and poured glasses of water from the pitcher in the center of the table. Felix glared until they all settled. Finally, he banged that ever-lovin' gavel on the tabletop podium.

"Let's have some order here. Since our Council President is out of town, I'll be presiding. We need to start this meeting." His eyes moved from right to left, traveling over the crowd until they came to rest on Claire. He squinted at her with suspicion. She sat up straighter as his eyes narrowed and leaned toward Patsy.

"The jig's up. He's on to us," Claire stage-whispered behind her hand. "He just doesn't know what yet. I swanney, even if all his brains were dynamite, he couldn't blow his nose."

"Stop. He's not dumb, just short-sighted and set in his ways."

"More like mule-stubborn."

Faye looked over her shoulder at them, scowling. Patsy nudged Claire with her elbow. "Hush. Somebody'll hear you."

The gavel banged again, and the crowd quieted. Felix called the roll, which was silly in Claire's opinion. He could look down the table and see everyone was there. Patsy's dad, Doc Benson, who chose a seat at the end of the table, smiled at them. Claire waggled her fingers at him and raised an eyebrow at Patsy, who nodded. Good that meant her dad was with them, too.

Tom sat on one side of Felix, hopefully to keep the man under control, but Claire doubted it would help. Eileen Carlson blushed as she took a seat on the other side of Felix and scooted her chair closer to his. Claire swore she saw Eileen bat her eyelashes at him. The others flanked Warren, with Ellie, who served as the town clerk, sitting at the end with her laptop.

After the roll call, Ellie slid on her glasses. The chain attached to their earpieces swayed and sparked in the light as she read the minutes of the last meeting. Claire wondered if it tickled. Doc took a drink from his water, Tom pulled out a handkerchief and blew his nose, and Ellie droned on and on.

Claire leaned over and cupped her mouth over Patsy's ear, earning her the evil eye from Felix. "This meeting won't be so boring once we get to the new business."

When the old business finally ended and Felix called for any new business, Claire jumped to her feet. "Mr. Chairman, it has—"

"You haven't been recognized, Claire." He pointed behind her. "Mr. Gordon? You have some new business?"

As the postmaster, Lester Gordon, stated his agenda, Claire took her seat and fumed. It wasn't Lester's dimples that won him the first speaking slot, or the cracked sidewalks under the postal boxes. Felix must have gotten wind of what they had in mind. For a precious ten minutes, the state of the postal concern was discussed.

For Pete's sake, if they didn't hurry up, she wouldn't get to speak at all. She glared at Felix, his arms folded across his chest and a smug grin on his face. If he was thinkin' to block her, he had another think coming.

Or was it "thing" coming? She'd read something about the debate between the two somewhere. Where had she been? Oh, yes. The dentist office waiting room the one and only time she'd had to have a root canal.

Bad thought. Moving on …

If *Felix* thought he would flummox her plans, she'd show him! She'd show him, even if she had to jump up and interrupt.

Only two others had new business. When they were done and with a sly smile on her lips, Claire stood and slowly turned around. No one else stood. "Well, Mr. Mayor, it would seem that I'm the last one standing."

Felix cast his scowl to and fro, obviously hoping someone had a question or comment. When he found no one, he huffed. "All right, Claire. What business do you have to bother this council with?" His condescending smile invited people to laugh but quickly faded when no one complied.

Her fingers curled. She'd remain pleasant if it killed her. "Mr. Mayor and members of the council, it has come to our attention—"

"Just who is 'our'?"

She gritted her teeth. "If you'd display some restraint, I'm sure all your questions will be answered. The people in question are business owners in Chapel Springs. There is a noticeable decline in the outward appearance of our town. There is also a corresponding decline in tourism and the influx of dollars they bring." She appreciated the murmured confirmations she heard.

"We believe the two are related and propose a beautification campaign, a revival if you like, of Chapel Springs. A few buildings need to make some minor repairs and paint. Then we'll add bright awnings and large pot gardens." Now for her zinger. "We'd also like to see the lamppost flowers brought back. They added so much charm to our village."

She paused a moment to let people remember. Once the chatter subsided, she swiped her hands down her sides and continued. "Lastly, we would like to propose the town get a website to promote tourism." Claire sat down to a round of applause.

Warren glanced at Felix, and at his slight nod, drew his brows together. "I'm a business owner in this town. Why wasn't I consulted?"

"Why touch a hot stove when you know it'll burn?" Tom asked.

"Just what do you mean by that?" Warren half turned in his chair and glared at the pharmacist.

"It's a known fact that you and Felix resist every proposed expense." Tom removed his glasses and polished them with his necktie. "I don't know what you're saving our tax dollars for. It certainly doesn't go to our salaries as council members."

"Good question." A woman's voice, strong and well modulated, carried over the laughter Tom's answer sparked. "Tell us, where exactly are those tax dollars going?"

Her voice had a familiar ring to it. Claire craned her neck to find the owner.

Felix pounded his gavel. "Not one penny has been misspent. Who asked that?"

"Jacqueline Ford, WPV, Channel 10, Pineridge."

The local evening news, of course. Claire couldn't have planned it better, but how did they get wind of tonight's meeting? She didn't come every time the council met.

"Did you invite her?" Joel asked.

Claire shook her head. "But you can bet Felix thinks I did. That glare of his could ignite a barbeque."

"So tell me, Mr. Mayor," Jacqueline said, "will tax revenues be used for this town revival?"

"We haven't decided if the town needs reviving. I don't think it does."

Felix's deepening scowl didn't seem to bother Tom Fowler. He reached for the microphone. "Paint's cheap, Felix, but we're not proposing the town's tax revenues cover the cost. We merchants have agreed to purchase our own paint."

"I didn't agree to pay for any awnings," Warren growled through his scraggly beard. "And the paint on my video store," he peered at Jacqueline, "*Front Row Seat*, is just fine, thank you very much."

Sure it was if you liked mud brown.

As if he heard her thoughts, he shifted his attention to Claire. "And I'd appreciate it if y'all and your nosy little committee would leave me out of this."

Bev rose. "My dear Mr. Jenkins, if you don't mind, I'd like to show some photos. In fact, if the deputy would get the lights, I've prepared a presentation for your edification."

Claire sat forward in her chair. She knew Bev had prepared something, but she'd kept it a secret. This had better be good.

Ignoring any objections from Felix, the lights went out and a PowerPoint presentation lit the wall above the council's heads. As they turned to look, views of each building appeared with captions bearing the names of the businesses. First up was *Front Row Seat*, not how it looked today but a shot from a few years ago, fresh and bright with flags flying in pots filled with red, white and blue flowers. Where had Bev gotten those? Claire glanced at Patsy.

"Tom supplied them from a Labor Day celebration," she whispered.

The next slide showed *Front Row Seat* with its drab brown paint. The large plate glass window had a crack in the lower left corner with a length of duct tape slapped over it on the inside. On the sill, dirt gathered in the corners.

In a clever demonstration, Bev started with Warren's store and ended with *Flavors*, owned by Felix. The photo of the ice cream parlor, shot in late afternoon, took advantage of the setting sun, which highlighted the streaked windows and obscured the Flavor of the Month sign.

Bev's PowerPoint spotlighted only the most unappealing sights, thus putting to rest any denials their once beautiful lakeside community needed a facelift. Claire hoped Jacqueline Ford was getting lots of notes. When the lights came back on, no one spoke for a moment, then everyone began talking at once.

Over the pandemonium, Claire studied Felix's face. He stared at her, not with the animosity she expected. If she could go by the slight twitch in the corner of his mouth, he held grudging respect for the committee. Then he chewed one end of his mustache. He was up to something. Tom leaned over and whispered in Felix's ear. He glanced at Warren and gave a single nod.

With a bang of his gavel, Felix quieted the crowd. "Do I hear a motion to set into action a revival program for Chapel Springs?"

Warren threw his arm up so fast Claire was surprised he didn't dislocate his shoulder. "I so move." He pushed his large bifocals back up his nose.

Were she a betting woman, she could have won money on that one. Doc Benson seconded the motion, and the vote carried with no dissenters. She turned to Joel.

"I guess we proved the old saying about what a picture's worth." She tried not to gloat, but it wasn't easy. Of course, now Felix would go around acting like the whole thing was all his idea. She'd have to ask Tom what he said to him. Probably something about reelection.

Joel tipped his head closer. "You did good."

Claire basked in the glow of the rare compliment. If he did that more often she'd think she *had* married the right man.

Felix banged his gavel again. "Vince, uh, I mean Doctor Bennett has the floor."

Claire raised an eyebrow in question to Joel, but he shrugged a shoulder. She turned in her seat to peer at her brother-in-law.

As Vince rose, Claire couldn't help but notice how Jacqueline leaned forward. She wasn't that much younger than him. It would be nice if she or someone like her could put the happy back in Vince's brown eyes.

Joel elbowed her. "Pay attention."

She tucked her thoughts away to listen.

"I'd like to bring another matter before the council, which I believe ties directly into the decline of the town. The springs' temperature is not at a good therapeutic level. It's fallen from where it was just a year ago. According to the caretaker, the temperature of the warm springs normally varies between thirty-six-point-six-seven degrees and forty-three-point-thirty-three degrees Celsius."

"What's the big deal about a couple of degrees?" Felix asked, putting voice to Claire's unspoken question.

"It's more than a couple. From the optimal therapeutic level, it's dropped by approximately twenty degrees." He walked to the front of the room to address the audience. "In other words, the water in our springs is normally around ninety-eight to one-hundred-ten degrees. Soothing and therapeutic. At the moment, it's sitting at ninety degrees." He walked to his seat but turned back to the council before he sat. "That's more than enough to feel the difference. But the big question is: will it fall more?"

Claire jumped up. "Lydia Smith recently opened her day-spa, which if successful, will benefit all of us when her clients stay here for vacations." She glanced back at the WPV anchor and lowered her voice. "If word gets out about this, she won't get the spa business."

"Do you have any idea what caused the drop?" Happy Drayton asked. "And will it affect the lake? If it changes temperatures, the fish could be threatened."

Vince shook his head. "The only way to know that is to hire a geologist."

Tom scanned the concerned faces of the town's citizens. "At what cost?"

"I have no idea." Vince took his seat.

It could cost a bundle. Claire leaned toward Joel. "Didn't you consult a geologist for something about the lake?"

"Ichthyologist. The guy studied fish."

Joel's grin was entirely too impudent. She swatted his arm. "Whatever. Couldn't the fish guy do something?"

He shook his head.

"Does anyone know about geologists?" Felix asked.

Ellie stopped typing on her laptop. "Yes, I do. A bit anyway. I have a friend in Atlanta whose cousin teaches geophysics at Georgia Tech.

Go Yellow Jackets." She grinned. "I can ask how one goes about hiring a geologist and the costs."

Faye Eisler tapped a book in front of her. "We don't get a large portion of the property tax revenues, you know. The lion's share goes to the county. What funds we receive," she looked pointedly at Jacqueline Ford, "are used for communal property maintenance and the workers' salaries. All of the council members are unpaid, elected positions."

Claire wished Faye would get to the point instead of making a trip around her elbow to get to her thumb. The point was Chapel Springs didn't have the money to hire a geologist. While Faye babbled, Claire dug out an old envelope from her SAK and jotted down some notes. She was ready when Faye finally drew a breath.

She held up the envelope. "I think we could do a fundraiser. I'll donate a few of my pieces to be auctioned."

Happy Drayton jumped up. "That's a fine idea, Claire. An' iffen we advertise it, we'll be getting the tourists back. An' iffen we tell 'em what it's for, they'll be more inclined to come 'round again. Count me in."

Felix beamed. He always smiled when his coffers weren't being depleted. "Well, Claire, that sounds like a right fine idea. I was fixing to suggest that myself."

Sure he was, the old goat.

He peered around the room, one brow lowered in his usual method of intimidation. "Now who's going to head this up?"

Chapter 9

Claire wiped steam from the bathroom mirror and ran the upcoming conversation through her mind. When she could see her reflection, she brushed the mascara wand against her eyelashes. Getting Joel to agree to the rehearsal dinner wasn't going to be easy. She had to use the right approach, and that could be tricky.

The shower turned off and Joel stepped out, wrapping a towel around his waist. He grabbed a second one and wiped the water dripping down his chest as he raised one bushy eyebrow in question.

"You're up early."

She screwed the wand in the mascara tube. "I need to talk to you before you leave for work."

"What'd you do now?"

In the mirror, she locked her eyes on his. "Why do you always assume I've done something?"

He picked up another towel and slung it over his shoulder, grabbed the other end in his left hand and rubbed it against his back. "Because you usually do."

"I wish you'd use a single towel instead of two or three. Every time I get out of the shower there aren't any clean ones. You've used them all."

He looked at the towels on the floor as if he'd never seen them. Maybe if she got one of those retractable rope things and sewed a towel to it, then when he threw it on the floor, it would be snapped back up to a hook and actually dry out. Right. Like that would really happen. "Anyway, I didn't do anything. Sandi's mother, Zoe, called the other day to talk about the wedding."

"And you're just telling me about it now?" He stepped up to his sink and ran his hand over his stubbly chin.

She picked up a make-up brush and applied blush, the soft bristles tickling her cheek as she stalled to organize her thoughts again. "I wanted to talk to Sandi first."

Joel peered sidelong at her through the mirror. "Why do I have the feeling I'm not going to like this?" He wiped shaving cream onto his cheeks and chin.

The man was entirely too astute. "Zoe said Sandi wanted the rehearsal dinner at our house. She doesn't want it in a restaurant."

Razor paused, he locked his eyes on hers in the mirror. "Does this mean you want to spend a lot of money massaging the house and buying new furniture? You know we can't afford that. Not with Wesley still in school."

"Who said anything about new furniture?" He always thought the worst.

"I know you, Claire. You plan a big wingding and want to make the house look like some magazine. Do we really have to have that thing here? And why are we doing it? I thought the bride's parents pay for the wedding."

"They do. They are. But the groom's parents are responsible for the rehearsal dinner."

"So what's wrong with the Krill Grill? It's a fancy seafood place."

Fancy to Joel meant anywhere with a candle on the table. If McDonald's had candles, he'd think a Happy Meal was gourmet.

"It's not intimate enough. Charlie and Sandi want to be able to talk to their friends without disturbing other diners. Besides that would be expensive."

Joel rinsed his face and picked up a fresh towel, tossing it on the floor next to the hamper when he finished. For all the basketball he played with the boys—

"Can't you at least make one shot into the hamper?"

He picked the towel up and dropped it in. "There's something you're not telling me about this dinner. Why would it be so expensive? How many people are we looking at here?"

Could she drop this bomb and retreat before it exploded? She stepped into the doorway, ready to escape. "Minimum of twenty-two, probably closer to twenty-eight." She zipped to the other side of the bedroom and opened the closet door.

"Twenty-eight!" The explosion echoed in the bathroom. He poked his head out. "How big is this bloody wedding? Our Charlie wouldn't want some grandiose hullabaloo."

Claire grimaced. "Apparently, Zoe is somewhat of a strong personality and overrode the kids' choices. Anyway, it isn't our decision. So," she steeled herself, "will you cook?"

Joel planted his feet apart and his hands on hips. "I told you before. No more than ten people."

That was better than expected. He must be getting soft. The question was, was it soft enough to push?

"Please?"

"Nip it, Claire. I don't have that kind of experience, and you know it. This is one pickle you'll have to figure out yourself."

Patsy opened an individual container of strawberry cream cheese and slathered it on the sesame bagel. The aroma of ground Kona rose from her mug, inviting a sip before tasting the bagel. Letting the richness of the coffee linger in her mouth, she closed her eyes. Palm trees swayed against azure skies while golden Hibiscus and fragrant Plumeria rode a humid breeze. She and Nathan honeymooned in Kona. On the edge of the volcano, he draped a fragrant lei around her neck and kissed her, declaring his love forever.

"Where are you?" Claire dropped into the chair beside her.

"Hawaii." Patsy opened her eyes, plopped back at *Dee's 'n' Doughs*. Her sigh was as deep as Kilauea. Life had been so simple then. They loved, they married.

Across the table, Bev dabbed her freshly glossed lips. "Now that we're all here, I thought we should go over the plans for the fundraiser. I suggest a festival similar to one I attended in Laguna Beach."

"California?" Lydia asked.

"Is there any other?" Icicles hung from each word.

"Actually, yes. There's one in Honduras."

Bev sat taller in her chair and repositioned her tablet and pen, her lips taut.

Something about her still bothered Patsy—more than just her domineering personality. Claire could rival her in that department only Claire was oblivious to hers. She didn't *use* it. It even went further than the way Patsy felt drab next to her. No, she couldn't put a name to it, yet. But she decidedly did *not* trust the woman.

"I only ask because I attended UCLA and went to the Laguna Art

Festival every year I was there." Lydia folded her hands and rested her chin on them, beaming. "It's amazing. The entire town is involved in presenting living pictures. People sit or stand behind a frame, dressed as the subject of the painting with a backdrop. Lacey was in one of them if I remember right." She turned to her sister. "Which one was it?"

"The Mona Lisa," Lacey said with a shy smile, her soft voice barely discernible.

Patsy couldn't help but think Lacey did bear a resemblance to the painting's subject. Other than the famous smile, the bland face held no remarkable beauty. Like the Mona Lisa, her nose was too long and her eyes too small to be considered beautiful. Poor Lacey was just plain … plain.

"Ahem, yes. Well, I was about to explain that." Bev retook control. "They turn the entire town of Laguna Beach into a large outdoor art gallery, including the living pictures." She nodded toward Lydia.

Claire cleared her throat. "We don't have actors, and while I love the idea of displaying my pottery and Patsy's paintings, not everyone here is an artist."

"Yes, Claire, I understand that. However, we can use that basic idea and expand on it for our own use. We could still have the living pictures too. It's very impressive and requires no acting skills."

Like Claire's Shiloh with a bone, Bev wouldn't let go. She remained determined to have her way and wouldn't discuss any new ideas. Patsy glanced at Lydia and Claire. Had they picked up on it? Neither seemed bothered.

The bell jangled and Vince Bennett strolled in. He raised a hand, greeting them before surveying the display cases.

Patsy excused herself. "I'll be right back. I need to talk to Vince a moment."

Claire raised her readers and telegraphed a what-are-you-up-to-now look. Patsy mouthed "later" and joined Vince.

"Good morning, Patsy."

"Do you have a moment? I need to discuss a private matter."

His penetrating gaze reassured her of his attention. "Of course." He gestured to a table across the room from the others. "How about there?"

Twisting a napkin, she sat and waited while he got his coffee and a pastry, her eyes scanning the floor. Dee's black and white tiled floor had seen better days, the scuffmarks and worn areas testifying to high foot traffic.

"I hope you won't need that."

Patsy stared at him. "What?"

His eyes twinkled with good humor. "That napkin. You've shredded it."

"Oh." Patsy pushed it away from her. "Vince, I'm worried about my mother."

Resting his folded hands on the table, he gave her his full concentration, leaving her to marvel at how he put his humor away like a wallet. "What seems to be the problem?"

She explained what happened at the dinner party. "Since you were there, I wondered if you'd noticed anything."

"Nothing out of the ordinary. I'm not sure what you're concerned about, Patsy."

Bev walked past them with a nod and smile to Vince on her way to the coffee refill bar situated behind them. Patsy lowered her voice.

"Alzheimer's." She hated to say the word aloud. Picking up a piece of the napkin, she tried to straighten it. "Mama seemed confused about things—talked to me like I was a teenager again."

"You said you startled her when you entered the kitchen?"

She nodded. "The way she pawed through the drawer, I thought she couldn't find something."

"Being startled can throw an older person for a loop." He raised his brow sympathetically. "I'm sure that's all it was."

She wished she could believe that. "Yesterday morning, I helped her clean and found one of my teaspoons and a fork in her jewelry box."

Vince took a sip of coffee. "Maybe she's working on a new technique for her art."

"With a fork? In her bedroom? That's really lame, Vince."

"Have you talked to your dad about your suspicions?"

She rolled the bits of napkin into one lump. "I tried but he flat out refused to even entertain the possibility."

"Can't say that I blame him. No one wants to think their life's partner is mentally losing it."

"There's something else. At the town council meeting, I overheard Kelly Appling saying a couple of things were missing from her gift shop."

Vince scratched his jaw, jutting his chin forward. "That could be anyone. Most likely kids."

"Look, Vince, I know it's probably nothing. In fact, if it were just one of those things, I wouldn't bother you, but combining the way she spoke and finding a fork in her bedroom—well you have to admit it's odd, even for *my* mother. Will you keep an open mind and an eye out for anything unusual? I know she comes in and out of Daddy's office during the day."

"I'll do that, but I think you're overreacting." He drained his cup, tipping it to get the last drop.

Patsy hoped she was, too. "Thank you." She rose. "I'm glad you're back in Chapel Springs and working with Daddy."

Vince stood and took her hand, stopping her. "Patsy, is there anything else bothering you?"

The drawback of this small town was everyone knew her so well. They'd all grown up together, played together, went to school together. Still, she wasn't ready to tell her problems with Nathan to anyone but Claire. She shook her head. At the coffee bar, Bev tossed a stir stick into the trash and returned to the other table. Patsy couldn't help wondering if she'd overheard their conversation.

"Well, if there is, you know you can talk with me. We go a long way back." Vince gave her hand a squeeze. "I suppose that can be a hindrance as well. After all, you knew me 'when' too."

His patients must love his attentive smile and bedside manner. Patsy cupped her hand on the side of his face. "You're a good friend, Vince." She gave his cheek two smart pats. "Even if you did push me off the dock every chance you got."

Vince's laughter followed her back to the table. Claire sent her another quizzical look but didn't press the issue.

"Now that we're all together again," Bev gave Patsy a pointed stare, "I'd like to recap. We'll hold the festival," she consulted her pad, "from May first through the third. Making it a May Day event will bring out more tourists."

Patsy couldn't deny Bev had good sense. "Did we decide on an auction?"

"Yes. Each merchant will donate." Bev tapped her pencil on the pad. "However, I'm concerned the auction alone may not bring in enough revenue."

"So what do we do?" asked Lydia.

Bev paused, tapping the pencil again, this time on her pursed lips. "What do you think of each person upping the donation to half of all they sell that weekend?"

Patsy sighed inwardly; she hated to admit Bev's ideas had merit.

Maybe she'd been too quick to judge. "I can do that. And I'll donate three pieces."

This time, Bev's smile was genuine. "I think that's generous and will help raise a lot, Patsy. Maybe it will be enough to include buying paint to refurbish the side of the gazebo that's burned."

"I'm all for that," Claire said, wincing. "Charlie's getting married July eleventh and they want to have the wedding there. If the festival is the beginning of May, then we only have ten weeks to do everything. I hope it's enough."

Lydia gathered the paper plates from the table as she stood. "Call me with my assignment, but right now I've an appointment. Bye y'all."

A few minutes later, while Claire unlocked the gallery door, Patsy faced the lake, gathering inspiration. Nathan's car drove down Sandy Shores. She threw her hand up to wave but froze as he drove past without a glance in her direction. His arm rested on the door through the open window. How could he drive past the gallery without seeing her? And what was he doing back in Chapel Springs? He should be at work by now.

"I'll be right back, Claire."

She walked to the end of the block. Across Hill Street sat the Spa and Nathan's car—and Lydia greeting him.

"Now just what business does he have with her?" Claire asked.

Absorbed in her own thoughts, Patsy hadn't heard her footsteps. "I don't know. Let's not jump to conclusions. Although, if it's what we think it is, I'd know how to fight that battle. It's the other one that scares me the most."

Claire grabbed her arm. "Let's go pay Lydia a visit. After all, we want to try out her—" She smacked her forehead with her palm. "We're about as thick as two short planks, Patsy." Her grin stretched from one end of Shores Drive to the other. "Tomorrow's your birthday, girlfriend. I'll just bet you get a gift certificate to the spa."

Chapter 10

Patsy sipped her coffee while turning the pages of the *Chapel Lake Weekly Voice*, but quickly set the cup down. After a restless night, her stomach was queasy. Mint tea would have been a better choice. She tossed out the remains of her cup. The sunlight streaming through the gauzy curtains over the kitchen sink did nothing to brighten her outlook. She felt like that old cartoon character that walked around with a perpetual rain cloud over his head.

On page two, she found *The Painted Loon's* ad alongside a three-column account of the council meeting and their plans for Chapel Springs. The reporter put a good spin on the story, and Charlie's design for the ad made it stand out. Claire's son inherited the family gene for creativity.

After folding the paper open so Nathan could see the story when he came downstairs, she went to the stove and turned on the kettle for tea. His soft breath on the back of her neck sent shivers of pleasure down her spine. With the shivers, a tremor of regret tagged along for what their supposed golden years would have been. What had she done so wrong that he turned from her?

"I didn't hear you come down."

"Happy birthday, Patsy." He wiggled a flat box with a blue bow, the kind that only comes from jewelers. "Dry your hands and come open your present." He set the box on the table, poured a cup of coffee, and raised the pot toward her. "More?"

His cheerfulness stung as sharply as the hornet she'd disturbed in the garden last week. Her forty-seventh birthday was far from happy. Instead of love, she had a cold bed and a philandering husband. If it was Lydia ...

She prayed a spa gift certificate lay hidden inside that jewelry box in an attempt to fool her. "No, thanks, I'm having mint tea."

She picked up the box. It was too heavy for paper. She glanced up and gave him a weak smile, then lifted the lid. Her heart shattered. Nestled against blue velvet was a silver bracelet with five charms. Three were for their children and bore their names and birth dates. One had a small diamond in the center with her birth date. The fifth was a small artist's palette, its paints depicted in gemstones. Noticeably absent was a charm for Nathan or their marriage.

He set his cup on the table. "I hope you like it. The jeweler said charm bracelets are all the rage. It's real gold, white gold—not silver."

"Yes, I can see it is. It's lovely, Nathan. Thank you." She rose and kissed his cheek, trying not to cry. Jewelry, especially expensive jewelry was, according to that magazine article, another sign of an affair. He was now up to seventeen of the twenty-one.

"Let me help you put it on." He lifted the bracelet out of the box and fastened it on her wrist. "It looks nice on you."

It did look nice, but its cool burn against her skin would always bring to mind his infidelity. "I need to get ready for work. See you tonight." She hurried upstairs before he saw her tears.

She couldn't go to *Dee's 'n' Doughs* this morning. It would take all her strength just to go into the gallery, when all she wanted to do was to crawl back into bed and pull the covers over her head.

"Where've you been?" Claire brought her potter's wheel to a slow stop, holding the clay steady so it wouldn't wobble out of shape. It was the first of several pieces she wanted to give Charlie and Sandi for a wedding present. When Claire asked them about china, Sandi said she wanted casual dinnerware, something that could go in the oven if Charlie were late, but still looked nice for company. Plus, each place setting would be a different pattern but all in earth tones. Claire decided she'd also do serving pieces for them. This one was a pitcher.

Patsy laid her handbag on a side table. "I couldn't face seeing Lydia."

Poor Patsy. She looked awful. Her hair laid flat against her head and her eyes lacked their usual sparkle.

"You asked Nathan? Did he admit to it?" Not that Claire could really see him having an affair. For that matter, she couldn't imagine Lydia as a husband-stealer. It didn't fit.

Patsy shook her head and pulled out a box from her tote bag. It held

Claire's gaze like a magnet as she first wiped her hands on a towel. She gingerly reached for the box, glancing at her friend.

"I'm almost afraid to open it."

"Not as much as I was. Go ahead. It seems he wasn't getting a spa certificate."

Claire opened the blue velvet box. Definitely not a spa certificate, but the bracelet was as beautiful and artistic as Patsy. Claire held it up, examining each charm. For a man having an affair, Nathan had chosen well. Maybe that was why. They, whoever "they" are, said men having affairs gave jewelry to assuage their guilt. Claire would kill Joel if he had an affair, expensive jewelry or not. And sure as clay's gray, she was ready to kill Nathan, too.

"I spent some time yesterday out at the cemetery, visiting Aunt Lola's grave. I thought about what she would have advised, and girl, I think it's time for our first spa treatment." Claire laid the bracelet back in the box and handed it to Patsy. "And if we don't get the answers we're looking for, I'll stake out Nathan's office and follow him. Come on."

Patsy slumped in her chair, her arms falling to her side. "You go. I don't want to."

Her listless voice nearly broke Claire's heart.

"Patsy, you're coming whether you want to or not. You're lower than a toad in a dry well. You need to get mad."

"I am mad. My mad is just different than yours."

"Uh-huh. You remember what my daddy used to say, 'My cow died last night, so I don't need your bull.'" That earned Claire the grin she'd been looking for. "Let's go."

She hoped they'd find out Lydia wasn't the husband-stealing hussy Patsy thought. Of course, if it wasn't Lydia, the alternative was worse. Claire cringed from the thought of Nathan with another man. How would Patsy live down the scandal? Her blood pressure went up a good ten whatevers. That was even more than Zoe's last phone call had raised it.

Could they get—"Do you suppose there's a way to poison a person and get away with it?" Patsy's horrified face stopped Claire. "All right, I was only teasing."

Sort of. She remembered a book she'd read about a dead body in a hot tub. The spa had hot tubs. If he and Lydia were carrying on …

"Come on." The spa was only a five-minute walk from the gallery.

Chapter 11

Claire hadn't been inside the old Candler mansion for years. Built in the late 1880s, it passed through numerous owners before Lydia bought it. As kids, she and Patsy believed it was haunted and wouldn't walk past it without crossing the street. Claire had been invited in a couple of times when it was owned by the high school principal, and even then, it gave her the creeps. What had Lydia done to turn the spooky old house into a spa? Curious, she increased her pace.

She and Patsy stepped off the sidewalk onto a brick path that curved through a garden filled with fragrant Hostas and Azaleas exploding in shades of pink. At the massive, mahogany door, Claire reached for the knob, but Patsy gasped and grabbed her arm.

Claire looked around. "What's wrong?"

Patsy pointed at the door's ornate carvings. Those drew Claire's eye upward to a half-moon panel above the entrance. A gargoyle leered down, its tongue protruding through its lips. Eew. Why would anyone want that hanging over their front door?

"It's not very inviting."

"They're downright creepy." Patsy shuddered. "People used to think they warded off evil. I never could figure out why."

Claire took the cool brass doorknob into her hand and turned. "They look so evil themselves, maybe the ghosts thought it was already haunted? You know, like another specter's territory."

Patsy's chin dropped to her chest and she shook with silent laughter.

"Stop it." Claire swatted her arm. "You asked. Come on, you're just stalling anyway." She pushed the door open. The moment they stepped inside, an enticing aroma of pears and lavender surrounded them. Piano music played softly in the background, and an old crystal chandelier towered above them. Pointing up at it, she elbowed Patsy.

"I remember that from years ago."

"Why are you whispering?" Patsy whispered.

"If Nathan's in here with Lydia, we want to catch him in the act."

"I ..." She started to back away. Claire grabbed her arm.

"Oh, no you don't. We're seeing this through. Don't you want answers?"

Patsy first nodded then shook her head no.

"Yes, you do," Claire whispered. "Now act normal." Whatever that meant.

She took in their surroundings. The foyer seemed larger than she remembered and had been turned into a reception area. A sage green loveseat nestled in the bay window. Two wingback chairs, upholstered in a dark green and burgundy plaid, flanked the fireplace across from the sofa.

Wait, what was a fireplace doing in the foyer? It may have been over thirty years since she'd been in this house, but she was positive it hadn't been there before. Lydia, or someone before her, must have knocked out the wall to one of the old parlors—maybe the gentlemen's—combining the rooms, which was why it looked so much bigger.

A large antique writing desk stood to Claire's left and held a display of brochures. She crossed the room and plucked one from the small wire rack. There wasn't a speck of dust on the desk. Hussy or not, Lydia kept a clean reception room. But what lay beyond?

"Come on, let's decide what we want done." She pulled Patsy to the sofa. Holding the brochure open between them, they studied it. Claire could deal with the facials and pedicures, but massages with hot rocks and full body exfoliation? She winced, envisioning a carpenter with sandpaper. Now, a bath in a Victorian tub was another story—as long as no one tried to bathe her.

Maybe this idea had been a mistake.

She glanced at Patsy, who looked like a kid with a toy catalogue. Poor thing, she'd rather pretend everything was all right than face trouble.

"What are you thinking about?"

"I've always heard mud baths are sheer bliss."

As if Nathan weren't with Lydia. Okay, Claire would play along. "Humph. Why pay someone when you can go roll in the mud in your backyard?"

"Hush, Lydia might hear you. You're missing the point anyway. This mud purifies your skin."

"Ha. There's an oxymoron for you." Claire waved the services list, quickly dropping her arm when her triceps undulated like ice skaters playing crack-the-whip. She needed a gym more than a massage. Her potter's muscles hadn't extended to her wings. "Purifying mud. Do they really fill a bath tub with mud and make you sit in it?"

Patsy pulled the menu from Claire's hand. "I have no idea, but let's try it. Since we're new to this, what about the reflexology thing they recommend instead of a full body massage? And facials." She flipped the brochure over. "They have pumpkin or cranberry peels."

Claire blinked. "They peel cranberries?" How odd.

"You nut. It's a facial peel."

"Oh. I don't care, but I want to do that paraffin thing—just the pedicure—my poor hands are a lost cause."

Patsy peered at her. "What about getting your upper lip waxed?"

Upper lip? Claire slid her tongue up over her lip. Yikes! "How long have I had a mustache?"

Patsy giggled. "Since you turned forty. Relax, it's not really that noticeable."

"Humph." Claire squinted at Patsy's lip. "How come you don't have one?"

"Deva waxes it for me."

"You let your daughter wax your lip?"

"Sure, why not?"

"Several punitive groundings come to mind."

Floorboards creaked from the hallway, and Lydia entered. "Welcome. I'm delighted y'all came by. I can give you the behind the scenes tour, but our grand opening isn't until next week."

Peeking past her, Claire tried to spot Nathan maybe sneaking out a back door or skulking around a corner. The hallway was empty. "Oh. We thought," she nodded toward Patsy, "we could come for ... whatever it is you do. Uhm ..."

Lydia failed if she was trying to hide her amusement. Her eyes twinkled, and her grin was infectious.

"I take it you've never been to a spa before. Normally, you'd need an appointment, but since we haven't had the grand opening yet, I think we can accommodate you."

She pulled what looked like a menu from the desk's center drawer.

She chewed the corner of her lip as she studied it. "I don't have a full team yet, but the massage therapist is here, setting up her rooms. Grace is ready to do facials & mani-pedis, so I think we can give you a nice afternoon." She pulled a sticker from the drawer and slapped it on the menu thingie. "On the house."

After making a few check marks on two of the cards, she handed one to each of them. "I need to take care of some business then I'll be right back. I'll send Grace to get you started." She walked into the hallway.

"Thanks, Lydia. That's really nice of you." Considering what she was doing with Patsy's husband. What did Lydia have to take care of right then, anyway? Something with Nathan, perhaps? Claire glanced down at her card.

"It's good business. You'll be my first advertisement."

As Lydia disappeared down the same hall she had come from, Claire felt another sniglet of doubt. How could she be so nice to them, not to mention the fact she didn't exhibit any signs of stress, if she were fooling around with Nathan?

A twenty-something with light brown hair, dressed in a beige lab coat monogrammed with the spa's logo, approached them. "Good morning, I'm Grace. Lydia asked me to get you started. May I see your services card?"

Claire exchanged glances with Patsy while patting her hand and whispering, "Don't worry. I'll find out what's going on here if it's the last thing I do." Flashing her best smile at Grace, Claire handed over her list. "Lydia chose these for us." Claire pointed to the selected services.

The technician nodded. "Yes, Lydia told me she chose your services. Let's see. Mud bath, full body massage, manicure and pedicure for Mrs. Kowalski, and for Mrs. Bennett, mud bath and massage for you, too. Ah, and I see you're getting a facial instead of the manicure. Excellent choices." She barely gave Patsy a glance, but her eyes settled on Claire's upper lip. "If you like, I'll wax your lip when I do your facial. Now, if you'll follow me, we'll get you started."

Terrific. First Patsy, now Grace. Who else noticed Claire had grown a mustache? Had Joel? No, if he'd noticed he would have said something. Then again, she doubted he'd notice if she had a goatee.

Grace led them to adjoining rooms and opened the doors, instructing them to remove their clothing, lay face down on the massage table and pull the sheet up over them. "You can hang your clothes in the closet.

I'll be back in a few minutes."

Claire watched her walk down the hall then whispered to Patsy, "Do we take off *everything*?"

Patsy stared, wide-eyed. Even her freckles looked pale. "I don't know."

"I feel so stupid, not knowing what to expect." Claire stepped inside and closed the door. The small room's décor was reminiscent of a Victorian bedroom. Lace curtains graced the window and the walls were papered in a soft green stripe. The same tranquil music they'd heard in the foyer was piped into the rooms. The overall effect was calming.

Before the technician arrived, Claire quickly removed her clothes and hung them in the small closet. Chill bumps rose on her arms. That sheet better cover her. She climbed onto the table, rolled onto her stomach and positioned her face in the cushioned oval, looking down at the floor. She giggled as she tried to shake the sheet open behind her back. It slipped from her fingers and fell on the floor.

Sighing, she leaned over the edge of the table but couldn't reach the sheet. She slid one leg off and grabbed it with her toes, a peculiar talent she'd perfected as a kid. Bending her knee, she moved her leg to the side, bringing the sheet within reach. Her fingers grasped the edge. Success! She slid the material over her exposed posterior. Feeling cool air on her shoulders, she pulled it up. Oh great, now her backside was uncovered again.

The door opened. Claire quickly snatched the sheet down.

"Oh, sorry."

The voice didn't sound like Grace and had a European accent, but Claire couldn't quite place it.

"If you are ready, I start your mud bath."

She lifted her head to see who it was. A brunette smiled back at her. Medium height, the young woman looked like she should be posed on the cover of a massage magazine. Do they have a magazine for masseuses? Her collared knit shirt fit snug at her upper arms. Uh-oh. Claire's muscles shrank in fear.

"I'm Olympia. Now, put head down and relax."

Olympia? "Do you work at The Pasta Bowl?" Claire had commented to Joel about her name. She was from Italy and had been here about two years, if Claire remembered right.

Water flowed into a basin. "*Sì*. I work here part time, also. *Il mio marito*, how you say ... my husband and I want to buy house."

What felt like sandpaper, dipped in warm water, scraped down her leg. "Yewouch! What is that?"

"To exfoliate, Signora Bennett," Olympia said in soothing tones. "We want to rid all dead skin before we detoxify and purify with red clay."

A yellow lump appeared in front of Claire's face. "See? Is like pumice."

That was supposed to ease her mind when her skin was being flayed? The tool of torture scraped over her heels and the bottom of her foot. Claire grunted. That was about all she could do with her face jammed into this foam rubber donut. She thought spas were supposed to relax you, not sand your skin off.

With a splat, cool mud landed on her back. Cheese Louise, couldn't they have warmed it some? She felt the spatula, or whatever Olympia used, spreading it over her back and legs. Boy, the things she did in the name of friendship. She felt like a layer cake.

"Roll over, please, Signora."

"Uh, I'm naked."

"*Sì*, I know. But to detox you properly, we need to do even bazooms."

Bazooms? Claire forced back the laugh and rolled over. It wasn't like she had *big* bazooms anyway. Olympia used her wooden spatula to spread the goo, hiding Claire's nakedness under a layer of red. Next, she wrapped strips of wet cheesecloth around Claire's legs, arms and torso.

"That's cold." Claire shivered.

"Not for long. I have warm blanket for you." It descended, enveloping Claire in a cocoon of delicious warmth. "I will be back in forty-five minutes. You relax and schmooze."

"You mean snooze?"

"*Sì*, take *poco pelo*—leetle nap." She wiggled her fingers in a wave, and the door closed, leaving Claire to mummify in her envelope of clay. Soft music lulled her into stupefaction. As she drifted off, she wondered how Patsy was enjoying her—*Nathan*! Claire's eyes popped open. She had forty minutes to find him and uncover why he was here.

Wrapping the blanket tight around her, she cracked the door open and peeked out. The hallway was clear. Thank goodness the spa hadn't officially opened yet. She tiptoed, as best she could without disturbing the cloth wound around her thighs, toward the hall where Lydia had disappeared.

Sneaking around wasn't easy trussed up like that Christmas pudding Ellie Grant gave her after reading a book about English traditions. The only difference between her and that pudding was its wrap had been soaked in brandy not Georgia red clay. Which itched as it dried. Using her elbow so not to drop the blanket, Claire rubbed it against her side.

Someone's heels clacked on the hardwood floors. She twisted her head right and left, spied a door, and dove through it just as a figure rounded the corner. Holding her breath, she listened to the footsteps pass by.

"May I help you?"

Claire jumped and turned around, dislodging her leg wrappings. They started to slide. She clamped her thighs together. A blonde in a white lab coat smirked at her as she folded a towel. Looking around, Claire realized she was in a large linen closet. How embarrassing. The woman must think she was nuts, and she probably was, creeping around like this.

"Uh, I was, uh, looking for the bathroom." Claire gritted her teeth, hoping she looked desperate.

"Of course, let me show you." The woman directed Claire back the way she came.

She smiled her thanks, mustered all the dignity she could and duck-walked back down the hall. She swore she heard a snicker before the closet door clicked shut. If she was going to find Nathan, she'd better get moving. One cheesecloth strip flapped against her calf. She reached under the blanket and tried to tuck it into another. The mud had dried and her legs itched. If she relaxed her thighs to scratch, she'd lose the whole wrap.

Had Lazarus felt like this when Jesus raised him from the dead?

Ignoring the irritation, Claire moved as stealthily as possible, considering her haute couture waddle. What would the twins say if they could see her now? She stifled a giggle.

A hallway stretched off to her right, but the one she was in continued. Now what? The new hallway had three doors. Keeping her knees firmly glued together, she padded to the first one and put her ear to it. Nothing. She cracked it open. With a massage table inside, it was just another room like the one she'd been in. The others were probably the same.

Lydia's office had to be around here somewhere. Claire returned to the main hallway and kept searching, keeping as close to the wall as she could. There was only one door and it was open. She peeked inside—a white-tiled bathroom. Not much help, but it never hurt to know a place she could duck and hide if necessary.

The hallway ended abruptly at a set of stairs and another hall to the left. This place was a maze of passageways and closed doors. Was Lydia's office up there? She glanced to the left. It was hard to decide which way to go, and she wasn't certain she remembered how to get back to her room. But she owed it to Patsy. She promised to find out what Nathan was doing. Looking up, she decided to go that way.

Placing her hand on the banister, Claire lifted her foot to the first riser, and a cheesecloth strip puddled around her ankle. Yanking at it only tightened it around her knee like a tourniquet. She was too close to her prey to stop, so she grabbed the trailing piece and looped it through another, tying a knot to hold it firm and took the next step.

Someone laughed. Her breath caught and she whipped around, losing hold of the banister and her balance. She fell hard onto her derriere and thumped down the three steps she'd come up. Grasping the blanket, she pulled it up over her head.

Chapter 12

Claire peeked through a slit in the blanket. No one was there. The laughter must have come from upstairs not behind her.

"Oh, thank you," she whispered. She rose and took the stairway one tread at a time. Flakes of clay from her chafing thighs and knees left a dusty trail behind her. At least she could find her way back to that hallway.

The top of the stairs opened into a loft with two doors. One was dark, but the other had light spilling out from beneath it. She crept forward.

"Where are the papers?"

Nathan's voice. He *was* here with Lydia. Claire flattened against the wall and inched closer to the door. If they had divorce papers, she'd stuff them down his throat.

A metal file drawer opened with its distinct rumble and papers shuffled. "Here."

"Thanks. Now I'll need to see the investment statements from Sam's estate. Don't worry, Lydia, I'll get this straightened out. This audit is standard routine. You've paid every penny you owed. I wouldn't be surprised if I find they owe you money."

An audit? Claire smacked her forehead. *That's* why Nathan was here.

"I'm so glad I met you and Patsy. Being new in town, I didn't know who to trust."

He was Lydia's accountant? Of course. Why hadn't they thought of that? Relief that Nathan wasn't having an affair with Lydia was quickly followed by guilt—heavy enough to qualify for Olympic weightlifting—for even suspecting her. It buckled Claire's knees and she sank against the door.

Which promptly gave way.

In what seemed like slow motion, she stumbled into the room. Her momentum carried her sideways three steps, before she lost the battle to keep her knees tightly clenched beneath the blanket. The mud-caked cloths dropped to her ankles, tripping her as neatly as an NFL tackle. Wide-eyed, Lydia raced to help, but Claire lost the war and went down hard on her hip.

Huddled in her blanket on the floor, she looked up into Nathan's startled face and grimaced. "Uh, ha, ha—"

Think!

Between her smarting hip, which would be black and blue by morning, and being caught, her mind went blank. She wasn't even sure she could remember her name at the moment. Which might not be a bad thing. Maybe she should claim amnesia.

"Claire, are you all right?"

Lydia helped her up. "What are you doing here? I thought Olympia was helping you."

"I, uh—where's the bathroom?" Oh, brilliant.

Nathan's face turned deep red as his shoulders shook with silent laughter. The traitor. Too bad he wasn't choking. Claire could imagine herself the center of the joke tomorrow at his office as he told his co-workers about his wife's crazy friend.

"Clairey-girl, you do liven things up," Nathan said, using her childhood nickname inspired by the Seekers' old song, *Georgy Girl*. Claire grew up thinking she was like the girl in the song and hated it, until she met Joel. He brought out the girl deep inside her and changed the way she'd always thought about herself. Now, the nickname held no sting. Her reputation, however …

She sent Lydia a silent plea for help, praying she'd never find out what they'd suspected her of. Her sweet smile reached Claire's heart as she helped her out of the room.

"I'm so sorry. I got lost and heard voices, so I followed them and found you. Uh, so where is the bathroom? And how soon can I get this gunk off me? It itches."

Lydia put her arm around Claire's shoulders. "If you can hold off using the restroom, I think you're ready to shower."

Amusement lurked beneath her words. Lydia knew, or at least she suspected. How utterly mortifying. Claire wished the floor would open up and swallow her. Should she explain? No, that wouldn't be fair to

Patsy. Then again, poor Lydia might think they really thought she was a husband-stealer. But Claire didn't, really. She'd always had doubts.

"I'm sorry, Lydia. I didn't really think you were having—" Claire clamped her hand over her mouth.

Lydia laughed until tears shone in her eyes. "If you could have seen your face when you fell into my office." She held her sides, doubling over.

In spite of her embarrassment, Claire chuckled as she imagined what she must have looked like. She plucked at the gauze bindings. "All this stuff is falling off me."

"It's not exactly made to walk in, you know." Lydia opened a door and ushered her into a large bathroom. Claire spied a thick terry robe on a hook by the shower door. It looked warm, and infinitely less scratchy than her current attire. She couldn't wait to get the clay off and put it on.

"Shower off, and I'll come back for you in a few minutes." Lydia removed the wrapper from a bar of soap and handed it to Claire. "We may be new ones, but we're friends. And friends don't go after husbands. Not even widowed friends."

Claire searched her face. "Can you ever forgive us?"

Lydia nodded, her eyes twinkling. "Besides, you're way too much fun to lose as a friend."

Her chuckling grew fainter as she closed the door and walked away. Claire groaned, disgusted with herself. Why had she let herself believe Patsy's wild imagination? She dropped the blanket and pulled off the remaining strips of loosened cloth. Small mud chips fell to the floor. Anyone could see Lydia wasn't a hussy.

Under the hot water, the dried mud melted off Claire's body, leaving her skin tingly. She picked up the soap and lathered. The tantalizing aroma of pears rose in the steam, clearing her mind of all thought. Finally, she turned off the water, stepped out of the shower and reached for the robe.

As she belted the snuggly terry cloth around her waist, a new thought body-slammed her. If Nathan wasn't having an affair with Lydia, their original suspicion gained credibility. Could he really be—?

The door opened and Lydia poked her head in. "You ready?"

Claire nodded, holding the towel she'd wrapped around her wet head from falling. Lydia escorted her back to the room where she'd left her clothing.

"Olympia will be in to give you your massage, then Grace will do your facial."

Knowing the drill, Claire removed the robe, climbed onto the table and held the sheet over her rump. Soon, Olympia came in and squirted cool lotion on Claire's back, making her shiver. Strong fingers kneaded her muscles. It felt pretty good until Olympia got near her sides. Then it tickled. Claire flinched and suppressed a giggle. After a couple of minutes, the massaging got harder. She tensed her muscles. Was she supposed to tell Olympia if it hurt?

Finally, it was over. Olympia assisted Claire into the robe and then escorted her to a lounge to wait. Almost as soon as she sat down, Lydia appeared, bearing a cup of hot herbal tea.

"How do you feel?" Lydia sat next to her. "Did you enjoy your massage?"

How could Claire tell her no after she'd basically accused Lydia of being a husband-stealer? "Well, I feel like I've been tenderized." Would her smile help ward off any more questions?

"Good." A phone rang and Lydia rose. "I'll see you before you go. Enjoy your facial."

Claire blew on the cup of steaming tea, more in relief that Lydia accepted her answer than to cool the liquid. The magazines all touted the benefits of massages and spas. Claire didn't want to be the one to yell the emperor was naked. If people liked to be pounded and pummeled, then let them.

By the time she finished her tea Grace came for her. Claire caught a glimpse of Patsy heading into the massage room. Her face bore a smile of tranquility. Claire hoped she was truly enjoying herself and not pretending. Of course, once she told Patsy where Nathan's true interest lay, that fragile serenity would split like an atom. How could Nathan hurt her friend this way?

As she lay back in the chair, more lotion was smoothed on her face. She'd had so many potions and lotions today she should be well-marinated. She had to admit Grace was talented at the facial. Her hands made firm, but gentle, strokes against Claire's skin. By the time she was done, every inch of her face tingled. It matched the way the rest of her felt. She dressed and found Patsy waiting for her in the foyer.

"You look gorgeous. Relaxed and glowing." It was a pretense, Patsy's stubborn refusal to meet her problems head on. Her "if she ignored it, it didn't exist" attitude drove Claire nuts.

Patsy peered at her with a strange expression. "You look very ...

rosy."

Claire felt her cheek. It did feel slightly warm. "I tingle all over. Did you enjoy it?"

"Mmm, I did." Patsy opened the door and stepped outside. "Lydia had to do something and said she'd see us tomorrow. Did you ... uh…"

Claire put her hand up. "Wait. Let's go to the gallery."

They walked in silence. Patsy fiddled with her manicure and kept glancing at her. Claire scratched her jaw, thinking how to tell Patsy about Nathan. Did she just blurt it out? Or should she ease into it? If she even mentioned—

"I can't wait any longer, Claire. What did you find out?"

Claire looked around, absently scratching her shoulder. They were alone on the street. "Nathan is Lydia's CPA. Period. Oh, Patsy, I made such a fool out of myself."

After Claire told her of her grand entrance into Lydia's office, Patsy laughed with her, but as they entered the gallery, her laugher suddenly stopped.

"But if it isn't Lydia ... it has to be a man."

"Auugh!" Claire screeched as she stared at her reflection in the mirror. She looked like she'd been attacked by a bunch of angry hornets. Red welts covered her face and neck. No wonder Patsy gawked at her when she left the gallery. Even Shiloh welcomed her with an odd tilt to his big head. He didn't recognize her until she spoke. Her wonderful makeover backfired. All she wanted was to look younger. Tears welled and spilled over, stinging her hives, as she stared at the caricature in the mirror.

"What's wrong?" Joel skidded into the bathroom and stared at her, scowling. "What in Sam Hill have you done to yourself?" He took her jaw in his hand and tipped her face up.

"Shouting at me isn't helping, Joel." Claire sniffed and wiped her eyes.

"Well this didn't just happen by itself."

"Patsy and I got massages and facials."

"You *paid* for this?"

"No. It was complimentary."

"Some compliment. You should've known better." He released her and slammed the medicine cabinet open then handed her a package of antihistamine. "I can't believe you did this, Claire. You've got allergies.

It's stupid to—"

"I'm allergic to grass. This was clay. I use clay all the time."

"Obviously not this kind. What else did they smear on you? Quit scratching." He opened a bottle of calamine lotion and plopped some on her face with his fingers. When it dribbled, cold and slimy, down her neck, Claire grabbed his wrist.

"I'll do it." She opened a drawer and snatched a cotton ball from its dispenser while Joel leaned against the doorjamb, arms crossed and still frowning.

Claire glared at him through the mirror. "I don't know why you're so mad. It's not your face that itches." She dabbed the soaked cotton on her neck. The cool medicine soothed the itching.

"No, but it's me who has to listen to you complain about it. It's irresponsible to get all that junk when you're allergic to so many things."

"Irresponsible? Oh, that's really nice. Thanks a lot." She tossed the soaked cotton ball at the wastebasket. It landed on the edge, leaving a drop of lotion trailing down the side. She flipped it in with her toe and reached for a fresh swab.

"Look ... honey ... I—" He blew out an exasperated breath, then clamped his lips together in a thin line and stomped back downstairs, muttering all the way.

She didn't want to know what he mumbled. Why did he always get mad when she hurt herself? Not that this hurt. It itched more than anything. So what was the big deal? It wasn't like it hurt *him*. Why couldn't he be sympathetic? He acted like she did it on purpose just to inconvenience him.

Maybe Sandi was right. If Claire had found the right husband, he would have held her and told her it would be okay and that she was still beautiful to him. And she wouldn't feel at fault all the time.

Chapter 13

B y morning, Claire no longer looked as bumpy as a dill pickle—
just sunburned. Thanking the Lord for Benadryl, she applied her
makeup, taking care not to irritate any sensitive spots. Hopefully,
her foundation would tone down the redness so no one would ask any
questions. A quick swipe with her mascara wand, a dash of lipstick, and
she was ready to paint the town—literally.

The awnings wouldn't be in until the following week, but that didn't
mean they couldn't get the flowers planted, window trim and shutters
painted, and complete any other small repairs. Felix surprised her when
he decided the town council should give the lampposts a fresh coat of
dark forest green paint. Most likely, Eileen had more to do with that
decision than Felix, but Claire wouldn't push the point. The lampposts
would be cheerful and welcoming when they each had a basket of
flowers hanging from their wrought ironwork.

After a glance at the bathroom clock, she shoved her makeup in the
drawer and pushed it shut. Time to go. Joel had left earlier and warned
her to watch the time. He and Happy were grabbing a couple of high
school boys to help them start the gazebo repairs. Wes promised to
come help. If he ever got out from behind that computer. She could hear
him tapping away at the keyboard and knocked on his closed bedroom
door.

"Wes, I'm leaving. Your dad's expecting you soon."

"I'll be ten minutes, Mom."

"No more, then. You need some fresh air."

She slipped on a lightweight sweater and ran downstairs. The dog
whined at the front door.

"No, Shiloh, you can't go. Not this time." Silly dog thought everyone in Chapel Springs belonged to his pack. They might love him but that whipping tail of his would be lethal around a can of paint. "I'll put you in the backyard."

His wagging tail stilled and he lowered his muzzle to the carpet. "Don't pull that sad doggy routine on me. You'll be fine." She grabbed a couple of jerky treats to entice him outside.

Not moving, he lay there with a look of betrayal in his eyes. Waving the jerky in front of his nose only made him drool. She weighed her options. Taking him was out. He chewed the windowsills last time they left him alone in the house. What would be next—the drywall?

She got behind him and tried to lift his back end. He slid but didn't get up. She blew her bangs out of her eyes. "Shiloh, I'm late. Daddy'll be mad at me. Come on, please?"

He looked up at her, his big head tilted to one side. Then he rose, took the jerky and with an air of dejection, padded to the door. Amazing. Who knew he'd respond to whining? She gave him an extra treat and patted his head.

"You can watch us over the fence and not feel alone. I'll see you later."

She was almost out the door when the phone rang. The caller I.D. listed Zoe Walker. Claire groaned. She didn't have time to listen to that woman's harangues. Zoe changed her mind as often as Claire changed her underwear. And called twice as often to complain about one thing or another that Sandi and Charlie had decided.

After locking the front door, Claire slipped her keys in her pocket and walked across Main Street to restaurant row's parking lot. In the background, Shiloh howled a few times but settled down when she called to him, and he could see her again. For a huge dog, he sure was a wuss.

In front of the restaurants, tables dotted the asphalt, filled with paint supplies, bags of potting soil, flowers, and large planters. Later, she'd make new decorative urns for the gallery, something eye-catching and amusing that made people smile. She pictured an ostrich with its head in the ground and flowers growing out of its back. The image of two rabbits holding forks and knives, ready to eat a bowl of flowers amused her. Moving to the flats of colorful flowers, visions of whimsy paraded through her mind. She could hardly wait to get back to the gallery and her clay.

"Claire! Over here."

Lydia's voice carried over the hum created by the small crowd of about twenty people. Where was everyone? They'd never get done at this rate. Lydia waved at her from the other end of the flower row.

"Glad you made it," Lydia said, giving Claire a one-armed hug, then she leaned back and inspected her face. "I'm so sorry about your allergic reaction. Patsy told me. I should have questioned you more closely."

Claire waved off her apology. "You were busy and we just popped in on you. No harm done." A huge variety of plants surrounded them. "Van Gogh's ear, that's a lot of flowers. Will we get them all planted today?" She looked around. "As usual, not many showed up to help."

Lydia pointed over Claire's shoulder. "Look behind you."

A herd of people paraded across Sandy Shores Drive, laughing and calling out hellos. Most held coffee cups and pastries from Dee's 'n' Doughs. Patsy waved from the back of the crowd. It looked like they'd get it all done after all.

Claire crossed her arms. "No wonder y'all are late. One of you better have something for me." Dee Lindstrom handed her a cup of coffee and a bag. Inside was a bagel slathered with strawberry cream cheese. Claire pulled it out and took a bite, closing her eyes. Dee's bagels were the best in all of Georgia. "Who's minding the bakery?" she asked around the dough in her mouth.

"Trish Halloran, an amazing young pastry chef I hired. Heather came home from college this weekend to help out, too. I'm thrilled about this, Claire, and I wanted to play in the dirt with everyone."

"When you bring me treats like this, you can play all you want."

Bev marched past them with her clipboard and a megaphone. She stopped beside a table and lifted her arm, holding her hand palm down like she expected it to be kissed or something. When no one responded, she put her free hand on her hip.

"Will someone please help me up? Where's Drew?"

"Last I saw, he was headed toward Dee's," Lydia said.

Bev's lips disappeared in a thin line. After a moment, she turned to Claire. "Help me up."

Why couldn't she climb on the table herself? It wasn't hard. You just—"Sit on the edge and swing your feet up. You don't need help."

Bev crossed her arms and tapped her foot. Claire rolled her eyes and cupped her hands. "Put your foot in here."

Bev narrowed her eyes at Claire like she'd lost her marbles.

"What? You want help? Put your foot in my hands and I'll give you a boost."

"That's what I'm afraid of. Where's Patsy?"

Oh, for pity sake. Claire grabbed Bev by the waist and hoisted her onto the table. "Now—stand up."

A snicker slipped past Claire's lips as Bev struggled to stand. For a little thing, she wasn't very graceful. From her tabletop vantage, she scowled at Claire then called for attention.

"I need about thirty of you to paint the lampposts and another twenty or so to get the pots ready for plants. Once the first few are filled, I have dollies to move them into place. Each pot is tagged with its location and what flowers to plant in it. Those painting, see Felix over here." In television-host fashion, Bev swept one arm to her left. "And those planting see Lydia." Again with the arm gesture, this time to her right. The woman fancied herself to be Vanna White. "Shall we begin?"

"Fill or plant?" Lydia asked as each person reached the front of her line. Claire chose "fill" and Lydia handed her a utility knife, directing her to the mountain of potting soil bags. Patsy slipped into line beside her.

"Oh, good. I wondered where you were." Claire turned to Lydia, pointing to Patsy. "She'll plant. She's much better than I am with flowers. They take one look at me and give up the ghost."

Lydia handed Patsy a pair of gloves, a trowel, and a list of the flowers to plant and in which pot to plant them. Claire took her knife and headed toward a line of ... wheelbarrows. Oh, dear. With her sadly lacking sense of balance, a one-wheeled bucket was not high on her lifetime list of things to conquer. She squared her shoulders and hoped this time would be easier. It should be. After all a parking lot was more stable than a dock.

"I'll fill the pots with soil while you get the flowers. How many are we doing?"

"Eight. When those are done, we'll help with the hanging baskets, if we're still needed."

Claire wrinkled her nose. "You can help with those. I'd rather paint the lampposts." She hoisted a bag of soil to her shoulder and dropped it into a wheelbarrow. After loading several bags on top of the first one, she grabbed the handles and lifted. It promptly wobbled to the right and tipped over.

That didn't go well. Eight-year-old Billy Lunn giggled from two tables over. She prayed no one else witnessed it. Her poor reputation couldn't handle another gaffe. She peeled off her sweater and tossed it onto a table. After removing two of the bags and a bit of muscling, she succeeded in getting the wheelbarrow upright.

Now, she eyed the hostile thing. A better approach was needed. Taking a deep breath, she set her feet at a wide stance—even with the handles to better equalize the weight—then hoisted upward. She waited a moment to feel the load's balance, and then took a tentative duck-waddle forward. It felt stable.

Filled with confidence, she tottered ahead, feeling like a pregnant loon. She'd only gone half a dozen steps before the wheel zigged again. This time she was ready for it and yanked up on the right handle to return it to the proper balanced path.

It refused to cooperate. Instead, it flopped over on its left side, tossed out another bag, and played dead. Claire glared at it.

"That only works with flowers and possums."

She tucked her hair behind her ears and pushed up her sleeves. Only she didn't have on long sleeves. Well, the wheelbarrow didn't know that, and anyway, it was playing dead. She wrangled it back to its feet and considered her options. Maybe she'd gone too slowly. Would moving faster make it quit careening off track?

Before it could figure out what she had in mind, she yanked up the handles and ran. It worked. With her destination in sight, she whooped in victory.

Suddenly, the front wheel hit a parking curb. Before she could scream or even whimper, Claire flew between the handles head first into the barrow's bed and split open the top bag of soil. She didn't stop there. Her forward trajectory tipped the cart and tossed her, along with the bag of soil on her head, out onto the parking lot. She landed with a thump, knocking the wind from her and the bag off her head.

"Claire! Are you okay?"

She heard the voice but didn't have the breath to answer and was barely able to spit soil out of her mouth. A big wet tongue slopped the side of her face, turning her cheek to mud. She grabbed for Shiloh's collar and sat up. Her lungs filled with air, plus a couple of potting soil particles. Ugh. She coughed.

"Shiloh! Stop it. How'd you get here?" He turned her ear to mud faster than she could shake the remaining dirt from it.

"He must have seen you were in trouble because he vaulted over your back fence just as you took your nose dive," Jake Dawson said, not letting her rise. "He got to you before any of us. Stay put for now. Do I need to get Doc?" His voice cracked in a failed attempt to cover his laugh.

At least he tried, which was more than she could say for her friends. Bev shook her head and giggled. Dee mopped her wet, red face. Warren was doubled over, slapping his straw hat against his thigh, guffawing and pointing at her. "That Claire! Always a million laughs."

She tentatively tested her shoulder and legs. The shoulder would be black and blue by tomorrow, but at least nothing was broken.

"I'm fine. Just help me up."

As she grasped his hand and stood, a cheer erupted. When she turned around, Pastor Seth, Kelly Appling, and Ellie Grant scribbled numbers on their instruction sheets and held them up. At least Kelly gave her a nine-point-five.

Claire groaned and dropped her head. Why did she have to have an audience? She remembered her old high school drama coach saying, "When you can't remember your lines, ad lib."

Standing tall, she grinned and made a sweeping bow. "Thank you. Thank you one and all. I owe this great accomplishment to my coach, W. L. Barrow. Without him, I never would've had this honor."

Assaulted from all sides by good-natured ribbing, she gathered as much dignity as she could recover, what with being covered in mud and dog slobber. Jake righted her wheelbarrow, refilled it and delivered it to a vacant table.

"You shouldn't have tried that, Claire. Not at your age. You could have hurt your back."

At *her* age? She scowled and raised a fist within inches of his nose. "Don't make me hurt you, Jake Dawson."

He held his hands up in mock surrender and backed away two steps.

Tsking softly, Patsy dusted the soil off Claire's back. "You forget she wrestles clay into obedient submission every day."

Feeling her cheeks grow warm, Claire blew out an exasperated breath. It'd be weeks before this was forgotten—if she got so lucky. And poor Shiloh. It looked as if it would take longer before he would be willing to leave her side. She bent over, taking his big head in her hands.

"Good boy. You rushed to my rescue, didn't you?"

Andy McMillan ran up to her and skidded to a stop. He threw his arms around Shiloh's neck and received a lathering for a kiss. "Can I take him for a walk, Miss Claire? Please? He's a hero!"

What a heartbreaker. "Honey, it would be Shiloh taking you for a walk. If I had a saddle you could ride him." Andy's little face lit up over that suggestion. She'd better be careful what ideas she put in his head or his mother would have hers.

"Why not let a couple of the high school boys take him with Andy?" Jake asked, tying a length of rope to Shiloh's collar.

It was a perfect solution. "Will that do for you, Sir Andy?"

His little freckled cheeks popped out with his grin and he nodded. She found two of the football players with enough muscle to keep the mastiff from dragging Andy all over town.

"Just keep him away from the painters." She hoped they heard her as they disappeared around The Pasta Bowl, Andy holding tight to Shiloh's leash.

They worked the rest of the day without any more mishaps. Even Shiloh managed not to get into any trouble, at least none that she heard of. She never knew for sure with him. When they were done, Chapel Springs resembled a queen decked out in her crown jewels, ready to welcome guests. The ladies stood on the beach side of Sandy Shores Drive and studied their labors.

Every lamppost in the village had a fresh coat of paint and held a basket of either bright pink and white petunias or mix of yellow, purple and blue pansies. The pansies were Claire's favorites. She pictured how they'd look on a bunny-table urn.

In front of each shop lining the Drive stood two large pots holding a colorful variety of annuals. Bright red and yellow something-or-others and white daisies surrounded golden Daylilies. In front of Sunspots, Nancy had chosen mini roses and sweet alyssum.

Wooden benches sat between the pots, inviting passers-by to sit and rest. Claire wanted to take advantage of one. She was hot and dripping from the humidity. Every one of her tired muscles complained.

"Once the awnings are installed, Chapel Springs will be the most picturesque village in the state," Lydia said. "The ads on the Internet won't be able to do it justice."

"We did a good job, but did y'all see how Felix strutted around all day? I swanney, he thinks he's the berries. He'll probably take credit for it all, too." He always did.

"No matter," Bev said. "We all know the truth and can be proud of what we've accomplished."

Claire would feel a lot better when her muscles quit arguing with her. They had more work to do tomorrow. If the men got the gazebo repaired, it would still need painting. And her reputation was at stake. But would the restoration there be enough to wipe out the memories of last year's July Fourth celebration?

Chapter 14

A dull pain pulled at the small of Patsy's back. She pressed her
fingertips into the ache and arched, working out a kink as she
inhaled the freshly turned earth and mulch. Preparing the beds
for the colorful petunias she'd plant in the sunny spots and the impatiens
where the Sweetgum tree cast its shade over the flowerbed was good
therapy. Spring always made her antsy, until the garden was a profusion
of blooms, and the pink-blossomed Cherry tree held hands with the
white Dogwood over beds of bright azaleas. The rhododendron bushes,
each with a multitude of buds, promised to bloom shortly after their
cousins. If the weather held she could begin in two or three weeks.

She was five—no, four—the first time she helped her mother plant
this garden, and the continuity of laying out the same flowers year after
year gave her a sense of security. She wished her life would remain as
predictable.

She stood, picked up the shovel, and laid it in the wheelbarrow.
Through a window, her mother's voice rose in a melody as familiar to
Patsy as her own heartbeat. *Que Sera Sera*. But her heart caught at the
words of its second verse. Would she still have dreamed of rainbows day
after day if she'd known what would happen in her marriage? Would
she have married at all? She held her face up to the sun's warmth. No.
Like the song said, it was best not to know. Another good maxim she
chose to adhere to.

She grabbed the wood handles of the wheelbarrow, careful to avoid
the rough spot near the edge that somehow always managed to give
her a splinter. Leaning forward, she gave it a shove into the open shed.
It clanked down on its wheel, knocking a rake down from the wall. It

lay across the wheelbarrow, teetering back and forth like a seesaw. She considered picking it up but shut the door instead. Out of sight, out of mind.

She climbed the stairs to her parents' apartment, knocked, and opened the door. "It's me." The scent of burnt sugar hung in the air, and the apartment felt warm, too warm. Another reminder her parents were getting old.

Mama ambled from the kitchen, wiping her hands on a towel. "Of course it's you. Who else knocks and walks in? The First Lady?"

At least her sense of humor hadn't been affected.

"I've got to go to Young Harris then to the art supply on the way home. Want to come with me?" Patsy followed her into the kitchen. "Mmm, Something smells delicious. What have you been baking?"

Mama opened her mouth then shut it. Her brows dipped, hooding her eyes as she squinted in concentration. "I can't remember the name. Some kind of cookies." She waved her hand dismissing the subject. "The recipe's on the counter. I'll go get my handbag."

Patsy picked up a cookie to munch as she read the recipe. Viennese Vanilla Cookies. Sounded good. As she read the recipe, she took a nibble. Crumbling cookie dissolved on her tongue, flooding her mouth with the taste of sugar, butter, and something that tasted almost like— she spit into the sink—vinegar! Using her hand as a cup, she slurped a drink of water to wash away the horrible taste. Mama used to be a good baker, but she'd obviously used vinegar instead of vanilla in these. Patsy would have to warn her dad before he ate them. Then again, if she didn't tell him, maybe eating one of these would open his eyes.

"I'm ready," her mother called from the hallway. "Put that cookie down and let's go."

The two-lane highway meandered through the mountains, the forest broken only by an occasional meadow. Cottages and large log homes nestled among the trees like roses on a wedding cake.

"Have you ever been inside one of those big old log ones, Mama?"

"A few times. Most of them belong to executives for summer homes. The smaller ones, though, are so cozy and quaint. I love them. Did I ever tell you the time your daddy and I rented a log house up in Canada?"

Several times. "I remember that story. A bear broke into the porch and raided the trash can, right?"

Never missing a beat, Mama kept the conversation flowing by relating stories from her childhood. Patsy loved them even though she'd heard them dozens of times. Her mother had been retelling the same stories more often lately. How could she mix up vanilla and vinegar, yet she remembered every detail of her own tenth birthday party down to the presents?

Patsy's stomach churned. She wasn't sure if it was nerves or the bite of cookie. Could her mother still be trusted to cook for Dad? What if she grabbed not just the wrong ingredient but something worse? They could be poisoned.

"Mama, why don't you and Dad eat with us tonight? I'm fixing to make his favorite, Shepherd's Pie."

"Your father would love that. Thank you, dear."

Good. Now all she had to do was figure out a way for them to eat with her every night. Behind her, a car loomed closer than she was comfortable with, so she pulled over into the right lane to let him pass. She could say she didn't like to eat alone. After all, it was tax season. But what would she say when tax season was over and Nathan still didn't come home for dinner?

As they rounded a curve in the road, the thick forest thinned as the outskirts of Young Harris came into view. Her mama wrinkled her nose.

"They've cut a swath out of the forest to build one of those subdivisions. Now, why come to the beautiful mountains to live in a cookie cutter house?" She clicked her tongue. "I'll never understand it. Why I remember when Young Harris was nothing but a whistle stop on the way to east Tennessee." She twisted her neck to look as they passed a strip mall.

A moment later, Patsy turned into the parking lot of Henderson's Organic Market. Her mama's mouth fell open.

"This huge place is Henderson's? My mama brought me here when I was a little girl. It was nothin' more than a little outdoor farmer's market." She chuckled. "I remember our old Ford barely made it up that mountain. Coming here was quite an adventure back then." She gazed at the market, shaking her head. "My, my, it's grown and gone indoors. Why, it's bigger than the Piggly Wiggly in Pineridge."

"But it still carries farm-fresh produce, Mama, and it has hard-to-find items, too. I need to get a few things in here I can't get at home. I also promised Claire I'd pick up the brochure about their cooking classes."

"Claire? In a cooking class? Oh, dear." Her mother rolled her eyes and chuckled. "Her picture belongs in the dictionary by the Sword of

Damocles. I've always loved her, but that girl gets into more jams than a bushel of strawberries, bless her heart."

"I'll go with her, Mama, to help keep her out of trouble."

Her mother snorted a chuckle. "You'll be busy."

After getting the brochure and the items Patsy wanted, they headed back to Pineridge and Artistic Expressions. The minute they stepped inside the art supply store, the owner, Max Zeason, rushed over to them, his hooded, Basset Hound eyes twinkling. Following him was a gentleman, who looked vaguely familiar. He took her mother's hand in his.

"I can't believe you're here. I was just telling Max I wanted to meet the famous Cooper Benson, and here you stand before me—in person." He bowed and kissed her hand, which he hadn't yet released. A lock of dark, wavy hair had dropped to his forehead. "Avery Chandler, ardent admirer."

Patsy blinked in surprise. Avery Chandler—art critic and collector. No wonder he looked familiar. The tweed jacket with leather at the elbows was the same one he had on in an interview last month in one of her and Mama's art magazines. What was he doing in Pineridge?

Her mother's cheeks turned pink with pleasure. She always did that no matter how often people recognized her, and it happened all the time. Chapel Lake wasn't the only draw to these north Georgia mountains. Mama's paintings were in notable collections and museums around the world.

"Mr. Chandler." Her mother's free hand waved the air like a true Southern belle, waving her hankie. "I've read your reviews of my work. You, sir, have made me blush."

Patsy hid a smile as her mother charmed the man. He was at least a decade older than than his picture in the magazine. She guessed him to be in his late forties, maybe early fifties, from the smattering of gray at his temples and in his trim goatee. A handsome man, he effected a British accent, but from what she'd read, he was raised in the Midwest.

Avery's chest puffed till Patsy feared his buttons would pop. "I finally acquired your 'Dawn at Moonrise' at auction last month. I've been after it for years."

Her mother extricated her hand from the collector's. "Did you now? How lovely. I hope it meets with your expectations."

"More than ever." He turned to Patsy. "Is this lovely lady your sister, perhaps?"

Forcing her eyes not to roll, she pulled her lips into a smile and extended her hand. "Patsy Kowalski."

He nodded with a blank expression. He didn't know her name. Well, who's to blame him? His attention was riveted on her mother. Max, bless his heart, looked fit to be tied at the man's ignorance, and Mama stretched to her full five-foot-eight height.

"My daughter's an accomplished artist herself, Mr. Chandler, although her style is much different than mine. She's a realist. I'm quite proud of her composition and technique."

Max rocked on the balls of his feet as Chandler peered at Patsy with new interest. "Really? Where can I view your work?"

She wished she had the nerve to tell him that he couldn't, but unfortunately, artists needed critics like him, full of themselves as they were, to gain exposure. "I share a gallery with a pottery artist. We're in Chapel Springs."

"A potter? Is she any good?"

"One of the best. Perhaps you know her work. Claire Bennett?" She handed him the gallery's card. "Now if you'll excuse me." She smiled apologetically. "I'm in need of some paints."

She left her mother chatting with him while she shopped. Avery Chandler had the ear of the art world and was the owner of a first rate collection. It would be a boost to her career if he gave her even a halfhearted review. A good one would put her on the national radar. Her heart picked up speed when she considered what could happen if he liked her work well enough to purchase one of her paintings. Her hand trembled as she selected tubes of Titanium White, Phthalo Blue and Yellow Ochre.

This could be a turning point for her, but did she want the kind of fame her mother had? Carrying her paint to the cash register, she thought back to her childhood, before her mother was discovered by the outside art world. That happened when Patsy turned six. Mama received an invitation to show her work in a prestigious New York gallery. She'd politely refused, telling them it was her daughter's birthday and she wouldn't miss it. And she hadn't. Nor did she miss out on the showing. They wanted her badly enough to move the date forward a week. After that, if she wasn't in the studio painting, Mama traveled to art shows, and often missed the special days in Patsy's young life.

Her mother had the freedom to travel because Daddy had his office at home. Still, she never saw much of him, either. He tried, of course, but patients demanded their doctor. She invaded his office occasionally, but the odor of medicine and antiseptic kept her out most of the time.

While she knew she was loved, she was lonely. Claire had been her lifeline. Patsy warmed at the memory, and she resolved to make sure Avery Chandler saw Claire's work.

Patsy slipped her debit card from her wallet and handed it to the cashier. As the girl swiped it, Patsy scanned the store, hoping to catch one last glimpse of the critic, but he must have already left. Now to find Mama.

"Psst, Patsy." From a side aisle, Max gestured for her to come to him while looking over his shoulder.

She sauntered toward him, smothering a smile. "Why the subterfuge, Max?"

His glasses wobbled from their perch on top of his head, as he wrung his hands and licked his lips. "I'm ... I'm ... I don't know how to say this."

What? Had her check bounced? She smiled in hopes of relaxing him. "If my check didn't clear the bank you can tell me. We're old friends."

His eyes, which always looked weepy, shifted downward. "No, no. It's not that. Patsy, I just saw your mama slip a brush in her pocket."

Oh, dear. "Are you sure, Max? Mother's never taken anything." Other than Patsy's knife and fork.

"I don't know what to make of it. It isn't even a sable brush but a synthetic."

She wasn't sure if Max was more upset by her mother taking an inferior brush or the theft itself. She patted his hand. "I'll pay you for it, Max. My mother hasn't been herself lately. Do me a favor, please. If she comes in alone and does something like that again, be sure to let me know. Don't confront her. It might send her into a tizzy."

"I wouldn't dream of it. Why, Cooper is my best customer and a dear friend. I'm just concerned about her." Above his worried eyes, bushy eyebrows, like twin hedgehogs, wove together in a unibrow.

"Me, too, Max. I just wish I knew what it was."

"Well, she is getting up in years, Patsy. We forget that because she looks so good and she's still painting so well. But she's what, seventy-three now? Do you think it's Alzheimer's?"

Patsy cringed. It was one thing to think it, but to hear the words out loud ... She swallowed a lump of anxiety. "I don't know, Max, but please keep it to yourself."

Now it was his turn to pat her hand. "Don't you worry, my dear. I adore your Mama and your daddy's my doctor. I won't tell a living soul."

"Don't tell any dead ones, either. It would be difficult to trace the gossip back."

He muffled his chuckle. "Claire's rubbing off on you, my dear. You have a good afternoon and don't worry. The secret's safe with me."

It might be safe with Max, but she couldn't follow her mother around all the time. If Mama did this in another store where they didn't know her, how could Patsy protect her from being arrested?

Chapter 15

"I'll be there in a minute. Put some music on." Claire closed the door to the master bathroom and opened a drawer, withdrawing a small Victoria's Secret bag. Inside rested a miniscule piece of slinky, diaphanous fabric. Good grits, she could wad it up in one hand. That tiny thing would never cover her body. That was the purpose, though, wasn't it—not to hide anything?

Was she a complete idiot to try this? Then again, she and Patsy had made a pact. Tonight began *Operation Marriage Revival*. She turned her back to the mirror and pulled off her sweatshirt. After discarding her jeans and underwear in the hamper, she slipped on the nightie.

One look down made blood rush to her cheeks. She was practically naked. Goose pimples rose on her arms. Even her toes were cold. Gulping, she gathered her nerve and turned to face the mirror, eyes squinched shut.

"Mirror, mirror on the bathroom wall, who's the biggest nutcase of all?" She opened one eye just enough to catch a glimpse of herself and grimaced. The daily sit-ups hadn't made her tummy flat, and five pregnancies left a roadmap across her abdomen. How would Joel view her? As the girl he married or an old has-been trying to recapture her youth?

He'd laugh. She just knew it. He'd laugh at her and she'd die of mortification. Egads, if she died, he wouldn't bury her in this get-up, would he? He wouldn't dare.

Would he?

She took a step back and buried her cold toes in the thick, soft pile of the bathroom rug. Men did weird things when their wives died. That's how Marybeth Wilkins ended up with that horrible tattoo. She never let Artie get those girlie mud flaps for his truck, and the day she died, he had the silhouette tattooed on her arm just for spite. It was all the town talked about for months.

Claire shifted to see her side view and sucked in her tummy. That looked better but her derriere had a slight droop. Maybe this was a mistake. She peeked again at her hunched figure. Just a cotton-picking minute. She was still this side of fifty and not an old woman. She stood taller. If she had to do this to invigorate their marriage, then so be it.

Taking a deep breath, she held her head high and her shoulders back. There, that looked better. Should she try a pair of heels? Her reflection shook its head. Bad idea. For sure she'd wobble or worse, trip and fall on her face.

She peered in the mirror. Her pale, scrubbed face was topped by flat hair—definitely not sexy. Maybe with a bit of make-up and her hair fluffed out, she'd make a decent vamp. Well, not a vamp exactly, but at least not a complete idiot. She hoped.

Using all her artistic talent, she applied the makeup she so rarely wore. She stared at her reflection in the mirror with a critical eye. Winking at herself, she whispered, "Not too bad for an almost-old broad."

After bending over and brushing her hair to add volume, she straightened and took a calming breath. It didn't help. Her heart continued beating at a pace almost in sync with the music Joel had playing. She cocked an ear. *Had* playing was the operative word. The music changed to what sounded like a Harley Davidson rally. She parked her fists on her hips. He'd better not have turned on that TV. He was supposed to be waiting for her, creating a romantic mood.

She cracked open the door.

The TV screen was dark and the herd of Harleys was only her husband—snoring.

Patsy glanced at the clock as she slipped into the turquoise nightgown and duster, its silky texture soft and cool against her skin. The Victoria's Secret clerk said the negligee was sexy, and Patsy's natural bed-head look added to the image. She hoped the girl was right, because tonight, she desperately needed to be sexy. This was the night she and Claire picked to begin their *Operation Marriage Revival*—dubbed O.M.R. for short. Patsy had to win Nathan back from this—she shuddered—

involvement he'd gotten himself into.

Now she wished it had been Lydia or even Bev. She knew how to fight that, but this ... this was unthinkable. She paused as she applied a soft pink lipstick. What she needed was a bit of Claire's spunk. She wasn't one to worry. In her mind's eye, Patsy saw Claire modeling that skimpy negligee for Joel. She'd probably jump up right onto the middle of the bed.

After pressing her lips to a tissue, leaving a pink kiss behind, Patsy went downstairs to wait for Nathan. She picked up a book and chose a seat in the front room's bay window. A tiffany lamp sat on the table between the wingback chairs, bathing the nook in a soft glow. From the entry hall, the grandfather clock chimed eight-forty-five. Nathan should be home soon. She artfully arranged the folds of her robe around her and picked up her book.

The story about a widower with four kids had intrigued her, but tonight she couldn't concentrate. Silence magnified the clock's ticking. She laid the open book on the table. A cup of tea might soothe her tense nerves.

In the kitchen waiting for the kettle to boil, she opened the pantry and reached for the box of her favorite tea. She stopped, her hand midway to the Chamomile. That box—well not that exact one, but *a* box of Chamomile had always been on that same shelf for ... well, for as long as she could remember. Her mother kept hers there. Patsy had other kinds but never drank them. Why not?

Because she always wanted everything the same. She never changed—anything.

Was that what Nathan wanted? Did he resent the constancy in their life? Her eyes zeroed in on a box of white tea with pear. She could change if that's what it took to win him back. She grabbed it before she changed her mind.

Armed with the steaming mug, Patsy returned to her post to wait. Her first cautious sip surprised her. It was good. How silly not to have tried it before. Even more ridiculous was the adventurous feeling it created. Claire would sure get a hoot out of that. Settling in to wait, Patsy picked up her book again, and this time, the story captured her interest. In the background, the clock struck ten. She leaned her head against the chair's wing as she read.

Somewhere a phone rang with insistence. Who would be calling this late at night? When Patsy won the battle to open her eyes, sunlight poured through the bay window behind her. She was still sitting on the chair, her half-finished tea and book beside her. How could it be morning? She raised her head and massaged the tight muscles in her neck. Ouch. Wasn't there some Chinese proverb about sleeping in a wingback chair? If not, there should be. What time was it?

The phone stopped ringing as the answering machine picked up, and a voice she didn't recognize asked for a call back to verify some appointment. She could replay it later. Right now she wanted to know why Nathan didn't wake her.

Since it was closest, she checked the garage first. Empty. She headed up to their bedroom. If he had gone to bed, why hadn't he awakened her to come up? The bedroom door was closed. She opened it carefully, in case he was still asleep. The spread hadn't a wrinkle in it. The decorative pillows stood where she'd tossed them yesterday morning.

Their bed hadn't been disturbed.

She leaned against the doorjamb and closed her eyes. Where was he? Not once in all the years they'd been married had he stayed out all night. Well, except for when he went to Miss Holly's every year for—her eyes popped open. Miss Holly!

She ran back to the kitchen and yanked the calendar off the fridge. There it was on April tenth in bold letters: Miss Holly's taxes. The domineering force behind a family dynasty in Macon, Miss Holly insisted no one but Nathan do the family's taxes.

Patsy shook her head. How could she not have remembered? She wanted to crawl under a rock and hide. And now she had to go report to Claire. Then again, that was less embarrassing than if Nathan had come home and ignored her. By the time she was lathered up in the shower, she could almost laugh about it.

Except for one nagging thought. Nathan had always invited her to come along. Did someone else accompany him this year?

Fifteen minutes later, Patsy pushed open the door to Dee's 'n' Doughs. She sighed in relief. Claire sat, waiting for her ... alone.

She looked up from her coffee cup. "Morning."

Her voice didn't hold the happy note Patsy thought it would. Maybe her O.M.R. hadn't been a success, either.

"How'd it go?"

Claire curled her upper lip and crossed her eyes.

Patsy laughed, picturing Claire falling off the bed or something equally silly. "What happened?"

"By the time I got up the nerve to walk into the bedroom, Joel was snoring up the window coverings."

How disappointing. "I'm sorry, but at least he was there."

"What do you mean?"

"Nathan never came home."

Claire's eyes popped open wide along with her mouth. "He didn't? Where is he? Do you know?"

"Yeah." She rolled her eyes. "At Miss Holly's."

"Oh, Patsy." Claire's giggles grew to guffaws. "How could you have forgotten?"

Patsy blew the paper cover from a straw at her. "How, indeed."

Claire batted the missile away. "Wait a minute. I thought you normally went with him."

She wished Claire hadn't brought that up. "Hmm, well the past few months haven't been what you'd call normal." Patsy eyed Claire's cup. "I need some caffeine."

She didn't want to think about the last few months. As long as Patsy didn't think, she didn't have to deal with it. But she knew she would sooner or later. Things like this wouldn't stay hidden for long.

Chapter 16

Sandy Shores Drive buzzed with activity. Patsy paused a moment after dragging a table outside the gallery and soaked up the cheery atmosphere of the street. The good Lord knew she could use some. The past few weeks she'd hardly seen Nathan, and the chasm was widening between them. But this morning was not the time to indulge in a pity party. There was work to be done.

"Hand me that frog, will you, Lacey?" Patsy pointed to a row of boxes behind her. The auction should bring a substantial amount toward hiring the geologist. She admired the way Bev had marshaled the entire town into action, coercing donations from every merchant right down to the bank that offered a complete framed set of uncirculated state quarters.

Patsy straightened, massaging her lower back, and lifted her face to the gentle warmth of the morning sun. The day had dawned bright and cool, promising mild temperatures for the first annual Chapel Springs Art Festival. For the past three weeks, the townspeople had repaired and painted all the shops in preparation for the day's event. There wasn't a cloud in the sky, and both lake and village sparkled.

Bev's committee and the merchants scurried around tacking bunting to the exhibit tables, checking off donations, and directing the preparations. Across the street on the lake's grassy beach area, scaffolding hid behind curtained frames, awaiting the actors, who would climb up to pose in the living pictures.

Everywhere Patsy looked, people scurried around, readying the town in expectation of the hoped-for visitors. Felix and Warren balanced atop ladders on opposite sides of the street, retying strings of colorful nautical flags from the light posts so they swung overhead, adding a jaunty spirit to the festival. From the *Dees 'n' Doughs* table, delicious aromas of coffee and yeasty pastries wafted through the air. Tillie Payne directed her nephew, pushing a handcart filled with boxes of books, to a spot three tables down the row in *The Tome Tomb*.

"Here you go." Lacey placed a green bullfrog vase on the table, in front of Patsy. "He makes me smile, and I've fallen in love. I want him." The frog's tongue protruded six inches and held a dragonfly in its grip. "I adore the gleam in his eye over his anticipated breakfast."

Patsy resisted the urge to lift her eyebrows. Lacey had never spoken so many words at once in all the years Patsy had known her. She was usually so quiet it was easy to forget she was there. Her delight over the frog animated her face, overcoming its plainness.

"Good luck then, but even if you lose I'm sure Claire would make you another."

Patsy turned her attention back to the display. She maneuvered a tabletop easel holding one of her smaller paintings to the center of the display. The eleven-by-fourteen canvas of Chapel Springs in the sixties rested within a red enamel frame. All the buildings looked pristine and the mood nostalgic. She'd painted two children, standing in front of the candy store holding dripping pink ice cream cones and peering in its window. If one could see the faces of the two figures, one would probably find strawberry ice cream smeared all around their mouths. It would be fun to see if Claire figured out who they were.

Bev approached with her ever-present clipboard. "Frog. Check. Loon platter. Check." She continued down her list of donations like an Army supply sergeant. "Chapel Springs in oil." She stopped and peered at the painting. "It's perfect, Patsy, exactly how we want visitors to view Chapel Springs. I'm sure it will sell high. Where's Claire?"

"Taking Shiloh home. He can't imagine a town festival without him as the main attraction." She laughed at Bev's wide-eyed expression of horror as she whirled around to look for a disaster.

Still chuckling, Patsy said, "Relax. The only catastrophe was that Shiloh timed his gallop into town just as Felix and Warren were lifting the string of flags from opposite sides of the street. The string caught on Shiloh's collar and slammed Felix's ladder into the light post and toppled Warren's. Fortunately, he managed to grab hold of the scrollwork and hang on."

Pausing to catch her breath, she could still see poor Warren, dangling from the light post, kicking his legs out in a vain attempt to connect with anything solid. It was pandemonium with Felix shouting curses down on Shiloh, and Happy Drayton's clumsy attempts to right the ladder under Warren while the rest of them were doubled over, helpless from laughter.

"She should be back in a few minutes." No sooner said than ... "In fact, here she comes now."

Claire carried a bag of frozen peas. "Where's Felix?"

Patsy pointed to the ladder across the street. "Up there. What are the peas for? Hungry already?"

"Felix's eye. I think it's going to turn black. He slammed into the post pretty hard." Claire looked around at the displays. "Everything looks beautiful, Pat-a-cake. Thanks for covering for me while I locked up Shiloh. I have no idea where Joel is."

"Last I saw, he was going to help Happy hang the new sign for the bait shop." Claire handed the frozen peas to one of the high school girls. "Would you take this to the mayor, please?"

Looking over the table, she repositioned the frog, turning it slightly to the left. Patsy held her breath, waiting. Claire stood back, tilted her head to one side then the other, and finally moved the frog back to its original position. Patsy said nothing as Claire tweaked their display, waiting for her to notice the painting. Suddenly she stopped with her hand mid-reach. Her eyes and mouth opened wide. Watching her lean in was a magical moment for Patsy. She let her breath out as Claire's mouth changed from an "O" to a sappy grin.

"It's us." She peered closer at the painting. "I remember debating whether the candy necklaces would have been as good as those strawberry ice cream cones."

"That's what sparked the idea. Every time I have one, I remember so many days like that when we were kids." Days free of care, and sorrow no bigger than losing at hopscotch.

Claire hugged her. "We did have the most ideal childhood. I never felt the lack of a mother thanks to your mom—at least when she was home."

Patsy didn't want to visit that old hurt. "She adored you and CeeCee. She always said she'd wanted twins. It's funny how our mothers were best friends and so are we. That doesn't always happen. Yet your sister always went her own way."

"Yeah—the domestic way. No wonder I never learned to cook. She was a tyrant, always pushing me out of the kitchen."

Lacey handed Patsy a box of donated items from *The Halls of Time*. Like everything else from the shop, the linens carried the distinctive musty odor of antiquity.

"Thank you, Lacey. Be a dear and see if Bev needs anything else before you have to get into costume and become Mona Lisa."

"You miss her?" Patsy passed Claire a Limoges perfume bottle and a trinket box.

"Who? Lacey?"

"No, silly. CeeCee."

"Sometimes. We were complete opposites in so many ways, yet when she died, I felt like I'd lost part of myself. If you remember," She stopped and looked at Patsy. "It was CeeCee who got me asking questions about God. She made me promise to meet her in Heaven."

What Patsy remembered the most was how angry Claire had been. And frightened. Cancer wasn't particular about whom it invaded.

Claire moved the trinket box an inch closer to the perfume bottle. "There. I think this table's ready. I need some coffee. We don't have too much more time until the festival opens and the crowds descend. *If* they descend."

"They'll come. I heard we've had several phone calls from the ads your Charlie designed. That reporter who came to the council meeting did a segment about it on the news last weekend and that's gotten the word out. Felix got Channel 10 to promise to cover the festival."

As they made their way to Dee's coffee booth, Claire lifted one corner of her upper lip in a sneer. "And we'll have to listen to him brag about it for the next year. Let's take our coffee to the gallery. I want to make sure it's ready. Is Avery Chandler really coming?"

She pumped coffee from an airpot into two cardboard cups, steam curling in the air above them, and handed one to Patsy.

"That's what he said. He wanted to see your work." It tickled her to see Claire so excited about the art critic. She worked hard on this festival, it was nice to give her something for a change.

Back at the gallery, Patsy opened the double doors and put stops beneath them. A light breeze brought fresh air in and with it, the scent of spring and the promise of summer. Standing in the doorway, she inhaled. Fresh air, clay, and oil paint mingled with the scent of old wood. Nowhere else on earth smelled as wonderful.

"If you keep inhaling like that, you'll suck a loon up your nose.

Here." Claire tossed a soft cloth at her. "Take a dust rag and get busy."

"We cleaned yesterday. How much dust could gather overnight?"

"I guess I *am* obsessing, huh?" Claire wiggled a feather duster at her. "I'm just nervous about Avery Chandler coming here."

"Why?" Something in the way she said Chandler's name bothered Patsy. "It's not like you to get nervous about someone looking at your work."

Claire continued to dust and didn't look at her. "I'm not nervous."

"And I'm not your best friend. Come on, spill. What's going on in that brain of yours?"

Claire stopped her frenetic dusting and faced her. Patsy hadn't seen her friend filled with this much kinetic energy since her nesting phase shortly before Charlie was born.

"Okay, I'm a little nervous. I Googled him last night, so I'd recognize him when he comes in." Her tongue poked out between her lips and she licked them. "He's rather good looking, isn't he?"

Oh, no. "Claire, you're not thinking of—"

"I'm not thinking of anything. I simply made an observation." She whirled around and swished her feather duster over a display of bowls.

"You've never 'simply made an observation' in your life. Be careful, okay? I don't want you or Joel to get hurt. Go very slowly." What was she saying? Claire had all the subtlety of a charging water buffalo.

"Don't be such an Eeyore." Claire waved the duster at her. Particles flew off into the air, and sparked in the sunlight. Like Claire's eyes, only her sparkle spelled trouble.

"I'm really only interested in what he can do for our careers. If he likes us—our work—he can bring the art world to our door." She looked down at her coveralls and back at Patsy. "Don't you think we should go home to get changed? The festival opens in thirty minutes." Claire turned on her heel and disappeared out the door.

Patsy shook her head, staring at the empty space where Cyclone Claire had been just a moment before. They needed Avery Chandler to love their work and give them a good review—and that was all. She'd seen that look in Claire's eyes before, and trouble usually followed. As she went to change, a sinking sensation filled her stomach, and she didn't think it was the coffee.

Thirty minutes later, she placed a guestbook on a small table at the gallery's entrance. She wanted to get email addresses on all their visitors and expand their client database. As she moved around the main room giving the displays a last minute check, she stopped in front of a mirror they used to reflect light into the room.

She turned a critical eye to her attire. The teal and coral broomstick skirt and matching peasant blouse flattered her light brown hair, although the colors didn't do much for her freckles. They stood out in relief against her pale skin. She needed some sun. A chunky silver necklace and bracelet, her only accessories, completed the outfit. Passing her own inspection, she gave the gallery a final visual sweep. They were both ready. Now where was Claire?

"I'm back." Claire bounced in the door and twirled for Patsy to admire her. She'd put on her favorite mid-length denim skirt. The gored panels and the elastic waistband let her move freely without binding. Why wear something uncomfortable? Her white blouse, its collar turned up, lay outside the skirt, and she added a wide leather belt over it, resting just above her hips. "How do I look?"

"Very stylish," Patsy said. "I'm impressed."

"Thanks and you look like a summer breeze—fresh and lovely." Claire pulled earrings out of her pocket and slipped them in her earlobes. The large, dangly chartreuse and orange baubles swung just above her shoulders, dancing like her nerves. "Do we have refreshments for people?"

"Yes. Tea and coffee for this morning, white wine, crackers and cheese for this afternoon. We're all ready, and just in time. Here come the first visitors."

A trio of ladies entered, laughing and chattering, followed by their husbands. Over the course of the next few hours, Claire and Patsy were kept busy greeting the steady flow of guests, showing them around the gallery, and answering their questions. As she rang up a fair number of sales, Claire kept a watchful eye through the front window, hoping to spot the art critic arriving, but Patsy downright hovered by the door.

Around three o'clock, the crowd thinned, giving them a break. Claire caught Patsy's elbow and pulled her to the back of the gallery. "Do you think Chandler's still coming?"

"I'm not sure. Maybe he's decided to come tomorrow instead. I'm trying not to get my hopes up too much."

"You look like you've lost that battle. Maybe he won't come at all."

"The way he fawned over my mother, I'm sure he'll be here."

"Then find your mom. She was here somewhere a while ago."

Patsy's eyes widened as she peered over Claire's shoulder. "I don't think we need to." She nodded toward the front of the gallery. "Look."

Excitement sparkled in her eyes, and Claire could see why. Dark hair with a sprinkling of gray at the temples complemented his blue eyes and strong jawline. Movie star handsome with suave right on its heels traipsed into her mind. She clenched her teeth to keep her jaw from dropping. The online photo did not do Avery Chandler justice. Why hadn't Patsy told her how good-looking he was? *My, my, my.* Claire's heart thumpety-thumped in her chest.

Chandler made his way to Patsy's painting of Loon Island. He cocked his head to the right, cupping his chin in his right hand while his left arm supported his elbow. After a moment, he switched hands and cocked his head to the left. Patsy grabbed Claire's hand and squeezed it—hard. *Ouch.*

She pulled her hand away. "Come on," she whispered. "Let's go greet him."

Patsy yanked her back. "No! Give him a minute to study my painting."

Trying to wrench free, Claire spoke through a tight smile. "I'm not about to let him get away."

"Claire Bennett, down, girl." Patsy tightened her grip.

"Are you trying to stop me from finding out if he's the one?"

"Shh. I'm trying to keep your feet out of your mouth and on the ground."

"You just want him all to yourself."

Patsy released her grip. "I can't believe you sa—"

"Ah-ah-ahem."

They whirled around. Avery stood three feet away, regarding them with undisguised interest. Heat rose in Claire's cheeks as Patsy stepped forward.

"I'm delighted you could make it, Avery. This," she gestured to Claire, "is my *friend* and gallery partner, Claire Bennett."

Spoken that way, "friend" didn't sound so friendly. Claire stepped in front of Patsy and put her hand out. "It's such a pleasure to meet you."

Avery clasped Claire's offered hand in both of his. "My dear, the pleasure is all mine. I had no idea a pottery artist could be so lovely." He tucked her hand through his arm. "Come, tell me about your work. I've never seen such unusual pieces before."

Okay, she knew flirting when she saw it, but he added a whole new dimension to the word. As he led her away, she couldn't help but toss a crowing smirk over her shoulder. She should have resisted. Trouble with a capital "P" was bearing down on her.

Chapter 17

Claire's ire grew dangerously hot as Patsy wormed her way in between Avery and her, guiding him back toward her side of the gallery. "Before you start on Claire's little pots, do you want to see mother's most recent painting?"

Little pots? Oh, that was low. Claire balled her hands into fists. And poor Avery, trapped, could only follow the traitor. Well, if Patsy thought she could get away with—Claire's eye fell on the wine and cheese tray. She grabbed it up and barreled across the room.

"Have a glass of chardonnay with some cheese, Avery?" She thrust the tray into Patsy's hands, lifted a glass in the transfer and handed it to Avery, who took it with great interest. Diverting him back to her influence was easier than she expected. With him safely in her clutches, she reached out and plucked a piece of Stilton cheese from the plate, popped it in her mouth and glared a warning at Patsy.

Patsy's eyes narrowed and she banged the plate down. She'd better not have chipped it. It was going into the auction.

Claire turned back to Avery as he studied her whimsy vases, his smile growing wider at the loons. "My dear, you have the best technique I've seen in years." He turned and leaned close. "Have you been hiding here all this time, and I didn't know it?"

Hiding? "Uh, no, I sup—"

"We must have dinner. I want to know all about your work. Every fascinating detail. How do you mix your colors? They're amazing."

Claire untangled an earring that had caught on her collar. When was the last time Joel asked her that? Had he ever asked? No, he wasn't interested in the details of her work. He couldn't care less about color.

Now if Avery would transfer that interest to *her*.

Avery continued to study her pieces. When he came to the turkey masquerading as a cookie jar, he laughed out loud. "You have a delicious sense of humor. I've never seen one translated into art so well." He took her hand, settled it through his arm, and gave it a squeeze.

Entranced by his chivalry, Claire mutely went along with him. How refreshing to be with a man who was honestly interested in her work. And in her, she hoped. With her mind in Fantasyland, she tripped on the step into the next display room. Avery steadied her, but kept his eyes on her work. It was so nice to have someone truly appreciate her art. Obviously, her gallery partner did not. In fact, where was her former best friend?

Looking around, Claire spotted Patsy, dragging her mother toward them, and gasped. Oh, of all the dirty tactics. And she had that look on her face—the one that meant Claire was about to be bested. Biting her lip, she searched right and left for a diversion. What could she do to stop Patsy? She needed help. She let go of Avery's arm and spun around, desperately looking for anything to ward off Patsy and her mother. Then, through the front window, she spied Bev, walking past the front door. Claire raced for the entrance.

"Bev! I'm delighted to see you. Come in and meet Avery Chandler." Claire pulled her into the gallery. "He's an art critic and collector. He's been admiring my work." She glanced back at Patsy, whose mouth hung open in disbelief. So, she didn't like losing, huh? Well, ha!

Claire turned and snagged Avery's arm just as he was reaching for the wine glass he'd set down. He looked slightly bewildered as his fingers missed their target, but she didn't have time to worry about that. If she didn't hurry, Patsy would have him.

As they approached Bev, he turned a shining smile on her. She all but batted her false eyelashes in return, but before he could speak, Patsy grabbed her mother's arm and rushed him, pushing Cooper before Avery. Oh, that was dirty.

"He came to see mother's paintings." Patsy glared at Claire.

Cooper looked back and forth between the friends, rolled her eyes and shook her head.

Claire wasn't going down without a fight. With her hip, she started to wedge herself in front of Patsy, regaining her spot by Avery's side, but before she could gain ground, Bev's hand reached past Claire's nose.

Avery obliged Bev, bowing and kissed the back of her fingers. "Such lovely ladies in Chapel Springs. It must be the water."

Bev smiled, lowered her head and batted her false eyelashes at him. "I declare! This is a pleasure, sir."

Claire blinked. What happened to her Boston accent? That little Yankee faked a drawl. And Avery was nearly drooling. Couldn't he spot a phony? Claire narrowed her eyes and peered at them, then face-palmed herself. It was her own dumb fault for letting in the hussy.

He tucked Bev's hand in his arm and led her away. "Let me get you a glass of wine, lovely lady, and I'll show you the paintings."

She splayed her fingers on her chest like she thought she was Scarlet O'Hara. "Why, thank you. Tell me, do you frequent art galleries all over the world? I have a favorite one on a back street in Venice."

"Do you? Say, I'm famished. What say we grab a bite somewhere and you can tell me about it."

"What about our review?" Claire asked.

Avery waved his hand in dismissal. "Later."

Later? "Now just a cotton-picking minute, buster." Claire stormed over to the man. Her finger poked his chest with each word. "Who do you think you are, coming in here, raising my friend's hopes for a review, then walking out with this tart?"

Bev's eyes shot open to the size of quarters. Uh-oh, maybe Claire shouldn't have said that. No stopping now. Not when she clearly saw *this* grass wasn't greener than her own. With each poke, Avery stepped back.

"You're about as low as a worm. Wait until I tell the newspaper about you." What would she tell the newspaper? She'd come up with something. "You think you're some big whootey-patootey? I'll tell you—"

With a loud thud, Avery's back rammed hard against a large set of display shelves. Claire's eyes traveled up to the top shelf as the prize turkey figurine wobbled and tipped. Everything slowed as the turkey tumbled off the shelf and somersaulted, beak over tail feathers until it struck Avery Chandler on the top of his inflated head and shattered into several pieces.

Claire clapped a hand over her mouth in disbelief. Avery's knees crumpled and he went down without a whimper, blood trickling from a scalp wound. Knocked out cold. Or was he dead? Her hands grew clammy and her breathing rapid. Could they convict her of murder?

Bev screamed and ran out the door.

Cooper opened her purse and pulled out her cell phone. "Walker, dahlin', we've had a bit of a mishap here at the gallery. Would y'all bring your doctor bag and perhaps Vince? I'm not sure, but Claire may have killed Avery Chandler."

Claire couldn't catch her breath, and her head turned to air. Patsy opened a drawer and slapped a plastic bag over Claire's nose and mouth. Now she really couldn't breathe. She pushed it away and her head cleared. Somewhat.

"I think it's supposed to be a paper bag, Patsy, but thanks. I'm okay now." She stared down at Chandler, watching for any signs of life. How many witnesses saw her clobber him? Would Joel come visit her in prison if they sent her away to the big house? Did they still call it "the big house"? Or maybe it was "the pokey" now?

Within minutes, Doc Benson and Vince rushed through the door. They squatted next to Chandler and took his vital signs. Claire's heartbeat increased until she thought she'd faint. She grabbed Patsy's hand and waited for the verdict while Cooper and Patsy told them what happened. Claire was sure she heard Doc snicker, but she could have been wrong on that count.

After what felt like hours, Vince rose and gave her a reassuring smile. "He'll be fine, but he's going to have one big headache, and about a dozen stitches. But you didn't kill him, honey." He patted her hand. "See? He's coming around."

Chandler moaned as he stirred. Vince talked to him until Chandler could tell him his name and where he was. From the floor, he glared up at Claire. Patsy slipped in front of her and set one hand on her hip until Chandler closed his eyes.

The ambulance arrived and the paramedics lifted him onto the gurney. Doc called ahead to the hospital and ordered x-rays, saying he'd be there shortly. Before he left, he hugged Claire.

"Don't worry, he'll live. That kind always does." He winked at her. "And it's been an interesting interruption to a boring afternoon. I've always been glad you and Patsy were friends, my dear. Life is never dull when you're around."

"Yeah, but you love me. I'm worried about what Chandler will do."

"Flummadiddle. Get your grits back in the bowl, girl. When I'm through stitching him up, he'll understand it was his fault. Why he's lucky you don't present him with a bill for that turkey." After kissing them both on the cheek, he picked up his bag and left.

Claire stared at the colorful remains of her prized pottery. "My turkey," she wailed. A turkey clobbered by a turkey. Her wail changed to a sniff and a giggle snuck out her nose. Did she really call Bev a tart? Her lips twitched and a snicker escaped.

Patsy picked up the turkey's tail section. "He was beautiful." She held the broom in her other hand.

"Who, Chandler or the turkey?"

"The turkey, you goof. Do you think you can make another one? He was magnificent."

"Yeah, a hero. He saved the day." Claire's laughter died. "Oh, Pat-a-cake, I'm so sorry." The one person whose friendship Claire treasured most in this life, and she'd almost tossed it out for a jerk. *She* was the jerk. "I wouldn't blame you if you never spoke to me again. I cost you a review and a chance to become famous."

"Oh, shut up. We both got carried away." Patsy chuckled. "He really was a turkey, wasn't he? Chandler, I mean. So full of himself." Her chuckle grew into giggles. "The look on his face when you backed him into that corner was hilarious. The little wimp." Her giggles morphed into guffaws. "And Bev—her eyebrows shot up so far when you called her a tart she looked like she'd had a face-lift." Patsy doubled over, holding her stomach, laughing.

"I knew ... I shouldn't ... have said ... that." She gasped for air between laughs. "I still can't believe I did."

"Oh, girlfriend, I can. You always stick your foot in your mouth."

Claire sobered. "She'll never forgive me."

"We don't know that. She may wake up to her ways over this. Poor Drew. I know her flirting embarrasses him. I wonder if he's ever said anything to her."

"Speaking of saying anything, thanks for not saying you told me so."

Patsy swept up the last of the turkey's porcelain shards, slipping them into a trash bag. She set the broom down and turned to Claire. "Aw, what's a decent argument once every decade or so? I've come to realize it's good for us—gets rid of any stale air." A snarky grin split her face. "Besides, you're really funny when you get mad at me." She ducked the chunk of dried cheese flung at her.

Claire picked up another but nibbled this one. "Let's go see how the auction is going. Maybe we can salvage our reputations. At least sell something before Chandler ruins us."

"Do you think he will?"

Her friend's attempt to not seem concerned broke Claire's heart. This was her fault. And Joel's. If he didn't take her for granted, she never would have looked at Chandler like that. And now their big chance to get a major art critic to review their work was ruined. All because of Joel.

Claire rocked the front porch swing and listened to the birds chattering in the huge cypress at the south corner of the house. A regular Audubon-condo, dozens of nests filled its branches, which were so thick with leaves, making it difficult to see the nests. The cacophony of twittering and whistles always brought visions of tenement houses in New York in the old movies, where women chattered in Italian, Gaelic, and Polish while hanging laundry out the windows, at the same time stopping a youngster from climbing out.

Joel joined her on the swing. "How about making some coffee?"

"Okay. In a minute."

He cocked his head and pointed at the cypress. "They're sure noisy tonight. Sounds like the fledglings are getting ready to fly."

"Hmm." Claire didn't feel like talking. She wanted to string Felix up by his toes for telling Joel about what happened to Chandler. Then Joel got mad about it. He acted like she'd planned it. Anyway, it was as much his fault as hers. What bothered her most was he didn't seem to care at all that Chandler had flirted with her.

Beside her, Joel sighed. They continued to rock in silence. One brave little bird hopped to the end of a branch. Five adults flew to the cherry tree in the center of the front yard, about ten feet away then flew back. They repeated this a few times, and then remained in the cherry tree, calling to the fledgling. The little one rocked on the branch, ruffling its feathers until all at once, it took to the air. Claire held her breath. Its little wings flapped hard as it closed the distance between them.

"I called Bev a tart today."

"You didn't."

"I did."

Joel's shoulders shook. Claire snuck a peek at him and relief at seeing his grin replace the earlier frown relaxed her tight muscles.

"What did she say?"

"Nothing. There wasn't time. Right after that, Chandler backed into the shelves and got clobbered."

Joel's grin faded. "I hope he doesn't sue you."

"He wouldn't dare. He should be glad I don't send him an invoice for the pottery he destroyed."

"I still don't understand how it all happened."

"He came to do a review of our work and Bev came in. He decided she was nicer to look at and more fun to flirt with than me, I guess." She glanced sidelong at him, but he didn't react. "He knocked the display as he was leaving."

"How could he be so clumsy? You sure you didn't touch him?"

That was a low blow. "Why do you always assume it's me?"

He stared at her, not saying a word.

"Just because I have a past, doesn't mean I caused it."

"He'll sue."

"You seem more concerned with him suing than with him flirting with your wife."

One shoulder shrugged. "You can take care of yourself."

What was that supposed to mean? "Why—"

Joel pointed. "Look, another baby's trying to fly."

This little one lost its courage and would only hop from branch to branch.

His remarks hurt, but knowing the conversation would only escalate to another argument, Claire rose. "I'll go make that coffee."

Chapter 18

The deep blue water of Chapel Lake shimmered and sparkled like a sequined gown worn at the Oscars, creating a hypnotic backdrop to the Festival auction. Psychology had been well employed, placing the event on the beach lawn. With the lake tranquilizing their senses, people would be likely to spend more. Too bad its powers didn't work on Patsy. She could still see the street from her chair.

Where was Nathan?

She nodded absently at Claire as she dropped into a chair next to her. He should have been here ages ago. His promises used to mean something.

"Why did Bev insist on setting up here instead of the parking lot? This chair's in a hole." Claire wiggled in her seat. "It keeps rocking. Move down."

Patsy lowered her sunglasses from the top of her head, settling them into place against the glare of the afternoon sun reflecting off the lake. Clusters of tourists sat chatting in the front rows of the auction, with townspeople interspersed among them. Felix played his mayoral role, moving among the crowd with backslaps and hearty handshakes. She recognized a couple of serious art collectors in the audience, who chose to sit toward the rear.

"We can't. Bev assigned us these seats." The scent of caramelized sugar floated from the cotton candy vendor, reminding her she'd skipped lunch.

"What do you mean we can't? Watch me." Claire got up and moved to another chair halfway down the row. "See? Nothing happened. Bunch of nonsense, assigned seats."

Patsy didn't move. A dark blue sedan caught her attention as it rounded the bend coming up Sandy Shores. Her hopes quickly died, though. It wasn't Nathan's Saturn. She dug deep into her pocket for a mint or a piece of gum to kill the bitter taste in her mouth.

"Oh, for Pete's sake." Claire huffed and came back to rejoin her, jostling the chairs in front of her as she passed them. The two women occupying the seats turned simultaneously and scowled at Claire, who grimaced an apology.

"You're more stubborn than Joel at times. What's wrong?"

Patsy couldn't tell her right then, but if she concentrated on the auction she wouldn't cry. "I just want to keep the peace. Bev had some idea of interspersing the auction donors with the visitors. She seems to think it would make them want to bid more."

"Well, shut my mouth. That's a sneaky strategy. May it take hold like Kudzu. How did we end up yesterday?"

"Pretty fair." Glad for the change of subject, Patsy reached in her skirt pocket and pulled out a folded sheet of paper. "You sold eleven pieces and three of my paintings went for top dollar. Here." She handed over the list.

"*Pretty* fair? Van Gogh's ear, I can't believe the bidding on my frog went that high. Why, it makes me feel almost guilty." Claire waggled her fingers over an imaginary cigar, like W.C. Fields. "Almost."

No matter how down she got, her best friend could always make Patsy smile. "I had the same reaction. I guess someone besides Lacey fell in love with Kermit's cousin."

"Did Lacey win? I wouldn't think she could afford it."

"No, poor thing. She was outbid." An overdressed tourist sat directly in front of Patsy. The woman's floppy straw hat, topped with a florist's nightmare, blocked her view. With half an open row, why did she have to choose that chair?

Claire craned her neck and surveyed the crowd. "Patsy, you don't suppose it could have been Chandler, do you?"

"Now why would he do something like that? You just caused him a head-full of stitches."

"I know, but the thought just leaped into my mind, and I can't shake free from it."

Patsy lowered her sunglasses, peering over them. "Sure you can. Just open your mouth. It'll fall out while you're changing feet." She pushed her shades back into place.

Claire elbowed her. "Be serious. What if he decided to"

"To what? Resell it? Good. Your name spreads. Hoard it? That certainly wouldn't hurt you. He could destroy it, but I think he loves art too much. No, there's no earthly reason for him to have bought it. You're just feelin' guiltier than a Baptist in a pool hall."

"So low I could sit on the curb and dangle my feet."

"Lower than pond scum?"

By Claire's momentary silence, Patsy knew she'd find a topper. "Guiltier than a Dairy Queen Moo-latte at a Weight Watcher's meeting."

Claire didn't disappoint her, and the cloud of doom hovering above Patsy's head lifted. "You win that round."

"Thanks, Pat-a-cake. You're right, too. He isn't worth the energy of feelin' guilty."

The opening bell of the auction rang out.

"Oh, they're about to start."

Visitors scurried to take seats and voices hushed. Patsy pulled out the day's catalogue. A portly man thumped into the stage. Behind the microphone, he hitched up his britches and popped his suspenders. He was the auctioneer? Patsy flipped the catalog pages to find his bio. Reading the fact he was from Chicago didn't compute with the hillbilly on the stage. Clenched in his gleaming white teeth, a long blade of river grass wiggled with each word. Why did people think just because Chapel Springs was in the north Georgia Mountains they were all hicks? But by the fourth item sold, counterintuitive as it seemed, his approach disarmed the audience. It was plumb amazing. He drove prices up, and they never realized they'd been played like a fiddle. Where had Bev ever found him?

Patsy had one more painting in today's sale, and Claire had two serving platters. With growing admiration for the auctioneer, she watched the prices go higher and higher.

"Too bad Chandler isn't here to see this," Claire mumbled. "What are you doing? You keep twisting your head like that and someone is going to think you're in need of an exorcist. What or who are you looking for?"

"What? Oh. Nathan." Patsy glanced at her watch. Her heart plummeted. It was past three. "He's terribly late."

"When was he supposed to be here?"

"Noon."

"Did you call him?"

She nodded.

"And?"

"He wasn't at the office or at home." Claire blurred as her eyes filled. "Miss Holly called this morning to confirm their changed date for her taxes. He wasn't at her house on the tenth." Patsy clenched her teeth. "I hate this—just hate it." She pulled out a hankie and dabbed her eyes. "Now I don't know whether to be mad at him or call the police or the hospital. If I didn't have these suspicions ..."

"Come on, let's go." Claire jumped up and pulled her along. "Nathan had better be in the hospital because if he isn't, I'll put him there for the grief he's inflicting on you."

Patsy scrambled to follow, bumping into the chair of a woman whose bottom was twice the size of it. She hoped her wallet was as large and she bid liberally. "Excuse me." She caught Claire at the end of the row. "Where are we going?"

"I don't know. I only know I couldn't sit there and—"

"Where are you two going?" Bev blocked their escape.

"I need to find Nathan," Patsy said.

"*No!* You *can't.* I mean, you can't leave yet."

Claire's eyes turned to slits. "And why not?"

Good thing she said it before Patsy had the chance. In her present frame of mind, she might have simply pushed Bev out of her way and asked questions later.

Bev looked back and forth between them. "We, we have to ... uh, we have a number of things left to auction." She flipped the pages on her clipboard.

Always cool and collected, Bev was in an absolute tizzy. Something akin to hot lava roiled in Patsy's stomach. Why had Bev lost her wits when Claire questioned her? For that matter, why did she freak when Patsy said she needed to find Nathan?

What. Did. Bev. Know?

"We'll be back. We're going to the restroom." Claire pushed past her.

When they were out of earshot, Patsy put her hand out to stop Claire. "We'd better visit the ladies' room. I don't want to add lying to our problems."

"Don't worry, we will. I just decided we should go to the one at the springs."

The springs? "Why?"

Claire pulled Patsy along. "Joel's there. They're finishing the last of the repairs and painting the gazebo. It's time we bring him into this."

Patsy gasped. "No! I don't want him to know."

"Have you thought of the possibility he already does know? He and Nathan are pals. They fish together."

"Men don't talk when they fish."

"Granted, but let's see if by chance, Joel knows where Nathan is."

They stopped by the springs' restroom then approached the gazebo. Patsy counted five masculine forms either hammering or painting. As they got closer, she identified Joel and Happy. The Applings' son, Trey, worked beside Joel and—she squinted against the sun—Bobby Eisler. She should have known. Wherever Trey went you'd find his sidekick, Bobby. Both nice boys. The fifth man had disappeared around a truck parked beside the gazebo.

From the gazebo's roof, Joel raised his hand in greeting. "Hey, girls. Here to give us a hand or just to admire our work?"

Claire sent him a saucy grin. "Neither. We're basking in the glory of great auction sales. Can you come down here a minute?"

"I'm close to done. Can't it wait?"

Patsy put her hand on Claire's arm. "Don't bother him. We can wait."

Claire ignored her. "Do you know where Nathan might be? He—"

"I'm right here." Nathan's voice came from behind him. *The fifth man.*

Patsy felt her blood pressure rise as she turned. "Why didn't you answer my phone calls?" His bewildered expression wasn't going to work on her. "I tried your office, I called home and your cell phone."

He wiped his hand on his pant leg, fished his cell phone out of his pocket, peered at it and then grimaced. "Dead. I'm sorry, honey, but you knew I was helping Joel."

"No, I didn't. You never told me that. As far as I knew, you went to work." She lowered her voice so only he could hear her. "And why aren't you there? You always work on Saturdays during tax season. Don't try to tell me you're through. I know better." He always had clients who needed extensions.

Nathan frowned. "I didn't tell you?"

"No."

"Well, what about Bev?"

Patsy's heart skipped a beat. "What about Bev?"

"I saw her a couple hours ago when I went to get me and the guys lunch. Didn't she tell you?"

Bev had seen him? She exchanged glances with Claire. Someone wasn't painting with a full palette. Why hadn't Bev wanted her to find Nathan?

He put his arm around her shoulders. "So what was Claire saying about your auction sales? Did your Loon Island sell?"

She looked up at him. His eyes weren't guarded. Either he'd become a very good actor, which she doubted, or he truly didn't realize he'd forgotten to tell her. His hair had more gray sprinkled through it than she remembered, but maybe it was the sunlight that made it seem that way. How long had it been since they'd been outdoors together during the day? It seemed like forever. She'd ask him about Miss Holly later. Right now, Patsy wanted to enjoy this moment.

She smiled up at him. "Well, never mind. You're fine and I can stop worrying." At least this time. "We'll leave you to your work. Will you be done in time for the Festival barbecue?"

"I think so. Hey, Joel, how much longer?"

"About an hour. All that's left is to shingle this last square of roof. The kids are finished painting."

Nathan's eyes met Patsy's and her heart warmed. That was how he used to gaze at her, his eyes filled with love. But if he loved her, why hadn't he made love to her in months? Maybe she misread him and he cared *about* her but didn't love her in a romantic way anymore. She felt the sting of tears at the back of her eyes.

"I need to go help get the barbecue ready. See you later." She quickly walked away, Claire on her heels.

"Patsy, wait." Claire huffed behind her. "What did Nathan say? I couldn't hear a word either one of you were saying."

Patsy shortened her stride. "It seems our friend Bev isn't so forthcoming. She saw Nathan at lunchtime. I want to know what she's up to."

Claire's eyebrows nearly met her widow's peak. "Are you going to ask her straight out?"

"No, but I'm fixin' to keep close to her during the barbecue. If she's saucin' her ribs, I want to know with whom."

Chapter 19

The auction was over. The barbecue was about to begin and with it, the official close to the festival weekend. The sun sat heavy on the horizon, sending its last rays like ballerinas to dance on the water's surface. Small paper lanterns, strung around each of the picnic arbors by the high school band members, swayed in the breeze, their lights twinkling red, orange, blue, and green.

Patsy shaded her eyes against the low-setting sun, peering beyond the grill where she painted sauce over baby-back ribs. Nathan had jogged home to shower and change, but he should've been back by now. Once again, tears stung her eyes. Smoke rose from the grill, the tantalizing aroma of roasted meat and onions wafting over the crowd that gathered around the picnic tables. Her emotions seesawed so often lately, she never knew when tears would betray her. At least if anyone noticed, she could blame the smoke.

"The Beethoven's Beans and coleslaw are on the table." Claire nudged Patsy out of her reverie. "What else are we serving?"

Boxes and coolers had been stacked in the beach picnic area. The tables wore bright red and white checked cloths held down by an abundance of food.

"Kelly and her team made tons of her special avocado potato salad, and there's Texas toast to go with the ribs."

"Oh, I love Kelly's potato salad. It has a Southwestern tang to it. Must be the cilantro and avocados. Where is it?"

"Beneath the table." Patsy pointed to the red and blue ice chests. "We'll wait to pull that out until the last minute."

"Can't I sneak a forkful?"

"No. We need to get everything on the tables. These ribs are about ready. Where's Jake? This is his job."

"Here I am." Curly, dishwater blond hair ruffled in the breeze. His colorful Hawaiian shirt with its red and yellow hibiscus design clashed with his plaid shorts. "Thanks for the break, Patsy." He didn't let go of Lacey's hand when he stepped up to the barbecue. "Sweetstuff, and I will finish these and get them plated."

That Jake adored Lacey was obvious to them all, but his nickname for her tickled Patsy. Lacey was as quiet as she was plain and often got overlooked because of it. But not by Jake. If she'd never met Lacey, Patsy would assume his wife was a knockout to hear him talk. She'd never seen him so much as look at another woman. It amazed her. But maybe it shouldn't. Her own Nathan wasn't movie star material. His close-set eyes were slightly too small and his nose a bit too large. But in her eyes—or maybe she saw through her heart—his personality outshined those small things. To her, he was Prince Charming and Mr. Darcy all rolled into one sweet Romeo.

Someone else thought so, too.

Everything blurred. How would she win Nathan back from whoever stole him? Especially if she didn't know the identity of her adversary.

Patsy turned away from Jake and Lacey and joined Claire at a picnic table. A lidded paper cup bearing *Dee's 'n' Doughs* logo occupied a spot next to her. "That for me?" she asked.

"Your favorite." Claire slid it toward her. "You looked like you needed something special."

Lifting the lid, Patsy inhaled the delicious smelling steam from the raspberry mocha, then took a sip. Sheer heaven and a definite morale booster. The caffeine didn't hurt either. She surveyed the cheerful crowd milling about the beach. "Why do things have to change? Chapel Springs is such a peaceful, happy place. Look at everyone. They feel good just being here."

Claire stared at her like she'd lost her marbles. Maybe she had.

"I remember when we were in first grade." Claire wrinkled her nose and waved her hand in a futile attempt to clear the smoke the wind kept blowing their way. "The teacher moved our desks around and you pitched a hissy fit until she moved them back."

"Wrong. *I* cried. *You* pitched the conniption fit because she made me cry." Patsy smiled at the memory of her self-appointed champion. "Wasn't that when they tried to separate us into different classrooms?"

She took a sip of raspberry mocha, holding the fruity chocolate in her mouth for a moment to savor its richness.

"I'll never forget that teacher, bless her heart. Poor woman shook in her boots seeing your mama barrelin' down on her. She folded like a Riverboat gambler spotting the sheriff."

"Speaking of spotting, I see my husband." Patsy's breath caught. "Claire, look." She pointed to where Nathan stood by the edge of the crowd. "Tell me I'm not seeing that." Bev had hold of Nathan's arm and stood way too close for Patsy's liking.

Claire's eyes bugged and her jaw dropped. "Why that little Benedict Arnold. If she keeps flashin' that syrupy smile, I'm gonna sic Waffle House on her. I know she tends to flirt, but that's plain wrong."

Patsy had seen enough. She jumped up, and Claire scrambled up behind her.

"What are you going to do?"

"I'm not sure, but I'm not about to stand by and let a so-called friend make a ninny out of me. Let's come up behind them. I want to get an earful before I confront them."

"Confront—you mean you think she's the one Nathan's?" Claire walked faster. "Why, that little lot lizard, I'll put something on her Ajax won't take off."

Patsy reached out her hand and caught Claire's arm. "Oh no you don't. This one's mine." If the situation weren't so dreadful, Patsy would have laughed. It wasn't often she managed to so completely surprise her best friend that she left Claire with her mouth hanging open. But then, she'd never had her husband stolen before. They made their way around the perimeter of the crowd until they closed in on Nathan and Bev.

Hanging on his arm, Bev flirted outrageously. Where was Drew? Patsy had seen her flirt before, but this was over the top. Poor Drew. She hated to be a part of this, not that she'd done anything. But maybe if she'd done something different, Nathan wouldn't have gone looking elsewhere. However, that didn't excuse Beverly McMillan for one minute from her culpability.

Patsy folded her arms and tapped her foot, strategizing the best approach. Murder flitted through her mind, but she dismissed it. Too messy. Too bad they outlawed confining convicted people in the stocks. In her mind's eye, she could see Bev with her head sticking through the hole and whining for mercy. Patsy and Claire would have a basket of rotten tomatoes—

"What is he thinking?" Claire whispered to her. "It looks like the little piranha's about to devour him."

Bev must have heard because she whirled around. Shock and horror froze her face into a gape-mouthed, guilt-ridden caricature of herself. Patsy almost laughed. Claire did, snickering through her nose. Nathan looked bewildered.

Bev gasped and rushed toward them. "Oh, dear, it's not how it looks, Patsy. Please, I'm so sorry. I was only trying to make Andrew jealous. Please believe me. Nathan had nothing to do with this."

Patsy stared at her then looked at Nathan. He shrugged his shoulders and lifted his hands, palms up, in a gesture of helplessness. He turned and joined a group of men gathered around the barbecue grills.

Patsy returned her attention to Bev. "I think you owe me more of an explanation. Let's take a walk. *Dee's 'n' Doughs* should be quiet." She put her hands on Bev's shoulders and turned her away from the crowd. Claire followed, for once silent.

Except for the teen behind the counter, the bakery was empty. Patsy pulled a chair out at their favorite table by the window. Bev sat opposite Patsy, twisting the tissue until it began to shred. She looked everywhere but at Patsy. The moment Claire opened her mouth to say something Bev began to cry. Melodramatically, Patsy thought.

"Andrew's trying to ruin my life."

Patsy exchanged glances with Claire. One corner of her upper lip rose slightly, signaling her distrust. She was right. Something rang false about Bev's display. Drew was the most married man Patsy knew. He paid more attention to Bev than the average husband.

"What are you talking about?" Patsy asked.

"He wants to leave." Bev dabbed a manicured fingertip at the corner of her eye.

"Leave? Bev, you're not making sense. Drew adores you. Why would he want to leave you?"

"Not leave *me*." She pulled a packet of tissues out of her pocket, unfolded one, and delicately blew her nose. "Leave the country."

"Didn't you say you wanted a vacation home in Mazatlan?" Claire asked. "Maybe he's going there to buy one for you."

"That's not where he wants to go." She drew a long shuddering sigh. "He wants to go to Africa."

None of this made any sense to Patsy, and from the look on Claire's face, not to her either. "Back up, Bev, and start at the beginning."

Patsy lifted the little tab on the miniature tub of cream and poured it in her coffee. Bev stirred hers, looking back and forth between Patsy and Claire. She sighed again, which grated on Patsy's last nerve. If Bev wanted to get her sympathy, sighing wasn't the way. Especially not after her blatant flirting with Nathan.

"Last week, Andrew came home from a missionary event at the church."

Uh-oh, this couldn't be good. The way Bev said "missionary," it sounded like a dirty word. What a shame she didn't share Drew's faith. Even little Andy tried to talk his mom into coming to church with them, but she always had an excuse. How could she say no to that sweet child?

"He said God was calling him to be a missionary," Bev raised her hands, palms up, "in Africa, of all places."

"I can see Drew doing that," Claire said. "He has such compassion for people."

Bev glared at her. "Doesn't the Bible say something about blooming where you're planted?"

Odd, how some people picked out only certain parts of the Bible to remember. "Sort of, yes," Patsy said. "It says for a man to remain in the situation he was in when God called him, but it's referring to when he first finds faith in God. It doesn't mean his situation won't ever change. What if God *is* calling him?"

"Well, he hasn't called *me*."

With her attitude, Patsy doubted Bev would hear him if he did. "Have you two prayed about it together?"

"That's another thing you people have wrong—praying together. The Bible says to pray in secret, in your closet, not together in the living room."

You people? For someone who rarely went to church, she sure threw around scripture. Although those could be the only two verses she knew. Too bad she didn't learn the context.

"Let me get this straight." Claire turned in her chair, squaring off with Bev. "Because Drew wants to be a missionary, you decided to flirt with Patsy's husband to make yours jealous. Is that about right?"

At least she had the grace to blush. "I'm sorry for that. I really am. If it's any consolation, it wouldn't have mattered who it was. Nathan just happened to be the closest man."

Consolation? Uh, no. It was downright insulting. Oh, she was so confused. First she and Claire thought he was having an affair with

Lydia, and that turned out to be untrue. Now Bev, and it turns out he's innocent again. Her heart stopped and with it, her last hope of her adversary being female shattered.

She stared past Bev and Claire to the scene out the window. The setting sun cast a glow over the crowd enjoying the barbecue across the street. While parents chatted over the remains of their dinners, children gathered around the fire pit and roasted marshmallows, sending the scent of caramel into the evening air. A few dads played catch with their children, and their laughter floated through the open windows. Nathan always rearranged the kids' baseball equipment, lining up the bats by size in their stand. The labels all faced forward, and the appropriate owner's glove sat atop their bat. He applied the same precision to their closet. His ties and even her scarves, were arranged by color. Scarves he picked out for her.

A mother called out a warning to her child. Did any of them know their lives could alter in a heartbeat? If one could capture this moment and keep it safe—she sighed. If only ...

A movement caught her eye, drawing her away from her wishing. On the fringe of the festivities, Nathan stood, head bent close and talking with a man Patsy didn't recognize.

Chapter 20

"Is that everything?" Claire lowered the back of her Chevy Trailblazer, chipping a nail she'd so carefully been growing out.

"Sure is." Patsy opened the passenger door and climbed in. "Let's get this show on the road. I'm looking forward to lunch at the Varsity. What time's the appointment with the geologist?"

Excitement accelerated Claire's heartbeat as she started the engine. "Two o'clock. I planned time for us to eat and check into the hotel." It had been at least four years since they'd taken a girl's road trip, and she looked forward to the time away from all obligations, including husbands. And chores and kids. Especially kids. She had foolishly thought when the nest emptied her obligation to do for them ended, too.

"How's Charlie's wedding coming along?"

"You've always had the uncanny ability to read my mind." Claire moved into traffic on the highway. "He's going to have his hands full with Sandi's mother, Zoe. That woman's driving me nuts."

Patsy pulled on her seatbelt and turned, leaning against the door, facing her. "What's she doing?"

"Calling almost every day, trying to foist her duties on me. She's the mother of the bride. I'm only supposed to host the groom's dinner not plan the bridesmaids' lunch, too. Why can't she call Sandi's friends herself? Have one of them do it?"

"I have no idea. Isn't she?"

Claire pulled into a gas station and parked beside an unoccupied pump. "No. She wants me to do it, and then let her know the date and time for her ladyship to show up."

She hopped out, leaving the door open, and swiped her credit card in the fuel pump. After putting in her zip code—why they needed that she never could understand—she inserted the nozzle into the Trailblazer's tank. The odor of gasoline rose from the hose. That wasn't all that rose. She eyed the numbers whirling around on the gas pump, dinging away her dollars. The rising price of gas didn't help to make her feel more charitable toward Zoe. Sandi's parents had more money than her and Joel, so why were they so stingy? Joel would pitch a fit if she had to pay for the bridesmaids' lunch. Besides, Megan and Melissa weren't even asked to be bridesmaids, only Adrianna. Of course, with the twins in college in Charleston, it was more difficult to arrange for fittings and all that went along with being bridesmaids. But Zoe had a lot of nerve to expect Claire to arrange and host the luncheon.

The hose shut off with a jerk. She hung the gas nozzle back in its cradle and mashed the button for a receipt. It whirred and wheezed but didn't spit out the promised slip of paper. She hoped this wasn't an omen for the rest of their trip.

Patsy leaned over into the driver's side and peered up at her. "What were you muttering about out there?"

"Zoe." Claire got back in the car and fastened her seatbelt. "What scorches my slurry is how I'm dragged into this when I'm working myself into an early grave with the town and—"

Patsy reached over and backhanded Claire's shoulder. "Would you listen to yourself? This isn't about you or Zoe. Charlie is getting married and you love Sandi. What's got you in such a snit?"

Claire glared at her. "Who appointed you my conscience?"

"You when you became my best friend."

"Yeah, well don't let it go to your head."

"So are you going to tell me or not?"

"It's all this junk with Joel. He's so—" A man, who looked way too much like Nathan crossed the street in the middle of the block. She jerked the steering wheel to the right and pulled to the side of the road and stopped. "Patsy, over there! Isn't that Nathan?"

Patsy peered through the windshield and paled. "It *is* Nathan. What's he doing here?"

"Could he be seeing a client?"

"He doesn't have any in Ellijay. I do his billing. I'd know."

Claire glanced over her shoulder, then whipped a u-turn and pulled into a parking spot. "Come on."

Patsy scrambled out after her. "What are you doing?"

"We're going to catch him with, with *whoever* it is." Claire grabbed Patsy's arm and pulled her across the street behind her. A horn blared as a car avoided them.

"I don't know about this, Claire. I'm not sure I really want to know who it is."

Not know? How could she not want to know? If it were her she'd want to know. Need to know. In fact, she did. Claire's blood pressure rose to dangerous levels. She faced her best friend.

"Yes, you do. You can't keep living the way you are. You're losing weight, you're depressed, and frankly not much fun anymore." She put up her hand to stop Patsy's protest. "Oh, I don't blame you. I blame Nathan entirely."

Grabbing Patsy's wrist, she pulled her through the building's front door into the empty marble lobby just as a pair elevator doors shut. Must have been Nathan. "Come on. We're gonna catch us a pair of testosterone challenged skunks." Her voice echoed off the walls.

A large directory on the wall next to the elevator listed the building's occupants. Claire studied it. If she were Nathan where would she have gone? To the window to jump out if he had a shred of conscience left. She glanced at the numbers blinking as they indicated to what floor the elevator had risen.

"Look. It stopped on the eighth floor." Claire glanced back at the listed names on that floor. They had several to choose from. "We can't really dismiss any of them. Let's start at the upper end of the hall with suite 875 and work our way back down." She punched the elevator up button. The light didn't come on and she mashed it again for good measure.

"I feel like I'm going to throw up."

"Oh, no you don't, Patsy. You're going through with this." She did look a little pale, though. "We'll ask the good doctor for something for nausea. A good punch in the nose should make you feel better."

Patsy gasped. "Why do I deserve to be punched? What'd I do?"

Claire rolled her eyes. "I didn't mean punch you. I meant when *you* punch Nathan's lover and then him."

Patsy covered her face with her hands. "I can't do this."

"You *can* and you are." She tightened her grip on Patsy's arm, pulling it away from her face as the elevator bounced to a stop. Claire's stomach lurched and she put her hand on the railing to steady herself. "Let's go."

She looked first to her left then right. The long empty hallway was broken every twenty feet with a closed door, each bearing a single brass number. The carpet's peach and pale blue pattern was right out of the eighties and hard to clean as a dark stain by the wall bore silent witness.

"The coast is clear. Come on."

Stepping out of the lift, the sign on the opposite wall pointed to the left for suites 875 through 862. Claire turned to her left and tiptoed down the hallway, with Patsy slightly behind her.

"Why are we tiptoeing?" Patsy asked.

"Shh. So we don't make any noise."

"Look down. That's carpet you're walking on. It doesn't make noise."

Claire glanced down. Right. Carpet. It had a cigarette burn left over from the days when people could smoke inside. One day, Claire would get her back for always being right.

"Okay, okay. Let's keep moving." She picked up her pace and soon stood before the door to suite 875. What she'd say when they got inside, she wasn't sure, but she'd think of something. She turned the knob and pushed the door open.

On more of the same peach and blue carpet, individual wooden chairs lined the walls. Three women of varying ages glanced up at her, but no Nathan. Maybe the doc hustled him inside to his office.

Claire approached the receptionist while Patsy hung back. Claire's eyes rolled again before she could stop herself. It was becoming a habit. That girl needed a good dose of gumption.

"Good morning. May I help you?" The receptionist, whose hair needed a good combing, didn't look up as she uttered rote words with false cheer. Good. She probably wouldn't even remember them.

"We're looking for my friend's husband. He said he was here already. Mr. Kowalski?"

The girl ran a long, blue fingernail down the appointment chart. If she snapped that gum any harder, the doctor may have to realign her jaw.

"Nope, no Mr. Kowalski." *Snap.* "Ya sure he was comin' here?"

"No, we're not sure. He has a couple of doctors, but we know he's on the eighth floor." She hoped God would see the necessity of that little misinformation. Besides, it wasn't a lie. Nathan and Patsy had more than one doctor, if dentists counted.

The girl snickered around her wad of green gum. "Well, I doubt he's visitin' the gynecologist. Try suite 872. That's the internist."

Claire nodded her thanks and pulled Patsy out the door. They tried the same routine on the internist's office and got the same response from yet another gum-snapper. Must be epidemic. Except this one had her tongue pierced. Claire rolled hers in her mouth. How did the girl keep the gum from getting tangled?

Back in the halls, Patsy pointed to another office directory. "Let's try this one."

"Okay." She read the name Patsy had her finger next to. Dr. Dubious - suite 841. Claire grinned at Patsy. "Dubious? That's as funny as when Joel's cousin on his mother's side Earl Cronic went into medicine."

They followed the signs to the lower numbered suites. As they turned down a long hallway, Nathan stepped out of a door into the hall. Claire stopped. Patsy ran into her back. "What's—"

"Shh. It's Nathan." She peeked around the corner. With his shirttail hanging out, he opened another door across the hall and disappeared inside. "It looks like your instinct was on target." She clutched Patsy's arm and pulled her forward. "He went into that door." She pointed to where Nathan went. "Looks like he used a private entrance. It's not marked."

They stood in front of the door. Patsy looked up and down the hallway. "What should we do, wait for him to come out?"

"No way. You don't know how many doors this office has. We're goin' in."

Patsy turned toward the office's main entrance, but Claire stopped her. "Uh-uh. We're going in the way he did." She pushed the door open and pulled Patsy in behind her.

Patsy's pulse pounded like a Led Zeppelin concert. The short corridor they entered was thankfully empty. Half of her wanted to flee. Wrong. All of her wanted to run, but Claire's grip on her wrist prevented it. Claire stuck her head into the hall facing them. With one hand behind her, she motioned for Patsy to follow.

Taking a deep breath, Patsy trailed her. Voices carried through the various doors. A faint ether-like odor, reminiscent of hospitals, made her slightly dizzy. Or was it her galloping heart? Suddenly Claire stopped. Patsy held her breath and listened. At the sound of Nathan's voice, her fear vanished, and anger rose in its place. She grasped the knob and pushed the door open, leaving Claire gaping behind her.

The room was in half-light, the window shades lowered. The doctor, taller than her husband, stood with his hands cupping Nathan's face. Her adversary's, looking like it had been chiseled out of granite, was slightly pockmarked and topped by dark wavy hair. Both turned and open-mouthed, stared at her.

Patsy's heart stopped then sank. Her fears were true. She couldn't find her voice but stared at the scene in front of her. The doctor dropped his hands. "What's going on here?"

At his challenge, she recovered. "My question, exactly." She turned to her husband. "What *is* going on, Nathan? Would you care to introduce me? Or will that ruin this little tête-à-tête?"

Nathan's mouth worked, but nothing came out.

"Are you Mrs. Kowalski?" the doctor asked, his frown disappearing. With a smile, he held out his hand. "I'm pleased to meet you. I've wondered when Nathan would let you in on his secret."

Now she was the one who gaped, unable to shake the hand offered. She'd heard of open marriages but not like this. This was way too open for her. Tears threatened, but she refused to let them see her cry. Turning, she grabbed Claire and headed to the door.

Nathan's hand on her arm stopped her. Patsy tried to shake free, but his grip was tight. "Sweetheart, I know I should have told you. I wanted to, but I was ashamed that I couldn't control myself."

She shook her head, unable to fully grasp what she'd suspected, but didn't want to admit. But now she had to know. She turned around but kept her eyes on his shoes. They needed polishing. "Why? Was it something I did?"

"No, I did it to myself. And now I have to pay the consequences. What kills me is that you have to bear it, too."

She couldn't stop them. Her tears spilled. Was he going to leave her for this man, then? A tissue appeared in front of her.

"It's not the end, Mrs. Kowalski. I've been telling Nathan there are things we can do to help him. This doesn't have to be the end of your marital relations."

Help him? *Marital relations?* Did this man think she would share her husband with him? She turned and looked at him. "Are you crazy?" She snatched the tissue he held out and dabbed her tears, which were quickly evaporating from the heat of her anger.

"There are drugs that will help him, if he takes them regularly and watches his diet."

This conversation was getting weirder by the minute. She turned to

Nathan. "What is he talking about? In plain English."

"I can control my condition with drugs. The side effect even has some chance of being reversed."

"I'm missing something here. What *condition*? I didn't know you could call infidelity a condition."

Nathan's mouth dropped open. "Infidelity?" It came out a strangled whisper. "Patsy, I've never cheated on you. I love you."

The doctor's eyes bounced to Nathan and back to Patsy. He looked as confused as she felt. "Mrs. Kowalski, Nathan has diabetes. We've been getting it under control by his diet, but the erectile dysfunction, often a side affect among others of this disease, still plagues him. I've been urging him to bring you with him to his appointments so we could talk about treatments."

"Erecti—then you're *not* having affair with the doctor?" Claire clapped her hand over her mouth, and her eyes shot to the half open door.

Patsy cringed and the doctor turned a deep shade of fuchsia at Claire's loud voice. It must have carried clear down the hall because a frowning nurse appeared on the threshold and pulled the door shut.

Nathan gasped. "You didn't think I was ... with ...?"

Patsy bit her lip as she thought about the escapades she and Claire had been through, trying to catch him. A giggle bubbled up. Another followed on its heels as she fully saw the absurdity of the whole thing. She covered her mouth but couldn't stop the laughter from escaping. She quickly doubled over, her arms holding her sides.

"Are you all right, Mrs. Kowalski?" He looked at Nathan. "Does she normally respond to news like this?"

"Honey?" Nathan put his arm around her and she leaned into him.

It felt so good to know he loved her. She looked up at him. His face was etched with dismay. Forgetting the doctor and Claire, Patsy grasped his face and pulled him close and kissed him. "I'm so sorry, Nathan. But you have to admit you never said anything. What was I to think?"

"You could have asked me."

Pulling back, she looked up at him. "When? You're never home. And anyway, think about it. It's a pretty hard question to ask."

"But ... but *why* with another man?"

She giggled again. "After we ruled out Lydia and Bev, I knew that you didn't really know any other women."

One side of his mouth turned up in a grimace. "I never needed to know any."

"Oh, Nathan, I love you, but I wish you'd saved us all a lot of grief by talking to me."

He slumped against the exam table. "I was ashamed. I'd eaten myself into this condition. Then when the side effects began to bother me, well I didn't want to admit it. I was afraid if you found out you'd leave me for someone who could still make love to you."

Uncertainty registered in his eyes, and her heart swelled with love for him. She put her hands on his shoulders. "Do you remember our wedding vows? For better or worse? In sickness and in health? I love you, Nathan. If we can never make love again, that doesn't change how I feel about *you*. There's more to our love than just that."

Nathan's eyes shone with moisture, and his Adam's apple bobbed. "I love you so much."

"Do you promise to never keep any secrets from me again?"

"I promise, sweetheart. I'm so sorry for what I've put you through."

"Will you tell me what happened the night you were supposed to be at Miss Holly's?"

He lowered his head and sighed. "I was working late, getting ready to go to her house. I'd forgotten to eat, and my blood sugar dropped really low and I passed out."

"Nathan! That's really dangerous isn't it?"

He wrapped her hands in his. "It's not good, but the cleaning lady found me, called 911, and the EMTs gave me an injection of glucagon, hooked me up to an IV and carted my carcass to the ER."

Tears fill her eyes, and she hugged him. "What we could have avoided if you'd told me."

"No kidding. I had a heck of a time getting them to allow me to drive myself home."

Patsy leaned back to look into his eyes. "But you didn't come home. I know. I waited up for you." She almost wished she hadn't told him. He looked so defeated.

"I went back to the office. I wasn't thinking straight." He tightened his arms around her. The faint scent of his Old Spice aftershave comforted her. "I'm so glad this is finally out in the open."

"And I'm sorry for not asking. I was afraid everything was about to change, and I hid from it. I won't do that anymore. It isn't worth it." She raised her face, and he kissed her. The safety of his familiar embrace never felt so good.

Suddenly, she remembered Claire and the doctor. She stiffened. Nathan's chuckle rumbled in her ear. "They slipped out a few minutes ago."

After Claire's less-than-tactful broadcast, Patsy wished they could, too.

Chapter 21

"You sure you still want to come with me?" Claire buckled her seatbelt and turned on the engine. She would understand if Patsy wanted to stay with Nathan after what they'd discovered in the doctor's office. Heat flooded her neck and cheeks as she thought about how she'd stuck her foot in her mouth once again and blurted out her thoughts.

"Absolutely. I'm not letting you go alone. No telling what might happen. Besides, Nathan went back to work, and later he's going fishing with Joel, so I wouldn't have seen him anyway."

They drove in silence for a few minutes. Claire slipped an oldies CD into the player and turned up the volume. She glanced at Patsy a couple of times, but her friend wore a sappy grin and tapped her fingers on her knee in time with the music.

Claire's thoughts turned to Charlie and Sandi. While she adored her son's fiancé, Sandi's mother was a different piece of artwork altogether. Maybe Sandi took after her dad. She hoped so for Charlie's sake. When Zoe called her about the shower, Claire couldn't get a word in edgewise. The woman refused to be interrupted.

"You keep muttering. Has Zoe got you bowed up again?" Patsy asked.

"She's stubborn as sand gnats, and she talks faster than Jeff Gordon drives. Before I could explain that it's bad etiquette for the groom's mother to host a shower, she'd said good-bye and hung up on me."

"Maybe she doesn't know."

Claire gripped the steering wheel tighter. "Well, she should educate herself. Iowa has libraries. Libraries have books. They can't all be about farming."

"She's probably stressed. How would you feel if Adrianna decided to marry someone from Nashville and have her wedding there?"

Not fair. Patsy always took the high road, leaving Claire feeling guilty. "Okay, okay. I'll call Sandi and find out who her friends are."

"You'll do nothing of the kind. I'll host the shower. As your best friend and Charlie's godmother, it's perfectly in keeping for me to do it."

Claire's grip relaxed. "Do you think I'll ever learn to be as nice as you?"

"It takes time for God to knock off the rough edges. You're a potter. You should understand that."

"When Charlie bought me my first Bible, some of the verses hit too close to home. I thought he had it written *for* me, a special one just for his momma. So I went back to the bookstore and asked for another version." She chuckled. "I went through four different Bibles before I realized that although the sentence structure changed some, God said the same thing in each one."

"You never told me that."

Claire pulled her mouth to the side. "Who wants to advertise their stupidity?"

"Naive maybe, but not stupid."

"Thanks, Pat-a-cake."

"Uneducated but not unintelligent."

"Okay, I get it."

"Tactless but not mean."

"I'm not tactless. I simply speak the truth."

"At inopportune times—like in doctors' offices."

Claire's face grew warm. "I'm sorry about that. I guess it was tactless."

Patsy aimed her air conditioner vent toward Claire's face. "Your expression almost made me laugh. You were more bothered about being wrong." She giggled. "Poor Nathan. He said with you as a friend, he shouldn't have been surprised we found him out."

Claire wasn't sure how to take that. Had she ruined the relationship they all shared? Would Nathan tell Joel what she did? They'd been friends for almost as long as she and Patsy. Had her clumsy efforts to help her best friend destroyed that camaraderie?

And what if ... "Patsy, if God has another husband picked out for me, will Nathan be his friend, too?"

"Why are you still worrying about that?"

"I just wondered. Hey, look. We're almost to Atlanta." The pines, cosmos, and coneflowers bordering the Interstate gave way to malls and office buildings with dogwoods and crepe myrtles strategically planted in the parking lots.

A black convertible cut in front of Claire, zipping from the inner left lane to the outer right. "Boy, I'd forgotten how crazy Atlanta traffic is." She focused on the exit signs until she found the one for Georgia Tech. Beulah, Claire's nickname for her navigation system, barked out the directions, and a few minutes later they entered the Varsity for the best chili dogs and fries in Atlanta.

After their thoroughly satisfying lunch and two antacid tablets, they walked into the Civil Engineering Building promptly at two o'clock. Claire sat on the edge of her vinyl seat, her eyes glued to the doorway the administrative manager said Professor Sokolov would come through. She pinched the clutch purse in her lap.

"If you keep opening and closing that, the clasp is going to break."

Tucking the bag between her hip and the chair's arm, she leaned back. "Do you think he'll look like a professor?"

"What do professors look like?"

"Don't be snarky. They look ... professorly. You know—brilliant, handsome, maybe a beard ..."

Patsy frowned. "You sound like a teenager waiting for a blind date to pick her up."

"Don't be silly. I'm simply hypothesizing."

The door opened across the room and through it walked a man who appeared to be in his late forties. His mustache and goatee—okay it wasn't technically a beard, but it qualified in her mind—was sprinkled with gray, neatly trimmed and framed a striking face—maybe not movie star quality but definitely handsome. And tall. He stopped in front of them. She rose and had to lift her chin to look into his face. As she shook his hand, eyes dark and deep as a volcanic pool peered back at her. She could get lost in their depth.

"Ladies, I'm Professor Leonard Sokolov. My assistant said you have a geological problem in Chapel Springs."

Patsy elbowed her, and Claire realized the professor was trying to extract his hand from hers. Embarrassment warmed her cheeks as she pulled her hand away.

"Thank you for seeing us, Professor. I'm Patsy Kowalski and this," she gave Claire a strange look, "is Claire Bennett."

Claire was glad Patsy made the introductions. She wasn't sure she could speak coherently right then.

With the flair of a nobleman, he put his hand on his chest. "Please call me Leo. Let me take you on a tour of the laboratories while you tell me what the trouble is."

He led them through a maze of rooms. The students took no notice of them as they bent over test tubes and equipment that looked like it could rival a NASA lab. One young man handled a dark brown rock unlike anything Claire had seen before. Was it a moon rock? Did university students get to play with those? And what were those other bags of dirt? She moved closer to see if they were labeled. They were, but the words were technical and looked like Latin.

She smiled at one lab-coated student when the girl glanced up at her. With a tilt of her strawberry-blonde head, she invited Claire to see her work. She stepped closer. In front of the girl sat one of those bags, its mouth open and dirt spilling out. To one side she had an arrangement of Petri dishes, filled with some sort of chemicals into which she plopped bits of dirt. It turned into unexciting mud. Flipping her long hair over her shoulder with one hand, she made a note on a chart with the other.

Not wanting to bother the young woman with her questions, Claire turned to ask the Prof—uh, Leo—and found herself alone. Where had he and Patsy gone?

The room had two doors at the far end. Neither gave any indication they'd just been opened. Choosing the left one, she hurried through it and found herself in another laboratory. She didn't see any students here. This lab didn't look at all like the last one—didn't smell like it either but vaguely reminded her of the zoo's nursery, where she once helped her zoologist cousin feed baby animals the mothers rejected.

Muted voices floated over a partition, the words muffling into gibberish. Claire ventured down an aisle lined with cages on both sides. Many sat empty, but at one end of the room, a small monkey chattered and bounced against the sides of its enclosure. What did monkeys have to do with geology? Curiosity won out, and she approached the cage.

"Hey there, cutie."

The animal leaped at its door, screaming at her. Claire jumped away, banging the back of her head on another cage. A screech rang out and fingers dug into her scalp, grasping a handful of her hair.

"Ow!" She pulled, but her captor had a vice-like grip on her, and banged the back of her head against the bars again. She couldn't see the ape that held her, but when she grabbed at its hairy hands, it bit her.

"Help!"

A ponytailed young man in a lab coat appeared from around a corner, running toward her as another door opened and Patsy and Leo raced to her side. Each time the student tried to pry the chimp's fingers loose, it yanked harder on her hair.

"Yeowch! Be careful! It's pulling my hair out!"

Patsy danced in Claire's peripheral vision. "Do something! Hurry!" Her hands flapped up and down. Like *that* would help. The creature pulled harder.

Leo tried to grab the ape's other arm, but it punched him in the face. "Oh!" He bent over, his hand held to his eye.

The bars on the cage pressed into her head. Tears flowed down her face, taking her makeup with them, but at that moment she couldn't care less.

"Be careful, don't break its arm," the student shouted above the din.

"Its arm? What about my head?" She clenched her teeth. "Get me loose!"

After wrestling unsuccessfully with the animal, the kid pulled a banana from his pocket and thrust it toward the varmint. The primate grabbed it in one hand—or was it a paw? Then with the other, it pulled with all its might, screeching in her ear.

Inside her skull, Claire heard each hair rip from its follicle. She jumped away from the cage and clutched her head. Patsy ran to her. She turned Claire around and gasped.

"What?" Touching her offended scalp, Claire felt dampness. "Am I bleeding? What did that thing do to me?" She scowled at the young man. Why couldn't he have shot it with a tranquillizer dart? Isn't that what Jack Hannah would've done?

Leo stepped up to examine her head. "It's just a slight amount of blood from a few follicles. It looks similar to a road rash. You'll be fine, and it should grow back. I must say, I'm sorry. Snowball has never acted like that before."

Snowball? If her head didn't hurt so much, she'd have laughed. What a misnom—*grow back?* Her hand flew to her head. "I'm bald!"

Patsy patted her shoulder. "It's not a big area, Claire."

She glared at her *best friend.* "It's not your head." She touched it again. "It's three fingers wide." She couldn't help it. She wailed. "It's huge. How can I cover that up?"

It would take more than Patsy's silent plea for forgiveness to get her back in Claire's good graces. She gingerly touched the spot again.

Leo reached over and took her hand. "Come on. Let's put some antibiotic ointment on that."

"Why? Do you think I'll catch something from that thing?" Did chimpanzees carry rabies or some other fatal disease?

"No, not at all, but with any wound, there's always the chance of infection."

"Oh."

"I'm terrible sorry about this Claire. I should have made certain you were with us."

Her anger melted. Wait. What? He wasn't *blaming* her? Well, that felt different. Nice. Very nice, being cared for. Protected. Not accused right off the bat. She met the professor's eyes. "It's my own fault for dawdling."

"What were you doing in here?" Patsy asked.

"Trying to find you. All I did was walk past that one." She pointed across the aisle. "It leaped at me then this one grabbed me."

Beneath his mustache, Leo's lip twitched, and Patsy covered her snickers with her hand. Sure, they could laugh. It wasn't their heads that had been snatched bald. Claire gathered the remains of her tattered dignity and straightened her spine. "Why do you have them here, anyway?"

"Earthquake research. Come on, let's go to my office. I have a first aid kit there."

"They work," Patsy said.

Leo looked confused. "What do you mean?"

"They sure alerted us to Earthquake Claire."

He turned and led them out of the lab. Patsy grinned at her as they followed. There were times she could make Claire as mad as the hatter in Wonderland. The professor must think she was a real ditz. Not the best way to start off a relationship.

The professor's office, which was painted gray, housed a generic metal desk with its sagging leather chair, overstuffed bookshelves, a four-drawer dented file cabinet, and a window in need of a good washing. She thought professors deserved a nicer office.

He opened a closet door and pulled out two folding chairs, setting them in front of the desk. After she and Patsy sat, he tenderly applied a soothing ointment to her stinging naked scalp. When he was finished, he took his seat behind the desk, and Claire explained the problem with the springs.

"Do you think you can find the reason the water's cooled?"

He didn't answer right away. Instead, he filled his pipe with tobacco, then stuck it in his mouth and sucked on the end.

What a strange way to smoke a pipe. "Don't you light that?"

He blinked and pulled it from his mouth, staring at it as if he'd never seen it before.

"Oh, that. I quit, but the habit of smoking while I'm thinking is ingrained, I'm afraid." He set it on his desk. "I won't say it's impossible for a warm springs to cool from natural causes, but it's highly unlikely. The source comes from deep within the earth's crust. It wouldn't be a significant drop. I'm not sure if I can do anything for you."

Claire exchanged glances with Patsy. They had to convince him. Something made the springs cool. "My brother-in-law documented his research on the temperatures."

"Oh?"

Funny how much skepticism a single word could hold, but Claire was confident she could overcome that. "Vince is a medical doctor and uses the springs for physical therapy. Both for himself and for his patients."

"I see. Well then, I suppose I could investigate it." He picked up the pipe again and tapped it against his chin. "It might make a good semester project for my graduate students."

And that would be good for Chapel Springs. She wouldn't mind seeing more of the professor, too. "How many students would you bring? And for how long?"

"I have eight registered for the summer semester. I'll need to introduce the course first, and we'll come to Chapel Springs on ..." He flipped a page in his desk calendar. "Let's say we arrive on the twentieth, and hopefully find an answer by the end of summer."

"That long?" The prospect of him being around all summer delighted her.

"We might find the source sooner, if it truly exists."

Oh, she hoped not. No, that wasn't right. She should be hoping they *would*. The town needed to deliver what their advertising promised or else they'd face a devastating loss of tourists—and their livelihoods. But a few weeks wouldn't hurt. Leo talked on about geological something-or-others. He had a small line beside his mouth just above his goatee where it met his mustache. She couldn't call it a dimple, but it played a charming game of hide-and-seek when he talked.

Suddenly he and Patsy were staring at her. "What? Oh, sorry. Wool gathering."

"Leo asked you what accommodations we have for him and his students," Patsy said.

"Oh. There're some cottages that would be perfect. That way, if they wanted to, they could cook some of their own meals. The town will take care of you, of course. Your time, I mean. And meals. And lodging." Why was she babbling? Her thoughts jumbled together, making her sound like an idiot. "Sorry." Even her laugh sounded nervous. "What I mean is the town will compensate *you* for your time and we'll cover your meals and lodging." Yes, that was better. "We can probably discount the lodging for your students." If he found the reason for the springs cooling, the town would be glad to pay.

Leo stood. "Then we'll see you on the twentieth. And once again, please accept my apologies for that little incident."

She felt vaguely disappointed the meeting ended, but the anticipation of seeing him again brightened her mood. She'd have to find a way to cover her bare scalp so he wouldn't feel so bad. When she shook his hand, she noted the smoothness of his palm. He must not be very hands-on with his research. But then, what did she know about it?

Patsy frowned at her but didn't speak as they left the building. Whatever her problem was, Claire was sure she'd hear about it soon. She didn't have long to wait. The minute her door closed, Patsy launched into her.

"You're playing with fire, girl. We already discovered how wrong we were about Nathan."

"Whatever do you mean?"

"You know exactly what I'm talking about. Your idea that God wants you married to someone other than Joel. Well, it's just stupid."

"What about all the stuff Sandi said?"

Patsy slipped on her dark glasses. "I don't know. I can't pretend to understand it all." She put her hand on Claire's arm. "Just be careful, please? I don't want you or Joel hurt."

Claire turned the key in the ignition and cranked the engine. "I'll be careful. And I'd never hurt Joel." Not if she could help it.

Chapter 22

"Claire, have you seen my swivel retractors?" Joel's voice resounded from the bottom of the basement stairwell.

"Hello to you, too." She closed the front door and set her overnight bag by the hall tree.

"How could I see them? I've been gone for two days."

"You were down here, cleaning after the twins went back to school Sunday night."

Just once, she'd like to come home without him blaming her for losing something he couldn't find. She took a deep breath and released it slowly, then descended the stairs. "Sweetheart, I know better than to disturb your things. I cleaned the rec room, not your work bench."

Joel stood with his hands on his hips, his cowlick sticking straight up. "Well, somebody moved them, along with my line clippers. Were the kids over here, playing around?"

One of the animal characters in a Richard Scarry book she read to the kids when they were little was Accusing Alligator, who could never admit its mistakes. They sounded alike.

"They're adults now, Joel. Charlie and Wes don't *play* with your tools, nor do they make fishing flies. And the girls certainly aren't interested. You've misplaced them. Come on, I'll help you look." She'd much rather soak in a hot tub after battling Atlanta traffic, but for the sake of peace, she started looking by the pool table.

"I didn't misplace them." Joel stood at his workbench with his arms folded across his chest. "I laid them down here," he stabbed his finger on the wooden surface, "where I always do."

"Oh? Then why are the retractors by the phone?"

He scowled. "Are you sure?"

She held up the tool and smiled, if you could call it that. It felt closer to a sneer. "I'm sure."

Joel frowned and held out his hand. "How'd they get there?"

"I wonder. Could it have been when you answered the phone, maybe?" Why couldn't he admit he did it? "Your line clippers are probably nearby. Look under the sofa. If you had them with the retractors, they might have fallen on the floor."

He knelt down and fished around under the couch. A moment later, he rose with the tool in his hand. "I still don't remember having them over here."

She resisted the urge to rub it in. "You were probably preoccupied. I'm going to unpack."

He stuck the tools in his pocket and followed her upstairs. "So how'd the trip go? Did you find the geologist?"

Did she ever. "He'll be here in two weeks." She didn't want to talk about the professor. "You should see the laboratory there. It even has monkeys to see if they can predict earthquakes." He'd followed her up the stairs, into the bedroom, and hadn't noticed the bald spot in the back of her head. The man's power of observation or lack thereof underwhelmed her.

Joel leaned one shoulder against the wall. "I remember my dad telling stories about the monkeys they used in the early rocket testing. He said they were kind of cute in a funny way."

"These weren't cute at all." She told him how the monkey grabbed her hair and ripped it out.

His jaw dropped. Then he clamped it shut and twirled his finger in a circle, gesturing for her to turn around. When she complied, his fingers probed the edges of the bald spot, sending stings radiating across her scalp.

"Ow. Be careful, it's still tender."

"I would think so." He chuckled. "Only you, Claire, only you. You absolutely defy logic."

It wasn't funny, but she refused to engage in an argument. She pressed her fingertips against the cold metal latches of the old suitcase and flipped them open, pinching her thumb. A small red indentation appeared. As she rubbed it away, she glanced up at Joel. "Have you talked to Nathan?"

"Huh?"

"Have you talked to Nathan since Sunday?" Examining a pair of slacks, she noticed a spot of catsup, from her Varsity lunch, no doubt. She dropped them to the floor to go into the laundry and yanked out a white shirt.

"We had lunch yesterday. Why?"

"Did he tell you about his—" How should she put it? She trudged into the closet for a hanger. "His little problem?"

"You mean the diabetes? I've known about that for a long time."

"And you didn't tell me?" She sat on the side of the bed and pressed the hanger to her lap. She twisted a loose thread poking out from the shirt's top button. "How could you not tell me?"

He shrugged. "It wasn't my problem. Why should I tell you?"

Men. "Because Patsy's my best friend, and she thought he was having an affair."

"Nathan?" Joel laughed. "That's like accusing Mr. Rogers or Andy Griffith."

"Maybe so, but that didn't stop Patsy from hurting."

Joel narrowed his eyes and scrutinized her. "What did you do, Claire?"

"What did *I* do? Why makes you think I did anything?" She slipped the hanger into the shirt, fastening the collar button.

"Because I know you, especially where your friends are concerned. You can't stand not to help. Unfortunately, you don't stop to think before you …" He waved his hand like he was trying to pick a word from the air. "… help."

"I don't know what you mean." Claire walked inside the closet. The problem was she *did* know. She bungled everything, even when she wasn't trying to help. Like in the professor's lab. She jammed the shirt onto the rack. Remembering her embarrassment, her throat thickened with unshed tears. Joel's arms closed around her. He kissed the side of her neck then turned her around.

"I'm sorry. Don't cry. I know your heart's big and you love the same way." His soft kiss sent butterflies across her skin. "You just need to learn to stop and think things out before you charge into these situations. But I have to say," he gave her a playful swat on the backside, "life's never dull with you, Clairey-girl."

His cheeky grin stayed with her after he went back downstairs to his fly-tying. He was such a turkey sometimes.

Beside the clawfoot tub, she knelt on the cold tile, the grooves digging into her knees, and turned on the faucet. A whoosh of water gushed out, and as the steam began to rise, she reran the conversation. Maybe she was at fault, but did he have to talk to her that way? Aunt Lola's third husband—or was it the fourth?—"turkey-talked" her only once, and she was out the door, leaving him flabbergasted.

Had his kisses made her aunt dizzy like Joel's did her?

Maybe that wasn't enough.

The next morning, after spending forty-five minutes arranging and rearranging her hair to hide the bald spot—and its accompanying red, pinprick scabs—as best she could, Claire walked into Dee's 'n' Doughs. Under an aromatic cloud of yeast and sugar, the place was packed and noisy with dozens of conversations.

Suddenly, all voices stopped. Lips twitched and all eyes riveted on her.

Why were so many people here? Every other morning, she and her friends were the only ones who came this early. Patsy sat with Lydia and Dee. Bev either hadn't arrived yet or was too embarrassed to face them after her flirting incident.

Claire let her gaze travel around the room. Lacey wove her way through the crowd, carrying an airpot of coffee. Ellie and Eileen shared a table with Happy and Glen. Ellie blushed when they made eye contact. What was that all about?

Attempting to keep her back facing the wall and away from prying eyes, Claire strove for nonchalance as she reached for a bagel and a cup. The door opened and Faye Eisler stepped inside. Her short red hair frizzed this morning, and her lips were set into a self-satisfied smirk until she spotted Claire. She gaped and clapped her hand over her mouth, then executed a fast about-face and left.

Okay, now she understood why there was such a crowd in Dee's this morning. Faye had spread the word. But how had that redheaded gossipmonger found out about the monkey incident? Claire's eyes swung back to Ellie, whose blush deepened, and the scene came together. She must have checked to see if they found the professor, and someone at the laboratory blabbed. Since she lived in the attic apartment at the Eisler's B&B, it was more than likely she told Faye.

Taking a seat next to Patsy, Claire tried to ignore the grating chuckles all around her. While Lydia dabbed her eyes, and Dee attempted to control her giggles, Claire groused and pumped a cup of Dee's special blend coffee from the airpot. Faye hadn't wasted a minute getting the story out it seemed. The monkey incident. Another one she'd have to live down. It hadn't been *that* funny. The blasted monkey ripped her hair out, for Pete's sake. Her scalp still hurt. Why did these things happen to her? She stirred sweetener and powdered creamer—another disgusting concession to the bulge battle—into her coffee.

She narrowed her eyes at Patsy, sending a "don't you dare laugh" warning. Patsy swallowed the suspicious tic at the side of her mouth. On Claire's other side, Dee's giggles picked up volume again. A change of subject was needed.

"I'm glad to see you join us, for once." Claire pinched off a corner of Dee's apple fritter. "How's your new helper working out?" She popped the tidbit in her mouth, enjoying the snap of the crystallized sugar that surrounded the chewy apple bits and pastry and the way it melted on her tongue. "Did she make this?"

"Isn't it wonderful? Did you notice there's a bit more cinnamon?"

Not from one bite. Claire debated a second but resisted. Apparently it had been a rhetorical question anyway, since Dee didn't wait for her response.

"Trish, that's her name, Trish Halloran—did I already tell you that? Anyway, she adds so many creative innovations into her baking. A little bit of this, a pinch of that and suddenly a plain old apple fritter becomes an extraordinary culinary experience." Dee closed her eyes, kissed her fingertips, and tossed the kiss to the air. Whoa, when had Dee turned into an Italian drama queen?

She opened one eye, looked at Claire and snickered. "Gotcha. That's for stealing." She slid her fritter out of Claire's reach. "But Trish really is very talented, and I'm glad to get out front for a change."

The door opened, bell jingling, and Lester Gordon saluted them as he sauntered in. "Morning, ladies. Y'all fixin' to paint the post office flagpole?"

"Does it need painting?" Lydia asked.

Worse than chalk on a blackboard, his condescending chuckle grated on Claire's last nerve. She gave Lester the evil eye.

"You have to understand him, Lydia. Lester thinks all women should be barefoot and pregnant or confined to the kitchen. The idea of a successful, female entrepreneur is totally foreign to his boxed-in pea-brain." She raised her voice on the last word.

Cackling, the cocky rooster selected a honey bun, dropped his money in the basket and winked at Claire on his way out the door. "New hair-do, Clairey-girl?" He barked a laugh and departed.

Good thing he did. Any more out of him and Claire would have gone public with the story of when Olympia, brandishing a cast iron skillet, chased him outside the house and down the street. He wasn't so chauvinistic then. Claire couldn't help the tug at her lips.

"So, is the geologist coming?" Dee asked.

Still smiling, Claire returned her attention back to the question at hand. "On the twentieth. His summer semester students are coming to help him as a class project."

Lydia pumped coffee from the airpot into her cup. It shooshed as she emptied out the last bit. "Does he think he can find the problem?"

"He seemed intrigued." Claire shrugged and tossed a sugar packet to her. "Said it was very unusual since the source is deep underground, but not impossible."

Dee elbowed Claire, her eyes twinkling with mischief. "I can't stand it. Give your closest friends the story. What happened with the monkey?"

Of its own volition, Claire's hand slipped to the back of her head, checking to see if her camouflaging held. "What's to tell? I got too close to a cage." How could she get them away from her gaffe and onto another subject?

Patsy's cup clanked as she set it down. "Have y'all noticed an increase in tourist traffic since we spruced up the town?"

Thank heaven. Claire sent her a tiny thank-you-smile.

"I have," Lydia said. "I've got more non-residents than locals in the spa now, and a few stayed at the Inn, coming back a second day. I'm thinking about the possibility of adding a three-day experience. Of course, I'd have to get Faye to alter her breakfasts and keep the clients out of here." She laughed as Dee's eyebrows nearly jumped off her head.

"I can offer … hmm." With her thumb and middle finger cupping her chin, Dee tapped her cheek with a forefinger. "What could I offer them?" She stared at Lydia. "If you came up with some recipes you wanted, we could make them. I've been thinking of adding sandwiches for those who don't want to go into the restaurants but have lunch on the beach."

"I have a book filled with ideas you could look at," Lydia said. "And besides the beach, they could eat their lunch in the gazebo at Warm Springs Park before going into the springs."

"Perfect." Dee glanced at Claire. "I noticed Joel and his team fixed the gazebo on our work day. Are you nearly ready for the wedding?"

At the word "wedding," the magazine ad from Henderson's Market popped up from Claire's memory bank. *That's it!* That's how she'd redeem her dignity and reputation. Not only would she serve a fabulous rehearsal dinner but could entertain her friends and gain respect as a competent cook.

The cooking class was her ticket out of dystopia.

Chapter 23

C laire stood on the corner admiring their handiwork on Sandy Shores Drive. The newly installed awnings gave the street an extra splash of color and her a metaphorical warm hug each morning as she walked to the gallery. Color gleamed everywhere from the dark green and gold strip of the gallery's awnings, to the urns flanking its front door. The whimsical pots were two bunny rabbits holding knives and forks, facing each other over a platter of wavy, dark purple leaves and deep yellow marigolds. It was a veritable bunny smorgasbord and made people smile, which was her objective. Chapel Springs never looked so inviting. Claire bent and pulled up a small weed from among the flowers.

Next door at *Halls of Time Antiques*, Eileen's awnings were two shades of cranberry. The grandfather clock pots Claire had made for her held bright pink azaleas. Up and down Sandy Shores, tourists received a colorful, warm welcome that promised fulfillment of all their summer dreams.

Opening the gallery's door, Claire sailed through to the workroom, ready to fulfill her dream of culinary success. A few moments later, she stared at the online registration form, filled with confusion. There was a whole lot more to cooking classes than she'd realized. Who knew? She thought they'd have a weeklong course, and she'd exit being able to wow her family and friends. Instead, each class was a menu for a single meal. So much for that dream. She didn't have the time or the money to pursue anything more than the rehearsal dinner.

Now her only dilemma was what to choose. And who. The teaching chefs all came from different restaurants around Atlanta and other

Southern cities. A few hailed from foreign countries. Claire was no foodie and didn't recognize any of the names. So, she wouldn't go by the chef. After all, she wouldn't be taking him home, just the food.

She read a class menu. Em-pan-ah-das. There wasn't a description, and since she couldn't even pronounce it, it was probably a bad idea to try that one. And it shouldn't be foreign anyway. Not with Sandi's parents. They only ate American cuisine. Claire pulled a face and rolled her eyes. None of her family had ever been picky eaters.

Twirling a strand of hair in her fingers, she continued to scroll and study the class list, until she zeroed in on one called Surprising Grill Sensations. Now there's an idea. Every bozo with a spatula could manage a backyard grill, even if it was just brats. Go meat! If they could do it, surely she could. A simple but delicious menu was the secret to redeeming her reputation. With a quick click of the mouse, she added Grill Sensations to her cart.

What else? Her finger rolled the little wheel on her mouse until Basic Kitchen Essentials caught her eye. The explanation said all she needed was a little know-how and some confidence. They'd teach her knife skills and cooking methods, and she'd leave with the ability to start making fresh and delicious meals at home. In one night? Exactly what she needed. She clicked and added it to her cart as well.

After looking over the selection of classes for desserts, she decided she'd pick up something from Dee's. Why push her luck? She clicked checkout, entered her credit card number and printed out her receipt and instructions. Her first class—the basics one—was next Tuesday night. Now she just needed to come up with a good excuse to get out of the house.

Patsy stuck her head in the back room. Her bed-head hair had new sun streaks. They made the freckles across her nose and cheekbones stand out more than usual. The overall effect was charming. "You've got a customer."

"Okay, I'll be right there." Claire closed the Internet browser and slipped her receipt into a file drawer. She wouldn't even tell Patsy she was going through with it, or else she'd want to come. Claire loved her, but if anything went wrong, she'd jump in to save Claire's bacon, and just once, she wanted to succeed on her own.

In the gallery, a tall man—he had to be at least six-foot-three—stood before her display of serving platters and large bowls. He had one arm laid across his ample belly and his thumb and forefinger supported the foremost of his two chins. He appeared in deep thought, and Claire hesitated to interrupt him. Finally he noticed her by his side.

"Oh. Didn't hear you. Do you always sneak up on people?"

Was he a relative of Felix? Rudeness ran in that family. "I didn't want to disturb you." She stretched her lips into what she hoped passed for a pleasant smile. "How may I help you?"

"I need some serving pieces. I don't want them the same. Nor do I want anyone possessing duplicates. They must be originals."

Claire bristled, flexing her fingers behind her back. "All my pieces are one of a kind."

His frank appraisal made her uncomfortable, but he finally nodded. "Fine. I'll take that platter …" he pointed to the top shelf at her favorite pansy design. "And that bowl. Do you have another one the same size? I need two."

Multi-colored, the ten-inch bowl had fruit painted inside and out. "What other colors are you inters—"

"I don't care about color. I asked if you have another in its size."

She wasn't sure she wanted His Royal Rudeness to own any of her work. Then again if she were going to pay for those classes, this would more than cover it. "I do, although none are exactly the same size since each is handcrafted and not from a mold. I'll bring it right out."

Pompous turkey. No, not a turkey. A peacock was more like it. She saw them at the zoo, wandering around, screeching so people would notice them.

She grabbed a bowl from her inventory, this one with a veggie motif, and after showing it to him, he grunted approval and she wrapped his purchases and rang them up. Though his money would pay for her cooking classes, she'd be happy to see the back of this customer.

Sighing with relief when the door closed behind him, Claire went in search of Patsy. She'd seemed preoccupied this morning. Claire found her standing at the workroom window.

"Patsy, is something wrong?"

Without turning around, she nodded. "It's Mama. When I walked into their apartment this morning, I frightened her." Patsy glanced at her with eyes glistening. "She didn't know me, Claire."

"Oh, no! Have you told your dad?"

"He was with patients."

Claire put her hand on Patsy's shoulder. "What did you do?"

"Nothing. After a moment, she frowned then blinked a couple of times like she was trying to clear her vision. Then she acted like nothing had happened."

"And she knew you then."

Patsy nodded and turned back to the window. "I don't know how to convince Dad to get her help."

"Hasn't he seen her have these … episodes?"

"If he has, he's ignoring them." She left the window and wandered to her easel, picking up her palette and brush. She stood in front of the blank canvas. "I tried to talk to her about it, but she's in denial, too."

How frightening to lose your memory. For someone as creative as Cooper, it would be devastating. Claire shuddered.

"I don't know what I can do, Pat-a-cake, but I'll keep my eyes and ears open."

Patsy slapped a wide swath of blue paint across the canvas. "Thanks. We've got to convince Dad before something happens to her."

Claire left the house Tuesday evening, breathing a prayer of thanks. She hated subterfuge, and after telling Joel she was going to the library in Pineridge, he asked if she would mind going into Young Harris and pick up a few things from Henderson's for him. She couldn't believe her good fortune. While she did have a book to return to the library, she didn't need to do any research and hadn't figured out how to account for the extra time. Now she didn't have to.

After depositing her books in the library's drive-through book-drop, she arrived at Henderson's Organic Market. She cruised the parking lot until she found a convenient spot, did her shopping, and stored the food in a cooler in the back of her Trailblazer.

Back inside, a sign for the cooking classes pointed to an elevator. She adjusted her deep orange tee-shirt, praying the evening would go well. With her tummy atwitter, Claire entered the lift with the enthusiasm of a death row inmate. Could she really pull this off? Every time she attempted to prepare anything beyond a PB and J or Jell-O, it resulted in disaster and somehow became a town joke. With the exception of her pottery, and even that was suspect, her life could be a reality show: Extreme Embarrassment.

She took a deep breath and released it slowly as the elevator stopped. The doors slid open and before her, a huge, loft-style kitchen, surrounded with windows, overlooked the market below. A slender woman, with short hair the color of summer wheat, sported a white apron and scurried back and forth from a huge refrigerator, bringing out what Claire guessed to be the ingredients for the class. A gigantic island with four stovetops, sat in the center of the room. Behind it, a long counter with two double sinks, ran the length of the wall and wrapped around two sides of the kitchen.

On the classroom side of the island, a flat screen TV hung from the soffit and faced three rows of long, bar-height counters. Two other women, students she guessed, hunched over some papers, scribbling. As she slid a barstool out from under the counter, the scrape of its wooden legs alerted apron-woman to her presence.

"Ah, another student. Welcome. I'm Judi." She handed Claire a piece of paper. "Please fill this out and sign it. Chef Thornton will be back shortly and collect them." She gestured to the others. "We'll do introductions when everyone has arrived."

Judi returned to her preparations, and Claire looked at the paper. At the top was the market's logo and just beneath were the words "Student Waiver." It contained words like "risk" and phrases like "safely follow instructions." If she'd learned anything in her forty-seven years, it was best not to read those warning things too closely. She signed it.

"I'll take that." A hand, bedecked with a diamond the size of Rhode Island, landed on her waiver and pulled it away, nearly clipping Claire's nose with the rock. An ink mark trailed off the page when she didn't lift her pen fast enough.

She regarded the strawberry-blonde—a home dye job if she ever saw one—and reached to take her paper back. "I thought the chef collected them. That's what Judi said."

"Oh, I always do it. Chef Thornton and I are old friends. I enroll in all his classes."

"Didn't the first one take?" Okay, that wasn't nice, but she couldn't help it.

The self-appointed queen-of-the-class stared at her, chewing one corner of her lip. Claire could almost see the wheels turning in her head as she tried to decide if she'd been insulted. Then she laughed and waved a hand at Claire.

"Oh, you're so funny. We're going to be the best of friends, I can tell." She sashayed over to a desk off to one side and laid their waivers in a box. Her capris looked like an Earl Scheib paint job, trying to camouflage a lumpy old chassis. She couldn't be a day under fifty-two.

When she came back, she grabbed her friend's arm. "Come on,

Eunice. Let's go sit with Claire. She's from Chapel Springs."

Terrific. The class queen was also a snoop.

They plopped their gear down, and Eunice took the seat next to her. Her congenial smile offered friendship, her gray hair wisdom, and the wrinkles around her eyes, humor. Claire liked her immediately.

"As you probably heard, I'm Eunice, and this is only my second time. I realized at the last class, I needed the basics. Never was much of a cook." She lifted her bifocals to peer through the bottom part at Claire. "Say, aren't you the lady that makes those whimsy pots?"

Claire winced inwardly. She'd hoped no one would know her here. Did she dare deny it?

"You *are* her." Eunice leaned closer and whispered. "I was in your gallery that day one of your lovely vases fell on a man." She patted Claire's hand. "He deserved it."

Oh, my.

Queenie leaned forward. "What are you two whispering about?"

"Nothing. I was admiring her necklace." Eunice winked at Claire.

Beginning to understand the dynamics, she smiled thanks to her new ally and relaxed.

Laughter and chatter announced the arrival of more students. A trio of twenty-somethings bee-bopped into the kitchen arena, giggling like high schoolers. Just what she needed—a bunch of silly girls, trying to impress each other or worse, flirt with the chef, when she needed life-changing instruction.

The newcomers chattered with Judi, met the Queen, and settled themselves into the first row.

Eunice nudged Claire. "Want to pair up?" Behind her bifocals, Eunice's blue eyes invited confidence.

"Pair up?"

She nodded. "They always have small groups, two to four, depending on the class size." She pointed to the island. "There are only four stoves."

Claire needed to focus to learn. The Queen would take over, and the trio giggled so much, she wouldn't be able to concentrate. She nodded at Eunice. "You've got yourself a partner."

A moment later, a pregnant belly waddled in, low and large, followed by its owner. Claire hoped delivering a baby wasn't part of the course. The young mother looked like she could go into labor any minute. She belonged at a childbirth class, not a cooking class. Her arms didn't look long enough to get around her girth to reach the counter. Judi must have said something when she handed her a waiver because she gestured at her stomach and laughed.

"Twins. I know I look about to pop, but I have another two months to go. Honest."

Looked more like triplets to Claire, but who was she to argue?

"I'm a flight attendant but had to take early maternity leave. I'm dying of boredom at home. That's why I'm here."

Queenie rushed over to her. "My dear, let's get you off your feet, at least for now. When Chef arrives, I'll help you." Like a tugboat escorting a freighter, she piloted the mother ship to port—a chair next to herself.

They'd just settled when the elevator door opened and a man barreled in, one hand buttoning his chef coat. In his other hand were Claire's platter and bowls.

Chapter 24

Claire squeezed her eyes shut. Please, it couldn't be. She slowly opened one eye. No! The teaching Chef was His Royal Rudeness? She groaned. Could she get away without being seen? She eyed the exit door to the market, but she'd have to go right past him. The elevator. Even if it made noise, maybe he'd only see her back. She reached for her tote.

Eunice's hand stopped her. "What's the matter?"

Chef Thornton looked up, frowning. He searched for the disturbance until his eyes locked with hers. They narrowed, then one twitched. Was he going to throw her out? Throw her bowl at her? Wait a potato-peeling minute here. She hadn't been the rude one. He was. Letting go of her tote, she straightened her shoulders, never breaking eye contact. One corner of her mouth rose as she tilted her head and gave him a half nod.

Thornton blinked. Then he bowed and made a show of placing her platter and bowls on the island. What was he up to? When he turned back to the group, he was all business. So … maybe he was sorry for his attitude in the gallery. Did her presence in the class embarrass him? If he was repentant, she didn't want him to be uncomfortable. She'd forgive him and move on into a professional relationship. She sent him a warm smile.

"I'd have been here on time, but someone parked their blue Trailblazer in my spot." The twitch moved upward into his right eyebrow as he scanned the room.

How was she supposed to know it was his? His name wasn't on it. It didn't say reserved, either. When his eyes landed on hers, she stared back. The twitch dropped back to his eye and picked up its tempo. How could he possibly know the Trailblazer was hers? For some reason she didn't understand, she knew she already had one strike against her.

"Hopefully it won't happen again. Now, welcome to Kitchen Basics. I'm Chef Thornton. You may call me Chef. I see a few of you I recognize. Trixie," he tipped his head to Queenie, "I don't know why you're here, but you can help with the new students. Eunice, welcome back. I'm glad you took my suggestion."

Next to Claire, Eunice hunched her shoulders and shifted in her seat. With her movements, a pleasant waft of lemon verbena floated from her.

"And beside Eunice is Claire Bennett, a local artist, who made these unique pieces." He gestured to the island where her platter and bowls rested. All heads turned to her. So much for anonymity. She waggled her fingers at the others.

"Katherine, my dear, welcome." Chef's whole demeanor changed when he addressed the mother-to-be. Claire glanced at her. Besides a flight attendant, who was she? Or better, who was she to the chef?

"We're the Joyce Club," said one of the trio, when Chef nodded to her. Her blonde hair had been gathered above her ears into two ponytails. "We're all named Joyce and have been friends since fourth grade." She giggled. "To keep us straight, I'm Joy, she's Jo," Joy indicated to the brunette on her left, "and this is Joyce. She's the oldest." Joy giggled again.

Claire would never get them straight. Hopefully, she wouldn't need to, but the giggling could get old fast.

"All right, everyone to the island."

Eunice stood next to Claire. In front of them lay folded white aprons and plastic bags containing a variety of knives. Claire reached for the bag.

"Don't open that yet."

She jerked her head up. Chef frowned at her. Oops. Was that strike two? She put her hands behind her back.

"All in good time. Now, the person to your right will be your partner. Trixie, you float between the groups, helping."

As they donned their aprons, Claire's fingers itched to get hold of the knives and begin. The kitchen still smelled clean. No pleasant aromas seeped from bubbling pots or goodies baking. Instead, Thornton droned on about safety. Yada, yada, yada. She'd heard it all before. They weren't kindergartners, yet the others paid rapt attention to his words. She had to stop her eyes from rolling. Finally he let them open the bags.

"Pull out the eight-inch chef's knife. We'll begin with learning proper dicing methods."

She could do that. She'd chopped lots of things for Joel, except she never held the veggies the way Chef did. She leaned forward to see around the Joyces, and peered at his hands. He curled his fingertips under his knuckles. Her eyes widened. He held the knife close to his fingers and moved it so fast she could barely see it. They were supposed to do that?

Judi handed everyone a small basket, holding four carrots, three celery ribs, and an onion, as the chef talked. "This is called *mirapoix*. This vegetable mix—often referred to as the mother vegetables—is the base for countless recipes, including soups, stews, sauces, stocks, etc. It's a perfect start for most dishes. Take out the celery."

As he demonstrated, Claire tried to curl her fingers like he said, but it felt awkward. She gripped the handle of her knife and took a tentative whack at the stalk. Her celery had a mind not to be cut and slid from her grip. She glanced at Eunice who had a small pile of diced celery in front of her.

Claire pursed her lips, rotated her shoulders, and walked her fingers forward a little on the celery. Chef said to leave the point of the knife on the board and move the back end. Her hand ached in rebellion at the awkward position as she wobbled the knife up and down, moving it along the celery. She gritted her teeth and forced her hand to behave. Her fingertips pressed down as the knife bit and the ribs cracked under its pressure. It worked … sort of. At least her pile grew fractionally. They weren't very small or uniform, though.

"No, no, no. That's all wrong." Queen Trixie's talons grabbed Claire's wrist, her loud voice alerting the chef to the errors, and he walked toward them. Why couldn't she stick her nose into somebody else's business?

"What seems to be the trouble, Ms. Bennett?"

"I have no idea. I was doing fine."

Trixie threw her hands on her strangulated hips. "You weren't, Claire. Your little fingertips were in danger. Why, you might have injured a nail."

Would it be a faux pas if she gagged?

Chef wrapped his furry hand around Claire's and pulled hers into a fist. Why did everyone have to grab her? The hairs on the side of his paw tickled her wrist. She wondered if it ever got into his dishes. For the sake of sanitation, he ought to shave them.

"Now try."

She thumped her fist on top of the celery.

"No, not like that. Use the back of your fingertips. Like this." He demonstrated again.

Claire scrunched down to look beneath his elbow. His clean fingernails rested on the celery but faced his wrist. She gave it a try and must have gotten the position right because he moved on to Joy. But as soon as Claire tried to move the knife like he said, her fingers slid forward again.

Oh, this was ridiculous. She'd been chopping vegetables for years and—"Yikes." She quickly glanced around, but only Eunice heard her.

"You okay?"

Claire nodded. "Yeah, I just got a little close." Too close. What had possessed her to take this class? Oh yeah, Sandi's mother, Zoe-the-Intimidator.

"You're trying to do it too fast. Forget what Chef looks like when he does it and just go slow. I'll help you."

Before Claire could tell her she wanted to do it herself, Eunice took the rest of her celery and quickly reduced it to a pile of uniform pieces. All Claire managed was to get one rib chopped. At least she didn't chop her fingers, as well. She didn't want to hurt Eunice's feelings, but helping her was the reason Claire hadn't asked Patsy to come. She needed to do it herself, although the carrots made her nervous. Those things rolled. And the pungent onions made her weep buckets. Maybe her reputation wasn't such a bad thing.

Uh, no. She sighed. Their Charlie had better appreciate this. Chef spent another ten minutes on the other knives and their purposes then moved on to the various pots and pans. When would they get to some cooking?

"All right. Now, look over the recipe Judi is handing out."

Well, finally!

"While you glance over it, we'll talk about *mise en place*."

Claire glanced at the recipe. She'd never heard of whatever-plas and didn't see any word that looked like meeze.

"By the look on Claire's face, I think you'd better explain *mise en place*, Chef." If Trixie was aiming to sound like Joy—or was Jo the giggler—it was a bad imitation. Then again, it could be her tight capris that made her laugh sound like a honking goose.

"Of course." Chef turned to Claire. "It's French and literally means 'everything in place.' All the various items you'll need to put together a recipe. Utensils, ingredients chopped and ready in prep bowls, pots, pans, blender—whatever." He twirled his hand in the air with a flourish. "So, gather your *mise en place*."

Claire forced her eyes not to roll by staring at the recipe Eunice placed in front of them. Hot and Spicy Salsa. It needed two limes, four peppers, two kinds, six tomatoes—why didn't they chop those instead of carrots? There weren't any carrots in this recipe. Onions. At least they already chopped those.

On her left, Joyce—at least she thought it was Joyce—pulled out a notepad and jotted down the ingredients. Why do things twice? It would be easier to carry the recipe to the refrigerator.

Claire grabbed hers and headed to the large industrial side-by-side, expecting to find more little baskets with the peppers and whatnot in them. She pulled the door open. No baskets. Maybe they put everything in plastic bags instead. Nope, no bags. When she opened a drawer, she found the peppers—two kinds, tomatoes, and cilantro. Arms loaded, she spread her fingers to capture the limes and dropped three of the peppers and a tomato, which promptly rolled under the island.

Terrific.

After picking up the peppers and depositing her whatever-he-called-it-plas back in the drawer, she walked around the island to the front side, got down on her knees and peered underneath. One rogue jalapeno she'd missed sneered at her, and the tomato lay just out of reach. With the clandestine stealth of an FBI agent, she peeked over her shoulder to make sure nobody was observing her. Fortunately, they were all at the fridge.

She lowered her head and tried to grab the tomato but felt only air. It must have rolled further. She stretched out, face down out on the floor. The little traitor laid a hand's reach away. She slid her shoulder under the island to capture it. When her fingers connected with the cool slick skin, she grabbed it.

A shoe appeared in her peripheral vision. A large, brown shoe. A large, brown, man's shoe.

"And what might you be doing?" Claire startled at his voice, and her fingers sank into the tomato's flesh, squirting seeds and juice onto her face—and the brown shoe.

If there had been any way possible, she would have slid all the way under the island. As it was, an arm reached down and Eunice, not Chef, helped her up. By the heat crawling up her cheeks, Claire knew her face looked like the tomato's twin.

"The other students preferred to gather their produce from the refrigerator. You, however, have chosen the floor." Chef looked down at his shoe covered in seeds and juicy bits of red tomato flesh. "I don't think I'll ask why." He turned and walked away, his left shoe squishing. Mutinous tomato seeds and a rouge piece of pulp abandoned ship, leaving a trail behind him.

Eunice handed her a basket. "Take this and get your veggies. I'll get the other things for you."

One Patsy in her life was enough, but Eunice turned away before Claire could stop her. After washing her hands and wiping her face with a damp paper towel to remove the tomato seeds, she filled her basket with the vegetables and limejuice. Back at her station, a blender had been set up and plugged in next to the bowls and spices Eunice collected.

"For efficiency in cooking, *mise en place* is recommended. That means," the Chef eyed Claire, "having all your ingredients measured, chopped and ready to incorporate. If there is any pre-cooking necessary, that should be done in advance, also." Thornton paced behind them like a general. "Today, we're doing a blender salsa, so you don't need to do as much prep work. However, because we don't want the salsa too hot, you should remove the seeds and veins first."

"And if we like really hot salsa?" Katherine asked.

"Then by all means, leave *some* in."

Claire glanced first at Katherine and then Chef, wondering what they classified as really hot. She loved Mexican food, and Joel often used jalapenos in his sauces. Leaving the seeds in avoided more knife work, too. Hot salsa it would be. She opened the top to her blender, tossed everything in, and slapped on the lid. Eunice stopped her before she could turn it on.

"Your lid isn't on tight. If you start it, everything inside will erupt all over you and the counter."

Claire gave her a weak smile. "Thanks." She clicked the lid in place, then hit the pulse button like the recipe said, letting it run for a few seconds, stopped and did it again, then once more for good measure. A muddy mixture of green and red, peppered with seeds, lay in the bottom. It smelled wonderful.

Judi emptied a pan of fresh tortilla chips onto a platter. Claire grabbed one, poured salsa over it and took a bite. It tasted fantastic. Hot and tangy. And she'd made it herself. Okay, she had some help from Eunice, but really, she did it herself. Exulting in her achievement, she poured the rest of the salsa into a bowl, wiping up the drips with her fingers.

Queen Trixie sauntered by with a chip in her hand. She waved it over Claire's bowl of salsa. "May I?" Without waiting for an answer, she dipped the chip in and took a bite. "Mmm," she mumbled. Then her eyes grew large and began to water. She danced up and down on her platform shoes. "Hot!" she managed between gasps.

Claire knew she shouldn't laugh, but when she opened her mouth to ask if Trixie wanted some water, it snuck out. She was still chuckling as Judi handed Trixie a glass of milk.

"That'll take the fire out better than water."

Claire lifted her hand to wipe the moisture from her eyes. Eunice grabbed her wrist. "You haven't washed yet. You touch your eyes with those fingers, and they'll burn worse than Trixie's mouth. You've still got pepper oil on them."

"Huh, who knew peppers had oil? Thanks."

Claire stood drying her hands. Maybe she did need a keeper. If Eunice hadn't stepped in tonight, she'd have been in a pickle for sure.

Chef Thornton concluded the class by having Trixie hand out the class completion certificates. As she gave Claire one, she paused and stared. Her lips twitched suspiciously, like she wanted to laugh. What was her problem?

"Is something wrong?" Claire looked over the certificate.

Trixie blushed. "No, I ... just wanted to say it was definitely fun, getting to know you. I've never known anyone quite like you."

The sarcasm dripped off her tongue faster than the tomato splashed Thornton's shoe. Just what she needed, another missile fired at her reputation. She gathered her tote and plastic bowl of salsa. On her way out of Henderson's, she chucked the bowl in the first trash bin she passed.

Chapter 25

Patsy turned out the bathroom light and crossed to the bed where Nathan sat, reading. Her heart swelled with love for this man. And with relief—sweet relief over the lifted burden of secrecy. While he still often worked late, he didn't prolong coming home until she was asleep. She lifted the covers and slid in next to him.

He set his book face down on his lap and pulled her close. "I hope that sigh was a happy one."

"A very contented one. Honey, I'm happy just cuddling with you. I missed that so much."

Doubt clouded his eyes. "You're sure you're okay with the … problem not being reversed?"

"With your blood pressure and arrhythmia, the medicines aren't an option."

"And you're not sorry you married me?"

She rose on her knees and clasped his face between her hands, his stubble prickling. "You listen to me, Nathan Kowalski. I love you. I've loved you since I was sixteen. I'll never love anyone other than you. I don't care *how* I have you, as long as you're here with me." She kissed him soundly, then sat back against her pillows.

Nathan put his arm around her shoulders and pulled her close. His book slipped off his lap onto the bed. With her head nestled in the hollow of his shoulder, his low chuckle reverberated in her ear.

"I knew you were the one for me the first time I saw you." His kiss landed on her temple. "Do you remember?"

The memory flowed over her like warm honey. "I do." She couldn't help but laugh at the mental image of Claire, moments before they first saw Nathan and Joel. "Claire had a part in that musical, and we were testing a prop I built."

"I never did understand why you didn't use a real trash can."

"Because of the noise it would make. I built it out of concrete forms for freeway supports. With paint, it looked realistic and strong, but most important, quiet. Too bad I didn't realize the lid wouldn't hold up."

Nathan threw his head back and laughed. She hadn't heard him laugh with abandon in months. "I'll never forget her dance partner's face. He tossed her, her bottom hit the lid, and she sank from sight."

Patsy wiped moisture from the corner of her eyes. "That's when I saw you and Joel watching in the wings."

"You were mad as a wet cat at us for laughing."

Patsy slipped her arm to Nathan's waist and pinched him.

"Ow. Not fair." He tickled her ribs in retaliation.

"Okay, I give. I give." She gasped. "Stop!"

"I was telling you how I knew you were the girl I wanted to marry. It was your loyalty to Claire. No teenaged boy was going to embarrass her—not on your watch."

"She's my best friend." Patsy smoothed the blue-and-chocolate duvet over them. "Next to you."

"Don't you think it's time to let her stand on her own feet, though?"

Where had that come from? "What do you mean?"

He picked up his book, slid the jacket flap between the pages, and handed it to her. "I mean you're still rescuing Claire."

"She needs it sometimes. She doesn't think first, she simply acts—or reacts."

"But isn't that Joel's problem?"

There was more to this than he let on. "Nathan, what is this about?"

He shifted his position, sitting up straighter, and with one arm, propped his pillow behind his neck. "Joel's worried about her. Says she's been acting strange."

She might not agree with Claire's chosen course of action, but she wouldn't betray her friend. "It's getting late." She rolled to her side and laid his book on her nightstand.

Nathan turned out the light then pulled Patsy close, spooning with her. "Okay, I get the hint. Subject closed. Just be careful, sweetheart. Let them solve their own problems."

She'd try, but she seemed to be the only one who could see what went on inside Claire's head.

Claire turned out the bathroom light and crossed the room. Sitting on the side of the bed, she set the alarm for five-thirty. That sounded awfully early. She changed it to six and turned off her bedside lamp. After tonight's fiasco, she could use a little extra sleep.

Joel closed his *American Angler* magazine as she slipped under the covers. "Want to reset that to four-thirty and come fishing with me?"

She hesitated. "Sure."

"No one's forcing you, Claire."

"Are you withdrawing the invite?"

"You had to think about it. You never used to. What's up with you lately, anyway?"

Tread carefully.

She set the alarm down and turned to face him. "Honey, I've had a long day. I'm tired. I was simply weighing my need for sleep with the lure," she smiled at the pun, "of fishing with you. I decided I could take a nap tomorrow."

"Oh." He dropped his magazine on the floor and turned out his light. "So, there's nothing else wrong?"

Who was this man? Not her Joel, who preferred to sweep problems out the back door, pretending they didn't exist. He was like Patsy in that. Too bad his timing was so off. Maybe if he'd asked months ago …

"Nope. Nothing some sleep won't fix." Sorry, Lord, but she was too tired to start that conversation now. Besides it would simply escalate into an argument.

Joel snuggled close, kissing her forehead, then pulled back as if he'd been burned. He plucked something from his bottom lip and examined it. "What in the world?" The light snapped on, and he sat up. "Claire, would you care to explain why you have tomato seeds in your bangs?"

She couldn't tell him. Not yet. That would spoil her surprise, and she had to rescue her reputation—by herself. "Tomato seeds?" Fingering beneath her bangs, she couldn't feel any seeds. "Are you sure?"

He held out his hand. On the tip of his index finger sat one lonely tomato seed.

"Hmm, must have been when I was checking the tomatoes you wanted for ripeness. One had a soft spot and squished."

Joel raised one scraggly eyebrow. "You never check for ripeness. You simply grab whatever's on the top of the pile and bag it."

She gulped. "Well, I'm trying to improve."

"I don't know what this is all about, Claire, but I think you're hiding something."

One blasted tomato seed had to betray her. But if things turned out like she hoped, he'd be glad in the end.

"It's a surprise, honey."

The skepticism couldn't be more plainly written on his face if he'd used a magic marker. "Uh-huh. For who?"

Who indeed? She worked for a bright, convincing tone. "You. And for Charlie and Sandi."

Joel rolled over and turned out the light. "All right, but coming from the woman who hates surprises, you can't blame me for being suspicious. Now go to sleep. Four-thirty comes early."

Long after Joel's snores rumbled, Claire lay in the dark listening to the tree frogs chirruping. She loved fishing at dawn with Joel. She'd really miss that if she had to marry someone else. *God, I don't understand all this. I thought...* what did she think?

What would Aunt Lola have done in this situation? She'd been Claire's only advisor on love after her mom died. If only Aunt Lola hadn't been so old, she might have been around today to help Claire figure this mess out. Maybe if she did a pros and cons list, like the twins did picking out a college.

On one hand, Joel was a good provider, a wonderful father, and had never been unfaithful.

On the other hand, he wouldn't—or couldn't, as he claimed—talk about his feelings or listen to hers. It was all Brussels sprouts to him. He played the blame game, always pointing the finger at anybody but himself.

On the other hand, he could be a lot of fun. He had a great sense of humor. And, she had to admit, he put up with a lot of embarrassing situations created by her. Laughed about them.

Cheese Louise, this didn't help her confusion. She pushed the suffocating covers away from her face, wishing God would just send her a telegram and get it over with.

Chapter 26

Claire peered through the windshield as they pulled into the parking lot at the marina. She stuck her head out the window and inhaled the fresh morning air. Eau d'Lake, with its undertones of piney woods, was her favorite perfume. When she opened her eyes again, Joel was grinning at her. No, wait. He was grinning *past* her. She turned to the open window. Across the parking lot, little Andy McMillan bounced on the balls of his feet next to his daddy, jiggling his fishing pole. She should've known they wouldn't be alone. Joel hated to talk about feelings and avoided it whenever possible.

"Drew and Andy?"

"Yep." Joel killed the engine. "I invited them yesterday afternoon. Andy hasn't been Crappie fishing yet."

Whenever he suspected she wanted to talk about their marriage, he invited people over. He knew with company in the boat, she wouldn't bring up private matters. No wonder he felt safe inviting her along today. He came from a long line of mules.

It wasn't that she didn't like Drew. She did, and she adored Andy, but she wanted her husband to herself this morning, even though she wasn't sure how to explain what she thought God wanted. Joel plopped his ratty fishing hat on his head. The lures hanging off it bobbled and clacked together. Maybe company along for the ride was for the best. Joel wasn't exactly on speaking terms with God, and he sure wouldn't take her word for it.

Joel jumped out and trotted across the parking lot while she still sat in the truck. His lineage lacked manners, too, although he wasn't really to blame for that. His mom never had a chance to drum things into him, like opening the car door for his wife. She died when he was ten, and no matter how often Claire reminded him, he never got it. He'd turn and stare at her like she was nuts if she waited.

She shook her head and got out, carrying the thermos of coffee and a bag of bagels. Andy ran toward her, hooting and hollering.

"Hey, Miss Claire!" He threw his arms around her waist and hugged her. "We're goin' fishing with you and Mr. Joel." His two-hundred-watt, gap-toothed grin rivaled the stars, still twinkling in the pre-dawn sky.

She hugged him back with one arm. "Good morning to you, too." How could Bev resist this adorable little boy's pleas to come to church with them? When it came to obstinacy, she wasn't sure who was worse— Bev or Joel. Come to think of it, Drew hadn't made any headway with Bev either. What was it with those two?

"I couldn't have asked for a better fishing partner. Will you be able to get to school on time?"

"My teacher said learning to fish is an important lesson, and I can be late." He glanced back at his daddy. "A little, anyway. Can I carry that?" Andy pointed to the bag of bagels.

She handed it over to him. "You sure can, sweetie."

He studied her then nodded. "I like your hat." He put his hand to the side of his mouth and leaned toward her. His breath smelled of toothpaste. "It hides your bald spot." He ran to help the men, the bagels bouncing inside the bag.

Van Gogh's ear, if Bev told Andy about the monkey incident it was probably all over the school, too. With a forced air of nonchalance, Claire touched the back of her head to make sure her old baseball cap still covered the spot. She'd be thankful when this episode of her life was past. Why did these things—

"Come on, we don't have all day." Joel's voice broke her thoughts.

He and Drew had their pontoon boat waiting at the dock. Little Andy made a big show of holding her hand as she stepped through the gate and onto the boat. Claire checked to see if Joel noticed the gentlemanly act. He didn't, or if he did, he ignored it.

"Thank you, sweetheart."

Andy beamed as she settled onto a seat near the bow. She pulled out life vests for Drew, Andy, and herself.

"Andy," Joel called from the wheel. "Want to help me steer?"

"Oh, boy! Thanks, Mr. Joel."

"You have to put on your life jacket first." He helped Andy into the orange vest.

With Joel seated and Andy standing between his knees holding the steering wheel, Drew used an oar to push them away from the dock. A school of minnows darted to safety in a bed of cattails. As soon as they were outside Moonrise Cove, Joel told Andy to open the throttle, and they headed toward Gosling Cove on the far side of Loon Island—the local favorite kept secret from the casual tourist-fisherman. Only the regulars, who Joel claimed as their bread-and-butter trade, were privy to the best spots.

As they skimmed across the open water, Claire studied Drew. He seemed quiet this morning, not his usual jovial self. To draw him out, she opened the thermos and poured two Styrofoam cups full of coffee. The invigorating fragrance of brewed French Roast wakened her senses. Eau d'Java challenged Eau d'Lake for favorite. Even Drew noticed and inhaled appreciatively.

As the sun shot recon-scouts over the horizon, she offered him a cup and a cream cheese-filled bagel. After taking a cup to Joel and orange juice to Andy, she rejoined Drew in the bow. "You seem preoccupied this morning." She took a bite of bagel.

Drew's sigh could have registered on the depth finder. "I'm really worried about Bev. All she talks about anymore is a home in Mazatlan. Says that will make her happy. She's never adjusted to Chapel Springs like I'd hoped."

"Did she say why she's unhappy?"

Drew blew on his coffee and took a cautious sip as he looked out over the lake. The recon-scouts declared conditions normal and the sun peeked over the eastern edge of the world.

"She resents what she calls my fanaticism over God." He glanced at Andy, who had a white-knuckle grip on the helm. "I was a casual believer when we got married. We attended church only occasionally, you know, weddings, funerals. Bev and I had the same goals back then, but that's changed now, and she's pretty angry." He bit off a chunk of his bagel.

"What made you change, Drew? I'm curious, since I keep hoping Joel will come to church."

Drew chewed the mouthful thoughtfully then swallowed. "I'd forgotten how most Chapel Springs residents were Bible-believing churchgoers. As a kid, I didn't think about that. All my friends went. It's what you did. But in Boston, it was easy to slip out of the habit. I was busy climbing the success ladder." He turned his cup around in his hands, staring into it, then dipped his finger in and pulled out a gnat. "When we moved here, I wanted Bev and Andy to get immersed in the village life, so we came to church. After listening to Seth say 'Christianity isn't a religion but a relationship,' and seeing how he lived what he preached, I knew I'd wasted years, chasing after the wrong things. When he asked if anyone wanted to enter into a relationship with God, I said yes."

Claire remembered Bev's caustic response when asked about church attendance. "What did Bev say?"

"She wigged out. When we got home, she blasted me for humiliating her. Said it was like saying we weren't Christians and called the church fanatical. She refused to go back. She also didn't want me to take Andy. I can't force her to go, but I won't leave Andy at home. He loves the church, and he loves Jesus."

Andy's hair blew in the wind, and he laughed at something Joel said to him and pointed toward Loon Island, rising in the center of the lake.

"How does she feel about that?"

"Right now, she tolerates it, but barely. Don't get me wrong. Bev's a good mother. She'd do anything for Andy."

"But not everything."

Sorrow etched Drew's face as he watched his son laughing with Joel. "No, not everything. Lately, she's enticing him with picnics on Sunday morning or a trip to Six Flags instead of going to church."

Claire taught Andy's Sunday school class. He never missed. "How'd you manage to combat that?"

Drew dangled his fingers in the boat's wake, washing off a bit of cream cheese, then dried them. "Didn't have to. Claire, you should've heard that kid. He said, 'I'd love to go, Mom, but I promised God I'd go to church, and you told me never to break a promise.' Poor Bev. She couldn't say anything. That was the last time she tried that. I hope she's given up."

"I know what you're going through." Ironic how Drew's wife and her husband both had a problem with God.

"How do you manage it, Claire?"

"Manage? I'm not sure I do, at least not very well. I keep asking Joel to come to church, but you've seen how unsuccessful I've been." She peeked over her shoulder. Andy had his hand cupped over Joel's ear. A moment later, he laughed and ruffled the boy's hair. "Maybe I need to hire Andy. He seems to have a good influence on Joel."

A shadow passed over Drew's face as he glanced at his son. "I guess we have to trust God and keep hoping."

Claire didn't answer. Who was she to give advice? She wondered if Drew ever thought he should be married to someone else. Bev's flirting had to hurt.

Fifteen minutes later, the boat drew close to Loon Island. Claire shaded her eyes against the rising sun and searched the inlet, but the loons had long migrated back north. She missed the males' yodeling. Joel stayed offshore about fifty feet and slowed the engine as they skirted the island's perimeter. When entered Gosling Cove, he maneuvered closer to the shore.

"We'll stop at McCabe's dock and get our gear ready first. Big bass like to hide there."

Ian McCabe had owned Loon Island. It had been in his family for generations. He used to let the local kids camp out on his property and kept an eye on their safety. Claire had loved the old man, and as teens, she and Patsy used to wonder why he never married. They made up romantic stories about his lost love. When he died, he left the island to Chapel Springs. The town chinked the old log cabin and rented it out to favored sportsmen. Now, every time she entered Gosling Cove and smelled the cattails and peat, she thought of romance.

Joel idled the boat up to the dock, and Drew looped a rope around a cleat. Claire pushed all thoughts of romance aside and scrambled for her fishing pole. She and Joel both loved to fish.

He pulled out a knife and opened the bait cooler. Andy peered inside it at the herring. "Where'd these come from, Mr. Joel?"

"I brought them. They're bait, Andy. Stripers love fresh herring."

"I thought we were gonna use those funny looking fuzzy things," Andy said.

"Those are flies for casting. We won't do that today."

"Why?"

Joel never seemed to run out of patience with Andy's questions. If only he'd save some for her. She put her hand on Andy's shoulder. "With four of us in the boat, that could be dangerous."

Joel guffawed. "You mean like last time?" He turned to Drew. "Felix went with us, and Claire sunk a hook into his backside."

She sniffed. "It served him right. I told him not to fish from the bow."

"He figured you were trying to keep the best spot to yourself." Joel patted Andy's head. "Pay attention, son. Stay far away from Miss Claire when you're fishing. It's safer."

"Joel!" Claire scowled at him. "Don't pay him any mind, Andy. You'll just drop your line over the side. The herring will swim down to deeper water."

While Drew helped Andy, Claire carefully hooked a herring without killing it and dropped her line in the water. She soon caught a striped bass, but it was small and she released it back into the lake. Drew coached his son until he squealed in excitement as he reeled in the first keeper of the day. After an hour or so, Joel and Drew each had a respectable sized bass.

When would it be her turn? She swatted at an insistent gnat buzzing around her face. After reeling in her line to check the bait, she found half the herring gone. She peered over the side of the boat. There was a real smart fish down there. She'd never even felt it nibble her bait. She removed the dead remains, threaded a fresh herring on her line, and lowered it into the water with a tiny slash.

A noisy blue jay squawked at its mate in the trees lining the shore. He hopped from branch to branch, chattering at the female as she flitted around a nest, adding pine needles. The male flew in and ripped one pine needle out and dropped it to the ground. He reminded her of Joel. Curious what the female would do, she continued watching. She knew what she'd do if she were that bird.

A hard tug bent her fishing rod until the tip touched the water, and the line zinged out. Her excitement grew as she jerked up on the rod, setting the hook. She set her feet in a wide stance and began the age-old contest between human and fish.

"Hang onto it, Claire," Joel shouted. "Start reeling it in."

What did he think she was doing? Right then, the fish had the advantage. She wanted to play it until it tired. The way her muscles strained holding the rod, it felt like a big one, but striped bass could be deceiving. After a few minutes, she could feel the fish tiring, and reeling became a bit easier. She pulled her rod up, wound some line in, and then lowered the tip again. She kept this up until she could see the bass.

"It's a big one! He's at least a twelve pounder!" Joel turned to grab the net.

Another large fish zeroed in, swimming around her catch. Did bass eat each other? When she pulled her striper out of the water, the other one leaped toward it. She screeched and jumped, jerking her rod into the boat and lost her balance. As she landed on her behind, the hooked fish flew past her head, smacked Joel in the face, and knocked him overboard. Her prize fish followed him, pulling the rod and reel out of her hands and into the lake.

After a few seconds of stunned silence, Drew and Andy burst out laughing. Claire clapped her hands over her face. Joel came up out of the lake, sputtering, his hat hanging over his face. He grabbed hold of the boat. As he lifted his hat, one side of his face was bright red and his eye was rapidly swelling. One of the hooks from his hat, dangled from his eyebrow.

She gaped down at him.

He glared up at her. "What did you do that for?"

"I didn't do it on *purpose*, Joel. Come on, I'm sorry." She reached her hand out to help him back into the boat.

He swatted it away. "You helped me *in*. I'll get myself out. It's safer." He hoisted himself up over the side and rolled into the boat, blood trickling from his brow.

"I'm really sorry, honey." She bit her lower lip. She grabbed a knife and cut the hook free from his hat. It still dangled dangerously close to his eye.

Andy wiggled in between them. "That old fish sure smacked you, huh, Mr. Joel? He hooked *you*! Are you gonna have a black eye?"

"Most likely." He frowned at Claire. "Why did you do that?"

"I told you it was an accident. A huge striper jumped at mine just as I pulled it out. It scared me and I reacted."

"I saw it, Mr. Joel. That ole fish came flying out of the water like a torpedo." Andy swung his hand in an arc. "Zoom! He was gonna eat Miss Claire's fish. I just know he was."

Drew handed Joel a towel. "It sure looked that way. I couldn't believe Claire's strength. She swung her bass out of the way. You just happened to be *in* the way."

He glanced at her. "Yeah, I guess." Joel's mouth turned up on one side in a sheepish grin. He winked at Andy with his good eye. "So, I guess I can say I had my bath today, right?"

Andy's giggles got the guys all laughing.

All but Claire. Even though it wasn't on purpose, this did happen because of her. Poor Joel. Maybe he'd be happier with a different wife. She hadn't thought about that before. She'd only been thinking of herself. Life would be a lot safer for him without her.

"Yep. You sure made a big splash. Hey, Miss Claire's fish came out and you went in."

Drew stood before Joel with the pliers in his hand. "This is going to hurt."

Cringing, Claire squeezed her eyes shut as Drew removed the fishhook. Joel didn't make a sound. Finally, she opened one eye. Drew had the first aid kit open and pulled out a gauze pad and a tube of antibiotic ointment.

"I'll do it. It's the least I can do." Claire reached for the ointment.

Joel put his hand on her wrist. "No offense, but … I think it's better if Drew did it."

When his wound had been bandaged, Joel used the towel to dry his hair. "So where's this big fish that tossed me overboard?"

Claire's stomach clenched. That rod was one of his favorites. "It followed you."

Joel's eyes grew wide—rather, the uninjured one did—but instead of getting mad, he stared at her, and then shrugged. "At least we all had a good time."

That bass must have knocked him senseless.

"Hey, look." Andy pointed to the water. The handle of the rod stuck out of the water, snagged on an old submerged tree trunk.

Thank you, Lord. Joel and Drew grabbed the oars and maneuvered the boat closer, then Joel reached for the rod. As he pulled it from the water, it bent and the line sang as it flew out. The exhausted fish was tangled in the end of the line. With a smile, Joel offered Claire the honors of landing it, but after subduing his anger the way he did, he deserved to reel it in.

"You go ahead. That fish owes you."

Once he had the bass safely onboard and on ice, she opened the cooler and pulled out a plastic bag of frozen peas she'd brought for Andy to feed the fish. They could forego their treat today. She handed it to Joel.

"Thanks. We better head back now. I—uh …" He held the bag on his eye and cleared his throat. "I'm sorry about getting upset, Claire." He turned and started the motor, leaving her with her mouth hanging open.

Once, when they were first married, Joel told her love meant not having to say you're sorry. She tried to explain that the adage and movie cliché meant if you didn't hurt the one you loved, you had no reason to say you're sorry—not that you never had to apologize. But he insisted on his version. Until now. Was he deliberately trying to confuse her?

When they arrived back at their slip in the marina, Joel, still holding his ice bag in one hand, and Drew picked up the cooler of fish between them and set it on the dock. Andy followed them as they climbed out, then turned back to Claire.

"I'll help you, Miss Claire."

"Thank you, Andy." She took his hand and stepped over the boat's side onto the dock. Looking back to see if she forgot anything, Joel's tackle box sat on the seat. She leaned into the boat and grabbed it.

"My word, it looks like there's been an accident. May I be of assistance?"

Oh, no. It couldn't be. Not here. Not now. Her smile felt weak, but she turned around.

Chapter 27

"Hello, Professor. You're here early." How did he know to find them at the lake? With Joel's tackle box in one hand, Claire tugged on her cap with the other to be sure it was still covering the back of her head. She didn't want to remind him of the monkey fiasco, although, by his smirk, he didn't seem to need a reminder. She felt heat in her cheeks that wasn't from the sun. He looked good, except she thought she remembered him as a bit more rugged, more outdoorsy. Behind him, a half-dozen of his students burst from a blue van.

Standing beside her, Joel shoved the bag of frozen veggies behind his back and nudged her with his elbow. "Joel, this is Professor Leo Sokolov. He and his grad students are going to investigate the springs." She smiled at Leo. "My husband, Joel, Drew McMillan, and his son, Andy."

Leo introduced the students, all of whose names she promptly forgot. After shaking hands, he pointed to Joel's eye. "What happened?"

Andy wiggled in front of her. "Miss Claire smacked Mr. Joel with a big ole fish. You should've seen it. It was cool."

Could the ground please open up and swallow her now?

Drew clapped a hand on Andy's shoulder. "Son, I think it's time for us to go. You're already late for school." Nodding to Leo and Joel, he steered Andy toward their car.

His little shoulders slumped. "But, Dad, I want to watch the 'fessor investigate the springs. Maybe I can help."

"I'm sure he has enough help."

"Awwww …" Whatever Andy said was cutoff by the slam of the car door.

Claire needed to take control of this situation before it deteriorated further. "Professor, my husband needs to open his business, so if you'll follow me, I'll take you to meet Felix Riley, our mayor."

"Certainly, but before we do, may I see the infamous fish?"

Joel opened the cooler. "It's a twelve pound striped bass. Claire nearly lost him to a bigger one. Fortunately, I was in the way and able to help." He pointed to his now swollen-shut eye.

She could always count on Joel never to pass up an opportunity to poke fun at her. At least this time, he included himself, which in all actuality surprised her. That fish really did clock him. Speaking of clock, she had to get to work. The Pineridge Art Show was next week.

"We need to get you and your students settled. Joel, I'll see you later. Call me if you need anything."

"You mean for pain?" His remark made the students laugh.

This was going to be a long summer.

Patsy fumbled to unlock the gallery's front door. The frantic call from her mother had made her late and left her hands shaking. Maybe this time Dad would quit denying Mama had Alzheimer's or dementia. The name didn't matter. Getting help did. So many advances had been made in the past ten years, and Patsy couldn't understand her dad's reluctance.

Then again, maybe she could. She'd spent enough time in denial about Nathan. Her heart warmed. Of course, in his case, her fears had been unfounded. She closed the door, bending to retrieve the mail from the basket beneath the slot in the door. But Dad's refusal to face facts had to be addressed and help found for her.

Patsy didn't want to repeat this morning ever again. Mama had been frantic. She said her daddy was missing. Patsy tried to explain that he was in the office, but she wouldn't accept that. Finally, Patsy said she would find Dad and bring him home. That seemed to calm her. When she called her back five minutes later, her mother was in her right mind again.

After tossing the mail on the desk, she turned on the computer. She wanted to have some concrete information to give Dad tonight. Vince told her that her dad hadn't done more than skim the medical updates on Alzheimer's.

While she waited for the computer to boot, she sorted through the mail, setting the clay and glazing advertisements onto Claire's side of the desk. A bill from the electric company went in the "To Be Paid" basket. As Patsy lifted the next envelope, the latest copy of *Art Review* magazine stared up at her and the words "Regional Artist Reviews."

Her throat dried like the Mojave Desert. Not sure whether to open the magazine or not, she simply stared at it. Several other stories had blurbs on the cover, but she couldn't seem to make her mind register what they were about. Only the words "Regional Reviews" stood out.

Avery Chandler's review might or might not be in it. Did she really want to know? If he wanted revenge for the turkey incident, he could destroy their reputation. She'd worked for years to surmount the comparison to her mother's art, and the recognition was hard won. To think she jeopardized it in a snit of competitiveness with Claire.

The front buzzer sounded and Claire's footsteps clattered through the gallery. "I'm here. I got the students settled into four Lakeview cottages and Leo into Sweet Dreams B&B, then I took him to meet Felix. The kids opted to explore Chapel Springs."

She finally stopped for air and dropped her tote on the worktable. Reaching for the clay advertisements on the desk, her hand paused and she stared at Patsy.

"Pat-a-cake, what's wrong? You look like you've seen a ghost."

How prophetic. "I may have. At least the ghost of our careers." She held up the magazine.

The color drained from Claire's cheeks. Her eyes grew large, and she took a step back, one hand clutched at her chunky silver necklace. "What did he say?"

"I don't know. I've been too chicken to open it. Want the honors?" Patsy held out the magazine to her.

In typical fashion, Claire straightened her shoulders, grabbed it and started to rip off the protective plastic. Patsy wished she had her courage.

The gallery door buzzer rang out again.

"Hello? Anyone here? Claire?"

Patsy didn't recognize the voice and fixed her eyes on Claire. No recognition there, either, but she quirked her mouth and tossed the magazine on the worktable.

"Come on." She grabbed Patsy's arm. "We'll both go. Then neither of us will be tempted to read without the other."

"Tempted? Right. I had it in my lap for five minutes before you came in. No temptation tickled me. Go see to your fan."

Claire stepped into the gallery. Holding court in front of the vase display was Queen Trixie, outfitted in five-inch stilettos, purple leggings and a hot-pink tunic that barely covered her backside. With her, were about a dozen of her lackeys-in-waiting. Okay, Claire didn't *know* these other ladies, so technically she didn't know they were Trixie-followers, but they hung on her every word. And from her waving, bejeweled hands and her audience's gaping mouths, it was clear that she was serving up the turkey incident.

Claire groaned. How did Trixie know about that? And how was she going to keep Motor-Mouth from blabbing about the class at Henderson's? With a backward glance at Patsy, Claire sent up a quick prayer. The last thing she wanted was to hurt Patsy's feelings, and if she found out about the cooking class before Claire was ready, she wouldn't understand.

Trixie's bracelets jangled as her hands moved as fast as her mouth. "Here she is, now. Ladies, I'd like to introduce you to my good friend, Claire Bennett."

Good friend? Claire donned a salesman's smile. "I'm sorry. Have we met?" That might not have been nice, but Trixie's bug-caught-in-the-flush look was worth it. She recovered fast enough, though.

"Oh, you." She turned to her friends with a conspiratorial hand-flap. "She's always joking."

Claire ignored her. "Ladies, what brought you here?"

"Trixie's van," a tiny blue-haired grandmother said. "She's the only one of us who has a vehicle large enough for everyone."

Was she kidding? Claire stared at her. Guess not. "I see. Well, what can I do for you?"

"We wanted to see your creations." A brunette, whose buckteeth could eat corn through a picket fence, grinned at her. "You're the only famous potter I've ever met."

Famous or infamous? With Trixie, Claire was pretty sure it was the latter. "Well, ya'll look around, and let me know if you see anything you like."

As they milled about the showroom, she mulled whether to ask Trixie not to mention the cooking class. That might be like baiting a hook. It invited the fish to bite.

"Ms. Bennett? I'd like to buy this loon bowl. It would be perfect on my kitchen island."

Claire prayed Trixie wouldn't tell on her and went to help the woman. The bowl—a loon on its back with the belly hollowed out—was one of Claire's favorite to make. Each had its own personality and made people laugh. This one did with its right wing positioned to select one whatever edible tidbit the owner put in it.

After ringing up the sale, she headed to another of Trixie's friends who gestured for help. Then another. Rounding the corner of a display, she stopped cold. Ahead of her stood Patsy and Trixie, deep in conversation. The Queen of Blab had her back to Claire, but Patsy wore that distressed look, the one where her facial muscles pinched together and her lips thinned. The hurt in her eyes as they zeroed in on Claire nearly killed her. She wanted to don a hair coat or whatever those Old Testament prophets did in repentance, and she would of if she had one. Anything to wipe away her friend's pain.

Trixie turned. Her lipstick had melted into the lines around her mouth. "Here's our culinary cut-up now."

Claire's mouth opened and closed like an oxygen-starved goldfish for a moment until she finally found words. "I'll explain later," she stared pointedly at Trixie, "after we're alone."

Naturally, Trixie didn't get the hint and giggled at Patsy. "If you could have seen her on that floor—"

"Excuse us." Claire turned her back. It might be rude, but she figured Trixie wouldn't get it otherwise. The woman was thicker than two short planks. She left them and joined her friends as they continued to wander the gallery.

Crooking her finger at Patsy, Claire whispered, "I'm sorry, but I had to do it on my own. You always save me from my pickles, and I love you for it, but I had to try just this once, alone. Please don't be mad at me. I never thought it would hurt you."

Patsy's eyes softened and a tiny smile turned up one corner of her mouth. "I have spent my life rescuing you, haven't I?"

Claire nodded. "And I needed it." She told Patsy about her and Joel's fight and how she planned to prove to him she could do something right. "But maybe you should come to the next one with me. Just in case."

"I wish I could have seen you crawling under that island."

Claire drew back and folded her arms. "I merely stretched my reach a bit."

Patsy quirked her right eyebrow and shut her left eye. Claire hated it when she did that, but only because she'd spent fruitless hours, practicing it in the mirror but never could get just one brow to rise.

"All right, my shoulder was underneath the island. But I didn't crawl under it."

"That's not what Trixie said."

"I can't believe my best friend would believe that Kewpie doll over me."

Patsy's eyes grew walnut-wide as she stared past Claire. "Joel just walked in. What happened to his eye?"

"I'll tell you later." They stared at each other, lips pulled tight and eyes bulged. "*Trixie!*" If she got to Joel, Claire's loon was fried.

Her heart hammered at a frightening pace. A heart attack might not be such a bad idea right now. Joel would not be happy she spent money on a cooking class. He'd considered that a lost cause. Before he found out, she had to prove she could do it.

"Claire?" Joel's voice carried over the hum of conversation in the gallery.

Patsy pushed her one direction while she went the other. "I'll take care of Trixie. You get Joel."

Claire nodded, raised her hand high and waved. "Here I am." She sailed across the room and hooked arms with him, directing him toward the back. He frowned and tried to pull his arm loose.

"What the Sam Hill are you doing?"

"Just going where we can talk. It's too noisy in here."

"Oh. Well, I'm not surprised, given the ar—"

"And who is this handsome gentleman?" Trixie shouldered her way between Joel and Claire, her heel grinding down on Claire's ingrown toenail. Sharp pain shot up the inside of her calf and radiated to her stomach.

She clenched her teeth. "Excuse you." Giving Trixie a not-so-gentle-nudge, Claire tried to extract her foot. Her Highness completely ignored her.

How Trixie had escaped, Claire wasn't sure. She searched for Patsy, who rounded the platter display in frantic pursuit. She skidded to a halt as Joel offered his hand.

"Joel Bennett."

Trixie's false eyelashes created more breeze than a ceiling fan. "Are you Claire's brother? And what happened to your poor eye?"

This had gone far enough. "This is my husband and we need a moment, if you'll get off my toe and excuse us." Claire bumped Trixie with her hip, dislodged her foot and whipped around, pulling Joel after her. She left Patsy to deal with that ... that woman.

"Have you ever seen my mother's artwork, Trixie? Trixie?"

Claire had no idea how she managed it, but once again, Queenie wedged herself between them and patted Claire's hand. Her night-blooming jasmine perfume made Claire sneeze. "Bless you. Your adoring public is mobbing this place, my dear. You need to attend them." She slipped her arm through Joel's. "I'll keep your dear husband occupied until you return."

Claire just bet she would.

"We do have an unusual amount of customers in today," Patsy said.

"That's what I was trying to tell you, Claire." Joel pushed Trixie's arm out of his. "That art—"

"Where's Claire? I need to buy a bowl, and I want one of Patsy's small paintings." Happy Drayton's voice boomed. He'd never come in the gallery before. Always claimed he could do all the artistic stuff he wanted from his hobby store kits. But one diversion was as good as another in Claire's mind—anything to get Trixie away from Joel.

Joel! Claire spun around. Where was he? And where was Trixie? Slipperier than Houdini, she'd somehow disappeared with him. Hearing a high pitch cackle, Claire zipped around her pitcher display.

Trixie had him pinned against the counter. Poor Joel. That vixen's long nails came dangerously close to his face with every gesture. Keeping a wary eye on her hands, hopefully he didn't hear a word she said.

"Claire?" Happy Drayton's voice boomed.

Claire waved. "Over here, Happy. With Joel." Throwing a scowl at Trixie, she took her husband's arm and pulled him back to her side. "Looks like Happy finally gave up on those paint by number kits and decided to get some real art."

"G'on with ya, Claire." Happy guffawed and snorted. "You're a hoot."

"She is that and more." Trixie stepped between the men. "Why you should have seen her—"

"Trixie, did you see your friends are outside?" Patsy took her by the arm. "Poor Miss Turner doesn't look like she's feeling well."

Trixie narrowed her eyes. "Are you sure?"

Patsy, the epitome of innocence, took her by the arm. "Oh, yes indeed." She winked over her shoulder at Claire. "Why, her breathing got labored and I had to get her ..."

Whatever Pat-a-cake said to Trixie worked. She left the gallery, at least for now. Claire turned back to the men.

"You pick out what you want, Happy. We'll give you a ten percent discount. Make that twenty. Now, dear," she turned to Joel. "What brought you to here? And don't tell me your feet."

Chapter 28

Claire still didn't understand why so many people were in the gallery today, especially Joel. He never came in—unless something was wrong. A couple of butterflies took up residence in her stomach. "One more time. Why are you here in the middle of a work day?"

"The same reason all these others are here, I think," Joel said.

Maybe that fish hit him harder than she realized. "What are you talking about?"

"To congratulate you. And Patsy."

The skin around his eye had turned a brilliant shade of purple. Maybe he had a concussion and Doc missed it. She peered at his pupils, then put her hand to his forehead. It was cool and dry. "You don't feel sick. What's this about?"

He jerked his head back but grinned. "What I've been trying to tell you. That art critic. His review's in the magazine."

Patsy skidded around the platter display. A strand of hair from her cowlick stood at an angle. "Well, I finally got rid of her. I had to—oh." She glanced between Claire and Joel. "Am I interrupting something?"

"The review. Joel said the review's published."

"Oh, dear."

"No, not 'oh dear.'" Joel slapped Happy on the back. "Ol' Happy, here, called me to ask if I'd seen it yet."

"Aw, I heard about it from Ellie Grant. She gets all those highbrow magazines at the library. She read it to me. It said—"

Claire didn't wait to hear the rest. She ran to the workroom with the others on her heels. Somehow, Patsy passed her and beat her to the magazine. She snatched it up and ripped the plastic off. As she flipped the pages, the wrapper fell to the floor.

Claire grabbed Joel's hand and held tight. "Hurry up!"

Patsy stopped her frenzied page flipping and held the magazine at arms length, squinting. "Give me your readers."

Claire handed them over. With the glasses perched on the end of her nose, Patsy's eyes flew back and forth down the page. She dropped into her chair, her expression never changing. Claire picked at bits of dried paint in her cuticles, bounced her leg, and tried to remember to breathe. Still Patsy's eyes went back and forth, back and forth. Back and forth.

Finally she stopped. "Do you want to hear it?"

Claire shook her head. "Yes." She nodded. "No. I don't know." She searched Patsy's face for a hint of what was coming. "Okay, yes. Definitely, yes. I can take it."

She hoped.

Patsy cleared her throat. "A tiny hamlet resides in the mountains of north Georgia. Chapel Springs is quaint and colorful—"

"This sounds like a travel guide. Are you sure it's the review?"

Patsy air-swatted her. "It's coming. Now hush." She lifted the magazine again, pushing the glasses up a bit. "… and home to some aptly named shops: The Happy Hooker," Happy preened and scuffled his shoe back and forth. "… where one obtains fresh bait for fishing if one is so inclined; The Tome Tomb, which carries old books, including some wonderful first editions; and Dee's 'n' Doughs is where the locals gather for gossip and the most delectable pastries this side of Denmark. Nestled among these is a little gem of a gallery called The Painted Loon—"

Claire's breath caught. "Oh, my goodness." It sounded favorable. "Read faster." If she escaped this with her career intact, she'd never compete for attention again. She'd trust more—in her ability and in God.

Patsy rose and paced as she continued. "… called so, apparently, because of the artists' favorite subject. Co-owners Patsy Kowalski and Claire Bennett could be dubbed the art world's Odd Couple. However unlikely this pairing of potter and painter is, each captures the loons, among other subjects, brilliantly in their own genre."

Brilliantly? Claire felt a tiny flame of hope begin to burn.

"Kowalski, daughter of renowned artist Cooper Benson, strayed from her mother's impressionism to realism. Her incorporation of light and movement breathes life into her work. Stand in front of her painting 'Loon Island' and you'll feel the breezes blowing across the water and hear the Loons' call." Patsy paused and gave them a dramatic bow.

She deserved every word, but Claire couldn't help feeling a teensy bit jealous as she high-fived her best friend. "Ouch!" She rubbed her stinging palm.

"Hold on to your husband, girlfriend. You're up next."

Claire held her breath as Joel squeezed her fingers.

"Bennett has experienced tremendous success in glazing experimentation. The depth and clarity of color she obtains through this secret process, and the drama of its mutability are unparalleled. Never have I seen anything like it in all the galleries I've visited. Bennett free forms all her unique pieces, but it's the whimsical vases in the shapes of Mother Nature's wild creatures that define this talented artist."

Talented? He called her talented. Claire's pulse beat all the way to her fingertips. Was it all right to feel proud over the review? She glanced at Joel. By his huge grin, she guessed it was okay.

"Vivid colors and imaginative form are the bywords for this extraordinary duo's art. I could rave on, but instead would encourage you to visit The Painted Loon. After my sojourn there, I understood their penchant for loons. Eccentric and unconventional, Bennett and Kowalski left a lasting impression on me."

"We certainly did that. I wonder if his stitches are out yet?" Patsy chuckled.

Claire threw her arms around Joel's neck. "I can't believe he didn't flay us alive."

"I can." His breath was warm in her ear. "I'm proud of you, babe." He leaned back, tipped her chin up, and planted a big kiss on her. She'd always read about love shining in a person's eyes, but she'd never really believed it. Just before Joel kissed her, she saw it.

How could one man be such a contradiction?

"You made Beethoven's Beans." Delighted, Claire lifted the fragrant casserole out of the oven, detecting the mouthwatering aroma of molasses and kielbasa. "I hope the professor and those kids get a chance to taste these before the others devour every last smidgen." She covered the pan with foil and tied it up in an insulated carrier. "After all, this shindig's in their honor."

Was it her imagination or did Joel's chest puff out a bit as he picked up the quilted tote?

"There should be plenty. I asked Patsy to make up a batch, too," he said. "You ready?"

"Just let me see to Shiloh while you sneak out. I'll be right behind you." Using a stick of doggie-pepperoni as enticement, she led the mastiff to his bed. "Here you go, boy. We'll be back soon."

She couldn't help laughing at the look on Shiloh's face. He dropped the treat on his bed, while the droop of his jowls gave new meaning to the expression "hang-dog." She tossed him a second doggie treat for good measure and met Joel on the front porch.

"Did you give Shi—"

"Yes, two."

"Good. Now, tell me about this professor. I didn't get to talk to him yesterday. You shuttled him off before I could say two words."

They set off at a leisurely pace. Claire loved evenings like this one. It was perfect for strolling. The sun wouldn't set until eight-thirty, but the air had cooled to a gentle sixty-eight degrees.

"He's ..." She searched for words that wouldn't raise any red flags. "... very interesting, I guess, if you can understand all the geology-speak." That seemed neutral enough. At least it earned a chuckle.

"Those academia types always have their heads in the clouds. Remember that writer who came here every summer a few years back? He was always trying to impress everyone."

"That guy was a novelist not a teacher. And he wasn't *always* trying to impress."

"I don't know what you'd call it, but every time I saw him, he'd ask if I read any of his books."

"That's called marketing, and it's no different than when you ask Warren if he's tried the new tackle you stocked."

Joel snorted. Now she'd have to think up some way to stroke his ego. *Men.* Up ahead, Earl and Kelly came out their front door. Kelly carried a box with a towel draped over the top. Claire waved and they fell into step with her and Joel.

"Hmm." Kelly sniffed the air. "Is that Joel's famous beans I smell?"

Claire could have hugged her for not asking about Leo. She didn't need that touchy topic reopened. "It sure is. What about you? Did you bring your potato salad?"

Joel and Earl dropped behind them, talking about fishing. They didn't seem to know any other topic.

"Not this time. I tried something new. Healthier."

"Healthy's no fun."

Kelly's throaty chuckle teased.

"Well, are you going to tell or keep it a secret?"

She shook her head. "It's one of those things that doesn't sound inviting, but once you taste it, you'll want more."

"I can vouch for that," Earl said.

"You can tell me. I promise I'll try it." Out of childhood habit, she stepped over a crack in the sidewalk.

"You better tell her," Joel said. "She'll badger you until you do. Claire can't stand being on the outside of a secret."

Looking back, she scrunched her nose at him. "Doesn't matter one bit to me. I can wait. I'll find out soon enough, anyway." They rounded the corner onto Church Street. "Of course, *if* it would help me find it on the table so I can sample it, you might want to give me a hint. At least what color dish you have it in."

Joel and Earl's laughter caused a few heads to turn in their direction. Patsy waved from the church steps. Leaving the men to fend for themselves for the moment, Claire followed Kelly as she joined the ladies inside. She still hadn't removed the towel that hid her secret. Still, the feel-good aroma of Potluck gave Claire a warm hug as she sidled up behind Patsy, who placed serving spoons in the various dishes.

"Psst, Patsy."

"Hey, girl—"

"Shh. Be sure to get a good look at Kelly's dish and tell me what color it is."

"What?"

"Quiet. You heard me." Claire leaned closer. "She made something new and wouldn't tell me what it is."

Gaping, Patsy planted one hand on the side of her face. "Well, I neveh! Of all the noive."

Claire wrinkled her nose. "Smart aleck. Never mind, then. I'll find it myself."

"No time." Patsy pointed over Claire's shoulder. "Felix is here with the professor."

Felix ushered Leo over to meet Pastor Seth while the students zeroed in on the buffet tables like ants at a picnic. Snatches of conversations rose and fell over the clink of serving spoons. Claire wandered around the perimeter of the room, stopping to chat with Ellie for a moment, then continued to slowly make her way toward the men.

She'd had the strangest dream last night. She stood between Joel and Leo on the dock near the day-launch ramp, talking. She didn't remember what they talked about, but she was trying to make a decision. All the while Aunt Lola stood at her side, whispering in her ear. The problem was, Claire couldn't make out what she said, but Aunt Lola had been clearly agitated, plucking at her rings and necklace. When Claire awoke, her aunt continued to hover at the edge of her thoughts.

Felix's barking laugh echoed. "Claire sure laid one on ya this time, Joel. I'm surprised you can get life insurance. Well, hey, Claire. Didn't see you there."

Sure you didn't. If Felix didn't shut up, not only would Joel prefer he had another wife, Leo wouldn't want anything to do with her, either. This called for drastic measures.

"Felix, I believe I saw Eileen set one of her fresh peach pies on the buffet table."

Who knew rotundity could move that fast?

With Felix gone, Claire turned back to Leo and Joel. "So, Professor, tell me, how's the investigation going?"

Leo stuck one hand in his pocket, and the other grasped his unlit pipe, which he used to punctuate his words. "We're in the preliminary stages of researching the surrounding topography with GPR." He pointed the pipe at the floor. "That's ground penetrating radar. It should reveal the subterranean support system, the angular unconformity."

Confused, Claire stared at him, and Joel scowled. If Leo noticed, he didn't try to enlighten any of them but carried on.

"Depending on what we find, we'll then search for cataclastic rock, which would evidence earthquake activity, examine the density current, the lake's feeder stream for bed-load until we reach a conclusion. Though yours is rare, most often in cases like this it's diastrophism."

Dis-what?

Joel recovered first. "I think it's time to eat. Professor? Claire?" He waited for Leo to precede them, then took her arm and held her back before escorting her to the end of the buffet line. Leo had joined Felix near the front.

"I told you. He's just like that writer fellow. Full of himself."

Others joined the line behind them. Pulling her arm from Joel's grasp, she frowned. Two dozen or more people stood between Leo and her. At least he couldn't overhear them. "He isn't either. He's just, just—"

"Academia. An obnoxious academic."

The line crawled. The smell of potato casserole wafted over them. Behind her, Earl grumbled, albeit good-naturedly, "Get a move on up there."

Claire shuffled forward. "Joel, just because you didn't go to college—"

"That's not it."

"Will you please let me finish?" They reached the table, and she picked up a plate.

Joel snatched one off the next pile, clattering it against his fork and knife. "Keep your voice down. You're yelling."

"I'm not yelling. We're simply having a difference of opinion."

"Well, this isn't the place." He scowled at her.

"Fine. We'll discuss it later." With everyone in a hurry to eat, she plopped a spoonful of whatever it was in the first dish onto her plate. Keeping his glare directed at her, Joel followed suit.

"There's nothing to discuss."

Moving down the table, another casserole looked interesting, and a helping landed next to the first mound. "Right. I know. Your way or the highway."

A third selection slipped on her plate, its long cheesy strands snapping off as it dropped. Joel didn't even look as he dished the same onto his. Claire paused. Wait a minute. That was squash casserole. Joel hated squash. He hated all vegetables except lettuce, corn, and tomatoes. He could cook veggies but wouldn't eat them. She grabbed a second spoonful.

"That's not true, Claire. I'm very open." He dropped another spoonful of the squash onto his plate.

"You're about as open as Fort Knox." Stifling a smirk, she served herself a large helping of broccoli salad and waited. He did the same. He still hadn't noticed. She couldn't believe it. Okay, what else was on this table? She bypassed the meats and reached Kelly's casserole dish, not believing her good fortune at recognizing the pottery. Zucchini casserole. With summer squash. Oh, how delightful. She inhaled, detecting garlic and parmesan. Gleefully, she dished herself a large spoonful. Joel was on her heels and a helping of zucchini landed on his plate.

"How can you say that?"

"Easy. You refuse to talk about relationships, emotions, feelings, dreams … shall I go on?" Lifting the serving fork, she heaped a pile of greens onto her plate. She nearly laughed out loud when Joel did the same. She couldn't wait to see his face when he discovered it.

"That's a load of codswallop."

Claire paused, serving spoon filled with black-eyed peas balanced midair. "Really? And when was the last time we discussed feelings?"

Joel scowled. She turned the spoon upside down on her plate, scooped up another spoonful and held it out for him. He took the spoon, dumped it on his plate.

"Hey, speed the line up. We're hungry back here."

Happy to oblige, Claire chose a few more selections to delight a vegetarian's sensibilities. It was hard to hold in her laughter as Joel matched her spoon for spoon all down the line.

"You women listen to those TV shows and mess up perfectly good marriages with all this 'share your feelings with me' hogwash."

They crossed to the dessert table.

"Joel, if you don't share, how am I supposed to know if …" she searched for a good example …"I said something that hurt you?"

"You never have, so don't worry about it."

Fine. She examined gooey cakes and selected a chocolate-frosted brownie with caramel drizzled over the top. Her Mr.-Vanilla-Only grabbed one, too. Oh, it was too delicious, and she didn't mean the brownie. She picked up a glass of sweet tea as she passed the beverage table on her way to find a seat.

With her eyes wide and hopefully looking innocent, she turned to Joel. "Where would you like to sit?"

He nodded in the direction of Nathan.

"Hey, you two." Nathan rose and took Claire's plate for her, setting it on the table.

"Thanks. Where's Patsy?"

"She's in the kitchen. She'll be right back."

Joel set his plate down and sat staring at it.

"What's wrong, Joel?" Claire tried not to. Really. But the shock on his face made her laugh out loud.

He frowned at her. "Why'd you put all this junk on my plate?"

Chapter 29

Patsy draped a towel around her neck to absorb the perspiration. The spa's aerobics class was tougher than she'd imagined, but to her amazement, energy flowed through her muscles. "I'm going to enjoy these classes … once I catch my breath."

"I'm glad you liked it." Lydia mopped her forehead with a terry wristband. "It's a fun way to keep in shape. Now get a shower and spend some time in our Jacuzzi. That way you won't be sore tomorrow."

"Easy for you to say." Claire, her hair plastered to her neck, limped toward the bench where their bags laid.

Lydia stopped her. "Please see Doc Benson about that ankle. I want to be sure it's not sprained. Have him send me the bill."

Claire waved her away with a wry grimace. "It's not your fault, and I'm sure it's just twisted. Really, the fall from an aerobics pad isn't far. Besides, the wedding shower is tomorrow. No time to see Doc."

Poor Claire. Even as a kid, she had balance problems. She kept the training wheels on her bike long after the rest of them abandoned theirs. Patsy grabbed both their totes as they headed for the showers. Bev tagged along behind them, an expensive looking towel draped around her neck. Patsy still wasn't comfortable in her company after the way she flirted with Nathan. It didn't matter that it hadn't been about him. It sill rankled. But for Drew and the sake of peace, she kept her feelings to herself.

"See you in the Jacuzzi," she said. After turning on the water, she stepped into the shower. She turned the faucet to cool and let the soothing spray bring her body temperature back down. In the stall next to her, Claire's singing carried over the sound of the spray. She may be a klutz, but she was the best alto in the church choir.

More than ready for the Jacuzzi's muscle-relaxing massage, Patsy hurried through her shower, slipped on a bathing suit and sank into the bubbling water. She leaned back and closed her eyes. A jet pulsated into the small of her back, sending shivers of elation through her muscles. Lydia's spa was a godsend for Chapel Springs. And so was Lydia, herself. The spa offered services they'd never had before, the town hadn't looked this good in years, and the tourist trade picked up more than anyone expected. But most of all, they all gained a wonderful new friend. Patsy smiled to herself. Lydia was the most gracious woman she knew, forgiving them for their misguided suspicions, and her gentle teasing dispelled the last vestiges of guilt.

Water splashed and waves rose around her chin as Claire and Bev lowered themselves into its liquid warmth. Something bumped Patsy's side. Opening one eye, she found Claire staring at her.

"What are you looking so pleased about?"

Patsy moved her legs under the water, letting them float over a stream of bubbles. "How great the village looks. It reminds me of how it looked when we were kids. Remember the Easter parades?" She turned her head to include Bev in the conversation. "The town put spring flowers in the lamppost baskets, and we wore our new dresses and hats. It was still traditional to wear hats on Easter up here in the mountains."

"There wasn't a dirty or skinned knee visible," Claire added. "We'd been scrubbed shiny just like the lampposts. Patsy loved it, but I hated it. I was a tomboy."

Bev gave a ladylike snort that sounded more like a cat, sneezing. "Why am I not surprised?"

Claire ignored her. "When did we stop having those, Patsy? Or maybe I should ask why?"

"I don't know. It's sad how some traditions seem to fade away. I'd love to see it revived. It celebrates the most important day of the year."

Bev sent her a look that Patsy could only describe as condescending. "You people bring religion into everything."

You people?

Next to her, Claire sat up straight. "What do you mean by that?"

"You said it's the most important day of the year. What about birthdays? To me, my Andy's birthday tops any other day."

Not sure how to answer, Patsy gave Bev a tentative smile. "Birthdays are important. But all Christianity hinges on Easter."

Bev shook her head, her short tight curls bouncing as she did. "That's not even right. Easter was a pagan holiday, borrowed by the church."

Barely controlled anger lay just below the surface of her voice, making Patsy squirm. Last Sunday, poor little Andy, his eyes filled with tears, told her in Sunday school that his mama and daddy argued about her not coming to church. He was worried about her. Couldn't Bev see that?

"I wish you'd come sometime. I think you'd find—"

She cut Patsy off. "What I find are people who turn down their noses at me because I don't go. Oh, they were happy enough to let me work on the town, but other than you two and maybe Lydia, no one's inviting me to dinner."

"Have you invited them?" Claire asked.

"I don't really know anyone other than the Dee's 'n' Doughs bunch. I'm not sure I want to. Not if they have the same attitude Drew's adopted."

He must be the real reason for Bev's anger. "Do you want to talk about it?"

Her red face reflected more than the heat from the Jacuzzi. "He's turned into a Jesus freak. All he can talk about is going to church. It's Jesus this and Jesus told him that. And that junk about wives submitting to their husbands? It's outdated and violates human rights. I won't have it." Bev shut her eyes and leaned her head back.

Patsy nudged Claire as she opened her mouth. Now was not the time for a debate on Biblical principles. Thankfully she got the message. Patsy followed Bev's example, letting the pulsating water relax them all. After a few moments, Claire's toe tapped Patsy's foot. She pointed to Bev. A drop of water slid down her cheek. Was it a tear or just a splash from the Jacuzzi jets?

Compassion overruled Patsy's distrust. "Bev? We're your friends. If we can help ..."

Her eyes remained shut. "I'm thinking of going back to Boston."

Patsy was speechless. Would she take Andy with her? Drew would be devastated. He adored Bev, as impossible as that seemed. Didn't she love him? The silence grew suffocating. "Are you sure?"

"No. But I'm thinking about it."

"What about Andy?"

"I don't know." Her voice was so soft Patsy could barely hear her over the churning water. "I only know I can't go on like this. Drew and I haven't had a conversation that hasn't ended in an argument in the last two months."

Patsy reached out her hand and touched Bev's arm, waiting for her to look at her. Finally she opened her eyes.

"Bev, I know you don't want to be pushed, and I won't. But would you mind if I prayed for you? Not here, I mean privately at home."

With a barely perceivable nod, Bev gave permission. "If you want to. I don't put a lot of credence in it, though."

"Didn't he used to have a rock group?" Claire asked.

"What?" Bev scowled, but Patsy sucked her lips in to keep from laughing.

"Credence. He had a rock group in the sixties and seventies. Credence Clearwater Revival. I think they broke up in seventy-two."

Bless Claire's heart. She was the best one for lightening a somber mood.

Bev stared at her and then laughed. "You're one in a million, Claire." She rose out of the water. "I'd better get going. Andy will be home from school soon."

Patsy followed her, grabbing her towel as she stepped out. "Me, too. We're taking my folks out to dinner tonight."

Claire splashed water at Patsy. "Well, hang on. I'm coming, too."

Ten minutes later, the three exited the spa. A wall of warm humid air smacked Patsy in the face and a ring of sweat formed under her arms. By the time she walked home, she'd need another shower.

Drew's car pulled under the porte-cochere. He rolled down the window. "Honey, you left these in the visor. I thought you might need them." He held out a glasses case.

For a long moment, Bev didn't move. "If I'd wanted them, I would have remembered to bring them."

Drew shifted in his seat, glancing first at Bev and then at Patsy and Claire. He raised a hand in greeting. "Hey. Uh, so what do you want me to do with them?"

"Whatever you want." She turned away from the car. Patsy's heart hurt for Drew as he drove away, his thoughtful act thrown back in his face.

As the three walked home, Bev fumed. "See what I mean? He's so controlling. *He* thinks I should wear reading glasses, just because some quack Optometrist prescribed them. Every chance he gets he pushes them at me."

After Bev left them, Claire exploded. "I can't believe she couldn't see

Drew's kindness for what it was. If that were me, Joel would say they're my glasses, and tell me to go get them."

"It shows you how important communication is between a husband and wife. If Bev explained how she feels instead of expecting Drew to understand her, I think she'd get further. I know Nathan and I fell into that mistake."

Claire sputtered air through her lips. "Why are you looking at me? Joel won't discuss feelings—'real men' and all that rubbish. If I try to tell him how I feel, he calls it psychobabble." Her shoulders rose then fell. "After a while, you quit trying."

Poor Claire. Joel did have a problem with sharing his feelings. "Nathan's willing to talk to him about that, honey."

She shook her head. "I don't give it much credence, as Bev would say, but tell Nathan to have at it. In the meantime, I still have my eyes open." Claire waved over her shoulder and walked away.

Lord, please watch over her. Keep her from making any foolish decisions.

Chapter 30

The woodsy aroma of smoked meat made Patsy's mouth water the moment they stepped inside Adam's Rib. They didn't come to the upscale Pineridge restaurant often, preferring The Rib Cage in Chapel Springs. Jake Dawson made the best barbeque sauces in the South, and the ribs were succulent and tender. However, Adam's Rib was a close second, and the restaurant was a client of Nathan's.

"Doesn't that make you hungry, Mama?"

Her mother shrugged one shoulder. "Jake's is my favorite place. My daddy's, too."

Patsy blinked in surprise. Her grandfather had died years before they built Restaurant Square in Chapel Springs. Dad didn't seem to notice, or else he was still ignoring Mama's symptoms, too busy waving at friends he spied in the restaurant. Nathan had a slight frown creasing his brow. He caught Mama's slip-up.

The restaurant's owner, Adam, greeted them personally and escorted them to a corner table with a view of the lake's south shore through one window and the forest through another.

"Look at that." Patsy pointed to both views. "I can never decide which I love most—our sunrises over the lake, or the way the setting sun casts interesting shadows as it sinks below the forest. The lower it slides, the more color variation in the trees."

Trey Appling arrived with an order pad, and pulled a pencil from behind his ear.

"Hey, Trey," Nathan said. "Your dad told me you were named the high school's starting quarterback for next year. Congratulations."

Trey's beautiful smile lit his face. Somehow, he'd avoided the teenage acne, and now with his braces gone, Patsy could see why the girls all adored him.

"Thanks, Mr. Kowalski." He scratched his head with the pencil tip. "Now what kind of ribs do y'all want tonight? Beef or pork? We have baby back, spare, and short. What's your preference?"

They gave him their order, and a young girl brought their drinks. A moment later, Trey returned with a complimentary platter of appetizers containing fried okra, stuffed mushrooms, catfish fingers, and onion strings.

Mama reached for a mushroom cap. Her hand hovered over several choices before settling on the fattest one. She considered it for a moment then popped it in her mouth. A speck of its breading caught in the corner of her mouth, and she licked it away. "Kelly and Earl raised that boy right."

Leaving the catfish for Nathan and her dad, Patsy took some of the sweet, crispy onion strings. Slightly greasy and hot, it crunched and dissolved on her tongue. She wiped her fingers on her napkin. Mama seemed fine now. She didn't miss a beat as the conversation flowed from the latest virus sweeping through the schools to the review of Patsy and Claire's art. When Dad told a story about their early-married life, Mama added comments and laughed when he got flustered. A couple of stories later, she nudged him.

"Let me out. All this giggling has had an effect. I need to use the ladies room before dinner arrives."

She hadn't been gone a minute before Trey served their dinner, and Amanda assisted, her eyes on Trey while he explained the various sauces from sweet to very hot. That girl had a crush going on.

"Let's wait another minute for your mother, then tuck into these ribs," Dad said, eyeing his plate.

Mama seemed to be taking her sweet time. "Dad, let's go ahead and eat before it gets cold. Say the blessing, please."

Dad prayed, and he and Nathan dug into their ribs. Patsy nibbled on one while keeping an eye on the hallway leading to the restrooms. What could be keeping her so long? Dad didn't seem the least bit concerned.

"Excuse me." Patsy set her napkin on the table beside her plate. "I'm going to see what's keeping Mama."

Nathan's hand stopped her. He leaned over and whispered in her ear. "Don't you think you should let your dad handle this?"

"He isn't handling it. That's the point." Her dad dipped a finger in a sauce bowl, licked it, and then spooned some over a rib. With his attention completely focused on eating, he hadn't even heard them. He's probably turned down his hearing aid, or could he be purposely ignoring them?

"Sweetheart, you can't fix everyone's problems. Your dad isn't going to wake up to this until you back off."

"She isn't your mother." As soon as the words left her mouth, Patsy wished she could snatch them back. The hurt in Nathan's eyes made her wince. "I'm sorry, honey. I know you love Mama, too. But I can't sit here and do nothing. She's been gone nearly fifteen minutes."

Before Patsy could slide out of the booth, her dad lifted his head from his plate and scowled at her mother's untouched one. A bit of sauce clung to his mustache.

"Where's your mother?"

Nathan nudged her with his elbow. Okay, he was right. Dad noticed. She blotted her lips with the napkin. "Do you want me to go see?"

"Tell her supper's going cold."

He continued to mumble as she hurried to the restroom. As she pulled the door open, silence greeted her. She entered the cold, tiled room and bent over. Not a single foot was visible under any of the three stalls. Heading back to the table, Patsy hoped she'd missed seeing her mother return, but her dad and Nathan were alone. She dropped into her seat and stared at her plate in dismay.

Dad looked past her. "Did you find her?"

"No."

"Could she have gone out on the porch?" Dad twisted his head toward the entrance as if expecting to see Mama walk through it.

"What would she be doing there?" Nathan asked, his voice soft and soothing.

"Who knows why Cooper does what she does? Her eccentricity is part of her charm." Dad picked up a rib. "She sometimes likes to sit and enjoy the view." He took a large bite.

Patsy pursed her lips. "Mama said she was hungry. She knew the food was about to be served." He had his head buried—again. Where she wasn't sure.

"Dad—"

Nathan frowned and shook his head. He mouthed, "Wait."

How could she wait? And wait for what? For Mama to get hurt? A small smile pulled at the corner of Nathan's mouth. He flicked his eyes toward her dad. Patsy followed his gaze.

Dad stood beside the table, his napkin hanging from his belt. "I'll find her." He walked to the front.

Nathan's hand on her knee stopped her from following. "Honey, let your dad do it." He chose a roll from the breadbasket and took a bite.

She picked up her water but set it back down when its contents threatened to splash over the rim. "I hope he sees now that Mama has a problem. The other day she didn't know me."

"A little confusion is expected as people grow older. It doesn't necessarily mean she has Alzheimer's." Nathan carefully wiped his hands and mouth with his napkin.

Patsy leaned her head back, closed her eyes, and counted to ten. "Nathan, she isn't old enough to have that kind of confusion … unless it's dementia or Alzheimer's. I've researched this."

"I understand that, honey, but you have got to let your dad do this."

She knew he was right, but it was so hard to watch Mama lose her mental capacity. As a doctor, Dad should know there were medicines out there now to help. So why was he ignoring it? They sat in silence as Nathan finished his dinner. Like Mama's, Patsy's sat untouched.

He approached the table, his napkin no longer hanging from his belt and his calm façade broken. "She's not outside. Adam said he'd look for her, too. I don't understand why she would wander off."

"Because—" Patsy clamped her mouth shut at Nathan's pointed glance. He rose and put his arm around her dad's shoulder. "Let's wait and see if Adam finds her."

Dad sat drumming his fingers on the table, one after the other as if ticking off time. With each one, the water in his glass rippled. He eyed them. "Daughter, has this happened before?"

Thank you, Lord. She nodded. "Last time, at least she was in Chapel Springs. Glen Tabor found her. She told him someone moved her house."

"Excuse me, Dr. Benson." Adam approached the table. "Your wife isn't on the premises. I've even been up to the office to see if she was there."

Patsy's heart fell. The tears she'd been holding back welled. She opened her purse, searching for the hankie Mama always insisted a lady carry. It wasn't there. She pawed through the bottom, but found nothing. She picked up her napkin, and as she dabbed her eyes, Dad patted her shoulder.

"We'll find her. After all, this isn't some big city. Everyone in Pineridge knows your mother."

As they followed Dad to the car, Nathan put his arm around her shoulders and squeezed. "I'm right sometimes, you know."

She smiled up at him and nodded. "It's just so hard."

He leaned down and kissed her. "I love your tender heart, but you aren't Superwoman."

"I'm not? Well, don't tell Claire."

Nathan chuckled. "Now, there's one person you may have to continue keeping an eye on."

"Come on, you two. We better find your mother before she realizes we haven't."

Chapter 31

Claire stared blindly at her Bible camouflaged behind a magazine while Joel watched the ballgame on TV. If he would come to church with her, he'd change and everything would be perfect. God would be happy with her choice, and she wouldn't need the professor.

She peered again at the passage on marriage—yoked, the Bible called it. She glanced at Joel. He was yoked to the game. They must play those subliminal messages about beer or potato chips or something to get men so channeled. Maybe that's what she should do—read verses softly out loud while he watched ...

"What in the Sam Hill are you doing, Claire?"

She stopped reading mid-word. Joel clicked the mute button on the remote and stared at her. She set the Southern Living magazine on her lap, her Bible beneath it, and blinked at him, hoping she looked convincing. "Doing?"

He lowered his chin and peered at her through bushy eyebrows. "Don't give me that innocent stuff." He laughed then reached over and snatched the magazine away. "Ha! I knew that didn't sound like a Southern Living article you were babbling. You're about as subtle as a bear in a trout stream, you know that?" He tossed the magazine back in her lap.

Her neck grew warm. "If you'd go to church with me, I wouldn't have to resort to subterfuge."

With a rush of air exploding from his lungs, Joel flipped up the footrest on his recliner and grabbed the remote. "Give it a rest, Claire. I'm not going to church. Not now, not next week. Not ever. You knew that when we got married. No use trying to change me now." He cranked up the volume on the TV.

"But Joel, God—"

"Nip it, Claire. End of discussion." The volume grew louder.

That went well. She closed her Bible, and with the Southern Living open to page thirty-eight, she stared at it, no longer seeing the beautiful garden. Now what? Joel needed some of the rough edges knocked off him, his stubbornness for one, and his temper for another. Plus he didn't own an ounce of patience. God could fix all that, but how could she get him to church? How did missionaries go about getting stubborn, thickheaded natives to God?

Claire turned into Patsy's and in her excitement over the bridal shower, ran over some of the boxwoods lining the driveway. Her firstborn—getting married! Unable to help what she knew must be a silly grin on her face, she jumped out of the car and propped up the hedge, stomping the dirt around its base. One broken branch listed to the left. Oh well, she'd buy Patsy a new one.

After brushing her hands together, she set a box filled with door prizes and games for the bridal shower on Patsy's front porch, rapped on the door, and then went back to her Trailblazer for the next load. The warmth of the late afternoon sun and the bright blue sky felt like God's blessing on the day. Using her hip to keep the passenger door open, she reached in for the table's centerpiece.

"You're early. Need a hand?" Patsy called out from the porch.

"Put that box by the door inside then come get the cake. Wait till you see it. Dee did a fantastic job." It would taste as good as it looked if she could go by its wonderful smell. It had filled the car with the sugary redolence of almond and vanilla, reminding Claire she'd skipped lunch.

She was glad the shower was today. It provided a distraction from the stress Joel put her under, not to mention Patsy's trying to convince Doc that her mama had Alzheimer's. Whatever happened to their nice quiet lives? Though Patsy tried to hide it, Claire detected the strain in her dear friend's eyes.

She slid the centerpiece aside and lifted the cake out of the car, handing it to Patsy. "How are your folks today?" She reached back for the floral arrangement and the bag containing the decorations.

"Better. Both of them are napping."

"When did you find her?"

"Not until this morning."

"Good grief, what happened to her?" She followed Patsy up the walk. "Doc must have been really shaken up."

"He was and finally gets it, but I feel bad for him. He was frantic when we couldn't find her, sure that someone had kidnapped her. We were up all night."

"I wish this wedding shower weren't today."

"I'm fine. I took a nap. Besides, I'm excited about this. It's our first wedding." Patsy's tired but sappy grin matched the way Claire felt. Well, not tired but definitely sappy.

She set her bag on the sideboard in Patsy's dining room and laid the centerpiece on the table. The floral arrangements were the one place Sandi let her mother have her way. All Claire had to do was pick it up. At least Zoe had good taste. Fresh red cymbidium orchids, and some white lily-type flower Claire didn't recognize, nestled in turquoise tulle inside a white straw container. It was interpretative of the bridesmaids' hats.

"So, tell me where and how you finally found her." Claire fluffed the netting where it had been squished against the side of the box.

"Max called us."

She turned the arrangement forty-five degrees to the left. "Our Max from the art supply?"

Patsy nodded. "He found her cold and shivering on the doorstep when he arrived this morning. When he woke her, she had no idea why she was there or how she even got there. It broke his heart when she began to cry and told him she thought she might be losing her mind."

She wasn't the only one. Moisture stung the back of Claire's eyes. How devastating to realize that soon your lifetime of memories would be lost.

"We hurried over and picked her up. Dad's finally agreed to take her to a specialist. They have an appointment with one of his colleagues tomorrow." Patsy dug around in the box of prizes. "So, what games do you have planned?"

"If I tell you, you'll cheat." Claire moved the box. "Quit peeking. I need to get these decorations hung."

They moved into the kitchen, where Nathan was pouring a cup of coffee.

"Hey, Nathan."

He looked more relaxed than Claire had seen him in months—

gone were the tight lines around his mouth. Apparently, Patsy was right about no secrets and more communication. At least it worked for them. If only Joel would learn to share his feelings.

"Hey there, Clairey-girl." He encircled one arm around Patsy, who smiled indulgently at her Romeo. "Do you two need me for anything before I go?"

Claire turned on the teakettle.

"We've got it covered." Patsy kissed his cheek. "Go have fun with Joel."

Claire opened a canister and pulled out a teabag. White with pear? Wrinkling her nose, she replaced it. "What do you boys have planned tonight?" She found a bag of Constant Comment and dropped it in a cup. As it brewed, she savored the rising orange aroma.

"We're going to get some pizza and play Spades with Earl and Glen." He sauntered out, his coffee still on the counter. In the doorway, he turned around, came back with a sheepish grin, picked up his cup, and left.

Patsy shook her head and Claire chuckled. "Does he do that often?"

"All the time." Patsy looked at the kitchen clock. "We'd better get cracking with the decorations. We'll have just enough time to eat dinner before everyone arrives."

With a nod to July fourth, Sandi had chosen red and turquoise for the wedding. Together, they'd searched Pineridge and the Internet until they found the perfect shades. Claire handed a package of balloons to Patsy. Once the turquoise ones were blown up, she clustered them with red crepe paper roses and white wedding bells. When they finished, the living and dining rooms looked festive.

Claire chewed a hangnail. "I hope everything meets with Zoe's approval. Each time we've spoken about the wedding plans, she's so picky. Makes me wonder if Sandi was adopted. They aren't at all alike."

"Don't worry about her, Claire. It's Sandi you have to please, and she loves you." Patsy gathered bits of string and tossed them in the trash. "I remember when we worried about diaper rash and teething. Now our first nestling is getting married."

"I'm glad it's Charlie and not one of the girls. This way, at least we get some practice in first."

"Come on, let's eat. They'll be here soon. Is Adrianna coming?"

"She's got some big presentation or something in Nashville. She sent a gift and will be here for the wedding."

Patsy removed two plates from the fridge, each containing a delectable looking salad. Claire's salads were plain old lettuce, tomatoes, cucumber, and if they had one, an avocado. Patsy turned salad making into an art form. Field greens, she called them. Besides the normal vegetables in a salad, she added walnuts, feta cheese, palm hearts—Claire poked her fork around the plate—and apples and berries. She took a forkful. Delicious. A few slices of grilled chicken topped the plate.

"Did you make the dressing? It tastes like raspberries." She forked another mouthful and munched happily.

"I'd offer you the recipe, but how about I make you some instead?" Patsy quirked one corner of her mouth upward. "You'd only try to substitute something totally inedible for one of the ingredients."

"You tease now but just wait till I finish my classes," Claire said around another mouthful of salad.

"Oh, honey, I'm sorry. I know you're trying hard."

Unsure of exactly why she was trying, Claire scooped up another bite. Joel didn't care about her lack of kitchen savvy. Just the opposite. It gave him the chance to do what he loved. He should have been a chef, but his daddy wouldn't hear of it. Called it a sissy-boy occupation. Ha! He never saw Emeril in action. *Bam!*

"What are you smiling about?"

"Joel's dad. Remember when Joel said something to him about going to culinary school? Roland hit the ceiling. I was thinking if Emeril had been on TV back then instead of Julia Child, he might have changed his mind."

Patsy picked up their plates. "What was it your Aunt Lola always said? Were ifs and buts candy and nuts ..."

"We'd all have a Merry Christmas," they finished together, laughing.

The doorbell rang. Hoping it was Sandi and not her mother, Claire reached for the plates Patsy held. "I'll take these to the kitchen. You get the door."

Patsy pulled them back and turned away. "Nothing doing. You get the door."

"But it's your house."

"It's your wedding."

"Rat."

"Brat."

Claire stomped to the foyer. Through the front door's sidelight she could see Sandi. Relieved, she threw the door open wide. She adored

Charlie's choice for a bride.

Sandi hugged her and whispered, "Did I make it here before my mother? I hurried, but got behind a slow truck."

She was going to be a wonderful daughter-in-law. "You did and I love you. I'm sorry I'm such a case of nerves."

"No worry. Mother does that to most people. You just need to stand up to her."

Easy for her to say. She didn't see the unspoken challenge. Zoe had drawn a line in the guacamole, and Claire didn't dare back down. Her— no, not just hers—the town's reputation depended on her.

She gulped and ushered Sandi into the large family room, where they planned for her to sit on the hearth to open her gifts. Patsy joined them, carrying a tray of cups.

"Chai?"

Sandi took one. "Hmm, smells heavenly, thank you, Patsy. I appreciate you hosting the shower for me. The decorations are perfect." She sat on her appointed pillow. "By the way, has the professor and his team made any headway on the Springs yet? I hope they're done by the wedding."

Claire shook her head. "I haven't heard anything. I'm going to look in on him, uh, them tomorrow. Oh, there's the doorbell again."

She ignored Patsy's pursed lips and let their guests in, thankful that it was Lydia and Lacey along with two of Sandi's friends. The more people who arrived before Zoe the better. She might be accustomed to being the big fish in her small Iowa pool, but she'd jumped into Claire's pond. And Claire's fellow pondites could be piranhas when one of their own was threatened.

As the house filled, the noise level rose with laughter and chatter. Just the way Claire liked it. She knew most of the young women, having met them over the years. Megan and Melissa snuck in a few minutes ago, surprising her. They hadn't confirmed if they could make it— something about passing a test first. They must have done all right on it. But what test could they both have at the same time? They didn't have the same classes.

"Megan, what were you and—" Claire froze. A woman dressed in the most expensive suit she'd ever laid eyes on stood in the arched doorway, waiting. For what? To be noticed?

It had to be Zoe Walker. She was a bit chubbier than Claire had expected, but that suit hid it well. It was the double chin that gave it away.

Fingers tapped her chin. "Close your mouth and go welcome her," Patsy said.

Welcome the enemy? Oops. She had to stop that. It wasn't fair to Sandi. Putting on her best smile and what Joel dubbed her "game face" Claire approached her.

"You must be Zoe. I'm Claire. Welcome."

Zoe stared at her.

"Charlie's mom."

Her gaze roamed from Claire's hair to her feet and back to her face. "Oh, of course. Claire. No one answered the door. I had to let myself in."

Late May in the north Georgia Mountains held warm days, but the temperature just dropped by a good twenty degrees. Zoe gave Claire a brain freeze. She slid one foot behind the other, hiding the worst of the scuffs from the boxwood. Thankfully, Sandi glided across the room, and hugged her mother.

"There you are. How was the flight?"

"Bumpy." Zoe passed her hand over Sandi's collar then raised the back to a peak. "What happened to the outfit I sent you?"

Sandi winked at Claire. "I exchanged it for this and two other outfits." She pirouetted. "This suits me better, don't you think?"

Zoe's nostrils flared, and her lips compressed into a thin line. "No, I don't. You've misplaced your sense of style." Her eyes flicked over Claire, making her feel like last week's fish sticks. Zoe had definitely seen that wink. "I see the influence, though."

"Mother! That was rude."

Zoe's right eyebrow rose a good inch. "I wasn't intending to be rude. I'll apologize if it makes you feel better."

Claire could do one of two things. The first wasn't really an option. It would ruin the shower, and the blood wouldn't do Patsy's floor any good, either. Taking the second choice, she smiled, hoping some warmth might defrost the woman.

"No offense taken. Let's go in so you can meet everyone." She took Zoe's arm and pulled her into the family room. "Everyone, here's the mother of the bride."

At that, Zoe transformed. She made a gracious entrance with a beaming smile. Claire stood back and crossed her arms, letting her have the spotlight.

Behind her, Patsy whispered, "I'm surprised you let her insult go by."

Claire shrugged one shoulder. "Sandi deserves a nice shower."

"Her mother deserves a fall from her self-made pedestal."

Zoe played the room like a politician, air-kissing the girls and traded limp handshakes with the women, all the while looking over the shoulder of the one she was speaking with for someone more important.

"Oh, I have plans for her overblown ego."

"Claire, you've got that look in your eye again. What are you going to do?"

Chapter 32

Running late because Shiloh forgot where he buried his latest bone and dug up her favorite hydrangea, which she had to replant, Claire jogged to the bakery. As she pushed open the door, she skidded to a halt and paused to catch her breath. The harmony of chatter and laughter accompanied by an ensemble of clinking spoons, clattering dishes, and jingling bells tickled her ears. Ah, the music of *Dee's 'n' Doughs.* Added to the heavenly aroma of yeast and sugar, it nullified her stress and boosted her mood better than Prozac. Dee was onto something.

Claire waggled her fingers at her friends, already gathered around their corner table, and zipped to the coffee bar. Choosing chocolate almond java, she added sweetener and half her normal amount of cream, then selected a triple-berry bagel that was a new item, and fat-free strawberry cream cheese. She'd lost three of those tenacious pounds and wasn't about to put them back on.

"It's about time you joined us, girlfriend." Dee scooted her chair over, giving Claire some room.

She was surprised to see Dee. It had been weeks since she'd joined them. "I could say the same thing. How come you're not slaving away in the back?" Claire spread the cream cheese over her bagel and took a bite. A blueberry popped between her teeth. "Wow, these are beyond delicious, Dee."

"Thank you, they're Trish's creation. Now that business has picked up, I hired a second part-timer, and with school out, Heather and Rick are helping, too." Dee's apple cheeks rounded with her radiant smile. Claire couldn't remember when she last saw her so cheerful, but then, the full cafe would make any baker happy.

Reviving the town had helped them all, if the parking lot at Lydia's spa was any indication. Her appointment book was always full. Even Patsy had the dreamy-eyed contentment of a newlywed. Yes, things were looking up for Chapel Springs. Now if they'd only turn around for Claire. Things still remained foggy in her life.

"It's hard to believe your kids are old enough to be of much help. I remember seeing Heather's little face, peeking through the glass case when she was too short to look over it."

They chatted for another ten minutes about kids growing older, the latest happening in their businesses, Bev complained about Andrew, Dee recited the summer menu, and Lacey said the bank manager was going to retire soon.

"I'd like to retire from this wedding," Claire said. "That nerve jockey has ridden her last."

"And Zoe seemed so nice at the shower." Lydia winked. "But then we all know appearances can be deceiving."

Claire wrinkled her nose at her, then laughed.

"I'm glad you brought up the wedding." JoAnn pulled out her calendar. "I'm organizing the July Fourth picnic." She tapped Claire's arm with her pen. "Since it's always held at Springs Park, I'd like you to consult with Nancy Vaughn, who's chairing the decorating committee. With Charlie's wedding the following weekend, maybe some of the decorations we use could stay up."

"Speaking of the Springs," Lydia stirred her coffee. "Have we gotten any answers from the professor and his team? I received a phone call yesterday from a woman needing physical therapy. She'd heard about the benefits of warm springs. If they find the problem and can fix it, I'm toying with the idea of hiring a certified therapist."

Claire swallowed the last bite of her bagel. "I'm heading over to see them this afternoon." She rose, ignoring Patsy's Eeyore expression. "I have some work first, before I'm free to go." Slipping her tote strap over her shoulder, she turned to JoAnn. "How about I have Sandi call Nancy?"

"That'll work," JoAnn said, making a note on her calendar.

Patsy followed Claire out of the bakery. "Want company?"

"Why?"

"I'm afraid you're going to do something rash and end up hurt."

Claire stopped, her hands fisted on her hips. "And just why would that happen?"

"This obsession of yours—you could lose Joel and end up alone."

"I won't."

"How can you be sure?" Patsy plucked a loose thread from her sleeve, rolled it into a ball, and tucked it in her pocket.

"I'll be careful. I won't do anything until I'm positive."

"But I don't understand how you can even look. You love Joel, don't you?"

"Of course I do. But, Patsy, what if Leo's the one I was *supposed* to marry—my soul mate?" Claire started walking. "I want to be able to share my deepest heart with my husband. Joel won't share more than his dirty socks." Still, her heart tumbled at the thought of leaving him. Unlocking the gallery door, she paused. "Don't worry, Pat-a-cake. I'll be very careful."

In the workroom, Patsy picked up her palette and brushed broad strokes across a blank canvas. Claire's pottery called for delicate work today. Too bad, she'd have loved to punch a blob of clay into submission. She could pretend it was Zoe. Instead, she set three pieces, a platter and two serving bowls for Charlie and Sandi, into her kiln and closed the lid.

A water pitcher in need of paint stood on her workbench. Jars of various colors scattered helter-skelter around it. Claire reached for a brush and fanned its bristles. Where were the professor and his team working today? She turned the pitcher around, looking for where she wanted to begin. It was important to the design to start in the right place. It had to flow. She squinted and tried a different angle. Finally, she laid her brush down, sighing. It was no use. Her concentration was shot.

"Patsy, I'm going to the springs." Claire pulled her apron off and dropped it on her stool. "See you later."

There was no activity outside the Springs House, and only silence seeped through the open windows. Claire shaded her eyes from the sun as she surveyed the park. Evidence of the team's investigation lay in small piles of dirt strewn across the landscape and heading into the forest. She followed the path, feeling a bit like Gretel following breadcrumbs.

A hundred yards or so into the woods, she lost their path. She stopped and then turned around slowly, eyes shut, and listened. A bird chirped, some leaves rustled high above her, but no voices reached her ears. Where could they be? Tramping into this wilderness hadn't found them. If she kept going, the path became steep and wound up a small mountain. The new highway was on the other side. If she was to find them she needed her car.

Jogging back to the house used all the energy she had left from breakfast. She fixed a quick salami sandwich and stood at the kitchen sink, eating, when Joel came home.

"Hey. I hoped you might be here." He eyed her sandwich. "Can I get one of those?"

"Sure." She held the last corner of hers out to Shiloh, who swallowed it in one gulp and looked for more. "Sorry, boy. You'll have to wait for Daddy's." A sandwich was the one thing she could make for him, and she made a mean salami sandwich. And coffee. "How come you're home for lunch?"

"Things are slow, and the twins can hold the fort until Wes comes back from lunch. I thought I might go to the springs and see what the professor and his team have found."

Claire's stomach, having happily accepted her offering of salami, now careened off her appendix. What she needed was to get alone with Leo to see if he was the one. She couldn't do that with Joel hanging around. She took a couple of deep breaths.

"Oh? And why may I ask, since you seem to find him … an obnoxious academic, I think your exact words were?"

"He is, but I'm interested in their findings, Claire. The springs are one of the town's biggest attractions. If we lose that, we all stand to lose tourist money, no matter how pretty you've made the town. Other lakes have quaint towns. The springs are what set us apart."

She couldn't argue with that logic, even if she wanted to. "You're right." She cut his sandwich in two. "They're moved beyond the park. I'm thinking they may be on the new highway. Sure you want to take that much time?" *Please say no.*

Joel grabbed up the sandwich and a napkin. "I'll eat this on the way. Let's go."

If nothing else, five kids had taught Claire to be adaptable. She drove as Joel ate. Twenty minutes later, they pulled off the highway. Down in the meadow, Leo and his team of students had some kind of equipment set up. Two young men supported a tripod of some sort that had a pulley on it, while Leo peered into something that looked like an etch-a-sketch. Joel loved stuff like that. They climbed out of the car, but before she could take a step, he'd left her behind, jogged down the embankment, and over to examine the tripod thingy. So much for announcing their arrival with a cheery hello.

Tires crunched on the gravel behind her. She jumped back and turned. Warren's old Corolla chugged to a stop. Felix sat in the passenger seat. What were they doing here?

Felix opened his door, grasped the frame with one meaty hand, and after three grunts and two failed attempts, hauled his rotundness out of the car, knocking his baseball cap askew in the process. "I wish you'd get an SUV, Warren. This thing's a girlie car." He tugged his hat back into place and shot a glance at Claire. "Came to see how the team you hired is progressing."

Behind him, bobble-head Warren nodded in agreement.

Sure you did. If Claire knew anything, she knew Felix came to find a reason to blame her. Leo and his team had been here fifteen days and found nothing to report yet. Felix was probably clicking off dollar signs in his head. She spun around and scrambled down to the meadow, where the professor was showing Joel his etch-a-sketch or whatever it was.

She hadn't seen Leo since the dinner at the church, but she pictured him a lot more handsome. Now, in the outdoors next to Joel, he looked pasty white. How could that be? Joel's skin glowed with a healthy tan from being outdoors. Where had Leo been spending his time? And what was with the dorky fedora? It couldn't be for sun protection. The brim wasn't large enough. He pushed the hat back and scratched his receding hairline, revealing deep crevices between his brows and on the sides of his mouth—the kind frowning caused.

"Have you found us an answer?" Felix asked. He stood behind Joel, peering over his shoulder.

"No one can pinpoint the exact cause of cooling in a spring." He held up a hand as Felix sputtered a protest. "We should be able to come up with any number of probable causes, however, and qualitatively rank each at a high, medium, or low chance of occurrence."

Felix snorted. "Sounds like a cop -out to me."

"Yeah. A cop out," Warren echoed.

Those two could make an optimist sound like a doomsayer. Claire crossed her arms and shook her head. "Let the professor explain before you two display your ignorance."

Felix glared at her and hitched up his pants as the professor continued.

"Once we realized a new highway had been built, we moved here to test for effects of blasting."

But how could—? Claire shook her head. "I don't understand. How could blasting over here affect the springs?" At least the highway hadn't been her idea. Felix couldn't blame that one on her.

Without answering her, the professor droned on. "All analysis has a degree of uncertainty. See this?" He pointed to the handheld screen. "This data will have to be calibrated with any nearby wells and direct measurement."

Blah, blah, blah. A bunch of techno-babble she didn't understand. Next to her, Joel picked up a couple of pebbles, rolling them in his hand. He didn't say anything, but his smirk said it all. He hadn't changed his notions about the professor. She grimaced at him, hoping he'd mask his expression. Like that would happen.

"Then we'll integrate it with surface mapping of the springs in the area and understanding a regional geology, i.e., fault/fracture, local aquifers, aquicludes, etc."

Although it was all geo-speak, Claire tried to at least appear intelligent as Leo nattered on and on. And on. Would a nod make her look like she understood? If only he used normal people language. It wasn't like he had to impress them. Maybe if she asked a question—

"Uh, Leo, why are you using radar instead of … well, instead of something else?"

He raised his chin and his eyebrows, heaving a sigh, and closed his eyes for a moment. Was he looking down his nose at her? Joel's shoulder touched her back as he moved closer.

"At radar frequencies, electrical properties are dominantly controlled by rock or soil density, and by the chemistry state, meaning liquid, gas, or solid, distribution, that's pore space connectivity, and content of water."

Blah, blah, blah, blah.

The heat flushing in Claire's cheeks wasn't from a hot flash. She might not be the sharpest tool in the workroom, but she wasn't stupid. Could Joel be right about Leo?

Blah, blah, blah.

Did the man revel in confusing everyone?

Joel stepped a little closer to Leo. The pebbles in his hand tumbled a little faster. "So what's the result of all this? It sounds like you're saying you really don't know what you're doing and don't have any concrete ideas."

Leo took a step back, his hat askew. "Not true. I have a supposition but won't give a quantitative answer until I have more backup data. We're getting there, but these things take time."

Felix tried to cross his arms over his belly, but they were too short. He gave up and put his hands on his hips. "Just how long do you think it will be before you get some answers?"

Leo heaved a loud sigh, and hollered over at a student working the radar thingy in the borehole. "Hey, Wingnut, got anything yet?"

As the young man looked up, his lips thinned and a twitch half-winked his right eye. He considered the professor for a moment before shaking his head. Forget that the poor kid came by the nickname legitimately, his ears standing out at a forty-five degree angle. The professor was insensitive.

"If you want to wait around, you're welcome to. Might be a while, though." Leo dismissed them, stalking off to another area where a trio of students was working.

How rude. Claire wasn't sure she wanted to consider him anymore. Aunt Lola definitely wouldn't have. Claire nearly snickered, thinking of what her aunt might have said to Leo.

They watched from outside the perimeter of the work area. About fifteen feet away, one student drove what looked like a four-wheel ATV with an apparatus on the front, resembling a Christmas tree frame on a box. The others walked around with something like metal detectors.

The professor stopped ATV-boy, and with a lot of arm gesturing, berated the youth for missing a gradient, whatever that was. As he queried each one, the others exchanged glances that included a lot of eye rolling.

Joel elbowed her. "Seems the kids even think your professor is obnoxious."

And kids, as Claire had learned from her own, were pretty good judges of character, at least in adults. Listening with half an ear, she mulled over what she'd seen and heard. Joel might have a lack of patience, and yes, he yelled a lot, but he never talked down to young people like the professor did.

The students went about their work, checking readouts and logging in data. She hoped they'd have an answer soon. A shadow passed over the sun, and the wind picked up. Small tumbleweeds skittered across the field. Joel scanned the sky, then pulled out his iPhone and brought up the weather.

"We're in for a fast-moving pop-up. No tornado warning, though." He scanned the open meadow and pointed back to the road. "The safest place is in the cars."

Even without a tornado warning, she knew pop-ups held dangerous lightning. They needed shelter and fast. Felix's belly bounced up and down and sideways as he hurried away with Warren right behind him. One fat drop after another hit Claire, and a flash of lightning was followed a second later by a deafening thunderclap.

A couple of girls huddled under a tree. It was the worse place they could be.

"You get those girls, I'll handle the others," Joel yelled over the wind. "Be careful!"

Claire ran to the girls while Joel headed toward the professor and Wingnut. She had to get that name out of her head. "Get away from that tree. It's a lightning magnet. Follow me."

They scrambled up the embankment to the car, along with the boys. After getting the girls in the SUV and the boys in the truck, she turned to look for Joel. Just as he came over the rise, dragging a protesting Leo, a blinding flash accompanied by simultaneous thunder rocked the car.

The girls screamed, clinging to each other. Even the professor momentarily lost his cockiness. Joel shoved him inside the truck, then he climbed into the SUV with Claire to wait out the storm. Blinding rain beat down, and lightning struck again and again, well within the vicinity, judging by the simultaneous thunder.

"Don't worry, we're safe here." She added a smile to her words, hoping to relieve their fears. "This'll pass over soon. They move through here pretty fast."

Joel peered through the windshield at the sky. "It's about over already. I can see lighter sky." Fifteen minutes later he opened the door. "Danger's past."

In the truck behind them, the professor got out. His former white complexion had turned puce. The boys tumbled out after him and stood, shuffling their feet, their hands stuffed in their pockets. Leo turned on them.

"You left expensive equipment down there. Do you have any idea how much that cost? You never leave it unattended." Leo slammed his hat to the ground. "You idiots!" He strutted up and down in front of them, spit flying from his mouth with each word. He stopped in front of Wingnut. "And you! You were in charge! There's over sixty thousand dollars sitting in that field and you left it for the lightning to hit. You imbecile!"

Claire couldn't take the abuse anymore. "That's enough." She stepped between Leo and the poor kid. "There's no need to be so ..." she glanced at Joel. "Obnoxious. No equipment is worth this young man's life."

"His life? Get real."

Joel held his hand up. "Watch your tone with my wife." He pointed down to the meadow. "Look. There's your 'get real' evidence."

A mass of twisted metal lay smoldering in testament to the lightning's power. Leo stumbled down the embankment to the mess. When the rest joined him, he had turned more shades of red than Claire knew existed. He opened his mouth, but nothing came out but a strangled screech.

He glared at Wingnut. "You're going to pay for this. Your irresponsibility cost my department thousands of dollars." Blobs of spit gathered at the corners of his mouth. "This isn't going to mark my reputation." He poked the young man in the chest. "You ... you moron. You just earned yourself an F in this course. You can forget getting a graduate degree or ever working in this field. I'll see to it if it's—"

Joel got in Leo's face. "Shove a sock in it, Sokolov."

Leo's eyes grew wide, and he took a step back.

Joel took another step forward. "We've all had about enough of your threats. How would your precious reputation look with a dead student? Not so pretty, huh?"

Leo backed up another step. "Don't you touch me."

What was Joel doing? He took another step forward.

Leo took another one back, frantically searching for nonexistent help. "You touch me and I'll have you arrested."

Joel's hands remained clenched at his side. Not speaking, he again stepped closer to Leo, who took another step back. And another. Then Claire saw what Joel was up to. With his next advance, Leo took one too many steps back and disappeared from sight where the edge of the meadow gave way to a sharp descent down to the river. His scream echoed in the silence.

The students gaped at Joel in awe. Claire stared at him, too. Maybe not in awe, but certainly with a new respect. He'd been right all along about Leo. The professor was a pompous little twit.

Joel shrugged. "He'll be fine. Wet but fine."

Felix stuck a finger in his ear and wiggled it around. "Well done, Bennett. But I doubt we'll get any kind of report now."

"Don't worry about it," Wingnut said. "I can get all the results from this." He held up a jump drive. "I backed up just before the storm. You'll have your report by tomorrow." He reached for Joel's hand. "Thanks, Mr. Bennett."

Joel grinned and shook his hand. "That's okay, kid. He deserved it. What's your name, anyway? I don't particularly like the nickname he gave you."

"It's Sean, sir. Sean O'Keefe."

"Claire? How about we take Sean, here, and all these young people home for dinner?"

If she wore dentures they'd have hit the ground. She blinked. Yep, it was still Joel.

Her hero.

Whether she was supposed to be married to someone else no longer mattered—she loved her husband. Always had. After all, he was a good provider. He didn't make millions by any stretch of the imagination, but they didn't lack for anything, either. Nor did he run around but came home each night. Okay, so he spent those nights in front of the television, but at least he came home. No, Joel might be a turkey at times, but he was *her* turkey. And she loved him.

She flashed him a big grin and linked her arm with his. "You bet! What should we make?" If he'd cook for that bunch, she could help.

After giving the kids directions, they left them salvaging the equipment and the professor and headed back to the car, discussing dinner. Joel leaned over and planted a kiss on her cheek as he opened the door for her. Who was this man?

But as they drove home, two things nagged her. How would she convince God that Joel was right for her? The second one was a bit dicier: Would Aunt Lola haunt her for staying with him?

Chapter 33

Running late, Claire grabbed the closest spot she could find in Henderson's parking lot. She was glad she'd asked Patsy to join her for this class. What do the kids call them these days? Oh, yeah—BFF—best friend forever. Patsy definitely qualified.

"You sure you want to come in with me? You might get a reputation." Claire laughed but slid her left hand beneath her knee and crossed her fingers. Tonight was crucial to her plans. If she had any chance of impressing Zoe—or Joel for that matter—she had to learn how to cook this dinner. And she needed her BFF to watch her back.

"Wouldn't miss it." Patsy leaned down and picked her handbag up off the floorboard, brushing off a dried leaf. "So, what are we learning to make tonight?"

"Actually I've forgotten, but I think it's grilled something. I figured if other non-cooks can grill out, I could. Right? I mean, how hard can it be?" Claire was out of breath by the time they climbed the stairs to the cooking school. She needed to get serious about Lydia's aerobics class.

The chefs' assistant, Judi, welcomed them. "Glad you're back, Claire." She seemed to mean it, too. Claire liked this woman.

She took an anticipatory sniff but detected nothing. Everything must still be in the fridge. After showing Patsy how to register, they both signed the waiver and then sampled the cheese selection while chatting with other arriving students. It was a new class. Not a single face Claire recognized, and most importantly, no Trixie. That was a relief. Ten minutes later Judi called for their attention.

"There's been a slight change to our class tonight. Chef Jacque Mynatt, who was scheduled to teach this class, had a family emergency, so Chef Thornton is filling in for him. Chef?"

Claire's mind went blank. Maybe numb was a better word—her limbs felt like they had ice water running through them instead of blood. The moment she needed her legs to act fast and head for the stairs, the traitors had turned into stone.

As Chef Thornton entered the room, Patsy turned to her, her mouth and eyes set in matching O's. She leaned close. "Tomato Man?"

Claire managed a single nod. Thornton had spied her and raised one twitching eyebrow. The tic slipped down to his eye as he stared at her. Her gaze locked with his. She swallowed. Undetected escape was no longer an option. Another class? How many weeks were left before the wedding? Claire couldn't make her brain compute with Thornton's eyes boring into it. Why, oh, why did Sandi's mother have to throw her into this predicament? The ice water in her veins rose to the surface. The cold sweat made her shiver.

"Chilly are we, Ms. Bennett? I'm sure you'll raise the heat soon enough. I see you took my parking spot. Again." Thornton cleared his throat. "Judi, please distribute tonight's menu." He crossed his arm, the challenge unmistakable.

Patsy whispered in Claire's ear, "Breathe or you'll pass out."

She inhaled, although passing out wasn't such a bad idea. At least they'd cart her off in an ambulance, and she'd evade mortification.

"Claire, I'm here to help you. Don't worry." Patsy nudged her. "Come on, girl. Where's your resolve?"

Dragging her eyes away from Thornton, Claire gathered her wits from hither and yon and turned a watery smile on Patsy. "You're right. After all, what can he do?" Other than make the next three hours miserable.

Claire looked over the menu. Pork chops and tenderloin. That should be easy enough. Corn and spinach salad. Yum. Of course, Joel would wrinkle his nose at that. She read on. Some kind of potatoes with herbs. Why not plain baked? Oh well, if she had any hope of wowing Zoe and her clan, herbs would probably help. Joel could suck it up for once. Besides, the appetizer was hot wings, and he loved those.

Claire skimmed down the page to dessert. Baked Alaska? Not even a chance. It was a good thing Chapel Springs had Dee. She didn't have to worry about the dessert.

"If you've all read the menu, turn to page two. You will see that you have the recipe for the brine. Ms. Bennett, can you tell the class what brine is?"

Her tongue cleaved to the roof of her mouth, not that she knew anything about brine. She shot Patsy a plea for help.

"It's a method of curing, preserving and/or flavoring certain foods such as meats, fish, vegetables and cheese by immersing them in a mixture of salt and water, or injecting the brine into them. It's also known as pickling."

Thornton stared at Patsy. "Yes. Well, very good, Ms. Kowalski."

His emphasis on Patsy's name singled out Claire worse than if he'd slapped a dunce cap on her head. Why was she doing this to herself? Oh, right. It was for her Charlie. Her firstborn. For his rehearsal dinner. His and Sandi's rehearsal dinner. Claire clenched her teeth. The dinner Sandi's mother, Zoe, insisted Claire cook.

"Tonight, since we don't have enough time, Judi has already done that step. You'll find the chops in bags of brine. Now go collect your *mise en place.*"

Thornton and his fancy words. Who was he trying to wow?

Patsy tapped her arm. "What are you mumbling about?"

Had she said that aloud? Claire grimaced. "Why can't he simply say get all your ingredients?"

"Because *mise en place* is more than just the ingredients. It's—"

"I know what it is, but it sounds pretentious." Claire grabbed a basket off the counter, and pulling Patsy behind her, headed for the huge, industrial refrigerator.

"Ms. Kowalski, where is your basket?"

Just because Claire had gotten a few tomato seeds on his shoe—okay, so she'd parked in his spot, too, but did that mean he had to make it his life's purpose to challenge her? She faced her nemesis.

"She doesn't need one. She's helping me."

Uh-oh. The twitchy eyebrow was boogieing above his right eye. After a couple of seconds that felt like an hour, he walked away.

"Suit yourselves."

She and Patsy leaned into one another, smothering giggles.

"Maybe you'll stay off the floor this time," Thornton tossed back over his shoulder.

Claire raised the wicker basket, but Patsy grabbed it away from her before she could launch it at his back. "Come on. Let's gather."

She gently extracted the list from Claire's tightly clenched fist and smoothed it out. "Let's divide this. I'll get the vegetables, liquids, and utensils. You get the rest."

"Oh, all right. Let me see that." Claire took the list back, eyed it, then ripped it in half. "Here's your part."

At the fridge, Claire glanced at the ragged list, tucked it in her pocket and filled her left arm with chops-in-a-brine-bag, loins, eggs, a ripe pineapple, and—she stopped. Balancing the lot—the pineapple's sides prickled her ear—she dug out the list. Good gravy, there were a lot of ingredients. She leaned into the depths of the fridge. That bowl of dusty-looking leaves near the back must be the sage. Reaching for it—

A tap on her shoulder startled her. "Are you about through in there? I need to get my *mise en place*, too, you know."

Claire jumped and bumped her head on the shelf, toppling the pineapple. No! The dingbat, who was responsible for its fall, dove and caught it before it hit the floor. All of four-foot-ten and badly in need of a root touchup, she deposited the fruit back on top of Claire's pile and stood with her hands on her hips, glaring up at her.

If her arms weren't full of pork … She reined in the impulse. "Thanks, I'll be through in a minute." She rubbed the painful indentation the shelf made in her scalp.

Setting her list on the fridge shelf for reference, she selected the rest of her items. Soon, she had everything, except the chicken wings. Her cache balanced in one arm while she poked around each shelf with no success. The wings weren't there. Someone had made off with more than one bag. Now she'd have to ask the chef.

With her chin holding the pineapple in place atop the pile, and cursing her own pride for not taking another basket, she slowly turned. The pineapple wobbled, but a fast jaw adjustment saved it.

"It's all yours." Short-stuff had disappeared. She must not have any patience. Claire fixed her eyes on her cooking station, took a step—"Ow!"

The tower of *mise en place* undulated in her arms like a slinky gone wild. She leaned one way then the other, trying to stay under the rolling, swaying pile. She caught the pineapple between her shoulder and her ear, and somehow maintained her balance.

Stepping back, Claire beheld the stumbling block she stepped on. Short-stuff's foot. Oops. Her hands still on her hips, Shorty glared up at her. Again. Didn't she have any other facial expressions? The woman sniffed, tossed her dark-rooted head, and stepped around Claire.

Under Shorty's left arm were two bags of wings. What Claire

wouldn't give for one ripe tomato and free hands about now.

"Don't even think it." Patsy took the pineapple from under Claire's ear. "I see that look in your eye." Relieving her of half her burden, Patsy urged her forward. "Forget about her. We're running behind."

She gave in, but she didn't have to like it. "I don't have the chicken wings. That klepto took more than her fair share. Now I've got to go ask Tomato-Man."

At the opposite end of the center island, Chef Thornton schmoozed with another student whose knife bounced up and down so fast it made Claire's fingers curl. Thornton's eye started to spasm the moment he caught sight of her approach. He took a step back, colliding with Short-stuff on her way back from gathering. Claire sucked in her lips to keep from laughing.

Thornton scowled. "What do you need?"

Not to be here. "There aren't any more chicken wings in the refrigerator."

"Go look in the freezer. There should be some more there." He waved a hand toward the huge walk-in locker.

She found the wings, frozen solid in bags of a dozen each, and took one. With no empty space at her station, she dropped the bag in the sink to collect later. Back at the island, everyone was busy chopping and dicing. The room filled with the scent of chilies, onions, and garlic.

"What are we supposed to do first?"

Patsy used her knife to point at the pork loin. "Get the meat rubbed with oil and chili powder. Be careful not to touch your eyes before you wash your hands afterwards."

"Right. Eunice taught me that last time."

While the rubbed tenderloin rested—why it needed a rest when she did the work was beyond her—they made the stuffing for the chops and the pineapple salsa. Thornton said when the meat went on the grill, they could make the corn and spinach salad. Why didn't they make the salad first? It was eaten before the meat. "Cooking doesn't make a lick of sense. For that matter, why not do the appe—"

"Talking to the food now, Ms. Bennett?"

Claire banged a lid over the pan of meat. "I …uh …" Where was Patsy?

"Chef, is this the correct ratio of nuts to fruit in this stuffing?"

He peered into the bowl that her-very-best-friend-in-the-whole-world held and smiled. "Lovely, Ms. Kowalski. You have an eye for perfection in dicing. Your pieces are neither too small nor too large." He kissed his fingertips.

If it weren't Patsy who saved her, Claire would have gagged. They were going to be chewed to oblivion not put on display. Who cared what size they were? Aunt Lola always said that only mattered in diamonds and men's wallets.

Thornton wandered off to answer another student's question. With Patsy's help, Claire got the rest of the meal prepared. Patsy worked on the baked Alaska, since she'd never done one before. So, now all that was left for Claire to do were the wings.

She picked up the recipe sheets. Heat oil. She poured peanut oil into the pan and turned on the heat to medium high. Check. Sauce? Already made and in a bowl beside the frying pan. Check. Wings? Ch—where were her wings? She lifted a towel and looked beneath it. No wings. Oh, wait—she left them in the sink beside the freezer.

She cranked up the heat under the pan of oil to high and went to retrieve the wings. By the time she got back, the oil shimmered and smoked. That looked right. She reached for the bag of frozen wings, turned it over, and dumped them in.

The oil bubbled like a fountain filled with soapsuds, rising rapidly up the sides of the pan. Was it supposed to do that? In the blink of an eye, the bubbles spilled over the pan and hit the fire beneath, and with a loud whoosh, flames shot high into the air as she jumped back.

She screeched, batting her hair. Patsy rushed to her side and started slapping Claire on the head just before the bulkhead above the island burst into flames. Lights flashed and a horrible sound, like the testing of the emergency broadcasting system, blared from a loudspeaker. Quicker than it takes to make instant grits, the overhead automatic fire extinguishers blasted powder over everything, quickly dousing the flames.

Other than the intermittent fire alarm, blat-buzzing through the PA system, and the automated voice telling everyone to walk to the nearest exit, silence reigned.

Claire blinked her eyes open. The entire place was covered in a thick blanket of white powder—the island, the appliances, and the people. They looked like pillars of salt. Not a bad analogy, really. Especially, considering she just about demolished Henderson's like Sodom and Gomorrah.

While they were all indistinguishable from one another under their blankets of Halon, could she sneak out before Thornton discovered who'd been responsible? Her hairline was starting to sting. She clutched Patsy's hand and inched slowly toward the door.

"Bennett!"

Chapter 34

Claire tiptoed through the bedroom after eleven o'clock. Guilt weighed heavy on her shoulders. Shiloh raised his head and looked at her, but Joel snored on, oblivious to her arrival. For that, she was most grateful. She motioned for the dog to stay.

As she scrubbed off the residue of Halon in the shower, she rehearsed how to tell Joel what happened. It would take the right words. Otherwise, he'd get all riled up and pitch a hissy fit. Aunt Lola never covered that. As glamorous as she was, men clamored for her attention, never wasting time on arguing.

Claire dumped shampoo on her head and gently worked it into her scalp, careful to avoid the burns on her forehead and hairline. The scent of coconut soothed her frayed nerves. Things could have turned out a lot worse. Because of Patsy they didn't. Once again, her best friend rescued her, and thanks to her fast talk, Claire wasn't going to be sued. Thornton underestimated her culinary deficit and never told her to defrost the wings before frying.

She turned off the water, slid a bath sheet around her body and towel dried her hair. It was Thornton's gaffe, but he hadn't taken the blame well. His eye twitched, his brows couldn't decide whether to be up or down, and he plucked at the right one. But it was his incoherent babbling that triggered the personnel director to call for an ambulance. Claire felt kind of sorry for him. After all, if she'd been more like Patsy, he wouldn't have had to tell her you don't fry frozen wings.

She fingered what was left of her burned hair—the former long bangs she'd spent months growing out. The ones she used to sweep to the side and tuck behind one ear were now frizzled at the bridge of her nose. She peered closer in the mirror. Until she could tell Joel, she'd have to do something about that.

By the time she got through trimming and evening them out, they barely covered her eyebrows. Those didn't look so good either. The hairs were stubby and curled, and the skin would take a few days to heal. Fortunately, Patsy slapped the flames out before she was badly burned. The paramedics said most were second degree but no third.

After dabbing some antibiotic ointment on her brows, she slid her nightgown over her head and turned out the light. Joel's snoring didn't miss a beat as she slipped into bed. She'd been granted a reprieve … for now.

The next morning, she rose early. She had to tell Joel before someone else did. Though Patsy wouldn't gossip, knowing this town somehow the news would have spread. Claire's stomach churned. Slipping on her robe, she hurried downstairs, tying it as she went. The aroma of pancakes greeted her in the kitchen. Joel stood over the griddle, a spatula in his hand. He smiled over his shoulder.

"Morning. I didn't expect you up this early." He stopped and stared at her.

Though it stung, she raised her eyebrows to keep them hidden.

"You cut your hair." He waved a hand around his forehead. "I like it."

She patted her hair as if it were all planned, sending a silent thank you heavenward.

Joel motioned to the griddle. "If I'd of known you were getting up, I would've made more batter." Using the spatula, he lifted one edge of a pancake to check its progress.

"That's okay. I just want toast." She poured herself a cup of coffee and dropped two slices of bread in the toaster.

"What kept you out so late?"

Her hand froze over the toaster's lever for a second. His question sounded innocent enough—normal conversational voice. She pushed the lever down. It was now or never. She turned on a bright smile.

"A surprise. For you. Well and me, too. I mean not a surprise for me, ha ha, but a surprise for you and something for me." Oy vey, she wasn't doing too well.

Joel flipped his pancakes onto a plate and turned off the burners. "Okaaay. Do you want to give me the bad news first and get it over with, or start with the good news and let me guess?"

Van Gogh's ear! He knew her too well. "Very funny. Remember

when Zoe came here for Sandi's shower?"

"Zoe? Hmmm. You mean that Wednesday two weeks ago? I believe my memory's still intact from then, so yes."

Turkey. "She reminded me that the groom's dinner is our responsibility, which I already knew, of course. I even planned for us all to dance in the moonlight after dinner. I've always wanted to do that. Dance in the moonlight, I mean."

"You knew." He put a dollop of butter on his pancakes. "And you're just now telling me about it? Just when *is* this dinner?"

Her toast popped up. While Joel poured syrup from a jug-shaped bottle, she spread her butter and recollected her thoughts. He flat ignored her suggestion of moonlit dances. She sighed with longing.

"I did tell you before. It's the night of the wedding rehearsal, but that's beside the point."

"We're responsible for a dinner but that's beside the point?"

"If you'll listen, I'll explain. The point is I know you normally don't like to cook for large groups." Brilliance struck her. "And after that sweet sacrifice you made to cook for the university kids last week, well, I thought it would be too much to ask you to do the groom's dinner."

Joel's loaded fork stopped halfway to his mouth. While he stared at her, thick maple syrup slid off the pile of pancake, through the tines and made its slow descent to the table. He quickly stuffed the bite in his mouth and wiped the drip with his napkin. "Too much to ask. Why do I have the feeling I'm about to lose my appetite?"

Claire took a seat across the table from him. She rotated her plate with the toast at a forty-five degree angle and set her coffee cup precisely at two o'clock to her plate.

"Claire?"

"Oh, right. Where was I?" She took a bite of toast, capturing stray crumbs from the corner of her mouth with her tongue.

"You weren't anywhere. What did you do last night?"

"Okay, so I knew we couldn't afford to have the dinner at one of the restaurants, although I do suppose if we had asked nicely and got Lacey to help convince him, Jake might have given us a discount, but then Zoe said Sandi really wanted to have it at our house, since she loves us and the homey atmosphere here. So, I decided I'd learn to cook, so I could either help you or do the dinner myself. That's where I was last night— at a cooking class at Henderson's in Young Harris. But it wasn't my fault. You can ask Patsy, she went with me. It was that awful Chef Thornton.

Ever since I took the first class, he's had it in for me."

Claire clapped her hand over her mouth. She'd never told him about that first class.

Joel gaped at her. He blinked then set his coffee mug on the table. He ran his tongue over his teeth and around the inside of his mouth like he was searching for rogue bits of pancake. "I see. Something tells me this—uh—cooking class didn't turn out like you planned."

Stalling, she stirred her coffee first clockwise then counterclockwise. "Not exactly."

"Well, let's hear it."

She put her hands in her lap, then sat on them, and took a deep breath. "The class was on grilling pork chops and a tenderloin. I thought that would be a good choice for the groom's dinner. Not too expensive but delicious. I know I loved the tenderloin you fixed a couple of weeks ago. That's one of the reasons I chose—"

"Claire. Get to the point."

"Oh, right. Okay, so I was doing pretty good. Then it was time to do the appetizers. Why do they have you cook things backwards? We had to start with the main dish, then make the veggies and last the appetizers. Why not have—"

"Claire!"

"Oh, right. The appetizer was hot wings. I was so glad because you love them, and—"

Joel drummed his fingers on the table.

"Okay. Sorry. It was really the chef's fault. He never told me I had to defrost them first. I mean, restaurants throw frozen French fries into the deep fryers all the time. Don't they?"

Joel's eyes widened. Her hands slid from their hiding place and her forefingers picked at the cuticles of her thumbs.

"Don't tell me you threw frozen wings into ..."

She nodded. He swallowed. His facial muscles tightened, and he clenched his jaw. His face grew awfully red.

"Joel," she whispered. "Say something."

"Was the oil hot?"

She nodded.

"Really hot?"

"Smoking."

He cringed. "I'm *trying* to see this from your perspective. Did you have any thoughts before dropping them into that hot oil?"

"Uh … not really."

"Did the oil—?" He turned his fingers in loops.

"In a whoosh, like a fountain."

His face lost all color. That scared her more than the red.

"Did you get burned?"

"Only my bangs and my eyebrows a bit." She brushed her bangs aside for him to see. "Patsy was fast helping me."

He nodded. "And what about the fire?"

"Powder sprayed from the ceiling."

"It's Halon."

"Right." Why wasn't he yelling at her? He usually yelled. Her heart picked up its tempo. The quiet voice with the measured words wasn't Joel.

"Tell me the Halon was contained to the room you were in."

She bit her lip. "Yes and no."

His eyes narrowed. "The market?"

She swallowed the rock in her throat. "Not the fire, just the Halon."

He closed his eyes. After a moment, he rose, put his plate still full with uneaten pancakes, on the counter. "I'm going out." He held up his hand. "Don't say anything."

The front door closed with a quiet click that reverberated in her heart. She sat for a long time, staring at the kitchen where Joel reigned. So many happy hours had been spent with her sitting at the table, watching him cook. Later when the kids got bigger, they began to help. Strange she never felt left out before.

So, why did she now?

Between God and Aunt Lola something disconnected. Had her aunt been right? Or was God? Did Aunt Lola ever pray for a husband? Somehow, Claire doubted it.

Determined to find out, she pulled down the attic ladder in the hallway and went up to find her aunt's journals. They needed a window up here, the humid, hot air was suffocating. She turned on the light. Aunt Lola's diaries were in one of the trunks under the eaves. A thick layer of dust covered every box and trunk, and dust motes sparkled in the light. The musty odor triggered memories of exploring the attic's depths together, when they first bought the house.

In a back corner, under the eaves, sat Aunt Lola's large travel trunk, covered with stickers from cruise lines and foreign countries. There was one from Paris in the shape of the Eiffel Tower. Claire remembered when Aunt Lola came back from Paris. She brought her a *cancan* doll.

Warmed by the memory, Claire opened the lid. As she hoped, the doll was still there, lying right on top. She lifted the much-loved toy out and cradled it to her chest. The paint on its cheeks was worn, its hair ratty, and its dress wrinkled and faded. She set it down and quickly found her objective. Aunt Lola's journals.

She carried the four gilt-edged volumes down to the family room. Armed with a cup of tea, she opened the first one.

Chapter 35

Claire closed the third volume, and took a sip from her mug, wrinkling her nose at the stone cold tea. She hadn't learned anything new about Aunt Lola. The first three journals simply chronicled her numerous husbands, her travels, and of course, her movies. This wasn't helping at all. She'd hoped to find some wisdom from her old auntie. Heaven knew she needed some.

After brewing a fresh cup of tea, she curled up on the sofa and picked up volume four. This one was red with gold braiding on the front and not as worn as the first three. This one wasn't as large as the others either, but by this time, Aunt Lola had been in her nineties. Claire lifted her cup to her lips, the fragrance of apple and ginger comforting. She took a sip and turned the page. Her aunt never lost her sparkle to the day she died. At eighty-seven, Aunt Lola had been awarded the Lifetime Achievement Award at the Oscars.

Most of the handwritten entries had been short, but near the end of the journal was a longer one. Claire set her cup down, intrigued. Aunt Lola's seventh and last husband had committed some unpardonable faux pas, and she'd left him, too.

Harold is gone and good riddance. After seven husbands, I've learned a thing or two. Like I enjoy my own company, and I don't hog the covers. Charlie, husband #4, tried to make me believe that one. I won't bother getting married again. I don't want to regret it. I've never regretted anything I've ever done.

No, that's not really true. I regret one thing and that's leaving Tommy, my first love. I got mad at him for taking me for granted, but looking back,

I realize it was a two-way street. Maybe even more of me than him. I was selfish and he hurt my pride. I didn't give him a chance.

But now, from the great age of ninety-five, I can say without a doubt, he was the love of my life. The rest were mere infatuations. Tommy really loved me in spite of my self-centeredness and tendencies to be wild. He loved me when I wasn't lovable. I never should have left him.

Claire reread the last line. At the end of her life, Aunt Lola finally learned what Claire figured out before it was too late for her. Husbands could definitely be turkeys, but it takes two to do the turkey trot. Out on that field, she'd seen the professor in a light that shone back on herself. She'd been awfully critical of Joel lately. That was easier than being a positive influence, like Patsy, who always tried to see the best in everyone.

Claire ran her thumb over the braided trim. It felt smooth to the touch, worn from contemplative rubbing. A change of thinking—an attitude adjustment was what she needed. There was a Bible verse about how to do that. It had to do with water and wells.

But would her changed thinking heal her marriage? If Joel weren't so stubborn about going to church that would help, too. Where was he anyway? She needed to tell him that Henderson's wasn't suing them. She picked up the phone and dialed his cell number. It rang in the kitchen. Great, he didn't take it. She tried the marina office. Melissa answered the phone.

"Hi, sweetheart. Can I talk to your daddy?"

"He's not here. Haven't seen him today."

"Is his boat gone?"

"Hold on."

The phone clunked and voices babbled in the background. He probably went fishing. Out on the lake was his favorite thinking place.

"Nope, his boat's tied up at the dock. Gotta go, Momma. Customers."

Claire put the receiver back in its cradle. Where could he have gone? She walked to the backyard to check the detached garage. The midday sun beat down on the grass. She'd have to turn on the sprinklers tonight. The garage door creaked as she opened it. A slight smell of gas lingered from filling the lawnmower. The car was there.

One o'clock had come and gone. He'd been gone since seven-forty-five. And on foot. Where could he be? She closed the door behind her and went back in the house. There was one place he might have gone.

The trail they used to hike together that ran around the lake. It was rarely used since the tourists didn't attempt to walk that far. Joel loved it out there.

He'd be hungry.

She grabbed a banana from the kitchen, peeling one for herself too, then ran out the door toward Patsy's. On this end, the trail started in the woods just past her house. She and Nathan had gone away for a few days on a second honeymoon. If Claire could pull off what she hoped to, maybe she and Joel would go on one, too.

As she jogged, pine needles crunched underfoot. Claire prayed he'd taken the path from the marina and she'd meet him head on. Unless he doubled back. She stopped, chewing her thumbnail. If she were following instead of intercepting him, she could be out here all night. A squirrel scolded her for disturbing it, and a blue jay squawked overhead. The trail went around the lake almost twenty miles, following the shoreline with all its coves and fingers. Joel could be anywhere.

She couldn't see a thing through the trees, had no idea where her husband was, or which direction he'd taken. Shoulders drooping, she turned around and headed home to wait for him there. As afternoon turned to evening, she paced the house, opened the door and looked down the street, then paced inside some more. Had he finally had enough of her and simply walked out of her life? How could she make amends? Tell him she'd change?

By six o'clock, she was ready to call out the National Guard. She opened the front door to look one more time. At the end of the street, a tired looking Joel trudged toward home. Relief drained her strength for a moment, and she couldn't move. Then adrenaline took over, and her feet barely touched the sidewalk. When she reached him, she threw her arms around him. Tears fell from her eyes.

"Where have you been? I've been *frantic.*"

He held her tight and didn't say anything—just squeezed her. After a moment, he kissed her temple. "Let's go home. We need to talk. No, that's wrong. *I* need to talk."

Those were foreign words to Joel. "Are you all right? Did I—"

"Hush. It's not you, sweetheart. It's me."

He had Joel's face. He even had Joel's woodsy scent, although it was disguised by sweat at the moment. But that wasn't her husband talking. She didn't say anything, but her heart ached at the exhaustion etched on his face, the pine needles tangled in his hair.

Inside the house, she couldn't hold it in. "Honey, what—"

"Do me a favor and fix some coffee."

"Okay." It was the hardest thing she'd ever done, not peppering him with questions, but if he wanted to talk, it would have to be in his own time. It took all her willpower not to tap the spoon on the counter, waiting for the coffee to finish brewing.

Finally, she handed him a mug and sat with hers across the same table where they'd started this morning. As she sipped, she drank in his face. Crows feet at the side of his eyes gave testament to laughter, and the smile grooves on the side of his mouth were deep. She never could have left him. He was truly her other half. If it took all night, she'd sit and not say a word until he felt ready to talk. She just hoped it was sooner than that. She wasn't sure she could hold her resolve that long.

"Clairey-girl, today I realized—no, that's wrong. I've always known how much I love you. But today, I saw how much I'd let familiarity and small aggravations color that." He yanked off his cap and tossed it aside. "This isn't easy, sharing feelings. You know how my dad was."

She reached across the table and placed her hand over his, entwining their fingers. His were as rough as hers, dried from hard work. "I know."

He looked into her eyes for a long moment. His Adam's apple bobbed as he swallowed. "I love you, Claire. More than you can begin to know. Way more than I can ever say. After I left, I walked the trail. I was mad about Henderson's, but for some reason, I began to understand how it happened. Mostly, I realized what *could* have happened. To you. And it scared me spitless."

Blasted tears made him hard to see. She came over to his side of the table and sat beside him. She leaned against him, and he put his arm around her, pulling her close. "I felt the same way this afternoon. You were angrier than I've ever seen you."

"I used to laugh at your escapades. When did I stop? I asked myself why I stopped."

A memory came with the clarity of a clear mountain sky, and she needed to confess it. "It's my own fault. It was when I tried to change who you were."

"What do you mean?" His thumb caressed her fingers.

"You remember when I started going to church? I wanted you to come with me and share what I'd found. But you wouldn't, so I started a constant barrage. I all but beat you over the head with my Bible."

Joel stirred his coffee, took a sip, and set his mug down. "I thought it was just a phase. I should have realized how important it was to you. You tried to tell me."

"Joel, you're not alone with fault here. I was self-centered. Definitely not an example of a Christian, much less a Christian wife." She wouldn't tell him about her search or the fantasies of a different husband. It wouldn't serve any purpose but hurt him, and that was something she never wanted to do again.

Lord, change me. Not him but me.

Turning to face him, she raised one hand in pledge. "I promise here and now, I will never try to change you again. I promise I won't keep asking you to come to church with me." She hoped she could keep that last one.

Joel laughed and hugged her, his warm breath as familiar as her own. "Honey, you'll never make it." He kissed her protests away. When he released her, he chuckled again. "I've decided that since it means so much to you, I'll check it out." He wrapped his hands around his coffee mug. "At least, I'll try it. I like Seth, and he's never made me feel like scum for not coming."

Claire's heart melted. They had other issues to work out, but at least they were on their way. Simply sharing like this left her plumb giddy. She laid her head on his shoulder, ignoring the scratch of forest debris left there by his hike. She breathed a prayer of thanks.

"I didn't get a chance to tell you this morning, but Henderson's isn't going to sue us. They put the blame on Thornton for not explaining all safety rules."

"I kind of feel sorry for the guy."

"You do? Why?"

Joel winked at her. "He'd obviously never come up against anyone like you before."

In his teasing, Claire heard love. And pride. Silly man. She bumped her shoulder against him. "We still have one problem."

"What's that?"

"The groom's dinner. Zoe expects me to cook it."

"Then let's not disappoint her."

Claire put her elbows on the table and cupped her chin in her hands, sighing. "Right. Me cook the dinner. You must have hit your head out there on the trail."

"I've got it all figured out, babe. Me 'n Patsy'll help you. We'll precook everything, with your help, then you'll follow our instructions." He wagged his finger at her, "To a 'T' under covert supervision that night."

She jumped up. "Joel, that's cheating."

"No, that's a campaign. Sit back down." He waited until she complied. "Zoe challenged you, and in this battle, all's fair. Your reputation is at stake."

"Everyone in Chapel Springs knows I can't cook. They'll give it away. I can't do this, Joel. And I don't need to now."

"Why not?"

She looked down at the table. "Because I wasn't really trying to impress Zoe. I was really trying to impress *you*."

"Yeah?"

He looked so pleased by her admission it nearly broke her heart. How long had it been since she'd flirted with him or told him how great he was? She'd spent the last few years pointing out his faults.

"Yeah." She grinned at him. "I'm a sap for you."

He grabbed her hand. "Come on. Let's you and me go—" He scratched his head.

"What?"

"Where'd we used to go on dates?"

If he kept this up, she'd melt into a pool of mush on the floor.

His eyes lit up. "I know!" The man actually waggled his eyebrows at her.

She started laughing. "Where?"

He took her hand. "Grab the CDs, Clairey-girl. We're goin' to Loon Island and dance in the moonlight."

Chapter 36

With the back of her hand, Claire pushed a strand of hair off her damp face. Ladies weren't supposed to sweat. They glow, Aunt Lola always said. But the rush to pick up Adrianna from the airport, and now the heat in the kitchen, plus nervousness, had Claire beyond glowing. But she was thankful for Joel and Patsy helping get most of the meal ready for tomorrow night's rehearsal dinner. The pressure was intense, and although the kitchen smelled heavenly with a test run of dinner rolls baking in the oven, she'd be glad when this was over, and she didn't have to pretend anymore.

In a bowl, she stirred together the dry rub ingredients Joel measured out for her. According to him, she technically *was* making the dinner, but if he and Patsy weren't there, she knew she'd fall flat on her face. It's a good thing Felix wasn't in the wedding party. He'd blab for spite.

Over at the butcher block, Patsy set her knife down and bagged the vegetables she'd chopped for the salad. A rogue piece of celery dove onto the floor. "Claire, where do you want these? The fridge or the cooler in the mud room?"

If she were a vegetable, where would she want to be?

Anywhere but here.

Joel stopped the mixer. "Don't look at me, Claire. You decide." He turned back and added cream cheese to the mashed potatoes, licking off some that stuck to his fingers.

She nibbled a thumbnail, trying to apply logic, an overrated value to her way of thinking. The kitchen fridge held the punch and the meat. It also had to house the once-baked potatoes waiting for their second baking. There wouldn't be room. The veggies weren't the squishy kind that got nasty overnight. "The cooler should be fine." She hoped that was right.

"Relax, Claire." Patsy zipped the plastic bag of veggies. "You're doing fine. Isn't she, Joel?"

"Sure is. I'm thinking of keeping her. Now come put these potatoes together, hon. Your sous chef is done and it's now ready for your mastery."

"What about this dry rub? Don't I need to put it on the meat first?"

Joel checked his watch. "Nope. That can wait."

She washed the spices off her hands and joined him at the table. Patsy had the potato skins already arranged on baking sheets. Joel had spooned the mashed insides into a pastry bag and handed it to her.

She swiped a finger through the potatoes left on his spoon and licked it off. Warm and creamy, the mixture tasted like garlic and summer. "Ooh, that's really good. What did you put in them?"

"Butter, a dash of milk, but the real secret to great mashed potatoes is cream cheese. That and a bit of roasted garlic. Now, do your magic."

"What magic?"

He took her hand and wrapped her fingers around the bag. It felt warm and squashy. "Pretend it's a paint brush and those skins are little bowls. It's all art, Clairey-girl, whether it's food, clay, or canvas."

She'd never thought of it that way before, but he was right. Bending over the table, she eyed the large tray full of empty potato halves, sitting there waiting for her to turn them into edible art. The fear of failure slid away like egg whites through fingers. She could do this!

After a quick test on waxed paper, she piped the potatoes into their jackets. When the first one was done, its scallops and swirls pleased her. Moving to the next skin, she applied a slightly different pattern to this one. Joel sat across the table, grinning at her.

"See? Art."

And it was. Now the challenge would be to see if she could make each one a little different from the last, like she did with her pottery. Not so easy with potatoes. But maybe, if she—"Hand me some of those left over veggies, Patsy. I've got an idea."

Since Joel called the skins "jackets," she'd make them look like jackets. Tuxedo jackets. All they needed were cummerbunds and bowties. She selected a small piece of green onion and laid it across the middle for the cummerbund. This just might work, she thought, and picked up a sliver of lighter green for the bowtie.

"I can't believe I'm doing this."

"What?" Patsy's chin appeared over Claire's shoulder. "Oh, those are so cute. Sandi's going to love them."

"I didn't mean this," Claire waved a hand over the tray of potatoes. "I meant all of it, the rehearsal dinner, the wedding. I'm too young to become a grandmother."

Patsy laughed. "They haven't had the wedding yet, and you're worried about becoming a grandmother?"

Put like that, it did sound sort of foolish. "It seems like yesterday we were sharing coffee and formula coupons." Where had their youth gone? "It makes me think of that song, the one that says something about turning around and they're grown." The potatoes blurred. "It's so true. Our babies are grown, and we're getting old. I'm not ready to be old, Pat-a-cake."

"Neither am I." Patsy stood with her hands on her hips. "We'll just tell the rest of the kids they can't get any older. Problem solved."

Claire picked up another skin, nestling it in the hollow of her hand and piped in the mashed potato. "Speaking of the kids, I'm concerned about Wes. He spends all his spare time in front of that computer. What do you suppose he's doing?" She added the embellishments to make the veggie-tux.

"Being social."

"Social? Being social is talking to people. Face to face."

"Not so much anymore, Claire. Not with all the social media sites and chat rooms. If you think about it, it's not all that much different than us with telephones."

"I guess, but at least with us, we talked to people we went to school with, not total strangers."

"True, but these days, horizons are broader. What about Kelly and Earl?"

"The Applings? What about them?"

Patsy stared. "Didn't you know they met on e-Love?"

"That Internet dating site?" Claire picked up a bottle of poppy seeds and put them down the center of the potatoes for the shirt buttons.

"They were one of the first success stories. I can't believe you didn't know that. They've been on the commercials forever."

"Well, imagine that. I guess I *am* getting old. I use the computer for research, not socializing."

"If our new website takes off, we may be socializing and selling over the Internet."

Claire bent, focusing on the poppy seed buttons. Cyber socializing, Internet dating. What would Aunt Lola have thought about all of that? Claire straightened. The old gal would have loved it.

Patsy poured them each a cup of coffee. "All this computer talk reminds me. Have you spoken to the professor or his team about the springs?"

Claire swallowed the mouthful of coffee she'd taken and set the cup down, nodding. "Sean, and that redhead, what was her name? Jennifer. That's it. They came over with Felix last night and brought the report." She carefully dropped poppy seeds on the last potato. "There. I'm done." She worked a stray seed from beneath her fingernail.

Patsy surveyed the trays. "Claire, they look adorable. They look delicious, and you should be proud."

"Tired is what I am." She rotated her shoulders to ease the kinks.

Patsy took the bowl from her to the sink. "Sit and tell me what Sean had to say."

If she sat, she might not get up. She joined Patsy loading the dishwasher. "Basically, he said they couldn't pinpoint the reason for the springs cooling. He also said that's not unusual in a case like this."

"Okay, but do we have any answers?" Patsy handed her another bowl.

"He gave us the probabilities of what happened. They think the blasting for the new highway caused some ground shifting, enough to reduce the flow from the springs' underground source." Claire moved a plate to fit in the bowl and closed the dishwasher. "Jennifer said an educated guess is by about fifty percent."

"What did Felix say about all this?"

"That's the strange part. The old goat surprised me. Instead of getting mad and blaming me, he got quiet, then thanked them for the report, and asked Sean to walk out with him. He's got some harebrained scheme hatching. I just know it."

"Whatever it is, I hope it works."

Joel came back into the kitchen. "Done?"

Claire nodded. "See?" She couldn't believe how nervous she felt as he silently inspected her work. When he turned a big smile on her, her heart skipped a beat.

"Before I know it, you're going to be fighting me for kitchen space." He kissed her cheek and slid the trays into the fridge for her. "I'm proud of you, babe." He closed the refrigerator door and headed toward the den. "There's a game on."

Claire and Patsy started putting things away. "I'm glad this part is over, but I'm still as nervous as Shiloh with a new bone. Cooking is definitely not my thing."

"But you did a wonderful job with the potatoes. They're unique."

"And only edible because Joel did the mixing and making."

Patsy hung up the dishrag she'd wiped the counter with and put her arm around Claire's shoulder. "Quit selling yourself short, girl."

"I'm not, really. I just know my limitations and interests, and I'd rather limit my interest to watching Joel or you do the cooking."

Warm Springs Park looked lovely, but a mosquito buzzed Claire relentlessly near the end of the rehearsal as she sat in the front row of chairs on the other side of the gazebo from Sandi's parents. She wafted at the pest with a cardboard fan, provided by Flannigan's Funeral Home. Why didn't they hand out wedding fans? Funeral home fans seemed so ominous and not at all appropriate.

After Pastor Seth signaled them from his place at the altar, she took Joel's hand and stood so they could follow Zoe and Bernie to the back where the rest of the wedding party gathered. Zoe must not have looked in the mirror when she put on that dress, at least not from the rear. The afternoon held a clothes-stuck-to-you type of humidity. With her free hand, Claire took hold of her own skirt and flapped as unobtrusively as possible while still being able to get some much-needed air around her thighs, which felt clammy at best.

Joel leaned his head close to hers. "Are you ready for your debut?"

"I'm as nervous as a long-tailed cat in a room full o' rocking chairs. I want to throw up."

"Clairey-girl, everything will be fine. Wait and see."

"What I can see is Zoe waiting for me to flat fall on my fettuccini."

Suppressing his laughter, Joel shook, silently. When they reached the gazebo steps, he pulled her away from the others. "With Patsy 'n' me at your back, you'll do great."

He kissed her cheek, but as he turned to talk with Bernie, another worry tripped into her thoughts. The wedding rehearsal had come off without a hitch. Claire frowned. An old theatre superstition went "bad dress rehearsal, good performance. Good dress rehearsal, bad performance." But did it apply to weddings? She hoped not but crossed her fingers just in case. After all, what could go wrong? It's not like Charlie would lose his way to the gazebo. The house he'd bought for himself and Sandi, which he already moved into, was across the street and five houses down from the park. The weather prediction was for sunshine and seventy-four degrees. No, she wouldn't borrow trouble from tomorrow as Aunt Lola used to say. Tonight had trouble enough.

She took Joel's arm and called over her shoulder, "We need to get a head start. We'll see y'all at the house."

At home, Claire pulled the potatoes from the fridge and slid them into the preheated oven to become twice-baked. A silly concept if she ever heard of one, but she had to admit they were cute. The doorbell rang, and she grabbed the back of Joel's shirt as he started to leave the kitchen.

"Don't you dare leave me alone for a minute. Disaster could strike. Wes and Adrianna can handle the door. Can you believe he actually shut down his computer for the evening?" She closed the oven door. "What's next?"

"Relax, that's what." Patsy entered the room, then set her sweater and handbag in the banquette and tied on an apron.

Her arrival helped Claire's stress level go down another notch. If she pulled this off, it would be due to Pat-a-cake and Joel. The two flanked her as she read off the menu.

"Hors d'oeuvres."

"Done," Joel said. "The hot ones are hot, the cold are chilled, and all are on the buffet."

"Thanks, honey."

"Don't thank me, thank Doc and Cooper."

Claire looked at Patsy. "Your mom and dad did that?"

"They wanted to help." She lowered her voice. "Everyone is pulling for you, Claire. As soon as they heard how Zoe challenged you, they closed ranks." Patsy winked. "Now what's next on your list?"

Still surprised by the moral support, Claire focused on the menu. "Salad. We need to toss it and add the dressing."

Patsy's hand stopped her as she turned to the fridge. "Not yet. We'll do that when Joel pulls the meat off the grill. We'll have a few minutes while it rests."

Rests? How tired could it get sitting on a grill? "The zucchini still needs to be halved and brushed with oil. Joel will grill those, too."

"Do you need my help with anything?" Zoe's flat heartland twang clanged in Claire's ear.

She whirled around, crushing the list behind her. How did she slip past the twins? They promised to keep her occupied. At least the kitchen smelled good from the garlic in the potatoes and the savory appetizers.

Patsy put her hands on Zoe's shoulders, turning her around. "Did you see the pile of gifts in the den? Let me show you."

Zoe nearly twisted her head off, looking back over her shoulder into the kitchen. She'd probably hoped to see the place a disaster. Claire sniffed. She might be the world's worst cook, but she kept a clean kitchen.

For the next twenty minutes, Patsy kept Zoe busy while Claire followed Joel's instructions. She'd just finished brushing olive oil on the halved zucchinis, when Zoe appeared in the doorway again. This time she snagged an apron and slipped it on, wrapping the strings around her waist and tying them in front—like she was Julia Child.

"I'm here to help."

Whooee, Claire was in trouble—and about to be exposed. Panic lassoed her tongue. *Think!* Where was Joel? Patsy? Anybody? "Uh—" Her mind kicked into survival mode. "The bread rolls need to go into the oven." She pointed to a baking sheet with a kitchen towel draped over it.

Zoe lifted the towel and picked up the pan. She reached for the oven door's handle but didn't open it. She just stood there.

"Is something wrong?"

"Uh, well … is the oven supposed to be cold or preheated?"

Was that a trick question? Claire narrowed her eyes. How should she know? Wait. They preheated for the potatoes, so … "Pre."

"What temperature?"

What was this, twenty questions? Pick a temperature. "Hot."

Zoe shifted from one foot to the other, her red painted toes gripping the ends of her sandals. "How hot?"

Claire squeezed her eyes shut. They did this last night. What temperature did they use? Where was Joel when she needed him? She had to slow her breathing or she'd hyperventilate. A tickling drop of moisture slid down her temple. Okay, she could do this. She licked her dry lips. Four-something. That was it! Four-hundred. Or was it four-twenty-five? It was definitely four, that part was right. If she got it too hot, they'd burn. She crossed her fingers.

"Four hundred degrees."

While Zoe started the second oven, Claire slid open the junk drawer where she'd stashed the instructions. Luck was with her. The rolls card was on top and said: Preheat oven to 400°. Claire pumped one fist. Yes!

"Is that long enough?"

What was with her and all the questions? You'd think she'd never been in a kitchen before. "No, it needs—" Needs what? She wasn't sure.

Claire was in over her head, and no one was coming to her rescue. She glanced at her adversary. But instead of triumphant at catching her in the lie she was perpetrating, Zoe looked ... lost. And her face was redder than the beets Patsy pickled for the salad. Claire's heart went out to her, against her better judgment, but then again, her judgment wasn't always that reliable.

"Zoe, are you all right?"

"To tell you the truth, no. May I sit down?" She didn't wait for an answer but slid onto the banquette bench. Claire bumped the drawer shut with her hip and joined Zoe, who acted like she'd run off with Moody's goose. She fidgeted with her collar then blew out a minty breath that reached clear across the table. Claire tasted her own mouth, checking for halitosis.

"I've been ... that is, Sandi said I ..." Zoe's eyes welled, and she lowered them. A tear slid over her lower lashes and trickled down the crease beside her nose, disappearing in the corner of her mouth. Her tongue licked it away. "I'm sorry, Claire. I've been so jealous of Sandi's relationship with you, I haven't been very nice."

She spoke truth, bless her heart, but jealous? Of what?

"Not only are you an accomplished artist, but Sandi always raved about the food at your house, how good it always was." She raised her eyes but quickly dropped them again. "I never learned to cook. The few times I've tried I failed miserably, and finally Bernie hired us a cook."

Claire couldn't believe it. And all this time, she'd been so caught up in her own pride she never saw Zoe's lack of self-confidence. Well, Claire knew what culinary failure felt like. In spades. Her lips twitched. She tried not to, but the chuckle slipped out as she pictured herself on the floor at Henderson's, reaching for that blasted tomato. Zoe stared at her.

"I'm sorry. I'm not laughing at you but at myself." If she'd learned anything in the past few days it was to be open, honest and communicate. It worked wonders for her marriage. Maybe it would work on in-laws, too. After all, Charlie would be married for a lifetime and this was her son's mother-in-law. Her decision became easy. It was confession time.

"Zoe, I can't cook anything but Jell-o, and that you don't technically cook. Joel does it all. All but the coffee. I *can* make great coffee."

"But … but what about," her gesture swept the kitchen, "all this?"

"Joel and Patsy. They did all the prep work and then they directed each step for me." She lifted a shoulder and quirked her mouth. "Without them, the meal would be completely inedible."

"Really? You can't cook?" Zoe's expression was so hopeful.

"Not so much as a hot dog."

Doubt narrowed her eyes. "Then how did you know what temperature to set the oven?"

"Recipe's in the drawer. I peeked. Yikes! Speaking of ovens, we need to get those rolls baking. Come on, Zoe. You put the rest of the rolls in the oven, and I'll take this zucchini out to Joel. We have a dinner to put on and wow our kids."

Just before she walked out of the kitchen, Claire turned back and winked. "And we'll keep it our little secret."

Chapter 37

Claire slid into bed. The mattress had never felt so soft and cradling. She was tired but a good kind of tired. The shower turned off. Joel would be out of the bathroom in a few minutes. Joel. Her hero. A shiver of pleasure wiggled her spine. Communication was definitely the key to marital bliss. And the way Joel championed her tonight won her heart all over again. Here it was, the night before their eldest child's wedding, and she felt like a newlywed.

The bathroom door opened, the light flipped off, and her hero-husband walked toward their bed, a smile on his face. It was the happiest she'd seen him in many moons. God was good and, in spite of her stubbornness, blessed her. She felt hope that Joel would one day believe too.

Cool air drifted over her as Joel raised the covers and slid into bed. He reached an arm around her and drew her close. His still-damp hair smelled of citrus shampoo.

"I was proud of you tonight, Clairey-girl. Ya done good."

Silly man. "What do you know, you're a hick."

"Southern chicks like Southern hicks."

She kissed his stubbly cheek and snuggled again him. "This one does."

He stroked her arm, his rough fingertips tickled her skin. "Charlie sure looks happy, doesn't he? Are you pleased with his choice of a bride?"

"Totally. She knows him well and loves him. They're best friends."

"I hope they each have another best friend, though. Like you do with Patsy."

"Why?"

"I couldn't handle all the girly things you women share." He pulled a thread from the lightweight quilt and balled it between his thumb and index finger.

Claire chuckled, yet he was right. She was thankful he liked Patsy. "It didn't hurt that Nathan was your best friend."

"True." He reached over and turned out the light. "We have an early morning tomorrow. Lots to do."

"And I want to visit Aunt Lola's grave before the wedding. I bought her a bouquet to commemorate the occasion. She would have been pleased with Charlie and Sandi."

"Too bad I never got to meet the old gal. I think I'd have liked her."

If he only knew. Claire smiled in the dark as Joel drew her into his arms.

Claire applied mascara to her lower lashes and willed the butterflies taking up residence in her stomach to quiet down. The morning had flown by so fast with all the last minute preparations, she'd barely had time to think. And now her firstborn would soon become a husband. The head of his own household. She sent up a prayer for God to bless his marriage. "Remind him of this day whenever he finds himself impatient or angry," she whispered around the lump in her throat.

After a last blast of hair spray, Claire lifted Aunt Lola's pearl earrings out of their case and screwed the old fashioned backs as tight as her ears could stand. She'd always meant to get them altered for pierced ears and give them to Adrianna when she got married. The right one was too tight, biting into her earlobe. She backed off the tension.

In the bedroom, she slipped her dress over her head. Its cool, silky lining caressed her skin as it settled into place. She never had a second thought about the dress. She loved how the deep aqua lining peeked through the islets of the lighter top layer. In the full-length mirror, the pale aqua made her skin glow. She smoothed the material over her hip. Not too bad for an old gal.

"Claire?" Joel walked into the room, fussing with his cufflinks. He looked up at her and stopped. "Wow. Honey, you look beautiful."

Love lodged in her throat and threatened to ruin her mascara. She swallowed. "You're looking pretty good yourself." She held out her hand. "Give me those." Taking his cufflinks, she fastened them and then straightened his bowtie.

They stood together, arms linked, in front of the mirror. Joel put his hand over hers and locked eyes with hers. "Remember our wedding day?"

"I was nervous."

"No more than me."

"We were so young."

"You were so beautiful." He turned her to face him. "You still are. I loved you the day we married, but I love you so much more now, Claire. I know I don't tell you very often, but I do."

He closed his arms around her and kissed her with the passion of a groom, making her dizzy. His grin and half-closed eyelids did funny things to her insides. She kissed him again. During this kiss, a chuckle rumbled in the back of his throat.

"We'd better stop or we'll miss the wedding and mortify our son." He released her. "I'll see you at the gazebo."

Yeah, the gazebo.

Oh! Claire jumped. The wedding. She turned fast and ran smack into the doorjamb. "Ow, ow, ow!" She slapped her hand over the sharp pain above her eyebrow, praying it wouldn't swell up.

"Claire! Are you all right?"

"I'm fine. I'm fine." She gently probed her forehead with her fingertips. No blood. Thank goodness it wasn't cut. That would be all she'd need to start the Chapel Springs gossip chain.

"Let me see."

She tipped her face up, waiting for an angry retort at her clumsiness.

"It's a bit red. Get some ice on it, and by the time you get to the gazebo, no one will notice." He kissed her cheek. "And be careful."

He really had changed. Praying she could as well, she slipped on her shoes and ran downstairs, grabbing the bouquet for Aunt Lola on her way to the car. She had a little over an hour, which gave her plenty of time. A quick glance in the rearview mirror revealed a little redness above her eye. She tentatively touched it. It didn't hurt much at all. If she were lucky, the red would fade and no one would ask.

She drove to the cemetery and pulled to the parking area for Aunt Lola's section. As she walked up the path, on the first knoll to the left, an open grave was waiting for its occupant. Strange, she hadn't heard about anyone dying. In a small town like Chapel Springs, death was hard news. When she finished putting the flowers on Aunt Lola's grave, she'd stop by that one and see if she could find out whose it was, so she could send a card.

She wandered past the markers until she reached Aunt Lola's headstone and placed the bouquet in the ground vase, pouring in the bottled water she'd brought. She stared at the inscription. Beloved wife. They should have carved that six more times. Poor auntie had been one mixed up lady.

And she had been as selfish and mixed up as Aunt Lola. For a while, anyway. Claire sat on a nearby bench, enjoying the warm sun on her back. Other than being at her pottery wheel, this peaceful spot was her favorite place to pray and think. The small hill at the perimeter of the cemetery wore a narrow stand of trees like a necklace between it and the road. The view was good, and not many people came there.

"I read your journals." She picked at a flower petal that was stuck to the bench. "They sure opened my eyes. I wish I'd read them sooner, but at least I learned before I did something really stupid. I love Joel, and I know he's the right one for me." She paused, gathering the rest of her thoughts. "I wish you could have known him." A bit of dandelion fluff, tumbled by the warm breeze, landed in her lap. "I sometimes wonder if, looking down from Heaven, you can see us, although, I suppose things here aren't as interesting as up there." She brushed the fluff off her dress.

Claire dawdled another few minutes, praying for Charlie and Sandi again. Then she prayed for herself and Joel, the twins, Adrianna, and finally, Wes. When she was finished, she glanced at her watch. The minutes had slipped by faster than she'd realized. She'd better get moving.

Walking quickly on grass wasn't easy in high heels, not that they were very high, but she didn't want mud and grass clinging to them. The rain had stopped yesterday, but the ground was saturated. She wobbled, tiptoeing, trying not to put her heels down. Her calves screamed in protest by the time she came alongside the open grave.

She stopped a moment to rest her legs and take a peek in the hole. Was it really six feet deep? Standing at the side of the chasm, she leaned over and peered into its depths. Something slid down her arm and landed at the bottom of the grave. What was that? She turned around but didn't see anything. As she looked into the hole again, a single pearl earring lay in its depths. Her hands flew to her ears. The right one was bare. Oh no! There had to be a way to retrieve it.

Claire looked right and left. No one was here but her. What could she do? She couldn't leave it here to be buried with some stranger. It was a family heirloom. *Gum.* That's it! She opened her purse, pulled out a stick of gum and unwrapped it. She stuffed it in her mouth and while she chewed it, she searched for a long stick. She'd need it to be really long, since she didn't want to lie down on the wet grass.

A nearby willow tree had long branches. They weren't hard, but the earring didn't weigh much. It would have to do. Choosing a likely one, Claire tugged on it. The branch didn't want to cooperate, but she was more stubborn. It finally broke. She stuck the gum on the end and returned to the grave. At the edge, she leaned over and dangled the gummed branch tip over the earring. It was like fishing.

She moved a step to the left to get closer. The ground beneath her right foot crumbled and gave way. The stick went flying into the air as she rotated her arms to catch her balance. For a moment, she teetered on the edge, flapping as fast as she could, but gravity won, and with a screech, Claire plunged into the open grave, hitting the bottom.

She stood for a minute in shock, then she looked down. She'd managed to land on her feet, but the bottom half of her beautiful dress was streaked with red clay. Not the whole thing at least, but how could that be? She touched the edge of the grave. Down here it was dryer. Up at the edge of hole, only about a foot was dislodged. Just enough to send her out of balance and down here. Great. She turned around, spying her earring. At least she got it.

After putting it back on, screwing it tight this time—her ear could complain all it wanted—she surveyed her situation. She was trapped. And her son's wedding would start in … she peered in the dim light at her watch. Fifteen minutes!

"*Nooooo!*" She reached her hands up and her wrists cleared the edge of the grave, but not enough to begin to pull herself out. She waved her hands.

"Help! Can anyone hear me? I need help!"

Birds chirped in the tree above, eyeing her. They'd better not do what birds usually do. That would be too much. "The least you could do is go peck someone. Help! *Help!*"

Jumping only exhausted her. Tears of frustration poured down her face. She was going to miss her own son's wedding.

"*Help!* I need help!"

Two faces appeared at the edge of the grave. She didn't recognize the red bearded face or the other dark stubbly one, but four muscular arms reached down, grabbed her hands, and pulled her up and out of her prison. Once she was on solid ground, they stared at her for a moment.

"Lady, it probably ain't any of our business, but for curiosity's sake, what were you doing in there?" Stubbles asked. He bent down and picked up a long handled shovel he must have been carrying, all the while never taking his eyes off her.

Claire touched her ear. "My great aunt's earring fell—well I was looking—oh, it's a long story." She was grateful for the rescue but—

Red Beard squinted at her. "You didn't put nothin' down there did you?" He looked at his companion. "I remember once, afore you worked here, a prankster put a firecracker in a grave and when they lowered the casket it set it off. Scared the rev'rend so bad, he ran off."

"No no," Claire took a few steps back and toward her parked car. "Look, I can't thank you enough for rescuing me, but I've got to run *now* or I'll be late for my son's wedding." Claire tapped on her watch with an index finger before she turned and sprinted to the car.

In the car, she pulled down the mirror to check the damage and groaned. Black mascara and red mud streaked her face. A few small clumps of dirt clung to her hair. The only things not muddy were—her shoes! Where were her shoes? They must be back in the grave. A giggle escaped her throat. Redbeard would think they were rigged. There was no time to worry about that now. At least her dress wasn't totally covered in mud, only the bottom half.

From the glove box, she pulled out some packets of wet wipes. She got the mud off her face and bangs. It left her without mascara, but no one would be looking at her. They'd be focused on Sandi and Charlie.

Her wheels spit gravel as she sped from the cemetery. When she reached Park Court, she eased into the space reserved for her. Relief that she was here left her weak. Then the whole episode played back through her mind as Joel approached the car. He opened her door, and she fell into his arms.

"Where have you—honey, are you all right? You're crying." He tilted her face up. "You're laughing." He put his hands on her shoulders and held her at arm's length, looking her over, head to toe. He stopped at her toes. "Claire, what happened?"

She couldn't stop giggling. Now that she was here and out of a stranger's grave, it was pretty funny. That poor family. They'd arrive at the cemetery to bury their loved one and find an ownerless pair of aqua high heels at the bottom of the grave.

Between spates of chuckles, she managed to get out most of the story. Joel's facial muscles twitched in his attempt not to laugh. He failed and soon howled.

"Shh, somebody will hear," Claire said, laughing as hard as him.

He clapped his hand over his mouth then lowered it. "I'll bet they're trying to figure out how to get your shoes out without touching them—just in case." He guffawed.

"You can't tell anyone, Joel." She clutched his arm. "I'll never live it down, not even if I live to be a hundred."

"Clairey-girl, your dress is gonna give you away, and there's no time to change. The wedding is starting."

Wes came around the side of the car. That boy looked pale. He needed to get out from behind that computer and in the sun more.

"There you are. The—what happened?" He gaped at her.

Joel repeated the story, and Wes laughed, shaking his head. "Only my mom, huh Dad?"

With a sigh, Claire mustered all the dignity she could, given she was barefoot and the bottom half of her dress was no longer aqua, but Georgia clay-red. At least she stayed in the wedding's color scheme. She slipped her hand through her son's arm, so he could escort her to her seat. She might not live down this episode, but Joel would have a great time telling their grandchildren about it someday while she sat quiet at his side.

Only, that is ... if she could somehow manage to keep her mouth *shut*.

The End

Patsy's Wasabi Salmon

Serves 4

1 Tbls wasabi powder

1 Tbls water

1 Tbls rice wine vinegar

1/4 tsp soy sauce

4 (6-ounce) salmon fillet pieces, skin removed

1 tsp Beau Monde

1 cup bread crumbs or Panko

1/4 cup Sesame oil

Orange-Ginger Sauce, recipe follows

1/4 cup toasted sesame seeds, garnish

In a little bowl, stir 1 Tbls of water into the wasabi to make a paste. Whisk in vinegar and soy. Place salmon in a Pyrex baking dish. Coat both sides evenly with wasabi mixture. Season lightly with the Beau Monde.

Put bread crumbs in a shallow dish. Coat both sides of the fillets evenly in the crumbs. You can press the crumbs to make them adhere. Line a cookie with wax paper. Lay the salmon on it refrigerate for 30 minutes.

Heat sesame oil in a large skillet over medium-high heat. Cook the fish until desired doneness, (medium-rare is best - 3 to 4 minutes per side depending on how thick the fillet). Plate the fish, drizzle with the Orange-Ginger Sauce, and dust with the seeds.

Orange-Ginger Sauce:

¼ C minced shallots

1 Tbls minced ginger

2 Tbls orange zest

1 C dry white wine

1 C orange juice (fresh squeezed is best)

½ C heavy cream

2 sticks cold unsalted butter, cut into pieces

1 tsp soy sauce

Salt

1/8 tsp wasabi powder

In a saucepan, combine the first 5 ingredients and bring to a boil. Reduce the heat to medium-low. Simmer until reduced in volume by 2/3. Add the cream and cook until reduced by half.

Whisking constantly, add the pieces of butter one at a time, waiting until each is completely melted before adding the next piece. Continue whisking until the sauce is smooth. Add the soy, wasabi, and salt to taste. Makes about 1 cup. If not being served immediately, place in a hot water bath, covered, and stir occasionally.

Beetoven's Beans

2	16 oz cans Baked Beans
1	32 oz can Pork 'n' Beans
1 lb	Kielbasa
1 lb	ground beef
1 ½ C	Hickory smoked Bar-B-Q sauce
1 TLBS	Yellow mustard
2/3 C	Brown sugar
¼ C	Molasses
1	Medium onion chopped

Over a medium heat, brown onion in some olive oil, add beef and Kielbasa. Cook until liquids are reabsorbed into the meat.

Drain juice off beans. When meat is done, add all ingredients together and mix well. Bake in a large baking pan, uncovered, at 350° for 1 hour (in a gas oven, cook at 400° for 1 hour)

Beans will be brown around the sides of the pan. This can be put together the day before and baked an hour before serving.

Serves 16-20

Corn & Spinach Salad

½ C chopped walnuts

1 T sugar

1 ½ tsp cider vinegar

1 6 oz pkg fresh baby spinach

1 med red bell pepper, diced

½ med sweet onion, diced

1 C frozen corn, thawed

1 C crumbled goat cheese

¼ C Craisins

Dressing:

3 T cider vinegar

2 T orange marmalade

2 T mayonnaise

½ t salt

½ t pepper

¼ t Worcestershire sauce

In a heavy skillet, cook walnuts over medium heat until toasted, 3-4 minutes. Sprinkle with sugar and vinegar. Cook and stir an additional 2-4 minutes, or until sugar is melted.

Spread out on some foil to cool.

In a bowl, combine the spinach, red pepper, onion, corn, cheese and craisins. Add in the walnuts.
In a small bowl, whisk together the ingredients for the dressing, then pour over salad and toss.

Serves 8

CPSIA information can be obtained at www.ICGtesting.com
Printed in the USA
LVOW07s1634121115

462271LV00007B/706/P